"A ghost from the French Revolution," she said, "haunting my dreams. . . . You believe in such things?"

He said cautiously, "I've seen enough not to disbelieve automatically."

"But Ricky, this is hardly a haunted house. There's never been a ghost here that I know of, least of all a French ghost. If we had an Indian, or some Conquistador . . . but French?"

"I never said the house was haunted, Dorothea. I propose that you are haunted, personally."

She began to laugh. "Ricky, love. I've never been to France. There's nothing French in my background. My mother was Austrian, my father was a Jewish confidence man from Poland, and I was raised in New York, on the Upper West Side. Where did I get a specter of the French Revolution?"

"That," said Ricky, "is the puzzle."

"As beautifully layered as Dorothea's wall . . . a very human story about love and loss and continuation."

—*Publishers Weekly*

"Compelling . . . a high burning talent!"

—*James Tiptree, Jr.*

DOROTHEA DREAMS

SUZY McKEE CHARNAS

BERKLEY BOOKS, NEW YORK

This story is entirely fictional, and no character in it is molded on or intended to resemble any real individual, living, dead, or reincarnated. Up to the time this book was written, no hospice service existed in Taos. Similarly, the "New Western Music Festival" alluded to herein does not exist and is not intended to bear any relationship whatever to the Summer Chamber Music Festival, now in its twenty-third season, put on in Taos each summer under the auspices of the Taos School of Music, or any other concert series.

This Berkley book contains the complete
text of the original hardcover edition.
It has been completely reset in a typeface
designed for easy reading and was printed
from new film.

DOROTHEA DREAMS

A Berkley Book, published by arrangement with
Arbor House Publishing Company

PRINTING HISTORY
Arbor House edition/April 1986
Berkley edition/January 1987

ISBN: 0-425-09475-8

A BERKLEY BOOK® TM 757,375
Berkley Books are published by The Berkley Publishing Group,
200 Madison Avenue, New York, NY 10016.
The name "BERKLEY" and the stylized "B" with design
are trademarks belonging to Berkley Publishing Corporation.

PRINTED IN THE UNITED STATES OF AMERICA

Acknowledgments

With grateful acknowledgment to all those who read this book in manuscript for me. Any errors that survive their attentions are to be laid at the door of the author alone. In particular, to Kay Weinrod for vetting my Englishman's transatlantic English; Rosalie Segura and Gerald Gonzales for dealing with some of my New York–type ignorance; Dr. David Bennahum for checking out the medical aspects of the story; Patricia Powers, who knows something about making a career in the fine arts; Bethinia Dougherty, who didn't like this book in an earlier draft and was at least partly right; Lynn Seligman, who didn't give up; Norman Thayer and Ray Schowers for legal advice; Mr. and Mrs. Ramon B. Gonzales, for helping with my Spanish; and others without whom the completed achievement, however that now measures up, would have been far less than it is.

This book is dedicated to Maxine, who never did have the painting career that she aspired to. She was too busy being a textile designer (and eventually the head of a studio) in order to keep us kids in Cheerios. And to every woman who feels that kind of creative urge, whether she gets to satisfy the craving or not.

One

DOROTHEA STRAIGHTENED WIRE, bent wire, coiled wire, using gloves, using her pliers. She looked up now and again, eyeing the place on the rock where the wire would go, next to a broad band of sparkling white ceramic (bits of broken bathroom fixtures) and glass condensers from old telephone poles. She shed the gloves and wound some adhesive tape around her fingers and palms as a rough shield against the rusted barbs but not tightly enough to constrict movement. Already the clear afternoon light had deepened. She went to the wall with a sponge and a brush and cleaned the surface she meant to use. While the stone dried in the arid air, she mixed some epoxy glue in an old paint can: not too much to use up before it thickened and dried. She stood on some carefully placed rocks and applied the glue with a painting knife.

While the epoxy set she looked over the wires, her world contracted to the prepared surface and the objects to be affixed there. Then one by one she took up the wires and pressed them into place, pausing to bend them to fit, making a wave pattern, working gingerly with bare fingertips. Her lips dried and cracked because she breathed through her mouth, sometimes humming a little (it was so quiet out here). A small area grew under her touch toward completion. She held the metal baking sheet over this patch of the work and tapped with the mallet, evening the tightly packed surface beneath the flat metal.

Embroidery, she thought, beginning a new section, laying one rusty thread alongside another, this coil here like an appliquéd flower. That was the extent of the thought process that the work allowed her: a single, peaceful, summary word—embroidery.

When the air grew cool and the light began to fail, she stopped using the mallet and the baking sheet. She allowed the barbs to stick out more and packed them more tightly together in burrlike clusters. Let the work project a little, a ragged and dangerous cropping-out like a growth of angry moss, the kind that would grow here if moss could live without water. This formation would need careful controlling so that it would not become too prominent and so too fragile.

She stepped back at last, rubbing together her sticky, rust-stained hands wound with ragged tape like a boxer's bloody fists.

On the wide, rugged shoulder of rock her handiwork winked and shone. The black rock itself, where it still showed, was volcanic, pitted and gnarled. Its edges could cut an ungloved hand. Over the two years and more since the work had begun, she had learned to be slow and wary in handling this surface, and she hardly used her cowhide gloves any more.

Ribbons of color and brightness, made of fragments she had fixed there in epoxy, ran like geologic strata along the rock face, sometimes touching—even fusing—with each other: glazed pottery shards, white quartz, pink granite pebbles, bronze fragments green with weathering, bright bits of steel, rusted iron, satin aluminum, thick blades of colored glass; mixed or homogeneous, flat or rough, the layers floated like solid clouds on a black and rugged sky.

She had begun with old things, odd bits of metal and glass preserved by the dry climate, castoffs from cars and homes, which she had collected idly and without any particular purpose on her long walks through the town of Taos and its environs. She had laid these finds out on a board in the back yard of her first Taos home for the pleasure of looking at the shapes and colors.

Later she had moved here to the outskirts of the town and scavenged her own acres, still on impulse, without further aim. And then walking one day in an unaccustomed direction, toward the lower ground instead of the higher to which she was habitually drawn, she had come upon this shield of anomalous rock, the wrong kind of stone for this area. She had seen it as a surface on which she would write her reply to the ancient Indian petroglyphs facing it on another rocky bluff across the arroyo.

No, not a reply exactly—she ran her hands over the strata, checking the soundness of the settings. A continuation, an amplified call forward that in its way would contain and expand the message of the petroglyphs.

Wind and water kept the face of the stone scoured of soil and the prying roots of plants. Still, in time her work would fall apart. In lots of time. She had no trouble with thoughts of its dissolution, so long as the completed work might stand awhile, jeweled, rising silently from the sandy soil.

She had built a rough, sturdy scaffold on wheels (with some help from a handy but incurious young man from a commune in the mountains) and trucked it out here to use at the cliff. Working on one of the scaffold's two platforms, she could only see one small, close section of the wall at a time. She could not climb down every five minutes and trot away to look and then climb up again, not at her age. In the selective blindness forced by the use of the scaffold she found the work to be like weaving and she liked it that way.

Suddenly, while she stood looking at it, the face of the wall seemed to fly apart. It became nothing but fragments, a lot of meaningless junk. In a panic, she saw the need for something big and bold to hold all the little pieces together or it would just lie there, a piece of bad weaving: not art, but craft at its lowest level, a shapeless assemblage of a lot of parts into a lot of parts, period.

The horror of it was that there was no longer any room for some kind of great unifying slash or meandering diagonal, not unless she applied something over what was already there. That kind of layering would add an element, a whole new set of considerations—she couldn't face the thought of it.

She began mechanically to clean up, and as she packed her tools and materials, her panic subsided. She ate one of the apples she'd brought, taking her time, thinking about getting hold of more wire, ignoring the faint taste of solvent that rubbed from her skin onto the apple's. She felt better, but exhausted.

These moments of panic came sometimes. They were nothing compared with the lasting and growing melancholy brought by the knowledge that soon, very soon, the work would be done.

Ricky drove slowly and carefully north toward Albuquerque. In his head ran the refrain of an old song: "Oh, where are you going, said Milder to Malder, oh, we may not tell you, said Fickle to Foes."

He didn't sing out loud any more (and no loss to the world in that). Breath cost him too much to waste.

"We're going a-hunting, said John the Red Nose, we're going a-hunting, said *John* the Red Nose."

We are not going a-hunting, he thought, we are going a-hunted, really, and no matter where or how we go we are driven in the end to the same earth. Ashes to ashes, and God knows these plains look ashen enough: barebones country. Every continent has its flat barrens, a memento mori. Appropriate surroundings for him now, he felt. Some comfort came through from this coarse pale land, where the sun left nothing but bleached pinks and browns and dusty, self-effacing greens. All the color hung in a sky as keenly blue as only inland sky could be, far from any thought of that other great blue expanse, the sea. The spareness of the scene suited his mood, dwarfing his preoccupation to barely significant proportions.

Well, doing that on and off, at any rate. Nothing could quite displace the fact that he was dying. That did tend to obtrude. A moribund man crossing a landscape that itself looked more dead than alive: fitting. Yet the landscape was not dead at all but teemed with hidden life (he knew deserts well), just as his body did and would continue to do, in altered form of course, after his death. Only consciousness makes the difference, he thought. But what a difference.

How, he wondered, did his old friend Dorothea Howard fit into this bony country? And where is she going, says Milder to Malder. . . . We are all going to the same destination, old boy, soon or late, bare bone and beetle. So let's stick to the limited speculation of the moment: Where, at this instant, are we going?

Bump—dead rabbit in the road. He opened his hands and moved them to fresh places on the steering wheel of the rented car.

Specifically, we are heading for Dorothea. A very sharp image of her came: that bright, thoughtful, narrow face, quietly expressing some kind of power.

What power? He wasn't just—well, curious? No. Had been attracted to her from their first meeting, and she had been warm toward him, too. But they had always been out of phase somehow (her marriage, and after that Ricky had been involved with someone, and then he was in Nepal, and then she'd come out here, and Ricky hadn't traveled recently through inland North America).

But what of it? The world was packed full with attractive women Ricky had never slept with and would never have the chance to if he lived to be two hundred.

"*Where* are you *going* said *Milder* to Malder. . . ." "Where" was not the question, he realized. The question was, Why are you going? One had alternatives. There was Bulton and his villa, an open invitation; or that little place in Iceland where one could be on one's own in earnest; or even home, for heaven's sake—cousins and young strangers. It would be an adventure of sorts merely to light down among his family at last.

No. Go to Dorothea, commanded impulse, across this bright, painful landscape. Apart from the peculiar and obscure drive to make the journey in the first place, there was nothing to it, really: first Albuquerque, tucked into the long seam of the Rio Grande Valley; sixty miles north along the river to Sante Fe; and another seventy miles should bring him to Taos, his destination, which he had already been told should be pronounced to rhyme with "house."

Go to Dorothea in Taos and see why.

Thursdays were her days in town, where she donated her time to the bookstore, Old Possum's. That was the name she and Nathan had playfully given the place when they'd started it, and though he was gone and Dorothea had sold the store, the new owners had not yet gotten around to changing the name.

It was a good day, golden with quiet. No one was in the shop all morning except a girl in a peasant skirt and blouse mooning over the astrology shelves. Sally Raines came in, agitated about an upcoming show at her gallery. Dorothea, listening to her outline the difficulty, was amused; we should all have such problems.

"Dorothea," Sally groaned, "what in the world am I going to do about Helen Macleary? She wants in, for God's sake, with those junky patio bells of hers, as if they were *art*! It's embarrassing. But now Betty is making noises about pulling her best stuff out if we don't hang Helen's things. It's some weird alliance they have from when they were both sleeping with that Volvo mechanic in Las Trampas or wherever it was."

There was more, old gossip laced with new spice. Dorothea liked having people come talk with her at the bookstore. Seeing friends here was preferable to having them come out to the house, from which they could be very difficult to dislodge. Meantime, she did her reading in the store, a good thing since there was no more room in the house for books unless she invaded the studio, which she would not do.

Dorothea said, "I think you could mount Helen's stuff very handsomely if you use all the bells she has, arranged in sized groups and hung together against one wall. A sort of waterfall effect."

"Ha," Sally accused. "You mean make her junk into art for her."

"Why not? It's a nice thing for one woman to do for another, and it would get Helen out of your hair and sweeten Betty for you. And I'll bet some Texan with too much money in his jeans comes in and buys the whole lot."

"It's kitsch and you know it, those bells."

"Come on, Sally, anything goes these days, including kitsch."

Sally grumbled something about standards. She yanked a thread from her raveled gray sweater. "Well," she said, "it might work out. Thank God there's somebody around here who keeps enough distance to be able to give a decent, unslanted opinion!"

Dorothea felt a faint stab of discomfort at this: Did people think that she kept her distance, think that she was arrogant, perhaps?

Sally invited her to a pot-luck dinner the next week, which Dorothea declined.

"Hermit," Sally said affectionately, and she left, bookless but cheerful again.

And of course it was true, to an extent. Once you started keeping to yourself, any time you accepted a social invitation anywhere that acceptance became charged with more significance than you could possibly intend. It was simpler to say no.

The wise woman of the bookstore, she chided herself, driving home that afternoon. But of strictly a private wisdom,

which was how she wanted it to be. She had not let herself
get caught up in local crosscurrents, social or political. She
was not here to take up causes and crusades but to leave them
behind: demonstrations against nuclear armament, against
American-packaged fascism in South and Central America,
against power's penchant for more power. All those struggles
she had thrown herself into when she had first found herself
free of her marriage, involved instead with Nathan and his
passionately political friends—timidly involved, full of indis-
tinct misgivings.

She had come here to be an artist, not an activist—especially
after Nathan, with his tendency to fly off into action instead
of completing a difficult piece of work, had left, and the
stimulus of his simmering anger was withdrawn.

She had deliberately turned away from the local problems
too, mainly the problems of Hispanic people and Indian
people trapped in the familiar maze of few jobs, poverty,
drugs and alcohol, poor education, no expectation. Politicians' promises on the one hand, exploitation on the other,
the old, old story. What a relief to drop all that after Nathan's
departure!

Better to play the wise woman, since people seemed to
wish that, and ignore the greater world and its upsets and
rages. Her work was huge, and more worthy, more significant, than any number of petitions and marches, that she
knew. The work left no room for all that seething and planning, all that excitement that left no mark but used up energy.

Not everyone, she thought against a vague doubt, is a
political animal, whatever Nathan and his friends said. I am
happy as I am.

She had a sudden flash that made her swerve off the road.
A dark wing had swept through her mind, leaving her lurch-
ing with terror. But what—?

A dream. She had dreamed last night, and woken from
some kind of nightmare. She'd forgotten until this moment,
and even now all she could recall was the image of someone
standing at a window in a sort of black nightgown and
looking out; that and the pale remnant of her fear.

A pickup truck rattled by with goats in the back. She
waved in return when the driver honked. That was Tomas
Vigil, who lived farther down her road. If she stayed here,
pulled over on the shoulder, he would stop and back up to see

what was wrong. Nothing, Tomas, just a bad dream. She got moving again.

By the time she got inside her front door, the black moment had faded. She made herself some coffee and took it into the living room, where she settled down to look over the latest crop of mail-order catalogs. Loads and loads of polyester clothes and electronic gadgets—who in the world bought that stuff?

The dogs, loafing on the front porch in the shade, began to bark. A gray car that she did not recognize (you knew people out here by their cars, as they had once been known by the horses they rode) had drawn up out in the yard. As she looked out the window, a man slowly uncoiled himself from the driver's seat.

She headed for the door, smiling: for God's sake, of all people! She knew that figure, the stick man climbing awkwardly out, all slack curves and clumsy angles and longer in the tooth than an old racehorse, which he rather resembled. Ricky Maulders, friend of how many years now?

"Ricky, I'm not dreaming, am I? That is you," she called, going to meet him.

The two dogs lolloped ahead. She watched him rumple their ears and give each of them, the Doberman and the big gray poodle, a good snuff of his hands.

"Oh, it's me, all right," he answered, smiling that half-averted smile that seemed always to be apologizing for itself. "Who else could track you down in this appalling wasteland?"

She embraced him lightly, inhaling the mixed scents of dust, sweat, and soap from his bush shirt. His arms like bony tree branches closed across her back, his throat emitted a soft sound almost like a groan as his cheek pressed against hers. She stood surprised for an instant by the warmth of his greeting, and gratified.

One of the dogs nosed her leg, and she laughed and stepped back to smile up at Ricky. "They get jealous," she said. "I have three visitors a year, and the dogs are jealous!"

"You look fit," he remarked.

"It's the appalling wasteland. It agrees with me." She put her arm through his and walked him to the house. "I can't offer you Nathan for a chat and a game of chess," she added, getting this part over with right away. "He moved out three years ago. Nothing messy, we just came apart, that's all. I hope you weren't set on seeing him."

"Nathan?" Ricky said. "No, not at all. I'm sorry to hear
. . . and after he dragged you out here into the hinterlands."

"That move was a joint project, Ricky, and I really do like
it here. Otherwise I'd have gone back to New York when
Nathan left."

Which was not strictly true. She could no longer afford
New York. She was not painting, let alone selling her work,
and the investment income that provided simple comfort here
in Taos would probably buy a life of flophouse nights and
dogfood dinners back east.

He stopped at the front door and faced her. "I ought to
have phoned first. I have no business turning up like this—"

"Oh, nonsense, Ricky. Come in and have a drink."

He held the door open for her on the relative dimness of the
big front room. His knuckles stood under his skin like the
bones of some other, larger animal.

"So," she said, pouring him a gin and tonic as requested,
"what brings you out this way? As I recall, you never travel
in the U.S.A. Didn't you once tell me you had enough of
America everywhere else in the world as it was?"

"Yes, particularly that all-too-movable feast, McDonald's,"
he said with a grimace. "I thought I might as well give up
and come to the source to make my formal surrender. You do
have one of them here in town, don't you?"

They sat in the shadowy, cool living room and talked about
Nathan, and her kids with their grown-up lives, and about
Ricky's recent travels in Nigeria, and about people they had
known in common back east. America per se Ricky had never
explored, but New York he had always accounted one of his
favorite cities.

He was not a handsome man, but oh, how welcome she
found his thin, homely face, with jaw and chin seeming to
shrink back from the brash beak of his nose. He was a
cartoon Englishman, out of Ronald Searle, until you looked at
his eyes. They were large, the irises an unfaded, startling
blue—wide, candid eyes, as if unaffected by a lifetime of
seeing what the wide world contained, best and worst.

How would he react to the wall? No, no, too soon to be
thinking of that.

He had just said something chilly but true about her elder
son, Bill.

"Heartless Ricky. Bill's not a bad guy, just—" She shrugged
helplessly. "Dull. He seems so intent on hurrying along

toward more money, more fancy possessions. I like him, in small doses, but I keep wondering what happened to the kid I raised.''

At that moment she saw what was wrong with Ricky. An explanation stared blindingly from the knobs of his knuckles, the steep angle of the jaw and the creased and sunburnt neck, the delicate bowl curve of the skull under an afterthought of weightless, colorless hair. The leather band of his watch had been replaced with an expanding metal one—or, rather, one that could contract to the shrunken circumference of his wrist.

He was being consumed alive. Dorothea knew what it was that ate people that way. Oh, no, she cried silently. Not Ricky. Oh, no.

"The kid you raised," he was saying, "decided to become Bill, inexplicable as that decision may appear. Well. How are you, Dorothea?''

"Drying up," she said briskly. "Moving a little slower, getting more and more absentminded—"

He hooted his too-loud, staccato guffaw. "Absentminded! Bless you, Dorothea, you are as absentminded as the Recording Angel.''

"Aha," she retorted. "Why do you think the Recording Angel writes everything down?" They laughed. "Damn," she said, "they should have knighted you or something by now, Ricky. It's long overdue.''

"Oh, I agree," he said. "Oh, absolutely." He crossed his legs, hoisting one pointed knee over the other. "You may not realize this, Dorothea, but you're looking at me exactly as I saw you look at Alice Boston that time we all stopped by to see her. Just before her kidneys finally killed her.''

"Oh, hell. Damn it, Ricky." She wasn't going to deny anything, and if she cried he might very well get up and go away in embarrassment. No option seemed to remain but anger. "Oh, damn it all to bloody hell.''

He sighed. "Well, yes; it's the usual thing. Not some unique affliction picked up in a wild byway of the world. Just cancer. Lungs. Smoking—I never could settle for a pipe. Anyway, most of the world still smokes cigarettes when possible, and when in Rome . . .''

"Are you—is it painful?''

"High marks for that," he said. "Most people are afraid to ask. It's not bad, actually, now that I've left off the treatments. No point to any of that except to make the doctors feel better, is there? Not in a case like mine, at any rate. I have some medicine with me for the rougher bits. They tell me that my stubbornness about treatment will hasten the end. I thought I'd better come to see you while I still could.'' He set down his glass on the ring-scarred table and added quietly, ''So you see, I really ought to have written first. But I don't do much reading or writing these days. The written word has lost its magic.''

And suppose he had written, with or without an explanation of his situation, and suppose she had not answered, or had answered no?

She said. ''You'll stay awhile, I hope?''

He looked away past her at the patio. ''I would like to, very much. Actually, I was hoping you'd ask me to. You have no idea how—constrained it all is, how frightened and solicitous most people become when they know or guess. And I find, very damned inconveniently, that I no longer take the pleasure I once did in the anonymity of hotels. All those days and nights in tents and inns and the homes of strangers . . . one would think I would be content to finish in the same style. But I'm not.

''Not,'' he amended hastily, ''that I mean to hang myself round your neck right the way through this. I just need a stopping place for a bit, and then I'm off again. And if anything should—come up, anything I can't manage, I've found out about a place near here; you know the sort of thing, these hospices run by various nursing orders where they take in the odd infidel for the last act—ever hopeful, I suppose.''

She had to smile. ''As a matter of fact, the local one's a lay operation, with clergy attached. It's not as casual as all that to sign on with them. But my doctor's on their staff, and if they're not overloaded I'm sure she can get you into the program. They're very good, the hospice people. Someone will come around while you're here and keep an eye on you and keep track of whatever medication you might need.''

He look alarmed. ''I wouldn't want to cause any sort of disruption—strangers traipsing in and out of the place.''

''Don't worry,'' she said. ''They're very flexible, and the point is to make an arrangement that suits you and keeps you comfortable. Beyond that—well, truly, Ricky, if I thought there'd be problems with your staying here—and I mean staying for as long as you want to—I'd say so.''

He cocked his head and his look measured her. ''I doubt

it,'' he drawled, ''but as I'm more or less in extremis, I'll take you at your word and damned gratefully at that.''

She got up, putting aside her own drink. ''Come on, let's go get your luggage. The guest bedroom will be a little dusty, but everything's in working order. You can settle in right now: nap, shower, stare out the window, go for a walk, sit and gossip—whatever you like.''

''All of the above, in due course,'' he said, ''but the nap first. I find that I tire ridiculously easily these days.''

The house felt different with Ricky in it. Visitors always made a difference, and he more than most. Of course she was nervous about having him here under the circumstances, and of course she would never say so. Thank God he had had the sense to understand that and ride right over it.

He would have no cause to regret coming here, either, she told herself vehemently. Should the written word beckon again, he would find this a comfortable place to work. He had made himself a modest but sturdy reputation with the travel and topical pieces he had been writing for more than twenty-five years from odd corners of the earth. Perhaps this was his last odd corner. Perhaps he would write something splendid here. Damn it, she hoped so.

There must be some carry-over of her own contentment. If it was not sharable, especially under these circumstances, what was the good of it?

''Dorothea?''

She thrashed to the surface with a groan and opened her eyes wide, washing out the images of her dream with light.

She saw her room, her ordinary room: rugs on the floor, stacks of books on the table, bathrobe slung over the back of the chair. ''It's all right,'' she croaked. ·

Ricky stood in her doorway, head craned anxiously forward. ''You're sure?'' he said.

She groaned again. ''Shit. No. Yes. It's not all right, that's what I'm sure of. Insomnia would be better than this.''

''May I—?''

She hauled herself upright on the bed, stuffing the pillows behind her back. ''Come in please. God, it's good to have some human company. Would you hand me my robe? What in the world is the matter with me, anyway?''

He crossed to the deep sill of the window and sat, pulling

his own faded flannel robe closer around his throat. "What were you dreaming of?"

Another dream, another goddamn dream. Her mind felt empty and flat. "A bunch of people, like a mob, roaring through a street, I think. Blood, too. Somebody watching, from a window. It's not enough to write down, even." She gestured toward the ring binder on the dresser. "I've got a couple of them down in there already. Or rather, the same one, I think, but changed a little each time. There's always the mob, though, and this person watching. Nasty stuff." A shuddering yawn gripped her for a moment. She rubbed her eyes. "Nathan used to try to get me to write down my dreams. He said you could learn a lot about yourself that way. I never thought I'd actually do it, but I don't know any other way to approach this—whatever's going on with me." She squinted at him from between puffy lids. "I wonder if it could be tied up with finishing—"

She stopped. This was certainly not the right time to tell him about the wall.

"Finishing?" he prompted.

She shook her head. "Just a vague notion, nothing." Another yawn. "Did I make any noise?"

"You cried out in your sleep," Ricky said. He fiddled with the frayed end of his bathrobe belt. "In French."

"What?" she said, sure she had misunderstood.

"I didn't know you speak French, Dorothea."

"I don't. I mean, I studied French as a schoolgirl, of course, and I used it in some art history courses in college, but I never learned to actually speak. What did I say?"

" '*Ils vont tuer la loi*;' which translates, I believe, as 'They are going to kill the law.' You spoke in a very agitated tone."

"What law?" she said stupidly.

"No details were mentioned."

She gaped at him, blankets hugged to her chest.

"And then you said, *'Je n'ose pas prendre leur parti.'* Twice. Which means, 'I dare not take their side.' "

She shook her head. "I don't understand."

"No pictures come to mind, no scraps of the dream?"

"Nothing."

"Just as well, perhaps," he said, sitting back again. The early sun scattered a brightness around the outline of his body. "Sun's coming up. Shall we have some breakfast?"

*   *   *

What an odd place Taos was, he reflected, sitting in the dining room of the inn on the southern edge of the town. She had brought him here—"You may as well begin getting the full flavor of the place, see if you can stand it"—for a cup of coffee. His appointment with her doctor had been postponed an hour because of an emergency case. Dorothea was chatting and laughing with the woman at the front counter.

An odd place, a straggle of low, jumbled architecture, raggedy dirt lanes, trumbledown fences, and empty fields cradled in the great circular arm of the mountains at which he now gazed through the plate-glass window. At the center of the town were a few large, ugly, official-looking buildings, a plaza lined with a covered boardwalk fronting the souvenir shops, and lots of large-windowed galleries along the narrow side streets. Then more straggle.

In here, she had led him through a huge lobby, a dim sort of mummy cave with sinister-looking objects hanging from the dark beamed ceiling: wrinkled leather saddles, harness, and stiff buckskin clothing, dusty Indian baskets, faded blankets, cow skulls and shriveled unidentifiable pelts, moccasins shrunk by dryness to fit dolls' feet.

Dry country, but look how green. The low bluish sage clung to the broad plain. Files of plumy trees marked the watercourses, and the shoulders of the mountains were dark with forest. It was the elevation, of course, that made the difference between this and the lower, parched country that he had crossed to get here. More rain through the same dry and sparkling air.

Two young people in shorts cycled by on the margin of the highway, the boy bent under a sagging knapsack, the girl carrying a bundled sheepskin in her basket. There came a honk of greeting from a pickup truck trundling in the opposite direction carrying in the back three blond girls and two black goats.

So many young people; he had noticed that in town too. The world was teeming with them.

He looked down at his skeletal hands, no longer young. But hungry. He knew he shouldn't think of letting himself lay these hands on Dorothea, not even in a last grasp at sensual joy. He did not want to claim her for his side, the gray side, the dying side, in this sunny country of the young where she had found herself a haven.

On the other hand, she was not young herself (nor, to give her her full and honest due, did she pretend in the least that she was). Her silver hair was cut close and caplike, no discreet curtains falling to hide the frank webbing of wrinkles at her eyes.

Here she came, leaving her friend, who was white-headed herself and sunk into that squarish, squat sort of age that took some people.

Not Dorothea. She would become slender as a deer, fined down to a ghost before she became a ghost. But I won't live to see that happen: blessing, or curse? His lips twisted with disgust at his own self-pity.

"So," she said, smoothing down the cotton tunic she wore over her blue jeans and settling herself across the wooden table from him. "Marian says she thinks you look very distinguished, and where did I get you?"

"What's so distinguished about a walking bone rack?" he said.

"I think Marian is a little jealous," Dorothea said mischievously.

"Jealous! What have you been telling her?" Do you read my mind, my silver-headed dear? Lord, how embarrassing!

"Only that you're staying with me for a while. She infers more from the sparkle in my eye and the rose in my cheeks, or is that roses, one for each?"

This has gone far enough, he thought. "Dorothea, I don't want to make problems by staying with you. It is such a small town, after all—"

"Tut," she said. "They had their chance to stone me to death when I came and lived here with Nathan. Actually, we'd have to do a hell of a lot more than drive sedately into town for a cup of coffee together to get noticed around here. You forget, if you ever knew it, that this is one of the nation's major centers for old hippies, and they do their best to uphold the reputation of the breed."

"Didn't think they had those," he observed. "It's an oxymoron, isn't it, an old hippie?"

"No, it tends to be a pseudo- or even really intellectual drunk at least around these parts. With beads and feathers and as much hair as they can produce." She made a face. "Sorry, the inn always brings out the worst in me. Something about the place. Did you order our coffees?"

"Couldn't. Nobody's come."

She leaned back perilously in her chair and shouted, "Marian! Can't you send somebody with a couple of cups of coffee for us?"

There came a hail in return, and Dorothea thumped down the front legs of her chair again.

"The service in town tends to be amateur and terrible," she confided. "They hire these kids, very cheap, who've come wandering out here for a taste of the high free life, or the skiing, or whatever. You just have to try to get their attention as best you can."

"You know," he said, "I didn't come for the place. I came for you. I could easily have lived and died without seeing Taos and its old hippies and its young ones, but I had a compulsion to come and see you while I still could."

She said quietly, "I'm glad you did."

"You were smiling and I made you stop."

"The hell you did." She sighed, looking past him at the doorway. "George did, and damn it, here he comes to do it some more."

Ricky turned to see a tall fellow in a three-piece brown corduroy suit and boots, wild brown hair frizzing electrically in the air, come loping down on them with a wave and a grin. Dorothea put on a soberly pleasant face but did not smile. Ricky thought of all the women he'd known to smile automatically when a man, any man, approached. It seemed suddenly not charm or courtesy in them but weakness and manipulation.

"George, this is Ricky Maulders, an old friend," Dorothea said. "Ricky, George Wilton."

Ricky shook hands and sat back, already not liking George.

George snagged a spare chair from the neighboring table and swung it around so that he sat spraddle-legged facing them, his arms folded across the top of the chair back.

"Have you heard?" he said. "They've thrown Rankovitch in jail. Well, dumped him in a psychiatric hospital with a 'breakdown,' which is the same thing." George rushed on, full of outrage, pausing only when a blond boy with a sleepy look ambled over to take their order at last.

Ricky took advantage of the gap. "Excuse me, but are you speaking of Yuri Rankovitch, the pianist? Hasn't he scheduled a tour of Canada and the United States next winter?"

"Exactly!" cried George, giving the table a thump. "And we'd arranged for him to come out here as a special engagement and play at our New Western Music Festival afterward." And so on, much enthusiastic verbiage about the festival, the benefits Rankovitch would have contributed and gained in return, the loss his absence represented. But George had an idea. George wanted to dedicate the festival to Rankovitch and to oppressed artists everywhere.

Clever George. What a puffed-up ass, Ricky thought. How does Dorothea stand him? But of course it was obvious; this was probably one of Nathan's acquisitions, just the sort of hanger-on he used to attract, and now Dorothea was too polite to tell him to buzz off and leave her alone.

But not too polite to deal with him, Ricky was pleased to note. "You want something from me, George," she said. "What is it?"

George grinned engagingly. Spoilt by his mother, no doubt, thinks his charm makes the world go round. Ricky wished he had insisted on waiting at the doctor's office after all.

"You're way ahead of me, Dorothea," George admitted ruefully, "as usual. I'd like something only you can give me: a picture for our program cover, for all our publicity. One real knockout of a picture for a knockout nationwide campaign."

Dorothea looked taken aback. "But George, you know I'm not political. I don't do protest art. Why not try Ernest Stimme, or some up-and-coming young Indian or Spanish painter who could use the boost?"

"Because their stuff wouldn't pack the punch that yours would," George said. "Face it, Dorothea: The retrospective show in New York has made you—well, a leading figure, like it or not. And you are an artist who's part of a sort of an oppressed population. The feminist slant would mean something."

"Um," Dorothea said dryly. "Happy housewife who left her family for art, led a wild Bohemian life, and now lives in the wilderness, heroically gives up her hard-won peace and quiet to come to the support of the Rankovitches of this world. Inspiring."

"You don't have to be so negative," George said plaintively. "What do you think, Rick? Doesn't Dorothea owe it to her own career, if nothing else, to get in on this? I'm talking about nationwide publicity, tremendous exposure for a piece of her work."

"Very valuable, I'm sure," Ricky said, "to someone who wants it."

"I am not in the message business," Dorothea said. "Matter of fact, I'm not in the picture business any more. I don't have anything to offer you."

"Yes you do. I've seen it."

To Ricky's astonishment and alarm, Dorothea blanched.

The odious young man pressed on, oblivious. "One time when I was out at your old place to talk to Nathan, this was just a little while before you two broke up, I saw some pictures tacked up in there—drawings, ink and wash, I think, I'm not sure now—a series: cliffs and stones and light, a few gnarly trees. Simple, powerful stuff, a perfect statement about the toughness of creativity under pressure."

Dorothea laughed. Ricky felt relieved for her. Whatever the threat was, it had not materialized. He hugged to himself the pleasure of knowing that there was some sort of secret and that it was, for the moment, safe from George.

"What you saw was old work, trivial work," she said with a shrug of dismissal.

The coffee came. George waited out the waiter.

Ricky saw George take a breath for a renewed attack and thought, Why am I so angry? Jealousy. I've come all this way, and there is only so much time, and here is this oaf crashing our private party. She is beautiful, my fox-faced friend, she is self-possessed and patient and alert, and everyone wants their piece. I've got my bit—the cheek of it, landing myself on her like this!—why grudge this twit a try for his? Especially when he's doing so damned badly. You don't want to let yourself turn possessive, old boy, not when you're within hailing distance of having to surrender the lot.

They wrangled on, but Ricky didn't listen. Dorothea could hold her own. She didn't need his creaking defense of her.

To his delight, as he watched, a rider came galloping up the shoulder of the highway outside, a young man on a buckskin horse. He wore overalls, a T-shirt, and an open-backed billed cap, and in his free hand he carried a coiled lariat. Ricky felt as if a breeze from a wilder, simpler time had blown briskly through his thoughts.

If he turns from the window, she thought in terror, I'll see his face.

She floated in a miasma of dread that indeed the figure at the window would turn, a warm glow of lamplight shifting among the folds of his black gown and then falling along jaw and brow and the rise of his cheek.

Some huge effort on her part, rooted in the knowledge that to continue this thought was to bring it into being shook through her with the sensation of a silent explosion. She was conscious of being without form in the sense that this man at the window had form, although she felt physically housed in some minimal way. Her senses functioned well enough. She heard voices, shouting, and clattering footsteps.

She was at the window herself now, right beside him, not daring to turn her head for fear of seeing his face.

Down below, the crowd moved along Sixth Avenue. She saw rapid shifts and the bob of colorful bits of clothing. It wasn't exactly Sixth Avenue because the buildings were of stone and not very large, and there was a hollow sound of wooden shoes on cobbles. In the middle of this thoroughfare, which seemed to have no sidewalks, some sort of clumsy cart was stuck while traffic honked around it.

Behind her a voice—a young voice, the voice of her daughter Claire—said scornfully, "You have already fallen."

The one beside her, whose confusion of anger and hurt she sensed as if it were her own, stirred, about to turn. His dark sleeve brushed her somewhere as if on the bare skin of her elbow.

Tearing herself free in a panic, she fled into the sky, struggling to fly higher, faster, to soar free, but feeling the power failing within her.

She woke drenched and panting. Her nightgown clung coldly to her back as she sat up and groped shakily for the bedside lamp switch.

Safe in light, she sat hugging her knees and trying to calm her heart. She went over and over the dream in her mind, tasting each time a more faded echo of the terror, a more tolerable fear. She was too old to start upright in a sweat of horror in her bed at three in the morning!

What, after all, was she so afraid of in the dream? An ugly face? Something scarred, modeled on news photos glimpsed before she could get the page safely turned?

And what in the world was Claire doing in her dream? After today's conversation she could have understood an appearance by George, come to badger her even in her sleep, but Claire? Haven't spoken to her in weeks.

Never mind, it's only a dream, remember? Claire is firmly

embedded in her own life, her own dreams, and here you sit safe in your own home, your dogs snoozing in the kitchen, your old friend asleep in the guest room.

Best, maybe, not to try to go back to sleep at once. She got up, threw on her robe, and wrote down the details she could remember from the dream.

Only that morning Ricky had asked her oh so diffidently whether she would consider letting him look over some of her dream notes on the off chance that he might be able to help. An outsider with a fresh viewpoint might be able to shed light on what was happening to her.

She was touched that he had offered her his time this way, his most precious possession: to throw it away on her nightmares seemed an act of generosity bordering on profligate madness. Why in the world should she allow him to involve himself in this?

Well, because he had asked, of course, and because without asking he had in a way already involved himself. Now and again, since that first night when he had been summoned to her bedroom by her outcries in French, he would keep a vigil by her bed at night. Nothing formal, nothing acknowledged openly by either of them, but she had wakened several times to find him sitting on the big blanket chest by the window, just sitting in the dark, breathing softly, sometimes rubbing nervously at the nape of his neck, making a dry sound of skin on skin.

To avoid embarrassing him or herself she had said nothing and given no sign of having noticed. But she was moved by his watchfulness, and his silent companionship made it easier for her to get back to sleep.

Now, casting over the accumulation of her nighttime scribbles, she felt embarrassed and foolish to have agreed. And a little bit afraid.

One thing was clear. It was always, in its essentials at any rate, the same damned dream.

Here was her first account of it, which now seemed to her curiously naive and chilling at the same time.

I'm watching a little scene. A man sits writing at a desk, wearing a dark sort of gown with a frilly white tie or something at the neck. A parade goes by in the street below—but it's not a parade, it's a noisy crowd, as if at some kind of holiday celebration. A face appears at the window in front of the desk, which is impossible because the window is, I realize, two stories up. The writer looks up, opens the window, and I see through his eyes that the greenish face with its gaping jaw is a human head fixed on a pole, one of several carried by the baying mob below. The people are looking up, they want something. If he doesn't give them something, he is in danger. He throws something out to the cheering mob, who are now in uniform, like soldiers of some kind, but very old-fashioned. I see suddenly that he's throwing his own inner organs, his guts, just scooping them out and heaving them down to the delighted crowd. Then I look down, and it's my own fingers that are red and slick.

Lovely.

Lying again in the dark and seeking sleep, she took refuge in thoughts of the wall. I miss it, she thought. I should be working; my mind is all at loose ends, restless, for want of occupation for my hands. No wonder I dream.

But with Ricky here—she realized with a small shock that though she was willing to show him the record of her dreams, she shied away from the idea of showing him the wall.

They sat together in the shade of tall trees in an enclosed patio eating piñon brittle from Señor Murphy's candy shop. This was one of the oldest blocks in Santa Fe, all little shops now around the green courtyard. She was thinking about a box of rusted iron hooks of various sizes, which she had collected but not yet used on the wall. The trouble was, some of them were too bulky to fix securely, too damned dimensional.

They had been talking about Santa Fe, about how far it was from the rest of the world. Ricky, as always, brought news of that rest of the world—famine, oppression, corruption, dirty little border wars, the usual patchwork of wretched modern history—in stinging detail from which she shrank. Partly to divert him from a caustic account of a summary execution he had inadvertently witnessed in some benighted desert province, she had begun defending this part of the country as having its own horrors, thank you: the murders of hippies by angry Spanish farmers whose stream and only water supply the intruders had merrily and ignorantly fouled, a priest kidnapped and found killed out on the mesa, the great prison riot of fairly recent memory, the latest rape murder of someone's little girl. . . .

"The big sky country," she said, "is no paradise. People will knife and shoot each other in the parking lots of bars, and bodies do keep turning up dumped in the country to dry up and blow away, although they don't, of course. But the scale is domestic, crude, and seldom political in the world's sense of that word."

"You'd never guess it," he murmured with irony, "looking at all these placid, God-fearing people of the soil."

"All these lost-looking tourists, you mean." She snorted. "I don't really like Santa Fe and I don't come here often. Only, in fact, when I have guests. It's pretty, after all, at least here in the center where the old architectural style has been preserved, bastardized, whatever you care to call it.

"But the place is so—well, you can see: Even before the season gets into full swing, rich or comparatively rich visitors more or less take over the town. Their presence, their interests, drive up prices, jam the restaurants and the parking lots, transform the place even physically—the new hotels, the pharmacy turned ice-cream parlor—into a machine for serving them instead of the people who live here. There are locals who won't go downtown at all till the tourist season is over."

Ricky shrugged faintly. "Modern colonialism in one of its guises: with a racist element, no doubt?"

"Yes," she said. "With the Indians and the Hispanics on the receiving end, as you might guess. But I don't really know much about any of it, Ricky, only what I read in the papers. I'm a newcomer myself, remember, an outsider by origin, and I've chosen not to try to become a local. Not to pretend. Living out in the country, beyond the edge of town—and not even this town that's the center of things, but a more peripheral town—that's my privacy, my solitude, my peace."

"Your studio," he corrected. "Your work, which I must not distract you from, much as I enjoy taking the local tour with you. I can't keep you on holiday forever."

Tell him now, show him when you get back this afternoon; show him what you chose for, when you chose against plunging into local issues. Instead she heard herself say, in an evasive tone that made her cringe, "I'm not painting, Ricky."

"Oh," he said. "I heard you tell that to George, but I thought you were just putting him off."

She shook her head, thinking, Why is this so hard to talk about?

"When did you stop, if I may ask?"

"A little while before Nathan left—about two years after we settled in Taos together." Better. Talking about Nathan seemed to restore her normal voice.

Ricky sat with one thin arm draped along the back of the bench between them, a line drawing of a man in a cotton turtleneck that bagged on his stick frame. "What happened?" he said.

"I don't know," she answered truthfully, offering more candy from the white bag: delicious, sinful stuff! She was grateful for this shift of the conversation onto accustomed ground (she'd been over all this with her gallery, with Claire, with many others besides George). "Coming here began the process. At first I thought a new setting would stimulate something fresh in me. I was fed up with doing all those damn bridge paintings—you remember my first pictures when I started out in New York, the ones that stunned me more than anybody by doing so well? I wanted something more 'authentic.' I hoped I might find it here, and Nathan encouraged me. The idea was to shake those bridges, which had become my signature image and could so easily become my prison, at least commercially speaking. But it didn't work. I petered out. I stopped."

He studied her with those remarkable blue eyes, ignoring utterly the tourists ambling past talking camera talk. "But then what in the world have you been doing with yourself?"

Dangerous ground again, but she felt ready to handle it this time. Infusion of sugar registering, probably. "Well, we had the bookstore, of course. After Nathan left, I kept it going. I only sold it last year, and I still go in and help out with stock and things once a week as part of the deal. And because I like to."

"Nice for you," he said, digging in the candy bag, spider-fingered, as she held it out for him. "And I suppose there's a very active artistic community, lots of coming and going, lots of demands on your time, especially after this 'retrospective' George was going on about. After all, this whole area is supposed to be an artists' colony, isn't it? Plenty of socializing and company for you."

"Not exactly," she said lightly. "I mean, yes, it exists,

but no, I don't get involved much. I'm a private person, Ricky. Even in New York I was that."

"Yes," he said. "I remember. You were shy. I suppose I thought if you're not painting, you'd welcome more social diversion than usual. Isn't it painful for you, having your talents just lie there, unexercised?"

Damn it, what was he probing for? It was none of his business, what she did with her talents, such as they were! "I wouldn't worry," she said. "Talent generally gets as much exercise as it's worth. Want to walk a little? I know where we can get some decent beer."

"In a minute," he said, not stirring. He was watching some fat tourist children rooting among the flower plantings. "Any of that lovely stuff left?"

She shook the last fragments of candy into his palm.

"I see," he observed, "it was Claire, in the dream the other night. You're sure it was her?"

"It was her voice. I didn't actually see her."

"Are you and your children close these days, may I ask?"

"Not especially. But we get along, we're even fond of each other. Claire's the hardest one for me. She's so . . . demanding: of herself, of me, of everyone. She writes me scolding letters, charging me with ducking my responsibilities as a 'prominent woman artist,' a public role model for other gifted women."

"And you reply?"

"That I haven't got time for all that stuff because my job is art, not politics. Anyway, what she means, I think, is that I walked out on the family, I ducked being her role model in the way that she wanted me to be."

"Ah," Ricky murmured. "The eternal cry of the artist's child: 'You never put me first!' Complicated here by the fact that of course you did actually walk away, for the sake of your career."

She licked the last sweetness from her fingers. "Come on, Ricky, do you buy that crap too? I know that's the accepted story, but you should know better. Well, maybe not, maybe I never made it plain enough. I didn't leave until they were grown, all three of them. Before that I was an amateur, and afterward I was lucky. A lucky dabbler without background or a decent education in art. You know why my friends in New York were all Nathan's friends, all poets, writers, musicians, anything but painters? Because I knew the painters would see right through me in a second, that's why. They'd all been studying with Albers and Kline while I was making prints in my garage after the kids went to bed, using an old press I'd picked up at a barn auction!''

Ricky crooked a dubious eyebrow. "And this retrospective?"

She laughed. "Oh, somebody resurrected some of those damned arches of mine and included them in a group show called Treasure Trove about women artists who'd been undeservedly passed over by the art-buying public. Somehow everybody in the show got labeled a 'major influence,' myself included. It's all a lot of nonsense. Claire makes much of it, the way George does in his way, and she wants me to do the same. I won't.''

"But you think it's really childish resentment left over from the breakup of her family?"

"She's the only one who reproaches me. I think daughters are more sensitive to these things than sons. Sometimes I suspect that sons take alienation for granted. They expect it.''

Not the most tactful thing to say, perhaps, to a man who was rather pointedly not going home to his own kindred even in extremis, but he had led the conversation onto this ground, and he had troubles a lot worse than a gauche remark from her. Her poor friend, who managed to sit there looking not at all poor but poised, collected, aristocratic as a wading bird at rest.

"I should think," he said, "that whatever the connection with Claire, the violence in the dreams comes from some other source, and I'm very puzzled as to what that might be. All that blood and gore. . . . What have you been reading lately?"

She grinned. "Letters of Sylvia Townsend Warner."

"Do you have a secret taste for spatter flicks?"

"Not a chance. A good visual memory can be a curse if you're not careful with it. I'm fussy about what I let my eyes look at.''

"Any history of nightmares?"

She shook her head. "Not since childhood. I was never even really scared of the dark, maybe because my mother used to come and sit with me if I woke up. She'd sing me Viennese songs, most of them off-color: girls going into the woods to pick strawberries and coming back pregnant, that kind of thing. She had a beautiful voice.''

"My people didn't believe in coddling children," Ricky

said wryly. "I took my lead soldiers to bed with me for
company, and I kept an old claw hammer under my pillow in
case of monsters."

She had a strong impulse to say to him, There's something
I want you to see; let's go home and I'll take you down the
arroyo and show you a surprise . . . so you won't worry
about me so much. So you'll know that, dreams or no dreams,
I'm functioning where it matters—in my work.

Instead she said, "How about that beer?"

Not yet, then. Maybe tomorrow.

It's because it's not finished; you never liked to show work
in progress, it's too vulnerable.

He cooked that night when they got back, a much more
elaborate dinner than she normally made for herself. She had
gotten into the habit of eating simply, like many people who
eat alone. He was lavish with the spices, and though he
scarcely ate anything himself, he watched her devour his
masterpiece with evident pleasure.

They talked about the old days back east, friends they had
in common. How in the tall bay-windowed living room of a
Greenwich Village apartment during one memorable party, a
well-known female concert pianist, a friend of the host's, had
worked over the poor old upright with great exuberance,
declaring at length with gusto as she banged shut the lid,
"Well, that's that!" And so it had been, as far as the piano
was concerned. Next morning it was found that six of the
wooden hammers inside had been snapped right off their
stems.

Dorothea put on some music, starting with the Mozart
clarinet quintet that always made her skin creep with a kind of
holy joy. Ricky made a fire on the hearth. They talked late
into the night. It was a lovely, lazy evening. At the end of it,
she still had said nothing to him of the wall.

So she was off to Albuquerque: to get supplies, she said,
though she was vague about what supplies exactly. Sensing a
closed area, he had backed off at once, wondering what
supplies she could need that were not available in Taos or
Santa Fe. Alone in the quiet of her home, he looked for the
hundredth time over the notes on her dreams. He was determined to spend enough time to wrest some insight from them,
some step forward in the disquieting puzzle they made.

He sat out in the back patio, the pages held down with a glass of fruit juice, for a light wind was blowing.

Serious reading was difficult for him these days. While not a Mickey Finn in its effects, the hospice prescription did tend to take the edge off his concentration. His mind would wander, turning over chips of memory one after another: the topiary lion in Grandfather's garden; slates falling from a rooftop and shattering on the walk so close that slivers hung from his bare knees, and the blood drops, starting; the way Miss Anstey rustled all the time as she walked, not cloth sounds but paper; the fat little Hotei figure, polished red wood with arms stretched to heaven in lazy joy, standing on the table in his room at Winchester; the lifelong repeats of that moment when he first knew that he was going to cut himself while shaving, and did so—letting his own blood, the very stuff that was now carrying death throughout his body, victor at last; seeing a play in London and knowing that there must be more to Kenya than paper palms and wicker furniture and khaki clothing!

He had enough stored up to go on with forever, if he chose. Would it be an error, to spend his last days foraging in the jumble of his past?

There were, after all, issues to be addressed. He had a letter from one of those issues in his breast pocket.

His sister Margaret wanted him to come home. She might have learned of his situation and his whereabouts through any number of chains of gossip; in any event, she had run him to earth here. A letter from her, via Nigeria, had caught up with him today.

She wanted to take care of him, in their parents' old place. Dark Devon green, streaming rain on window glass, watery light and brittle, clever conversation. Christ.

He loved the high places of the world, and this place of Dorothea's was a glorious one: a plateau eight thousand feet up, covered in low, thick brush, with a grand stage of a sky full of cloud processions in the afternoons. He would not be here long enough to have to breast the full flood of summer tourists, let alone the winter ski crowd, so he enjoyed a comfortable sparseness of human figures in this vast landscape.

Stop dodging about, you pathetic nit. There was only one figure, Dorothea, jaunty in slacks and boots with her dogs at her side, mistress of her slice of this country. She would keep running out after him to clap a hat on his head, as if he had

time to develop skin cancer from the sun! Give her up for
Margaret?

He had written, of course—one was not a beast—*Dear
Maggot, not to worry; the ailing badger has found a warm,
dry lair.* And so on, as if they were still children together.
Well, it was as a child—an imaginative tyrant—that he had
loved Margaret, not as the prissy, moralistic, high-minded
woman she became.

Having refused her plea for his return, ought he not at least
to dwell on her in his thoughts as she once was; indeed, honor
all that was good in his past by ruminating on it? Not for the
first time, it occurred to him that much of his strenuous
traveling had been done to avoid just that sort of reflection.

Sitting here on the white wrought-iron chair in Dorothea's
patio, he was traveling still, in a way. He could feel the
shrinkage inward. (How could that be, since there must be
tumors growing inside and the sensation should be of swell-
ing, of crowded space?) He had grown skillful at gauging just
how much strength he had. His periods of feebleness were not
steady and unrelenting yet, thank God, but they were bad
enough when they came. The body was heading for death and
taking him with it.

He caressed the bony back of his neck with his palm. Not a
bad body. He had given it a hell of a time, after all. Frozen
and starved and roasted and soaked and desiccated, scraped
raw with blowing sand, chewed up by insects, half poisoned
with villainous water and flyblown food, it was a wonder the
poor beast had lasted.

And five-star feeds in France, let's not forget that; wines
with more pedigree than his whole family put together; endless Oriental feasts; and the comforts of fine hotels. To offset
abstinence in some places, he had allowed himself indulgence
in others—for instance, with a brilliant blond economist in
Brussels, an old connection often reaffirmed over the years,
to whom he had considered going with his horrible news
before his impetus toward Dorothea had become clear. With a
doctor's widow in Wales, although he had known her in the
biblical sense well before her bereavement. Homely as he
was, he had not done badly in that department. Too well,
perhaps?

Abstinence and indulgence had probably done the carcass
in. Drove it round the bend with too much right-hand, too
much left. Now here it was bending the knee to its own tyrant

cells run amok. His initial rage at this treachery was long since spent. He had torn up the reams of bitter outpourings that had relieved those feelings and had begun to develop a mood of rumination, judgment, a weighing and sorting and searching for patterns.

But I don't care about my past, he objected. How could the already-lived past compete with the allure of exploring Dorothea's dreams?

He sipped lemonade and read the latest account. *A man sits by a window, hearing the mob below, and he writes and writes and shakes with terror. . . .*

That evening he had an attack of the horrors, brought on by nothing more evocative than feeding the dogs and letting them out for the night, as instructed.

When he shut the door after them, his solitude struck him with sledgehammer force. He stood clutching the counter edge in the kitchen, unable to let go of this anchorage. His consciousness spun in a heavy black vortex of fear. He whimpered and clung there, bent over his grasping, white-knuckled hands, trying desperately to take deep breaths and pull out of it. But every breath made it worse, as if he breathed in the panic with the air.

I can't stand this, he thought, not again, I've been through this; why again, isn't it ever done with? How much worse can it get, how long can it last, what is it?

Mad, he thought, sweating; I'm going mad, Dorothea will come back and find me raving.

Eventually, undramatically, the dark, pulsing dread simply withdrew, leaving him racked and gasping while the electric clock on the wall clucked faintly to itself as the second hand jerked another fraction forward.

He dragged in the deepest breath he dared to, wary of triggering the damned cough, and shuffled out into the back patio, where he whispered his curses at the moon; croaked his curses, finally shouted them with all the meager power of his diseased lungs; and cried. And then felt not better but simply too exhausted to feel worse.

Call her up, she left the number of the hotel, ask her to come back, tell her you're leaving, something—

Next to the phone in the kitchen, on the pink pad, she had left him a message. It was an invitation to walk down the arroyo behind the house and find something, she didn't say what. A little map was added, firmly and clearly drawn.

Well. He never could resist a map. He took his medicine and went to bed.

In the morning he walked down the arroyo.

And she dared to question whether she was an artist or not! Ricky, confronted with the mosaic wall, was outraged. What was the matter with the woman? Just *look* at this bloody thing! How could anyone doubt?

He moved toward it and away from it, muttering and swearing and groaning to himself under a sky so rich with cloud that only vagrant gleams of sunlight reached the coruscated surface of the work. A woman's work, he thought—a myriad of tiny details adding up to one stupendous gesture. Oh, she would bridle to hear him say that!

He chuckled and wiped his forehead on his cuff, stepping back and back so that he wouldn't have to crane his neck to see it all.

Lord, what hubris! What a gigantic action to take in the midst of this sweep of dry land and mutinously fulminant sky!

A god's work, a myriad of tiny details adding up . . .

No wonder she kept it a secret. Wait until the environmentalists saw what she'd done to a grand, handsome chunk of rock.

Not his style, of course. He was a lover of Dutch painting, all domestic clarity and northern light. No matter. He couldn't stop looking at this, trudging forward to caress the river of chipped and sand-blasted glass marbles she had made, the hot chaos of a bed of bright copper scraps not yet verdigrised over.

By God, I could write something wonderful about this, he thought. It makes me want to sit down and drive my pen across the paper, but what words could I possibly find? He coughed, drank from his water bottle, and wiped his mouth on the back of his wrist. Better than the great Egyptian sphinx, he thought. The sort of thing one always hoped to stumble on in some trackless barrens, relic of a lost civilization no one had ever heard of before, marker of some hitherto undreamed-of stage of humanity's development. Why, he might be on Mars at this moment, stumbling upon some arrogant testament to the existence—once—of the builders of the canals (which were a figment, of course, but what the wall did was mine the imagination so that one could not look at it without visions bursting before the mind's eye).

His chukka boots had sand in them. He sat on a rock in the

shade of a withered tree. As he worked at the knots in his laces, the wall seemed to move. She had somehow endowed it with an ability to shift when one wasn't looking.

He felt a sudden wave of gratitude engulf and warm him. He was reminded of a time when, walking in England, in the south somewhere, he had entered a church in some nondescript town to rest. On the organist's bench a young fellow in a sagging suit had played—practicing, it soon became apparent, for some future recital or ceremony, and unaware of anyone being in the church. Had played and created such a joyful, romping glitter of beauty that Ricky found himself brimming with this same undirected gratitude: not to God, in whom he did not believe, nor yet to the young man himself, who was not giving anything, only practicing; just gratitude.

Dorothea sat on the floor in the front room sorting books to be contributed to the library sale into a carton: a soothing activity, since it was a wet day and she could not go out to the wall. The group of plastic dashboard saints that she had acquired in the flea market in Albuquerque would contribute their hands, perhaps, somewhere or other in the design, a whole patch of blessing, pleading, bleeding plastic hands. But first she must look at the wall with the hands laid out in front of it, and she could not do that today.

Ricky had greeted her return with the presentation of a gift, something he said that as a guest he liked to wait to bestow until he was sure he had the right item for the host in question. He had given her a small metal charm of beaten silver from North Africa in the form of an eye. It was supposed to ensure good sight, he said, although in her case he had seen with his own eyes that her vision—in artistic terms, at least—was excellent.

Perhaps he would come and keep her company while she worked. This prospect aroused not the anxiety she would have expected but a shy eagerness instead. Knowing that he had seen the wall and admired it made her feel not that she had handed the work to the world but rather that she had drawn him into the world of the work with her.

See, she told herself, nothing to it. What a way to show the thing to him, so childish! Six steps from the hollow tree, five hops to the right, and find the treasure—while I'm gone, safely distant from your reaction in its first freshness. So, now, human eyes other than her own had looked upon the work and not only done no harm but had found it good.

On the other hand, Ricky wasn't just anybody, any old pair of eyes.

She stared at the book in her hand: *Disturbing the Universe,* Freeman Dyson's autobiographical reflections. One of Nathan's better choices, which she might dip into again. Keep it.

People say we're all dying, but dying sometime-or-other is not the same thing as dying progressively, recognizably, moment by moment toward a painfully foreseeable end. Not exactly, of course; Ricky had set her straight on that, stressing the maddening unpredictability of cancer, the falsehood of doctors "giving" one this much time or that much time. But he had told her too that he thought his horizon was not far.

Sometimes his doses of the hospice mix made him so chipper and bright-seeming that she almost could not believe that he was dying at all. At other times she had only to glance at him, to listen to the uncertainty of his step, to know it for truth all over again. Each time the knowledge hurt as much.

God, these books were dusty! She managed to grab a tissue out of her pocket and jam her nose in it just in time for a fit of sneezing.

How long is he staying with you? someone had asked her at the bookstore the other day. I don't know, she'd answered. But that's awfully hard on you, isn't it? Dorothea remembered herself saying, It's hard any way you do it, I guess. She was a little embarrassed now at having presented herself as some sort of heroine about this. How could anyone know how good it sometimes felt to have Ricky here in the house? How pleasing to come upon him browsing these bookshelves or brushing sleek Mars till his black coat glowed?

Miss Kelly, that lovely old book about the talking cat that each of her kids had treasured in turn. Give it, pass it on.

And on the subject of kids, there was this matter of the art class coming up here sometime soon on a "field trip." Mary Morgan, a teacher in the Taos schools when Dorothea had just arrived, now headed an alternative high school program down in Albuquerque. She had run into Dorothea at the flea market, where Mary was hunting cheap but colorful objects for a still-life for the art class.

"Let us bring them up to see you," Mary had begged. "There'd be only nine of them and two adults, for an afternoon. I found them a fellow to visit down here, who shall remain nameless, and while I was looking over the drawings on his walls I heard him wandering from comments on art to stories about artists and their hangers-on, and the next thing you know he was describing some model of somebody's as the kind of 'girl' who really needed to be raped for her own good. No kidding, I heard him with my own ears. I need an antidote, Dorothea. Those kids need an antidote." And when the other teacher had wandered off to look at some jewelry, "You can see that even little Miss Stern from big bad New York is still pale from that moment. Please be our antidote, will you?"

Have to ask Ricky, of course; in some way so that he must answer truthfully rather than as the always accommodating guest. Unless of course she herself could really not stomach the idea and needed a good excuse to avoid the class visit.

Sneak.

"What subjects did you read at university?" Ricky said, looming suddenly above her, pad in hand.

Taken aback, she blinked up at him from among the books. "English Lit, of which I remember next to nothing. Why?" And why were his cheeks flushed and his head reared back and his eyes so bright? She scrambled to her feet. "Ricky, is something wrong?"

"Something's pretty queer, I can tell you that," he said. "Your having done literature instead of history makes it all the queerer. I was rereading your notes on the dream you had down in Albuquerque—"

She grimaced. "Yes, so much for the therapeutic effect of distance! Right there in the Plaza Hotel in glorious downtown Albuquerque, up pops my mystery man-at-the-window, and this time he throws them a cat, a tortoise-shell cat like the one Claire used to have. Don't tell me that makes some kind of sense to you?"

He tucked the note pad under his arm and stood rubbing his palms together in slow satisfaction. "Not that bit," he drawled, "but put together some other factors: the pieces of layer cake your crowd members are wearing on their hats, red, white, and blue layers—the soft red cap the fellow with the pike is wearing—the cart in the middle of Sixth Avenue—"

"Ricky, what is it?" She spoke more sharply than she'd intended: scared?

"Cake, cake," he said triumphantly. "Don't you remember?

'Let them eat cake.' And the colors are those of the French Republican cockade worn by the revolutionaries and then the soldiers of Napoleon. The red cap is a liberty cap, the cart is a tumbril—you're dreaming about the French Revolution of 1789, my girl!''

She chortled. ''Aw, Ricky, come on!''

''It's perfectly evident.'' He drew himself up and regarded her sternly. ''Believe me, Dorothea. I'm not a brilliant analyst, but the pattern is too clear to ignore.''

My God, she thought in dismay, I've hurt his feelings. And after all the study he's put in on my damned dreams. ''How—how absolutely *weird*, to quote my daughter on any number of other subjects. The French Revolution! How about a sherry or something, to celebrate this breakthrough? I'm not making fun of you, you know. This is the first thing to come out of those blasted dreams besides interrupted sleep and plain, nasty fear.''

He patted her arm. ''No, thank you, I'm feeling quite high as it is.''

She hugged him. She wanted to cry. To have been able to give him something that made him feel happy and strong was wonderful. She had wanted to help, knowing there was nothing to be done. But maybe the rotten dreams were good for something after all. Well worth it, then.

Unless now that he's labeled them, they stop, she thought. And if they stop, maybe he'll leave, to avoid ''presuming'' on me or something.

She admitted to herself the one disgraceful moment on her way back from Albuquerque when she had thought, Suppose I get back and find he's discreetly packed up and left in my absence? A note of thanks, a plant or a book on the table as a thank-you gesture, and my house all to myself again, my time to myself. Not to see him walking around with his death inside him, peering confidently out now and then, not to have to hear what he thinks of the wall—recognizing this final cowardice as the true, devious spine of her feelings, she had rejected the whole mess of them.

And with what pleasure and relief she had seen his gawky body framed in the front doorway on her return while the dogs whooped and capered around them both.

Right. But if he wants to go now that he's shaken something out of the dreams, now while his body still serves him and his triumph is fresh, I mustn't selfishly make it harder for him to do it.

"Well," she said, standing back from him again, "heartiest congratulations. It looks as if you've cracked the code."

"Oh, not at all," he demurred. "I may have located the ball park, as you might say. But the big question is still wide open."

Ah, the big question. He would stay for the answer to that, she was sure. "You mean, why. Any theories?"

"Not a clue," he said cheerfully, "but perhaps your dreams will honor our progress by pointing the way more concretely now. At least we've made a start."

She stooped and fished a book from the carton. "Well, we certainly won't need this, will we? He'd never have gotten as far as you have, not distracted as he was with his cigars and his rampaging libidos and whatnot."

"What's that?" Ricky said, squinting.

She grinned. "One of Nathan's. He left me tons of books. This is Freud's *The Interpretation of Dreams.*"

❧ Two ❧

Cousin Bobbie was younger, smaller, and neater than Roberto was. If I'm a Phantom jet fighter, Roberto thought, Bobbie's a Cessna. Bobbie sat tucked together on the rock, his arms around his shins. He looked pale, as if living up in the Heights with the Anglos had bleached him out.

Their parents' houses had been next to each other on Pinto Street down in the valley part of Albuquerque. As kids the cousins had shot basketball together for hours with other guys outside Joe Lopez's garage. A rusty hoop had hung there for years, until the house and the garage had both burned down from a water-heater explosion.

You wouldn't expect Bobbie to go hoop-shooting now in his fancy jeans with the stitched designs on the back pockets. His shirt had an alligator on the front. His motorbike gleamed in the shade of the willows deep in the canyon below. What the shit had Bobbie ever done to deserve that beautiful bike?

If I had a bike like that, Roberto thought longingly, I'd go to work every day just to show it off.

Bobbie was talking about school, this special school for Heights kids he'd gone to last summer. He was going again now for a three-times-a-week class.

"There's nothing to it," he said. "It's all free credit, as good as. There was this kid in the southwest history class, he told his teacher he had a block about writing reports, so they let him report orally. He put together this little speech the night before class while he was watching TV. Got a good grade for it, too.''

"It's still school,'' Roberto grunted. To tell the truth, which he wasn't about to with Bobbie, he kind of missed the hanging-out part of school. He missed the guys he didn't see any more because they were still in school while he was out loading sand and wrestling prickly trees and bushes for the landscaping company.

"It beats hanging around being bored all summer,'' Bobbie said. "Or working at some crappy job.'' Quickly he added, "I mean, like the jobs they give kids, if you can get them— they're all pretty bad.''

Roberto said nothing. He never talked about his work with Bobbie. Bobbie might say the wrong thing, and they'd have a fight, and there'd be no more rides on the bike.

Roberto tossed a stone into the canyon. It clicked on the boulders all the way down. Beyond the canyon the land sloped swiftly down to the murmuring spread of Albuquerque with the dark meander of trees along the Rio Grande winding down the heart of it, parallel to this long, crumbling mountain that formed the eastern boundary of the city.

"Some of the guys are okay,'' Bobbie continued, back on the safe topic of this fancy school of his. "There's some foxy chicks in my class, too.''

"Stuck-up *gringas*,'' Roberto sneered. "Fuck 'em.''

"Some,'' Bobbie said, turning red.

"Don't give me that shit, man.'' Roberto hooted. "Only thing you sleep with is that bike of yours, I bet.'' That was another thing: It wasn't so easy to find girls when you were out of school, except the retards, the pigs laying around in wait to marry a father for some other dude's kid.

He prodded his crumpled beer can with the toe of his boot. The can slid off the rock and clanked faintly down into a clump of brush, where it hung, gleaming in the brilliant sunlight.

"How many cans you think it would take to fill up this whole canyon?'' he said. "We should go to one of those recycling dumps and load up a whole lot of cans in a truck— shit, a plane—and come bomb those cans down, let them loose. *Wham!* No more canyon, everybody jumps out of bed yelling, 'Hey, what was that, earthquake?' ''

Bobbie said, "You can get money for those things.'

Shit, he'd gotten yellow living in the Heights, yellow and

prissy. Won't even come down for the street-closing next
week, too busy filling a garbage bag with cans to help keep
his neighborhood clean.

"Penny-a-can, garbage man," Roberto sang, pushing Bobbie's shoulder. "What's the matter, litterbug bit you? I got a
right, man. There's nothing here that didn't belong to us first.
Why they call this Juan Tabo Canyon, after some damn
Anglo, you think? Just because those fuckers put a fence
around half the mesa and say it's theirs!

"Now if it had of been me, I'd have snuck up the canyon
with a rifle and when the sheriff came to throw me off my
land I'd shoot hell out them all, blow them away into the
sunset, *blam, blam!*" he yelled, sighting along the barrel of
an imaginary gun. "*Boom!* Blow their brains out, *ka-pow,
ka-pow,* Rambo, get them all!"

He stopped, embarrassed to be playing shoot-out like a
little kid.

"Your land?" Bobbie said. "Hey, bro, you grew up in the
city, just like me. If this land was yours now, all you'd know
is to subdivide it, just like they do."

"What if I did?"

"I've got to go to class pretty soon," Bobbie said, getting
up. He looked at his watch. "Shit, I'm going to be late!
Look, I don't have time to drop you back at Pinto Street
first."

Roberto got up too, brushing the dust from the seat of his
jeans. "Okay, just leave me off where I can thumb a ride."
Shit. You'd think with that fancy watch of his, Bobbie could
keep track of time better—Anglo time.

Already starting down the steep back-slope, Bobbie turned.
"Listen, bro, why don't you come to class with me? It's only
drawing, everybody's pretty terrible at it, and you don't have
to know anything much. I'll run you home after."

"Shit, no, man, I'm allergic to school."

"This is different, I told you."

"It's all the same."

Bobbie stepped back, elaborately casual. "You're not scared,
are you? Come on, man. I'll come down to help you close
Pinto Street next week, okay? Cut class to be there too. I'll
do that. You scared to come to a little art class with me
today?"

Hell, when he put it like that— Roberto shrugged. "You're
crazy. The teacher won't let me in anyhow."

"Yes she will. They're real cool at this place, nobody gets fussed up except maybe if you did dope right on the doorstep."

Bobbie's life, Bobbie's kind of friends. Roberto was curious. He was a little nervous too. Nervous about some Heights kids in some kind of play school? No way he could really be scared of that!

"I don't know about pictures, art, that stuff," he said.

"So what? That's what they're supposed to be teaching you."

Blanca's sister Mina had her ride to work already. Their mother put on her long, sagging sweater coat. She left early on the mornings that she went to work in the discount store, because sometimes the old clock in her bedroom slipped a couple of minutes.

Blanca, finishing her cereal, said nothing. She was afraid she would let out the secret if she spoke: Today was the day, and Mom didn't know. That suited Blanca. She would rather die than tell. She was furious with her mother over this asthma camp that her mother had gotten her into somehow. What a bummer—a whole camp full of asthmatic brats, and they made you go swimming and climbing and all kinds of things they thought you should be able to handle. Blanca had had enough of that with her phys ed teachers in school.

Mom insisted that these camp people were experienced, they knew. Hell they did. Nobody knew, not even the doctors. Look at all the different things the different doctors at the clinic had told them over the years: exercise, don't exercise, take this medicine, take that one, you're taking too much, you're not taking enough, don't overprotect your daughter, she's being allowed to do too much. Nobody knew.

Blanca had refused to talk about it at all. She kept silent to avoid bursting out with the anger that would probably trigger an episode.

What if the camp people gave her the wrong medication, or they had some doctor there with a whole new plan and it was wrong? Here in Albuquerque, Blanca knew the dangers. What if there were different pollens up there in the mountains to set her asthma off?

Her own mother wanted to expose her to these dangers: her own mom, who was supposed to understand. Boy. She watched her mother hunt for bus tokens in the cracked sugar bowl on the sideboard. All she understood, Blanca thought bitterly, was how mad and scared it made her when Blanca had an episode. You didn't have to be a genius to guess how sick Mom was of the whole thing, years of it now. Let's push it all off on some strangers for a while, give the family a break.

The only one who never got a break was Blanca.

Besides, imagine leaving Albuquerque in summer, when there was so much to see: people living on the porches and in the yards of Pinto Street to escape the heat, and the exciting business today of the street closing that Mom didn't know about and Blanca wasn't supposed to know about but of course she did. Knowing things was her best protection.

At the door her mother looked back. "Quita, you're sure you don't want to come to the store with me today?"

"I want to finish a book, Mom. It's already overdue at the library, and I can't read at the store. It's too noisy there."

"All right, but you stay inside, Blanquita, hear me? No running around. And don't forget your relaxing exercises and your medicine. You know where the doctor's number is. You sure you feel okay this morning, *mi hija?* I don't like how you look."

"I'm sure, Mom."

At last Mom was gone, and Roberto was slamming drawers in his room looking for something. All you had to do was be patient.

Blanca washed her cereal bowl and went into her own room. She shut the door and then opened it a crack again, quietly. She listened to her brother getting ready to leave. Her older sister didn't know she was alive, her mother fussed over her too much, and her brother thought he could boss her around. That was how it was, being the youngest and having asthma. With Mom and Mina gone to work, Beto acted like he had the whole place to himself.

"Hey, Quita!" he yelled finally. "You got a pencil? I can't find anything to write down license numbers—shit, there's nothing in here but a bunch of stupid crayons!" She could hear him rummaging furiously in the kitchen drawer that served as a catch-all.

"Here," she said, tossing him a pencil. "Where are you going to be?"

"At the ditch," he said. Pinto Street ran east at right

angles to Fourth, the major road up the north valley, and ended at the big irrigation ditch that ran along Second Street, parallel to Fourth. The access to Pinto from Second, across the plank bridge over the ditch, was to be Roberto's station. "Me and Horacio and John Archuleta. I could do it myself, but it's going to be more fun with some other guys around."

He left running, but slammed back in again almost at once. He grabbed a bowlful of cold potatoes out of the refrigerator and dashed out again, hollering with his mouth full, "Hey, Horacio! Wait up!"

At least he'd remembered to take food. They were supposed to guard the two entries to Pinto Street's short length, Fourth on the west and Second on the east, all day long. The chances were pretty good that Beto would not come barging back in here at lunchtime and find her gone.

Blanca waited a little before she went to the kitchen to get herself something to eat outside: a chunk of cheese and an orange. She hated cold cooked leftovers.

Back in her bedroom, she took off her good clothes, a red sweater over a cotton blouse and skirt. Out of habit she looked in the long mirror on the closet door, the mirror that her sister Mina liked to use for her preening. To Blanca it showed nothing new and nothing good, reminding her merely that there were reasons why her mother babied her and the others bullied her or forgot she existed.

Her arms and legs were sticks like broom handles. But that was better than before, when the doctor had her on corticosteroids and she had swelled up and couldn't stop crying. Another doctor had finally taken her off that stuff and given her cromolyn powder to inhale instead. Now she was thin, little and thin, and they said—she wasn't supposed to hear—that she would stay little. The corticosteroids had permanently stunted her; that was what the new doctor had said in a roundabout way until Mom pinned him in a corner and he said it straight out.

There was another doc at the clinic who said that Blanca would begin to grow again now and "fill out." That was what they always said, meaning, Start looking like a cow, like Blanca's sister, Herminia. As if you weren't a human person, if you were female, until you got great big tits. That was going to be a while, because Blanca was fifteen and still didn't menstruate.

Mom never gave up. She said, You'll be like other kids, give the doctors a chance. She had even let Great-uncle Tilo try the old trick of getting a Chihuahua dog and tying it to the bed that Blanca slept in so the dog would take the sickness from Blanca. Blanca remembered being devastated when it didn't work. That was back when she still thought Great-uncle Tilo could do things, before she realized what being a drunk really meant.

Mom always said, I'm not mad at you, *mi hija*, I'm mad at the asthma. A lie, Blanca could feel it.

Mom said, You're a girl like the other girls, Quita, and you have to learn how to live like them. They had had a huge fight about that, because Blanca had voiced her own thought: that she wasn't a girl, not really. A girl is somebody who grows up and gets married and has babies of her own. Nobody was going to marry Blanca. If she had babies they could be sick like her, so why would anyone want to have them with her?

I will always be a kid, she thought, staring at her knobby knees in the mirror. But people forget about kids when important things are going on. People pay no attention to kids.

She shivered with excitement over what she intended to do. Actually, she was pretty scared, but you couldn't just lay around being sickly, not when everybody was gearing up for this big effort and even dumb, punky Beto was in on it.

She put on one of Roberto's old T-shirts, a pair of bleached-out jeans, and sneakers on her bare feet. The sneakers dated back nearly two years now. She had not outgrown them yet, although her toenails had worn a hole in the rubber rim of the left one. The thing was to look like some anonymous boy from a neighboring street. Otherwise some well-meaning pain in the neck would spot her and take her home to keep an eye on her until Mom got back.

Her thick hair she stuffed into a baseball cap that Roberto had worn one summer. The cap still smelled of his hair stuff, ugh.

She put her medication in her jeans pocket, the one without a hole. She was not sure she would find water if she needed to take her pills, but she'd taken them dry before, throwing her head back hard and working her throat.

A soft cotton flannel shirt, long-sleeved and faded, completed her outfit. It was a hand-me-down from Roberto that her mother wouldn't let her wear out of the house because it was too boyish-looking. That was why Blanca loved it. She wore it whenever she could. With her lucky shirt she put on an identity so far from her own that she felt her asthma could not follow.

Dust still hung in the air of Pinto Street from somebody's car or truck passing through. The houses looked so quiet in the morning. School was out, but most of the kids had gone to the church-sponsored teen outing today. Blanca could see two little kids playing by the sagging fence around the trailer park. Betsy Armijo was feeding the ducks in her yard, all dappled with the shade of the thorny Russian olives her parents had planted before Blanca was even born. Betsy liked to play invalid when she had her period, as if her cramps were the end of the world. Too bad she didn't know what being really sick was like.

Blanca could hear water running and dishes chinking in the Romeros' kitchen as she walked by. Vallejo's dog came scuffling out of his dusty yard and grinned at her, trotting along beside her for a little until Mrs. Ruiz's big mutt began barking from inside her fence, and Vallejo's dog veered off to go yell back.

Estelle Ruiz, the widow, was out watering her flowers in front of her place, a converted trailer with trumpet vines all over that were now beginning to blossom. She was old and ugly, but nice. Blanca walked fast. Mrs. Ruiz had sharp eyes.

Then that place the Ortegas kept working on while they lived in it, slowly patching it together over the seasons out of adobe, cinderblock, and faded black panels of rigid insulation board nailed over two-by-fours. They had a great big wood-pile made from the dozen Chinese elms they had cut down when they started building. Slimy-wet and iron-tough under the bark at first, the wood had finally dried out so it would burn long and hot, and last winter the Ortegas had sold some off to their neighbors. Beto used to pretend he had black widow spiders from that woodpile to turn loose in Blanca's bed.

The sawhorses were still out in Mr. Lopez's yard where he'd been working yesterday, building a new coop for his chickens. He said Vallejo's dog had run off with another hen, and next time he saw that dog he would shoot it. Nobody ever saw Vallejo's dog kill anything, but Mr. Vallejo never fed it and it was very fat, so it was assumed that whatever ran loose and disappeared on the street, Vallejo's dog must have gotten it.

Blanca thought it was a pissy little dog, always digging its way out from under Vallejo's chain-link fence around his bare dirt yard. She wouldn't mind if Mr. Lopez did kill Vallejo's dog.

Somebody had a TV on loud, soapy music. And there was the big old salt cedar that leaned out of the Roybals' yard near the corner of Pinto Street and Fourth.

Blanca saw the young men gathered at the joining of the streets. They were lounging together, half hiding the orange traffic cones behind their legs. Jake and Martín Maestas, Ramon Romero from Truchas, and for goodness' sake, Great-uncle Tilo! He sure looked dried-up and funny with the younger men, but he looked sober too. Somebody must have pushed him to leave his eternal card games and his bottle-passing cronies and come stand with the others like a man. He seemed dignified even, in spite of that beat-up old hat of his and his crippled arm hanging like a knotted rope. He'd almost lost that arm years ago, working for the railroad.

The one who looked best, though, was Martín Maestas. He always looked beautiful to Blanca, at least until he opened his mouth to talk—something he did seldom—and you saw the gap where he'd lost his front teeth. It wasn't from fighting, as most people assumed when they looked at Martín's wide shoulders and strong arms and the tattoos on his smooth brown skin. He'd stood too close behind the batter in a sandlot baseball game when he was younger. Sometimes Blanca thought his shy, quiet manner was all because of those teeth, but other times she knew it was his nature. But he was a tough guy, too. Nobody messed with the Maestas brothers.

Today Martín wore a sweat shirt with the sleeves torn out to show his biceps, and pressed bluejeans, and boots. He had on his tooled leather belt with his name on it and the brass buckle in the shape of a charging bull. His hair gleamed black in the sun. He looked ready to take on a whole army.

Only nothing was happening. They just stood around and smoked and talked, and after a while Ramon Romero turned on his portable stereo so they would have some music.

People going to work had gone. No cars turned off Fourth or even slowed down. The young men looked bored.

Blanca, bored herself, headed back toward the ditch end of Pinto Street. She would run a risk that Roberto, stationed there, would recognize her. Even that would be better than a lot of dull waiting around.

She went through the yard of the abandoned Estrada house and under the fence around the lumberyard in the next street. From there she could trot down to the ditch and come toward Roberto's end of things from Second Street.

The ditch was wide and deep, and those who still farmed in this part of Albuquerque's north valley drew irrigation water from it. It ran alongside Second Street in a rough parallel to the Rio Grande farther west, from which its mud-colored water flowed. Every spring the machines came by and dredged the ditch out and smoothed down the dirt along its banks. A fat new growth of weeds was already reclaiming the ditch banks, and straggly elms gave a ragged shade.

Somebody was with Beto and the other boys from the street. It was Bobbie, Blanca's cousin who lived in the Heights. He had an Anglo kid with him, a brown-haired boy with work boots on and corduroys and a torn T-shirt. The stranger had a big pad of paper under his arm. Bobbie was taking Horacio Ramirez for a ride on his bike up and down the ditch-bank trail, the bike shooting thin gray smoke and making a sound like a machine gun.

Blanca sat under the trees and ate some of her cheese, thinking about asking Bobbie for a ride. Maybe he wouldn't even recognize her. He hadn't been down here more than twice since his parents had moved to the mesa that sloped up from the river valley to the foothills of the Sandia Mountains— the new part of the city, full of new people from the East and West Coasts. Anglos. This Anglo kid must be one of Bobbie's new friends from up there. He didn't look like anything special.

She decided to have one more look at the Fourth Street group. If nothing was going on she would come back here and try to get a bike ride out of the day anyhow. It wouldn't trigger an episode, not a little thing like that, just riding around.

She heard men talking as she neared Fourth. The orange cones had been lined up across the end of Pinto Street and backed up with sawhorses. A car that said SHERIFF on the side was parked there, and Eddie the cop was leaning against the car and talking with the young men. Blanca moved into the shadow of the Roybals' twisted salt cedar and listened.

"I'm telling you," Eddie was saying patiently, "you can't do it. Look, the street belongs to the city. You aren't allowed to just block off a street like that. What if there was a fire or something, and a fire truck needed to get in, or the Emergency Rescue people?"

"We got no fires today and no emergencies except what we're trying to handle ourselves here," Jake Maestas said. He had a fierce black mustache and a bandana tied *cholo*-style around his head. "It's our street. We're closing it to outsiders today."

Eddie, who was short and stocky and crew-cut, pushed his cap back on his head and looked past the young men. "What is it, you having a block party or something? All you do is, you call the city people and let them know, and everything is okay."

Jake said, "But everything is not okay. That's the point."

Ramon Romero said to Martín in a tough voice, "What's this guy got to do with this anyhow? He's with the sheriff, right? I thought we were in the city here, not the country."

Ramon was a newcomer, sent down from the mountain village of Truchas to live here with his aunt and uncle for a while. He didn't know Eddie, who so often came by to drop off Great-uncle Tilo when he'd found him wandering drunk on Fourth Street.

Eddie answered for himself. "I know folks on this street and I see these barriers up and I stop, that's all. I don't think you want city cops swarming all over the place, do you? Not if you don't have to. Let's just talk about this, okay?"

"That's what we're going to do," Jake said. "I just called the TV news from Mrs. Roybal's. They said they'll come up here. We figure if the guys that are after our homes here won't come to us, we'll go to them via the media and tell them our message: Lay off our homes, lay off our street, quit trying to rip us off."

"Lay off what?" Eddie said. "What's going on?"

"Some kind of scam," Jake said. "Some guy has been coming around here daytimes, you know, when there's not too many men around, and hassling people in their homes. I mean telling them, Hey, lady, I am a city inspector for the zoning up here, and the zone rules are changed because of that new YMCA building going up across Fourth Street, so I got to inspect your place and see if it conforms. And then they go, Hey, your wiring's no good, or, Your plumbing's not up to code, or this or that, so we're going to have to condemn it. Only this guy is saying, I've got a buyer, somebody who wants to buy your place and put the money in it to bring it up to code and then sell for a profit. This buyer would buy cheap, but it would still be a better price than the city will give you if they condemn the place, this guy says. And then he goes, Don't tell your neighbors or it's no deal; my buyer can't have everybody trying to get him to buy their place at a better price than the city would give. How does all that sound to you, Eddie?''

Blanca hugged the knobby trunk of the cedar. She liked the way Jake talked, quiet like his brother, but hard, too: no crap.

Eddie scratched the back of his neck. ''Sounds like you got some kind of real problem.''

Great-uncle Tilo spoiled it all by moving forward and saying humbly, ''We just want to make our statement, Eddie. You can see no harm is being done.''

''The harm, the only harm,'' Jake said, ''is being done to us, man. That's why we're taking this action.''

A city police car drew up with two cops in it. They got out in a carefully casual manner and came over to join the group. Jake began explaining again about the man who called himself an inspector. Mrs. Roybal came out of her house, drying her hands on a dish towel. She hung frowning on the edges of the knot of men, listening. Somebody came over from the trailer park. Soon a small crowd had gathered, listening to Jake and the cops talk.

One of the city cops got back in his car and used the intercom. When he returned, Blanca could see the patches of sweat beginning to darken under the arms of his shirt. He was nervous, she thought. Funny to think of the cops, who made everybody else nervous, being uptight themselves. But there were only the two of them and Eddie, and all these people from Pinto Street.

Martín Maestas was talking to Mrs. Roybal and several other neighbors now. Mrs. Roybal was not liking whatever he was telling her. She looked mad. She shouldered into the crowd and started talking over Jake as he talked to the police, all on top of the racket from Ramon's portable stereo.

One of the cops asked Ramon to turn the sound down. Ramon sneered. He didn't turn the sound down.

Here came Roberto, running down Pinto Street with the Anglo kid tagging after him. Blanca watched him work his way into the crowd to be nearer to Jake. He really worshiped Jake Maestas. And he better not see her here, or he'd send her home.

She swung herself up into one of the lower branches of the tree where the bark had been polished smooth by a lot of kids sitting there. She sat panting slightly, triumphant to have had the strength to climb at all and to have gotten up this high without setting off the asthma.

The speaker in the city cop car jabbered loudly. With that and the people talking and Ramon's radio blasting away, it was hard to hear what people said. She noticed the Anglo kid moving around the outside of the group, sketching on his newsprint pad.

One of the city cops came back from another conversation on his car speaker and walked over to the Anglo kid.

"Hey," the cop said, "you don't live around here, do you? Go on home."

"I was invited," the Anglo kid said. He put the pad behind him.

The cop said, "This is no place for sightseers."

The Anglo kid's voice creaked with nerves and anger. "You can't just run me off like that. I got asked if I wanted to come here."

"You got asked into a lot of other people's trouble," the cop said. "Go on over to my car there. I'm going to get you taken home." He gave the boy a pat on the shoulder that was partly a shove. The Anglo kid stumbled and dropped his pad and pencil. He went on his knee to pick them up, just in front of Mrs. Roybal, who was coming out of the crowd talking angrily with Estelle Ruiz, the widow. Mrs. Roybal stopped and said loudly, "I saw you. You hit him. He hit that boy."

Blanca heard the quick silence, attention yanked tight. All the faces turned.

"I didn't hit him," the cop said. His face was red.

The Anglo boy straightened up, looking from face to face with a scared expression. "Hey, it's okay," he said. "I just dropped some of my stuff, that's all."

Jake Maestas said loudly to the red-faced cop, "What you

picking on a kid for? There's grown men here for you to try and rough up, if that's what you're looking for.''

Beto, with his big mouth, jumped out right at Jake's elbow and hollered, ''Yeah, man, leave my friend there alone. That's my friend, I asked him down here. You got a problem with him?''

Beto watched too much TV.

''Come on, guys, relax,'' Eddie said.

The city cop turned and looked at Jake, arms akimbo. ''I know you,'' he said. ''Dope charge, couple months ago.''

Jake shook his head. ''Not me, man. Or maybe me, but not you. That was Officer Walter Tate that took me in that time, you can ask him.''

That was when the TV people came. They piled out of their truck laden with equipment. It was almost as exciting as if there'd been a fight after all. Only some stupid woman ended up right in the middle of the crowd holding out a microphone for Jake and Martin to talk into, and Beto had to stick in his two cents, scowling and playing the big honcho.

When the TV people moved on, leaving the cops talking with Jake, Blanca skinned her shin scrambling down out of the tree. She hurried up the street after the camera team. She caught up to them outside the Vallejo place.

''That's my house over there,'' she said, pointing. ''Roberto Cantu, who was telling you all about what's been going on? He's my brother. My name is Blanca Cantu.''

She pulled off Roberto's cap so that her hair tumbled out around her face. The TV people looked at each other. Both turned toward her, one with a microphone he had just been talking into and the other with the camera that hung on his body like a huge black insect.

Thing about this Miss Stern, Roberto reflected, was she had boobs, man: big ones, for a small lady. Him and Bobbie had laughed their heads off about that, whooping and roaring over the Death Race game down at the arcade in Coronado, for almost an hour yesterday.

But she was out of it, man. Just fooling around out here for the summer and teaching a class—what a jerk. Why should a teacher teach on her vacation? Like if I spent my free time digging holes in the yard and piling up rocks to look pretty. And art wasn't even her subject, it was some kind of literature; she'd even come out and told them that. Weird.

The class was sometimes interesting, though. It was going to be especially interesting today.

Sure enough, soon as they walked in (a little late), she looks up and says in this cut-you voice, "Ah, the three musketeers. Where were you three during our last class?"

Three because it was Roberto and Bobbie and Alex.

Bobbie said, "We did some drawing, Miss Stern. Alex did, anyhow, and we did ours after. We just didn't come to class to do it, that's all."

What a wimp, look at him holding out the big newsprint pages like they were money to buy the teacher off. At least he hadn't let Roberto down at the closing, in front of the Maestas brothers and all. He showed up and he stuck around till everybody went home. But look at him now.

Miss Stern frowned at the papers, dismissing them. "That you can do without bothering with school at all," she said. Huh, damn straight, Roberto thought; hope everybody else is listening. "But then why did you sign up here?"

"This was something special," Alex said.

"Too special to share with the rest of the class?" she said, taking the papers.

"You wouldn't have let us," Bobbie said.

"How do you know if you don't—" She stopped, looking at the pictures they'd made. The rest of the kids waited, their faces full of curiosity. Wait till they heard. Bunch of jerks. Fat Paul who couldn't draw a straight line, and that brown-nose Joni Reed who had an answer for everything, or skinny Jeff who looked like he was someplace else most of the time. And those two blond foxes who giggled all the time, and sour little Angie who was always late. Alex was the best of the bunch, and he wasn't so great.

Nine people in a class, so everybody could always spot you, especially the teacher. He was glad he wasn't part of it, only a sort of guest of Bobbie's.

He tried to catch Angie's eye. She wasn't so bad, Angie, except she wouldn't admit he was alive. Too stuck-up from living in the Heights. He wrinkled his nose at her. That skinny dope Jeff saw and snickered behind his hand.

Miss Stern didn't even notice. There she stood, looking at the pictures Bobbie had handed her. Her dress was loose and cool today, not one of those clingy ones that really showed off her tits. Too bad.

She looked up—not at Roberto; she never looked at him

directly, and he knew and enjoyed knowing that it was because she was a little scared of him.

"What is this, boys?" she said, speaking to Bobbie, of course, the wimp.

Roberto answered for his cousin. "That's pictures of the cops hassling people. We closed my street down that day, and the cops came."

"Closed it? What do you mean? Who's 'we'?" Now she looked at him.

He straightened his shoulders and resisted an impulse to run his hands over his hair. He was neat enough.

Keeping it casual, he said, "Somebody's been coming around conning people on my street to try to get them to sell their houses. A couple of our guys went to the building inspection office to complain about this inspector, but all they got was a runaround—the guy you want to talk to is in a meeting, come back later, can you wait; all that shit—so we decided to take care of it ourselves. We decided to keep this inspector out. We closed the street and called the TV, and they came and talked to us."

"That was you on the news, then," one of the blond chicks said, and the other one giggled.

Alex said, "The cops tried to give me a hard time about making those pictures."

So then Stern did this thing she did sometimes, she grabbed what was going on and turned it around into something she wanted instead of what it was supposed to be. She said in this clippy voice like she was pissed off but trying not to show it, "So you boys made a field trip. Well, maybe it's time we gave some consideration to the subject of field trips. There's no reason to confine the class to this room all the time, assuming we can manage to all take our trips together as a class after this. I've been thinking about going out to the zoo one day to draw the animals, and maybe a session in the foothills for studies from nature. Any other suggestions?"

Nobody said anything at first. Then that little bitch Joni Reed piped up, "How about one of the big shopping centers, like the Coronado Mall? There's always stuff going on there, people moving around; or we could draw the trees they have growing out of the planting boxes."

"Good," Miss Stern said, nodding. She laid the boys' drawings on the desk, and that was going to be that for them, you could tell.

Bobbie sat down with the others. Alex shuffled over and stood behind Angie, leaning against the wall and scowling. Roberto stayed where he was, near the door, angry about how things were turning out. Okay that's enough for Pinto Street, let's talk about the zoo. Shit.

"Jeff, you have a suggestion?"

Jeff said, "Maybe we could visit a car dealer and draw the new models in the showroom."

The foxes groaned.

"Good idea," Stern said, all light and smiles again. "Any others?"

Roberto said, "The jail."

Everybody looked at him. Good. Now tell me it's a good idea, Miss Stern.

"The jail?" she said in this squeezed voice.

"Yeah," he said. "If you want to draw people, why don't you go to the jail where there's people that have to sit there and let you? Like going to the zoo if you want to draw animals."

"I don't think we'd be allowed to do that," Miss Stern said. "But look, people, I'll bet we could go visit one of the courtrooms and draw the judge and the jury and the lawyers in a trial, the way professional artists do sometimes for television. Is that the kind of thing you had in mind, Roberto?"

I got you something real, lady, from my real street, but you don't even want to look at it. Out loud he said, "It was just an idea."

Shit, he wished he could just holler out what he felt, but school was school, like he told Bobbie, and the chance always just slipped past him. He sat down next to Angie.

She whispered, "I saw that news report on TV. Was that really your sister? What's wrong with her?"

"Nothing."

Goddamn Blanca, sticking her nose into everything. They gave her more time on the TV than anybody else. You always got shorted with a cripple next to you.

"There is one field trip," Miss Stern was saying loudly, glaring briefly at him and Angie to make them shut up, "that might work out, a really important one. I wasn't going to tell you until it was a sure thing, but since the subject has come up—"

She wanted them to go spend a day with some old lady painter living in Taos.

Shit, not me, lady, Roberto thought. He stared at the worn blue carpeting. You want to get rid of me, this is sure a good way to do it. Summer school was just a joke anyhow, man. He was only along to keep Bobbie company. He hadn't dropped out of school to go on any stupid field trips.

He'd had his field trip the day they closed Pinto Street, just like Miss Stern said. Too bad for the others that they missed it.

❧ Three ❧

SHE WATCHED THE man go to the window, and she saw with him what he saw: There they were, the mob outside, yelling and jeering and shaking their fists.

She was aware of a terrible constriction, a suffocating horror of seeing the same scene play itself out again.

The man threw the casement wide, lifted something from his head—God, was he going to throw his own head to the mob? No, only his hat. He had on a cylindrical black hat with a strip of ribbon around the base. He threw it down and bowed to the crowd, now a group of men in frock coats who applauded.

But what's so horrible about this? she thought, confused. The scene was comic rather than awful, the figure at the window a caricature rather than a demon: stick limbs and a whiskery head sticking out of his absurd dark gown. But a caricature should not move, bend, wave to the crowd, act like a living being. It's like the puppet in *Dead of Night,* she thought, the ventriloquist's dummy that speaks on its own: unspeakable—

And he's going to turn now and show me his face . . .

She woke, gasping but triumphant with discovery. The figure at the window was lifted right out of a source she knew well, she was sure of it: Daumier, the Daumier prints satirizing the legal profession. That gowned and oddly capped figure, so familiar!

Ricky was in the chair by the window, head sunk on chest, gently snoring. Silently, so as not to waken him, she put on her robe and slippers, took her notebook, and went into the chilly living room. She turned on a lamp and dug out her books on Daumier.

Like that, she thought, studying a long-nosed tyrant leaning from the bench to bully a young witness. A judge? Come to judge me, my judgment on myself?

But then what's the French Revolution doing mixed up in it all? And why do I sometimes get traces of Claire?

There came a scratching at the door to the kitchen. She let the dogs come in and curl up with her on the couch. Hugging their comforting largeness and warmth helped settle her mind again for sleep.

Ricky's going to love this, she thought. It's almost worth waking him to tell him: Here come de judge. She giggled. Brillo licked her ear.

"And what do you dream of, my fine fellow?"

Having Ricky at the wall with her was a pleasure; she'd been a fool to have feared it. He settled always in the shade of a thick, twisted juniper with her dream notebook and his yellow pad. After a while the dogs would get tired of snuffling around and go lie down with him.

The wall, too, pleased her immensely. She had set the plastic hands. They were like small creatures from deep under the sea, a cross between coral and sea anemones with their tendril-like pink fingers. But what next? She could not seem to see what was needed next.

She walked back and forth, the shadow of her body and her wide-brimmed hat sliding over the sandy ground with her. The pleasure of looking seemed almost enough. Almost. Perhaps it was the habit of action that impelled her to do something, even if it was only using sandpaper on some of the plastics to try to tone down the more acid colors.

She hummed. Pages fluttered softly in Ricky's hands. She forgot him for a while, remembered again when he brought her some coffee from the thermos. The realization that he was here always came with a little kick of pleasure: To have this companionship at her work, a companionship that demanded nothing, was a luxury she had never imagined.

Well, she deserved some luxury, by God. She was tired today. Maybe that was why the wall offered no essential next step for the moment. The constant interruptions of her sleep by the dreams were telling on her, she knew. Ricky had commented with concern this morning on the black marks under her eyes, the tracks of her nightmares.

He seemed to sleep decently, when he didn't suffer from the spells of small, dry coughs that she hated to hear. Look at him dozing now, his head pillowed on his arm. She noted with tenderness the slackness, the vulnerability of sleep.

Thank God the wall was good, worth giving him. Thank God she had saved it up, not squandered it on anyone else. It was Ricky's and hers and would remain so for a while. He said it was time for her to make its existence public, but she preferred to share it only with him for now, not with the greedy world.

At lunch, as they sat over apples, cheese, and bread, Ricky said calmly, "Well, I've thought it all through again in the light of your identification of your dreams' protagonist as a legal gentleman. I think you've got a ghost."

"A ghost!" she said, charmed. "Really? Of all things. But where do you see a ghost in all this?"

"In your accounts. This fellow you watch in the dreams, the judge at the window—he's always the same person; he has a continuous existence."

"Yes," she said slowly, trying to think herself back into the dreams. "Though I don't know much about him. I've never seen his face, of course, but he's not very big, and he's older, I think—his hair's gray—and under his gown he has on street clothes and these neat, small, very shiny black shoes. He's vain, I think. Those shoes."

"Citizen X," Ricky mused, "of the Revolutionary Republic. Afterward, perhaps, Magistrate X under Napoleon? A man of substance, of influence: The crowd in the street seems aware of and interested in his actions, however ominously. Someone who lived through interesting times."

She had a curious sensation of dropping through a hole in the bright afternoon.

"A ghost from the Revolution," she said, "haunting my dreams. . . . You believe in such things?" How would it feel to be dying and to believe in ghosts? Had Ricky only begun to believe as death drew nearer?

He said cautiously, "I've seen enough not to disbelieve automatically."

Who was she to question whatever comforts he might find

for himself? He can believe what he damn well pleases, and if he wants to chase a "ghost" through my dreams, more power to him!

"Okay," she said, "let's say, for the sake of argument, a ghost. But why in my dreams?"

"Why not, if the ghost feels it can get through in dreams?"

"Seems an awfully roundabout route to me. And what would he be trying to get through with?"

"He has a story to tell, a lesson to teach, I should think. Perhaps even a warning to give, in traditional ghostly style. Nothing as simple as knocking on the walls or drifting across the patio of an evening. A complex haunt, Dorothea, to go with a complex hauntee."

"But Ricky, you've been in my house for nearly two weeks now. It's hardly anyone's idea of a haunted house. No one's ever been afflicted by a ghost here that I know of, least of all a French ghost from the 'best of times' and the 'worst of times.' Now, if we had an Indian ghost chanting its grief over the Spanish Conquest, that might fit. Or some eager conquistador searching for gold. But French—" She shook her head. "I just don't see how it works."

He looked modestly victorious. "I never said the house was haunted, Dorothea. I am proposing that it is you who are haunted, personally."

"*Oy,*" she said. "*Vey . . . is . . . mir.*"

"I beg your pardon?"

She began to laugh. "Ricky, love, look: I've never been to France in my life. There's nothing French in my background. My mother came from Vienna in 1915 and my father was a Jewish confidence man from Poland. Nobody knows when he came. He traveled on his mysterious affairs, showing up now and again with money or worn-out shoes, depending. Mama raised me on the Upper West Side of New York and supported herself making clothes for other immigrant women from Mitteleuropa. How do I get this French ghost, this specter of the Revolution, from a background like that?"

"That," said Ricky with relish, "is the puzzle."

She cut a bruise out of an apple with her painting knife, reflecting wryly that in all probability the wall was a great deal less important to Ricky than the more mysterious artistry of her dreams.

She would never have expected him to be so imaginative. He had always been, after all, a man of surfaces: a traveler crossing and recrossing the rumpled skin of the world, an observer and reporter of the exotic, not an interpreter of the mind's fantasies. Yet she had had hints of interior complexities. There had been stories about him even when she had first met him years ago in New York: of a beautiful heiress who had followed him into wild bushland, to no avail, her own sorrow, and the disapproval of Ricky's two matchmaking aunts; and of a young cousin, a girl who sent him a sheaf of poems and then perished in a terrible fire at a country house. Afterward Ricky had retreated to some modest mews apartment in a comfortable backwater of London, from which he had eventually emerged to sail without explanation for South America. All long ago, but it is our past that makes us.

"You know," she said, "I think I've underestimated you."

"Oh," he scoffed, "we English are wonderful at ghosts, it's part of our heritage. I'm just interpreting the phenomenon in terms I feel at home with, that's all." He turned to gaze at the wall. "Call it my own poor sort of creativity, roused up to meet your own."

"I'm very glad you've come," she said.

"This must be treated in absolute confidence," Ricky said. "It concerns someone else's secrets. *Silence.*"

"Agreed," Frank said.

Ricky, stretched out in an old lawn chair behind the hospice building, looked not at Frank Sanford but at his own steepled fingers. He knew from experience that he could learn little of the trustworthiness of someone from a culture other than his own through visual inspection. But an aura was often to be felt, if one attended to it. As one might expect of a hospice volunteer, Frank radiated reliability.

The man knew Dorothea, although not well. Taos was socially as neatly structured and interlocked as any village anywhere. That was the crux of the problem.

Nevertheless, Frank was a skilled counselor, a sort of priest manqué, and for the first time since his illness had begun Ricky felt in need of good counsel.

"I am very worried about Dorothea," he said finally, taking the plunge. "Something strange is happening to her—or, rather, something is not happening."

He stopped while an enormous truck trundled past with a sound like a dragon clearing its throat. The hospice had established itself in an old motel on the edge of town which had, unfortunately, a major trucking route along its frontage. But diers can't be choosers.

"Look here," Ricky went on, "do you believe in magic at all?"

"What kind of magic?" Frank said, not with the cautious hedging of the clever but with honest interest. He had a quick mind. Ricky liked him and would have enjoyed spending more time playing chess with him and talking about other things. Did, sometimes. But not today.

"I don't know what kind of magic," he admitted. "I hope you can tell me. I've seen some odd things here and there, but I've not come across this before.

"She says she's quit painting, and by my observation, she has. She says she's content, and seems to be, but not because she's doing nothing, not because she's 'retired,' as I've heard her put it. That's an evasion, if not an outright lie. Although in a sense—well, you'll see when I tell you the rest.

"There's this great—great *thing* she's been working on for upwards of two years. It's absolutely splendid, Frank, a great achievement, I think. And it has her enchanted."

Frank leaned down and picked up a stick and fiddled with it in his neat, small fingers. He was a pipe smoker, Ricky knew, and a faint odor of tobacco clung to his clothes, but he refrained in company. He also refrained now from answering. If he'd had his pipe lit, no doubt he'd be sipping smoke and gazing slit-eyed into the middle distance.

"Mind you," Ricky said, "her paintings alone have finally begun to bring her the recognition she deserves. And that's part of it, you see. Letters come from galleries begging her for material to show. She refuses them. She hides out here with this great, secret piece of work. She hides *in* it, I think."

"You mean she spends all her time closeted with this—this project?"

"No, but when she's away from it, she often thinks of it." He pictured her bending to retrieve some bit of scrap from the ground, the thoughtful expression he saw whenever she looked at any set of objects arranged in series or in a group—even silverware laid out for polishing. "It's as if it rides silently on her shoulder and whispers in her ear. And when she's working on the thing—"

Yesterday at the wall he had observed her with growing concern. He hardly knew how to describe his feelings and

their cause without sounding foolish, oversensitive, a prying
old busybody.

"The fact is, she barely works on it at all. I mean, she may
add a bit here or there, but most of the time she just moons
about admiring the damned thing."

Frank looked puzzled. This was not getting across. Ricky
tried again.

"I think she's still looking for more work to do on it, but
there isn't any more. It's finished. I told her so and she
disagreed, but the work itself rejects further alteration. And
she can't fiddle about with it and ruin it by overworking it;
her own artistic judgment won't let her. Her eye knows I'm
right, you see? But she denies it. She won't let anyone see the
thing. She won't let it go, she won't let it be done."

"Maybe she keeps looking because she sees things you
don't," Frank ventured. "Some loose ends only the artist
could catch."

"Naturally she sees things I don't," Ricky said impa-
tiently. The hospice cat lumped itself into his lap. He stroked
it absently. "But if you could see her, wandering entranced in
front of that damned, beautiful thing, you'd know. She's
be-spelled."

"It's that powerful?"

Ricky nodded. His feelings about the wall had progressed
to a point where he suspected that it was in some way the
focusing agent that had drawn him to Dorothea in the first
place. This was not something he chose to say to Frank. It
was too personal, and it had to do with—oh, say, the spirit
mazes he had seen drawn on the sands of certain deserts. He
didn't want to get off on that kind of thing. Besides, he
wasn't sure he really believed it. Only sometimes, looking at
the wall, he would think that its completion included him in a
way that had compelled his presence. As if I were part of the
spell, he thought. One doesn't presume on Frank's cheerful,
patient acceptance with that type of prattle. What I've said so
far is quite enough.

The cat drooled on his hand. He left off stroking it and sat
holding its vibrating warmth.

" 'And I awoke, and found me here on the cold hill side,' "
Frank murmured unexpectedly. "You think an awakening
like that is crucial for Dorothea?"

"Exactly. I think she's trying to be in some sort of artists'
heaven without having died, and she can't. There's got to be

more for her to be and to do beyond this single great accomplishment; she can't let it just stop her life! Might as well be dead then, eh? Rapt in some golden stasis of completion. You can't have that, no one can, not without going rotten or petrifying where you stand.''

Was that what he thought? Yes, hearing his own words, he recognized the rightness of them.

"Does it help, do you think, to worry about her future?" Frank said gently. Meaning, Does it help *you*, thinking about her future instead of your own?

Ricky snapped, "It distracts me, yes, you clever bastard." For God's sake, the man's doing his sweet, decent best. "It's true that I may be avoiding some—some work of my own by concentrating on her, if that's what you're thinking. But that doesn't alter the facts of her situation."

He stopped on the brink of mentioning the dreams. One could only go so far with another's secrets. The wall was intended to be public property one day. The dreams were not.

Frank snapped another twig into segments with crisp, tiny sounds. "I think I'd feel a lot better about dying if I thought I could help a good friend to escape or avoid another kind of death, a spiritual death."

"So would I," Ricky rejoined with some asperity, "but the problem is, I don't see any way to do that. I'm a guest, after all; one doesn't want to presume."

"On the other hand, she may accept comments from you that she wouldn't take from anyone else."

Ricky poured the cat out of his lap and leaned back, shutting his eyes. "Perhaps I have made it all up to divert myself, if that's what you're suggesting."

He heard rustling of grass as Frank hunted about for another twig to torture.

"Do you know," Frank said thoughtfully, "some of the Indians out here always include a deliberate imperfection in the design on any of their pots or rugs or whatever. They say it's to let the maker's spirit out, so it doesn't get trapped in the work."

Ricky shivered.

The minuscule snapping sounds started again.

"Oh, for God's sake, Frank," he said, getting up, "go and smoke your pipe, will you?"

She took a bath. She was tired, having spent the morning

mending the fence around the pasture of Horace, the fat
buckskin gelding she never rode any more. The fence posts
were rotting so badly they would hardly hold the staples, and
she was going to have to seriously consider either divesting
herself of Horace or having those damned ugly metal posts
installed.

Grumpily she soaped herself, white body and dark-tanned
limbs. Mars was pawing at the door, wanting to come in and
lap at the bathwater, which would make it scummy and
smelly since he always dipped most of his face in.

The phone rang. It was perched on the toilet lid within easy
reach, but she wished this time she'd left it in its usual place
in the hall, because here came George's eager voice. She
sighed and leaned back in the hot water to listen to his
harangue about the picture he wanted.

"—capitalize on the New York show and make some
sales, Dorothea. You don't have to be painting right now to
realize the worth of things you did earlier. You could sell old
work and give your kids whatever amounts of money are
allowed without being hit by a gift tax, which would reduce
the tax bite on your estate—"

Tactful George. "I've thought about all this. Every artist
does."

"Then you're not thinking enough! Let me have a signature piece for my concert series. It goes into every program
book, every piece of major publicity, nationwide advertising,
the works. We'll do it in posters, too. The exposure will be a
tremendous boost for other work you'd like to market. And of
course there'd be a fee for our use of your work."

"Are you proposing a bribe now?"

"Sure, if you want to think of it that way. Though I can't
see why anyone should have to bribe you to allow the public
access to your work. Go and look at those old pictures again,
Dorothea. With the pictures in front of you, see how you feel.
I'm getting grant money, I can pay. I never meant you just to
hand something over for free."

Unless maybe I'd lost my marbles and agreed to do it, she
thought, exasperated and amused. "Look, George, I told you
I'd think about it. I'm still thinking about it. Settle for that,
will you?"

"I will," he said, "for now."

She did think about it, soaking in the tub. She thought
George was a royal pain, as her son Arthur would say. Well

connected, knowledgeable about art, full of good causes with
solid commercial potential—and a pain.

What is it about giving George a picture that brings out this
stubbornness in me? she thought.

I don't want the attention. If they really begin taking notice
of you, they come mooching around for answers, for judg-
ments about other people's work, the state of Art today, the
whole schmeer. You get distracted, you get tempted—come
and teach here; we want six weeks of your life so we can do a
photo essay or a book; we need you at a conference of women
artists—she had lived through some of this already and wanted
no more of it, for all the financial advantages.

But at the same time here I am working on this unmis-
takably large and commanding piece of art out in the desert,
two years in the making and not done yet—hardly the action
of a person who craves only obscurity. What goes on with
me?

It can't be as simple as just not being able to stand the idea
of George getting his mitts on my work.

The woman who had the nerve to walk out on Jack is the
same woman who fled from the success of the bridge paintings, which might have led to something better. The woman
who came to Taos to start over, living in—um, passionate
unwedlock with Nathan and opening a bookstore in a new
place, she's the same one who stopped painting out here
because—the work showed too much promise?

Baloney. I like a private life, that's all. I like it, and I've
earned it.

But.

Does it count that I've said yes to Mary Morgan's blasted
art class coming to visit? Probably not. Small potatoes, evasive action (an image came instantly of a school of pink new
potatoes executing a swift underwater maneuver). Ricky says
you're a hermit. He probably feels guilty, thinks you're beat-
ing off your friends for the sake of his peace and quiet.

"Mars, shut *up!*" she yelled, and the scratching and whining at the bathroom door subsided. She rinsed her hair, her
skin, and climbed out of the bath. "Shit," she growled.

Dried and dressed, she collected Ricky from his nap to take
him to the studio with her. "If there's a ghost around, that's
where we'll find him," she said, digging the key out of her
desk drawer. "The ghost of my painting career. Actually, I

just want to check and make sure that there really is nothing
for George.''

"Since you put it that way," Ricky said, "I don't give
much for his chances. Love to see the place, though, and any
of your work that you'd care to show me.''

The studio was the entire north wing of the house. Its long
outside wall was a bank of tall windows with iron grillwork
guards. The other long wall was faced with cork for pinning
up papers. One end of the room held a slop sink and a small
bathroom; the other was fitted with racks for canvases (more
canvases that she remembered). The pale oak floor was ran-
domly stained with faded splashes of pigment. Two easels
leaned in a corner.

She had not been in this big, bare room with its fullness of
light for months. The air smelled of sunny staleness and
turpentine. Ricky sat down in the big green velvet armchair in
which Nathan had sat for his portrait more than once, in the
other house, down in town. Ghosts, she thought; I've got my
share, and more to come. Ricky, eventually.

Swiftly she whipped through the contents of her portfolios,
feeling detached from the work. Some of the drawings were
worse even than she remembered, but some were better. A
few might even do for George.

Then she turned up a pen-and-ink piece, a man's head seen
full face, a coarse and even brutal visage with wild hair and
some sort of neck cloth and odd stand-up collar, on a background of rough cross-hatching. The picture jolted her. She
said hastily, "This doesn't belong here," and skimmed it
onto a heap of discards.

She had forgotten those, that last series, the set that had
brought her to a dead stop. They were not what George was
looking for or what she had wished to find.

Ricky leaned down and picked up the drawing.

"I didn't know you did this sort of work," he said.

"I'd forgotten it myself," she said, truthfully. She stood
up, straightening her back with effort and wiping her dusty
palms on her pants. "This was something else that—happened
when we got out here. I was trying to be spontaneous,
looking for what was really mine. The drawings we've been
looking at were only exercises. I started producing images of
faces, people I'd never seen. Yet they were as detailed as
portraits from life, and they brought with them a sort of

charge, a negative charge. Anxiety. That's when I stopped, almost three years ago now.''

"The picture of this man is full of power and poignance,'' he said in an accusing tone.

"I knew that at the time," she said, "but I didn't know why, and I had a feeling that I didn't want to know why. So I stopped." Her heart was pounding. Leave it alone, Ricky, why pursue it?

"You do know who this is, don't you?''

Reluctantly she stepped nearer to look again. The portrait showed the face of the head in her dream, the one that was thrust up on its pole outside the judge's window.

"From my dream," she said, dry-mouthed. "A severed head.''

"He's from reality. This is a recognizable likeness of Danton, one of the architects and leaders of the Revolution and later one of its most illustrious victims. He was guillotined during the Reign of Terror.''

Dorothea was hardly listening. She stood hugging her crossed· arms to her body. She did not doubt him for a moment. But how could she have made this picture? How long had this intrusion from the past been brewing within her, scarcely noticed? Funny; now she remembered that she had nearly flunked out of college, her sophomore year, because she'd been reading all about Danton and Robespierre and the rest instead of doing her course assignments.

"You said there was a series?" Ricky said. "Where are the rest?''

"Destroyed," she said forcefully, glad that this was so.

He made an angry, impatient sound.

"They scared me, Ricky. I produced these disturbing images, I didn't understand where they came from then any more than I do now, and I quit. I threw out most of the work.''

"They ought to have been taken away from you," he snapped. "Someone ought to have been posted to snatch each piece from you as you completed it. What disturbed you might enlighten others, didn't you think of that? If you're lucky enough to have visions to set down, you shouldn't complain that they aren't pretty or soothing or entertaining enough! You should have the courage of your gifts, but instead you've denied your own creative impulse. I'd give a great deal to see the rest of this group, do you know that?

And I'm sure others with educated eyes would agree with me.
You had no right, you know. You had no right, in this world
that tears down so much, buries and drowns so much, to
obliterate your own work."

He set the drawing on the seat of the velvet chair and
stalked out of the studio, leaving her openmouthed.

What the hell had happened?

Mortality, she thought grimly. The man is dying, what do
you expect? He would leave nothing like this work behind
him. She remembered once urging him to make a book of the
best of his essays, but he had protested that his pieces weren't
worth republishing. His writing gift was not great, she had to
admit, and she had admired him for recognizing his own
limitations.

She was an artist, he was not. The feeling behind this
outburst had had to come out somehow: the fury of the dying
at the continued existence of those around them who were
dying much more slowly, or, worse, wasting the ability to
leave something behind them that was valuable enough to be
"undying."

Well, what did you expect? she asked herself bitterly.
Good cheer and roses all the way?

The Danton portrait compelled her eye. God, it gave her
the shivers to look at that blunt and passionate face, risen
from some inexplicable depths of her consciousness years
before the damn dreams ever began.

His regular evening coughing fit was past, but Ricky felt
faintly nauseated and could not sleep. His unpardonable be-
havior in the studio weighed on his mind. He was ashamed,
and afraid of what his outburst might have done to their
friendship.

Much of her attraction for him now, he realized, was that
she needed help. At first he had resented this—he was the one
who was dying, after all—but now he was beginning to find
vastly liberating the idea that he was here not so much to take
as to give. He felt retrieved from the rubbish tip, infused with
alertness that had nothing to do with his earlier frantic grasping after each moment in anticipation of the end of all moments. One had not yet become one's own complaining,
lingering ghost. One had the trust of a friend materially
beneath one's hands, there in her dream pages, just as if one

were still a companion in life, fit for consultation over the puzzles of living.

Perhaps today he had thrown all that away. This unbearable thought circled in his mind.

At some point he surfaced, listening in the quiet of the night and the uncomforting confines of his bed. He heard her in the kitchen moving softly about, the muted clink of a spoon on china. The illuminated clock at his bedside table read 4:15 A.M.

He got up, shrugged into his robe, and went to join her. She was standing at the stove stirring something in a small saucepan with a long-handled wooden spoon.

"Dreams wake you?" he said awkwardly. Was he forgiven?

"Yup. Wait till you read my notes. Oh, not now, it can wait."

"I'm sorry," he began, "about my outburst—"

"Yes," she said. "I know. Want some hot milk? It always helps me to get back to sleep."

He was distressed to see the smudges under her eyes, the hollows in her cheeks. He accepted a cup of milk knowing he would not drink it and thinking how she had ankles lean as a whippet's under the hem of her robe.

"You know," she said, "you mustn't feel apologetic about this afternoon."

"Having cancer does not excuse one from basic ordinary decency," he said.

"Having bad dreams doesn't justify grabbing up all of somebody else's time and energy, either. I feel guilty when I see you working so hard on my damn dreams."

"I work hard," he said, "because I think the matter is urgent."

She looked down at the pot of milk. "I'm very grateful, Ricky. Have I said so? Grateful, and bowled over by what you've gotten out of that mass of scribbles. I couldn't do a damn thing with any of it, and here you are wrestling it all into submission."

He was painfully conscious of the inadequacy of his labors. After all, nothing he had done so far had alleviated the problem of the dreams in the slightest; they still came.

She poured herself a mugful of the hot spiced milk and padded over to join him at the table.

"This may sound peculiar," she said slowly, "but do you

think the dreams might have something to do with you rather than with me?''

His head was clearing of some of the hazier mists of his medication. Trying to get rid of the dream stuff, was she, the closer it got to herself? Trying to fob it off on him? He could well understand the impulse, but he was not going to make it easy for her. Frank never helped him slough off what was properly his own.

''I don't think I see how that could be,'' he said cautiously.

''Maybe my interest in the Revolutionary period, the interest I've had in it on and off since I was a kid, makes me receptive to something you're carrying around from your own background, do you see?''

''I'm not sure I do.''

''Well, to begin with, maybe there's a hidden connection with France and the French language through you. Is 'Maulders' a French name, for instance?''

Interesting; he rubbed his chin, thinking. ''In its oldest form it's probably German; that is, Saxon. It meant something like 'big mouth,' related to 'maw,' I shouldn't wonder. Became a French name, normally used as a Christian name, 'Mauger,' which was brought over by the Normans in 1066. That, at least, is what I recall from the reports of my sister Margaret, who once made a study of our family background. By the time we became 'Maulders' we were thoroughly English, and that was well before the 1789 Revolution.

''And I did have an ancestor who was particularly interested in those events in France. He stayed closeted in London throughout the Revolution, writing an interminable tome on ancient Roman history. His book was intended to refute the Revolutionaries' claims to have reconstituted the Roman Republic in France. You realize that in those days of nearly universal monarchism, any sort of Republican sentiment was considered violently radical by solid citizens. This kinsman of mine thought the French Republicans utterly depraved and mad, at the same time that he revered the ancient Romans whose state was the model for the French Republic. But he's not our ghost. He was a good-for-nothing gentleman, not a judge, and he spoke no French, never went to France, would not have dreamed of contaminating rational analysis with subjective experience. And I'm afraid that's the best I can come up with.''

''But couldn't we still be dealing with something that's

trying to communicate with you but approaching through me because it can't reach you directly?''

''Why bother?'' he said. ''Anything supernatural that wants to talk to me can do it face to face, or whatever one has in place of a face, if it will be patient for a bit. Unless there's something it wants done, something only a—well, living person can do.''

Dorothea sighed. ''To hell with that kind of talk, Ricky. If we're going to converse in the kitchen in the middle of the night, let's discuss something else: art, for instance. It's less mysterious. Most of the time, anyway. Claire wrote me, did I tell you? Among other things—the usual exhortations to stand up and take my place in the leadership of the Amazon rebellion—all about a show of Turner paintings she saw in Seattle. Wonderful stuff, she says.''

''I never cared for old Turner,'' Ricky said, ''till a few years ago. I'd shuffled past acres of sixth-rate rubbish at the Tate, was really feeling very impatient, stepped into the first of the Turner rooms they've got there, and burst into tears. All that *light*.'' He shook his head. ''There. I'd never thought to tell anyone about that.''

Don't yawn and blink, dear friend, don't amble off to sleep and leave me alone with the rest of the night.

''Your secret is safe with me,'' she said. ''You know, once early in my marriage I was fooling around with my older son's India ink and a couple of watercolor brushes from his paint box. He was going to be Picasso in those days. I was supposed to take his kid brother to the doctor for some shots that afternoon.

''I never did, not that day. I made one image after another, used up a whole tablet of paper and most of a bottle of ink. I didn't stop until Bill came and took his toys away from me, very indignantly.

''I was glad of it. I looked around me and I thought, in absolute terror and confusion, But if I do this, how can I have any sort of a normal life? I wasn't thinking of the unwashed dishes, the missed appointment, that sort of stuff. It was the awful chill of coming out of that completely absorbed state back into the plain afternoon: home, kids, phone ringing, the whole schmeer. I thought if I had to make that transition very often, eventually I'd refuse to come back at all and I'd end up in the nuthouse—belong there, too.''

That was how Ricky had always felt returning from his

travels: the reentry into the drearily familiar airport, the end of enchantment. But return he always did. She was still at the wall.

Do you hear yourself? he thought urgently. Do you hear yourself telling me that you are bewitched by your own work, lost in it? That what you foresaw has in a fashion come about? Do you hear these dreams shouting to you that there are other matters demanding your attention?

She sipped her milk and began to speak of Turner.

She came back from taking the dogs for their summer shots. Mars, cheerful and unfazed as usual, went bounding off around the corner of the house on business of his own, but Brillo came inside to lie down and sleep off the effects of the vaccines.

"Oh, you're so sensitive," she chided, smiling into his reproachful amber eyes.

Ricky came in from the back patio while she was putting away the groceries she had picked up. He watched for a moment without speaking. Then he said, "You had a visitor."

"Not George?"

"No." Ricky sat down at the table and described a woman from the university in Albuquerque who had stopped by on a return trip there from Denver. She had wanted to discuss with Dorothea the possibility of a teaching position at the university, a studio class or a class in the history of women in art.

"I told you, people think they have a perfect right to pester the life out of me, ever since that damn New York show," she said irritably. "She should at least have phoned me first."

"Her name is Violet Harding. She said she made an appointment to speak to you this afternoon."

"Oh, Lord!" Dorothea checked the calendar by the telephone. "So she did. I completely forgot."

"Dorothea," Ricky said quietly, "what's going on here?"

"I don't know—early senility, you think?" She put away the English Breakfast Tea she'd bought for him.

"No. I think faintheartedness. You're hiding. Why?"

She turned to look at him, shocked. "Hiding? From what?"

"From the part of the world that wants you, the people who can use what you have to offer. This woman and this job, among others."

"Haven't you ever forgotten an appointment?" she said.

His clear blue eyes were fixed steadily on her: Inquisitor's eyes. She resented that unwavering stare.

"What is it?" he said. "Some kind of shell shock? If it's battle fatigue, the only war I know of that you've fought lately is your artist's war with the wall. And you've won that. But you act as if you've lost. You act as if you've been routed or, worse yet, as if the damned wall has fallen on you and buried you out there with it."

Her dismay flashed hotly into anger, but she swallowed it. A dying man gets some extra latitude. "I don't think you understand, Ricky. I have my work to do, and that's how I want to spend my time. The wall isn't finished."

With a suddenness that made her jump, he slapped his palm down on the tabletop so that the salt shaker jittered. "Yes it is! You can't stay here with it forever like some stone guardian of a temple lost in the jungle!"

She tried to turn her rising anger to lightness. "Come on, Ricky, I'm not as petrified as all that. This is ridicu—"

"It is not. I am deadly serious, and so should you be."

Her anger rose on a wave of conviction that he was being unreasonable, he did not understand, he was abusing his situation to intrude suddenly in this overbearing manner on her life. What the hell did he know about art anyway?

"Look, what is it you'd like to see me doing, would you mind telling me that?"

"Kiss the wall goodbye and walk away into the rest of your life," he said promptly.

"Jesus," she said, glaring. "What is this? I open my dreams to you and you take that as a mandate to run my whole life?"

"Your dreams!" He stood, catching the back of his chair in time to prevent it from toppling over behind him. "I don't know who the ghost in your dreams is, but I can tell you this, my girl: You need him! You need a shock, a jar, a revolution of your own to heave you clear of this—this enslavement to your own work!"

Brillo came whining to her side and thrust his sharp wet nose into her palm. "It's all right," she said. "Go lie down." All right, stop; stop now. "Ricky, I'm sorry. This is crazy. What are we fighting about?"

"We're not fighting. I am concerned, that's all. I'm concerned, and I'm a sick man; I don't need extra worries."

His querulous tone set her off. She could feel herself slip

the moorings of control and conciliation, and goddamn it, so be it.

"Christ almighty!" she blazed. "Whoever asked you to worry about me? I can worry about myself."

"Ah, but you don't, you see. You don't. You wander about hypnotized by the wall, in full flight from whatever living impulse it is that sends you these dreams of rebellion and raw feeling. You're like a little old miser, hoarding yourself out here, saving your talent for a project that's done."

"What?" she said. "What?" She was stuttering with rage.

"You're not lived out yet, you understand? You can't construct yourself a paradise of beauty and then crawl into it and zip it up after you. Christ, look at me, learn from me, if you can't find it in yourself. I'm spent to the last farthing, but that just leaves me the lighter for leaving."

"Goddamn it," she said through clenched teeth, "you're not dead yet, so don't pull this know-all, see-all crap on me, all right? If we're talking about my life, then let's talk about my life, my work, my future, not yours. And by God if there was any kind of paradise around here it's in shreds now, between these damned dreams and the demands people keep making on me, including your demands, *yours.*" She stopped, breathless and appalled at what she had said. But he had asked for it. He had no right to tear her whole way of life down around her like this because she didn't like to live the way he had, out in the world and meeting people, mixing, frittering time away in aimless wanderings and trivial half-understood conversations with strangers. Don't say that to him. Finish. "So you tend to your life and I'll tend to mine, all right? I'll keep my own accounts and I'll thank you to stay the hell out of it."

He lowered his head. "I went too far. I'm sorry."

"Good," she snapped. She felt wobbly and a little sick. "So am I. God. Are we finished with this?"

"I am," he said faintly. "I need to sit down."

"Go inside. I'm going to get a drink."

They sat facing each other over the drinks she had brought. She did not want to look into his face again for a while. But was that in part because there was truth in what he'd said? Why had she become so angry? Not in years, not since before Nathan left, when things had begun going bad, had she felt like this. It was horrible, dizzying, and exciting too in a sickly way.

You asked for it, for his judgment on you. Can't let somebody only halfway into your soul.

"Do you want me to go?" he said.

"At the moment, yes. But not enough."

He coughed. She waited, not going to him, not speaking. When he was done coughing, he picked up his drink and silently raised it to her.

❧ Four ❧

BLANCA KNEW RIGHT away that Mina was ticked about something by the way she snapped her high heels on the floor when she walked: *crack, crack, crack,* like a whip.

"Where's Beto?" Mina said, looming in the doorway, all red lips and red nails and furious black eyebrows.

Blanca was sitting at the kitchen table putting a month's worth of bingo counters into the bingo sheets from the supermarket. She'd already pocketed two that got you a dollar for just turning them in. "He's down the street, playing with the pieces of Horacio's busted motorbike just like usual."

"Where's Mom?"

"Visiting. Mrs. Atencio has some cousins in from Las Cruces."

"Good," Mina said. "Maybe I can do this without getting hassled, then."

"Do what?"

"Split. Leave. For good. I'm moving in with a girlfriend from the office."

Blanca hurried after Mina and stood in the doorway of the bedroom as her older sister pulled an old suitcase from the top of Mom's closet and started throwing her own clothes into it.

Blanca watched with envious eyes as the pink sweater she'd been hoping to grow into and appropriate went into the case with the rest. There didn't seem to be a lot to say. Mina hadn't been spending much time around home lately anyhow.

"Goddamn it," Mina said, holding up a belt. "Did you do this?" The end of the belt had been cut off neatly at about the third hole.

"Well, I borrowed it, and it wouldn't fit me otherwise," Blanca said, hunching back a little in case Mina started to throw things.

"I told you a million times, I don't care if you borrow my stuff, just don't ruin it so I can't ever use it again," Mina shouted. "I can't wear this now, it's too small, and look at it, it looks like shit!"

"Well, you weren't using it, and it was too big on me."

"I ought to use it on you," Mina said. She threw the belt. "Take it. It's no good to me any more, you fixed that."

Roberto walked in, wiping his greasy black hands on his jeans. "Hey," he said to Mina, "you packing? Where you going?"

"Moving out."

"Out? Where, out? Does Mom know?"

Mina glared at him. "She will. I'm moving to the Heights, permanent. I'm not going to stay around here and carry the whole job of supporting this place now that you got fired off your job. I can't afford it."

"Job," Beto sneered. "What job? Fucking slavery is all it was. I couldn't wait to get out of it."

"I'll bet." Mina slammed the empty drawers of her bureau shut. "You skipped one day too many and got canned, and now I'm supposed to take up the slack, right? Well, think again. You can just go and get yourself some other kind of slavery, and damn fast, if you want to stay around here eating off Mom's table."

She banged the suitcase shut, latched it, and pushed past the two of them. "Hey," Beto yelled, but Blanca noticed he didn't put a hand on her. Mina could hit like a prize fighter; both the younger kids knew that from experience. So he just stomped after her into the kitchen, talking hard. Scared, Blanca thought, because of what Mom would say. She hurried after them, not wanting to miss anything.

"I didn't just skip work," Beto said hotly. "I had business to take care of right here on the street. Remember our street, where you used to live?"

Mina thumped the bag down and went rummaging under the cupboards. "I heard all about it," she said harshly. "You must think you're some kind of hero, right? 'Closing the

street.' Big deal. A lot of people are pissed off at you and
those *cholo* friends of yours, the Maestas, did you know that?
They don't want downtown looking around and making trouble because people up here are fussing. Linda Aguilar told me
some of the neighbors wanted to get the cops themselves, to
throw you and the Maestas in the slammer and get you out of
everybody's hair.''

She put pots and silver and her own mug with the pig on it
in a plastic bag to take away. Trying to make herself disappear. Boy, Blanca thought, imagining herself doing the same
someday.

"Sticking your nose in everybody's business," Mina went
on. "Getting the TV up here. You think people like having
their place on TV just like that, with no chance to clean it up
or maybe put a few things away out of the sight of strangers
first? Nobody told you to shut down the whole street like that.
It was just an excuse for you to hang out with the big boys
and stay off work. If you're going to do something dumb like
that, the least you should do is make sure you get paid for
it.''

Beto said, "Hey, you don't know what you're talking
about, you know that? Mr. Escobar is with us now, he's
president of Pinto Street Protection.''

"Right, a man who owns a feed store is going to make a
real big difference," Mina jeered. "You dummy. You're
going to need real big guns if you're going to hold off
whoever's after this street. Where's my saucepan, that little
one with the lid that fits?''

"They went to Santa Fe," Beto yelled. "They talked to a
guy up there, and he only let them into his office on account
of the street closing.''

"Great," Mina snapped, "and talk is all he'll do. Don't
you know what's going on? Some real estate sharks are trying
to tip you all out of your homes cheap so they can renovate
and landscape and slap a wall and some gates around the
street. They'll sell it all to a lot of rich Anglos who want
security and real old Spanish charm. Call it something cute,
you know, like Gato Lindo Lane or Poquito Nido, some
damn thing like that, and make a killing. Big money, Beto.
Big money buys what it needs to get what it wants. And if
they want Pinto Street, they'll get it, and no bunch of ex-cons
and grain peddlers and lazy high school dropouts with nothing
else to do is going to stop them.''

Suddenly she grabbed Blanca and hugged her hard and kissed her head. Blanca stiffened in surprise, overwhelmed by the sweet cloud of Mina's perfume.

Beto said, "We know that, we figured all that out! But we're not going to just let them push us around. This is where we live, man. This house is where Dad wanted us to live, remember?"

Blanca gasped. You didn't bring Dad into things around here unless you were dead serious.

Mina just glared at him and said in a low voice, "When it comes to Dad, I remember more than you ever did and don't you forget it. And where he wanted us to live was not in some dumpy little dirt street full of losers."

Beto turned brick color. He grabbed a chair and banged its feet down hard on the floor. "My dad would be proud of me, being in Pinto Street Protection," he said hoarsely. "What the hell do you know anyhow, hiding up there in the Heights with your Anglo pals? How many Anglo boyfriends you got already? It's a good thing you're going because you sure don't belong here, *Mindy*."

Mina lunged at him, swinging at his head with her suitcase, and he stumbled out backward through the living room onto the porch and down into the yard. She dropped her stuff on the porch and tore down after him, punching at his head. He hit back. Blanca heard the smack of his hand on the side of Mina's face. Mina backed off a step and reached down and yanked off one of her high heels, holding it by the front and waving the spike heel like a weapon.

There was a car waiting at the curb, a maroon Cutlass, with the trunk open. The driver leaned anxiously across the seat to watch.

"Get out of my way," Mina said to Roberto, who stood between her and the car. Over her shoulder she called, "Blanca, bring my stuff!"

"It's too heavy for me," Blanca said, shrinking back onto the porch. Her heart was pounding. She was scared and excited.

"*¡Vendida!*" Beto said. "Chicken! Whose side you on, anyhow? When you going to start pretending you don't know Spanish?"

"As soon as I can damn well get away with it," Mina snapped. "I'm not staying on this shitty street so I can end up pushing a fucking big belly into church with some bum who spends all his time buried under his fucking car and thinks it's a kick in the balls if I don't make him a goddamn baby every year until my guts fall out. I'm going to marry some nice guy with a house big enough to turn around in and a pool and two cars that both run.''

She spat and crackled like a downed power line. No wonder Beto faced her but kept his distance, no wonder people were at their doors and windows listening. This time when Mina yelled for her bags, Blanca obeyed. She wanted to see if the driver of the car was a man or a woman.

"What's the matter, what's going on?" breathed Great-uncle Tilo odorously, stooping beside her to take the heavier bag. She hadn't even noticed him coming.

"Mina's leaving," Blanca said, raising her voice over the barking of Vallejo's dog, which had joined in the racket.

Beto gave ground, glowering and furious. "Don't come back," he said. "Just don't bother ever coming back, you hear? Nobody wants you here, nobody cares where you go, with your Anglo friends and your swimming pools."

Mina grabbed her stuff and slung it in the trunk of the car. Blanca got a look at a skinny blond girl in glasses at the wheel, wide-eyed and blinking with fear, while Great-uncle Tilo made a last-ditch effort to argue Mina out of going. Mina shook him off and got in and slammed the door. Beto leaped forward, yelling something Blanca couldn't make out, and smacked the hood of the car with his fists. The car began to roll forward, slung itself suddenly around, and took off.

Blanca watched it go, full of confusion. Her eyes were smarting. She wished she were in the car with Mina, bad temper and all. She ran back into the house and shut herself in her room, but even with the door closed she could hear Mom when she got home, crying and carrying on.

And later on, in the middle of the night, she had an attack.

It wasn't her first mad dash to the hospital at night, but each one always felt like the last one. I'll die, she'd think, in a furious, resentful panic. I can't breathe, I'm going to die, and it's all their fault.

The first two shots didn't work, but the third one did. By then Blanca had been admitted through the emergency room. She was wheeled into an open ward where they put curtains around her bed. Good. She hated being stared at by other patients in the middle of the night while she lay there slowly getting her breath back, slowly loosening up into the warm, drifty exhaustion that always followed an attack. There was a good part, though. The same doctor was there, the round little man from India. Even without him, of course, they would have taken care of Blanca in a hurry. One thing about being carried in wrapped in a blanket with your lips and your fingernails turning blue and your breathing sounding like something out of a horror movie: They paid attention to you right away.

She heard them talk, her mother and the doctor, sifting through all the possible things that might have triggered the attack: smoke, cleaning fluid, paint or paint thinner? Cold air? Peanut butter, fish, chocolate? Climbing the stairs too fast, laughing too hard, getting too mad—always coming back to the one the doctor favored: stress, emotional tension.

Her mother said, ''But she was just sleeping, doctor, she was only sleeping!''

It's all crap, Blanca thought scornfully. Crap, crap, crap. Tension! I don't let them throw me into the asthma with a little yelling. If I did, I'd be here in the hospital all the time. Mom and Roberto, me and Roberto, Mina and everybody—we fight. Everybody fights. Vallejo's dog barks, Rosa Romero's boyfriend is hitting her again, but you can't let things like that upset you. If you did, you'd just have to go live in the Arctic with nothing but sled dogs, like the Eskimos on TV. Nothing going on, just cold all the time, white all around, nothing to bother you, no yelling or anything.

For a minute she lay thinking about that, about peaceful whiteness, aloneness, someplace really far away with none of her family there. It felt nice.

So what was she going to get instead? More grief from her mother now that Mina was gone, more thunderclouds and strutting from Beto, and for her—asthma camp, some dumb place full of mosquitoes and crips.

She could explain this attack herself, if anybody asked her. I didn't use the nebulizer. I was playing cards with Dolly Armijo before lunch, and I didn't feel like leaving the game and spraying powder down into my throat like a creepy old invalid. Dolly might get nervous that I was going to have an attack, or she might tease me about it. Even Dolly might do that. Nobody wants a sick friend.

I forgot, that's all. Anybody can forget.

Right away the meeting went sour. It was like a jinx, Roberto thought. His mother had only agreed to let Mr. Escobar use her living room for Pinto Street Protection because he was Mina's godfather and because Father Leo was supposed to come. But Father Leo had an emergency call on Thomas Street, and only about seven people showed up anyhow. Now Jake Maestas was saying they couldn't really get started until something else got straight first.

Which turned out to be something about Pete Romero. Everybody sat crowded into the little front room, looking at Pete. He was not the kind of guy who went to meetings anyhow. He was usually out of work, got into fights a lot, and disappeared for days at a time, nobody knew where or what for.

Jake said, "What's this construction outfit that gave you this new plastering job, Pete?"

Pete stared back at him. He had plaster dust in his hair still. "J and K Builders, and I been working there almost three months now. Why?"

"Because in Santa Fe we looked up J and K Builders, and the same guys that run that company are on the board of Valley Reconstruction."

"Valley Reconstruction?" Pete said loudly. "What's that?"

"You should know," Mr. Escobar said. "You sold your house to them five months ago. And they're the ones that's trying to buy all the places on the street, dirt cheap, through this 'inspector.' "

Pete Romero stood up. He wasn't very tall, but he had the reputation of being a mean fighter. Roberto avoided his mother's anxious eyes and moved closer to the kitchen door. He could see the knives hanging over the sink. His stomach throbbed faintly with tension.

"Who says I sold my house?" Pete Romero said.

Rudolfo Escobar, who was little and round and bald, said in the same dry voice, "The papers are on file. The sale is recorded, Pete. It's a matter of public record."

Romero's face went dark with a flush of anger. "What the hell gives anybody the right to stick their goddamn nose into my business? It's my own business if I want to go and sell my own house!"

Mr. Vallejo said harshly from the wicker chair in the corner where he sat, "Sure. And all of a sudden along comes a nice job for you so now you can afford those fancy boots you're wearing, and that's your business too. I think they gave you the job to keep your mouth shut. Nobody's heard till now that you sold your place, Pete, the place you're still living in. Nobody's heard you asking around for a new place to move to—have they?'' Heads shook; there were negative murmurs around the room. ''Maybe that is other people's business. Why are you trying to keep the sale a secret?''

Romero glared around at them all, his thumbs stuck into his belt. He took up a lot of space in the crowded room.

''These buyers offered me good money and I took it, that's all. A job comes along, I take that too. None of it's anybody's concern but mine, you hear? And if I want to take my time finding a new place, that's nothing to do with anybody else either. I don't have to stand here and listen to a lot of goddamn accusations. I don't even know what I'm supposed to have done that's hurt anybody.''

Roberto put his own sweating hands into his pockets. His mom would have a fit if there was a fight here and things got busted—lamps, pictures, anything. He wasn't so scared for himself, not really. He'd been working out with Martin Maestas, lifting weights in the yard. Too bad Mina wasn't here now. She'd see if it was all a lot of nothing.

Mrs. Ruiz said, ''Sit down, Pete, don't run away.''

Romero began fiercely, ''Listen, *mujer*—''

Old Mr. Garduño banged on the floor with the tip of his cane. He said in his husky voice, ''I guess I better say this before anybody else does. I was the first one to jump on the young men for closing the street. That's because I sold my place last month. This 'inspector' is supposed to come around here with some papers and money for me. I didn't want anybody stopping him from delivering. I sold to those same people, Valley Reconstruction.''

Wow, Roberto thought, how did they get him to sell? Mr. Garduño was a mean and stubborn old man, not a pushover. Roberto had grown up to the sounds of Mr. Garduño's kids yelling when he whipped them.

Mr. Lopez said to Mr. Garduño, ''But you've lived here all your life, Tomas. Why sell to anybody? Where will you go?''

''I'm getting too old to live by myself,'' Mr. Garduño said. He shifted his twisted hands on the head of his cane. ''You need a lot of money to get into a decent home for old people.''

''A home!'' Mrs. Ruiz cried. ''But what about your relatives, your kids?''

"Don't tell me about them," the old man snapped. "I wouldn't live with any of those bums."

Mrs. Ruiz, pug-nosed, hair combed high on her head, gave Mr. Garduño a look of outrage. "I can't believe it," she said. "You'd go to one of those old people's places? Why not ask your neighbors to come in and help once in a while? People would do it, if they knew you needed help. You don't have to leave the street."

Mr. Garduño shook his head. "There maybe won't be any people here, not people I know, and I've got no special love for Pinto Street. It's just a place I live. Besides, I'd rather pay money to professionals. That way you know what you're getting." He gave a hitch to the crease of his faded pants. "The thing of it is, I feel like I've been had by those bastards. They're paying me chickenfeed compared to what they can make off this street if they buy up the whole thing and rebuild. They're giving me a goddamn tip."

Pete Romero, who had slowly sunk back into his seat, said angrily, "You can feel like a fool if you want, Garduño. I got a good price for my place."

"You think so?" Mr. Garduño looked him in the eye. "Well, I got twenty-two thousand for mine, half down and half when I vacate."

There was a moment of silence. Then Mr. Ortega said, "For that shack? I just put on a new porch and a new water heater, and they only offered me seventeen fifty!"

Mrs. Ruiz stared from face to face. "My God," she said, "how many people on this street have already sold out?" Her sister, anxious-looking herself, patted Mrs. Ruiz's arm.

Mr. Escobar said, "I don't think we should talk any more about this with Pete Romero here. Anything we decide, he'll just run and tell those Valley Reconstruction people."

"That's right, he's a spy." Mrs. Ruiz said. "Get out, spy. Nobody wants you here."

Everybody stared at Pete Romero. Oh, shit, he's going to fight, Roberto thought. The Maestas brothers thought so too; they stood up. Roberto saw his mother lean over to whisper anxiously to Mr. Escobar. Roberto avoided looking at his mother. His mouth was dry. Nerves. Pete Romero would have a knife on him, maybe worse. He was only one guy, but even one knife can do a lot of damage. I'm ready, he thought. I can't leave it all to the Maestas; this is my house, my mom's place. I'm ready.

Pete Romero shrugged contemptuously. "I don't stay where I'm not wanted," he said. "You could all learn a lesson from that." He stomped out, slamming the front door behind him.

"All right," Jake Maestas said, when everybody had settled back down again, "we need to think about what we can do to save our street. If just a few of us refuse to sell, whatever these sharks have already bought up won't be worth a damn to them. Can you imagine some fancy Anglo family paying a hundred thousand dollars to come live next to the Ortegas' place, or Tom Chavez with his goats?"

People laughed, nervous laughs.

Roberto chewed his thumbnail and tuned out the talk. He felt jittery and let-down, getting ready for a brawl like that and then ending up with nothing but more damn talk. He looked admiringly at Martín Maestas's strong chest and shoulders under the tight T-shirt and wondered if maybe Martín might go for a little trip to the offices of this J and K Builders company. No spray-paint cans, either. Crowbars, maybe a pick-ax, and some sledgehammers, bash the place apart.

Somebody had to do something besides talk.

Blanca and her mother got back from the clinic and found Father Leo waiting on the porch. While the two adults sat in the front room to talk, Blanca made lemonade in the kitchen. From here she could listen easily to what they had to say.

After the stiff greetings and vague comments on the weather, Father Leo got down to what was bothering him: that stupid meeting, of course. It really bugged Blanca that she'd missed it, being sick and all. The asthma made her miss out on everything interesting.

The priest had a pleasing, mellow voice that Blanca liked. To look at, he was nothing much: a small, quiet man with a perpetually worried look that didn't say a whole lot for the comfort he got from the faith he represented. People respected him as a dutiful and concerned priest, though Blanca had heard elderly neighbors sigh over the loss of old Father Diego to a different parish.

Father Leo came seldom to the Cantu house, perhaps because when he did he always ended up lecturing Mom. Blanca's mother had sworn not to go to church ever again until Blanca's asthma went away. She sent her kids, of course, but she stayed home herself. She said God had loaded her with more trouble than was fair, and she would not be argued out of it. Father Leo was no match for her. Blanca took pride in this.

Today he was complaining, in that sad, roundabout way he had, how the people Mr. Escobar had asked over here had carried on their meeting without their priest's presence and even had decided things, things having to do with a wedding that he himself was going to perform, without asking him. Cecilia Baca was getting married, and everybody was going to go to the party afterward in the big field across the street, next to the new YMCA construction. Pinto Street Protection had decided to use the amplifying equipment of the party's band to talk to everybody about the problem of the fake inspections and the land grab that was going on.

"It's not suitable," the priest was saying. "I'm very disappointed by what happened here in my absence, Mrs. Cantu, and I'm trying to communicate that to everyone who came. We have other ways to handle this problem. Our political people, the city government—"

Blanca knew the answers. Great-uncle Tilo and Mr. Escobar had been chewing it all over together practically every night on the porch since the meeting. The politicals weren't interested, they said, they couldn't be trusted, they didn't have the clout. The city government had already said they would "look into" the question of the false inspections, but everybody knew what that meant: the round file, the wastebasket. And the man in Santa Fe had kept Mr. Escobar and Jake waiting for two hours and then only made the same kind of promises.

She whacked the can opener on the countertop; the thing stuck all the time. There, done; the container came open. Now she had to shave the frozen plug of lemonade to be able to fit it into the neck of the bottle.

She heard Father Leo shift his ground. He didn't approve of some of the membership of the protection society. He didn't approve, to be exact, of the Maestas brothers, and he was unhappy to see Roberto Cantu hanging around with them. They were older, ex-convicts, troublemakers. They would drag Roberto into trouble with them.

Mom protested that she couldn't get Roberto to listen to her any more, he was too big.

Well, the priest said sadly, he was not surprised to hear that. "You must realize that in a household where the mother avoids her church and its authority in her own life, the

children lose their respect not only for that church but for all
authority, including their own mother's.''

Here they go, Blanca thought. Nothing would be said that
she had not heard a dozen times before. She licked up a
dollop of the frozen concentrate that had slid down the side of
the mixing bottle. The sharp, icy taste made her shiver with
delight. She began vigorously shaking the bottle. Each time
she stopped to uncap it and stir the contents with a spoon, she
could hear the argument proceeding.

''Make a promise, Mrs. Cantu, promise something to God
if He would mercifully decide to lift the burden of Blanca's
sickness. Think of that young man who promised to walk to
Santa Fe if his wife at last conceived a child. God heard, and
now that young man has a beautiful daughter and the pleasure
of showing our Heavenly Father his gratitude.''

The low voice of Blanca's mother: ''I made my promise,
Father, when my Eddie went into the marines, and you see
what came out of that.''

Blanca's father had been killed in an incident on the border
between North and South Korea years before. Probably Mom
didn't even remember him any more, she just had these habits
of thinking and talking about him. Blanca didn't remember.
Beto sometimes pretended that he did, which Blanca was sure
was just an act. Beto could be such a jerk. Mina did remember but wouldn't talk about it.

Shake, shake, shake. The stuff tasted awful if the frozen
slush wasn't fully dissolved.

''You can't hold your soul hostage in order to get favors
from God, Mrs. Cantu. Our Lord will not be blackmailed. By
this stubbornness of yours you cut yourself off from God
when you most need Him.''

''I pray every night to the Virgin, Father. She was a
mother too; she understands what I'm doing. She speaks to
our Lord for me.''

''We must not elevate the Virgin above God and His Son,''
the priest said with real distress in his voice.

Blanca poured herself a cupful of lemonade and went into
her room and shut the door. She was in the middle of reading
a book from the school library about a wild horse that a girl
tamed all on her own, someplace in California.

Later, when the priest had gone, her mother called her to
come clear up the mess she had left in the kitchen. Besides,
they had some dishes from breakfast to wash. Blanca dried

each plate and spoon as they were handed to her. Her mother's silent rage depressed her. The same small pretty woman who smiled at people in the discount store and wished even the crankiest old shoppers a nice day and cried at home so much was the same one who could stand up to the priest and make conditions with God Himself. Mom was a crier, but she knew how to win in the end.

Any day now, Beto would leave, like Mina. Great-uncle Tilo would die, and nobody would be left with Mom but Blanca, the invalid, the one who had nowhere to go.

❧ Five ❧

THE SINGING AND shouting mounted in volume. The dreamer, place on the page lost yet again, rose to look out of the open window.

Dorothea, watching against her will, saw someone look back in. A head on a pole, bobbing high above the heads of the mob below, gaped in at the window. This time she managed to blur her vision so that she didn't have to see it clearly. The others, the members of the mob, she saw more clearly than ever.

The people in the crowd had been looting. They had loaves of bread, armloads of garments. A man carried a small, neat, child-sized chair extended in front of him as he swept along on his roller skates at the edge of the crowd.

"Hey, *citoyen!*" The man at the window was hailed. "What is your trade?"

"I study the law," he replied. The shadow of the pole and its burden jiggled across his worn woolen sleeve.

A woman bawled, "Look well, then, *citoyen,* for we are the law now!"

People laughed. Dorothea had just time to notice that the woman who had shouted was Claire, and then someone lobbed something up at the judge. For a nauseated instant Dorothea expected him to catch a bloody collop of flesh. If he flinched from it they would call him a traitor and rush up the stairs to tear him to pieces. Don't flinch, she begged him silently.

He caught a peach, hard and green.

She woke up whimpering and lay awhile with her head buried under the pillow. It's getting worse, she thought. Maybe we're making it worse, not better. She blew her nose, sat down at her desk with her robe pulled on over her shoulders, and wrote.

Ricky sat back with his fingers interlaced behind his head and stared at the beamed ceiling. On Thursday Dorothea had found for him at the bookstore a wonderful work by Richard Cobb, a classic study of Revolutionary and post-Revolutionary France titled *The Police and the People*. Ricky had read it once before, for want of anything better at first but with increasing fascination, during an illness one winter in London. Having just used Cobb's book to refresh his memory, he was clear on the details of the judge's period. At least I know enough, he thought, to fill in the gaps in Dorothea's wretched American education.

The French Revolution had produced a police state, as revolutions historically do. Workingmen had to carry passbooks, called livrets, signed by their employers. The police made constant searches of travelers, stopping coaches on the roads, even bursting into homes and lodging houses in the middle of the night, Gestapo style. If a country relative came to stay with you in town, you were supposed to report this to the police. A veritable mania about disguise spurred the authorities to harass the life out of used-clothing peddlers.

The point of making mobility so difficult was not primarily to inconvenience spies and counterrevolutionaries, nor to entrap fleeing aristocrats. It was simply to control the roving bands of beggars and deserters, from the Revolutionary—and later the Imperial—armies, which plagued the countryside, spreading alarm and unrest.

Before whom would they bring someone picked up for unlawful travel? Or a workingman caught without his livret? Or a merchant charged with hoarding food by spiteful neighbors? Or anyone accused by his enemy—another farmer who covets one's lower pasture, a rival tradesman who desires one's clientele—and charged with unenthusiastic support of the Revolution or the Emperor Napoleon or, for that matter, later, the returned king? Who would be responsible for fining, imprisoning, or deporting to the Seychelles in the Indian

Ocean these victims of official paranoia and repression? The
ghost in Dorothea's dreams, of course: the judge.

Worse still—there is always worse—some provincial judges
aided and abetted outright murder. The death toll of the Red
Terror, the relatively short-lived reign of Madame Guillotine,
was probably far exceeded by the death toll of the counterrev-
olutionary reaction.

This movement, called the White Terror for the white lilies
of the deposed royal Bourbons, was a wave of killings that
began as soon as Robespierre was brought down. His place
was taken by more moderate Republicans who withdrew the
protection of the government from Robespierre's radical
followers.

The country people had remained throughout both royalist
and devoutly Catholic. They now turned with fury on the
radical firebrands who had been sent from Paris to rule the
provincial districts under Robespierre and also on any locals
who had collaborated with these strangers. Fleeing ex-officials
were arrested in neighboring towns, where many were butchered in their cells by rampaging mobs.

Some judges, informed that an ex-official was to be brought
back for trial, would deliberately release the details of the
homecoming (often set for midday, when people had free
time). The townspeople would meet the shackled wretch at
the town gate, wrest him from his unresisting military escort,
and beat him to death on the spot.

Ricky reflected on the way Dorothea's ghost repeatedly
threw offerings to the mob (or to the soldiery, men in uniform, officialdom of all sorts). This is a ghost, surely, like so
many of its ilk, with a guilty conscience! He played no noble
part in these events. No Scarlet Pimpernel here.

If he could be identified by name, what a coup that would
be, what a legacy to leave Dorothea! Pity it wasn't as easy as
saying, It's famous old Judge Whatnot, my dear, everyone
knowledgeable in the field knows his name; nothing simpler.
The dreams were not so direct as that. Anyway, suppose the
judge was important enough to show up in the written histories of the time, how to recognize him among the many like
him? One would need to sift the stories of hundreds. I haven't
the sources, not here, probably not outside France itself. And
I may not have the time.

Ridiculously on cue, the chipped Seth Thomas clock on the
mantel gave out a series of muted chimes. The afternoon was

nearly gone. Ricky looked down at the blue tracery under the thin skin of his wrist.

Who was it, awaiting execution, who remarked on how wonderfully the approach of one's death concentrated the mind? In one afternoon, this new pattern had fully emerged and clarified itself: our judge as an official functionary, perhaps even an Eichmann-like monster. And the occasional accusatory young voice that Dorothea thought was Claire's? The judge's own younger, more idealistic self, perhaps, making its own judgment? Too complicated.

A motor roared and died outside. Ricky sat still. Go away, no one is home. He and Dorothea had made their peace again, and he wanted nothing and no one to disturb it.

Whoever it was rapped briskly on the door. Ricky struggled up out of his chair—how could his shrunken body weigh so much?—and went to answer, to his immediate regret. There stood George.

"Hi, Dick, how're you doing? I had a message from Dorothea—"

"She's not in just now."

"But she left word she had some pictures for me to look at."

"I'm afraid you've missed her, she's gone out."

"Well, can you tell me where—"

Here came Mars hallooing round the corner of the house and practically leaping into George's arms, with gray Brillo trotting daintily in his wake, and of course Dorothea behind them both. She must have stopped at the shed to clean up and drop off her tools, for she came empty-handed and wiping her fingers on her shirttail.

"I got your message," whooped George. "Dorothea, you're terrific! I knew you'd wake up and see it my way. Dick, here, was just telling me you'd gone out."

"I was taking a walk," she said calmly, "with the dogs. Come on in, George, and I'll show you what you can choose from."

The drawings were taken out of the bureau in the living room and exclaimed over—black and white, wonderful, not expensive to reproduce and of course they would do a class job, nothing cheap, this one was clearly the best, and George had brought a contract with him. They headed for the kitchen and the back patio, George carried ahead by his long, ebullient stride.

Ricky stayed behind, his thoughts locked in black anger. All that energy, all that life, stuffed into a bounding ape who hadn't the first notion of what to do with it. *Intolerable.*

She built a fire because it was cool even on summer nights, up this high, and she knew he was susceptible to the cold. They watched Dr. Who, caped and capped like Sherlock Holmes, take on a giant rat (that is, a regular-sized rat in a small metal tube seen very closely by the camera) in the sewers of Victorian London.

"My God," Dorothea said, "it's such nonsense, but it's actually literate. Those are lines the actors are speaking, not comic-strip captions. Doesn't it make you homesick?"

"Not a bit," Ricky said. "The most popular television show in England isn't *Dr. Who.* it's *Dallas,* didn't you know that?"

"Doesn't anything make you homesick?" she persisted gently. When he did not reply she added, "Was that another letter from your sister yesterday?"

"Yes."

He didn't want to talk about this, that was obvious. But it needed talking about. "She wants you to come home, doesn't she."

"Of course she does. She is a perfectly conventional creature, and convention has it that one comes home to die. Therefore, I must come home."

Apprehensive about the answer but determined to get one, she said, "Are you considering going?"

"Would you like me to?" he said, not looking at her.

"Maybe you should regardless of what I'd like. You tell me not to hide here, Ricky, but am I the only one who does?"

Pause. He watched the flames. She had difficulty imagining herself sitting here watching the flames alone, with him gone away out of her house. The fire spat. Now he looked at her with his wide blue gaze.

"You mean that I'm hiding?"

"Yes, with every good reason, but even so, I don't think you can do it forever. I don't think you should. Do you realize that you never talk about yourself? I mean your life, your travels, your family, your childhood. You came to my house like a man without a past, and you live here totally concentrated on the moment—the dreams, or whatever we're doing—as if you were a ghost yourself. Already. And you're not, that's the point.''

She stopped, but he said nothing. She forced herself to go on.

"You have family, Ricky, and friends, and I don't know who else, people you haven't seen in years but who probably need to see you, people maybe you need to see. Everyone has those people clustered in their lives. I can't believe that you don't. If you have time before you die, you try to see them and settle things with them, say what needs to be said, or write them long letters, or think about them. You don't just toss your whole past life over your shoulder like a worn-out sock and sink yourself in somebody else's doings.''

"How do you know what I think about?" he said.

"I know what you talk about: art, music, the country up here; the dogs; what you see around you from day to day; the dogs. Me, my dreams, my life. Are you going to tell me that all that is a smokescreen and that behind it you're thinking about your own affairs?''

He sipped juice from the glass on the table at his elbow and he did not answer.

Dorothea looked into the fire. Well, you've started this, you might as well get along to the end of it. You don't want to go through this strain and tension for nothing.

"I feel as if I'm—unlawfully detaining you, do you understand?'' she said. ''When there are other matters belonging to you alone that need your attention, now of all times. I feel like a thief, when I see those letters from your sister. There must be others, too; people must be trying to get in touch with you while they still can.'' She swallowed and said more softly, ''You accused me not long ago of hoarding myself. But I feel as if I'm hoarding you.''

"Well, don't,'' he said brusquely. ''To start, you've got the thing wrong-end-to. It isn't that I'm avoiding some sort of deathbed accounting by meddling in your life. It's that when I look back, there's really very little to examine. In a sense I'm using your dream dilemma to fill a void, do you see? Not as a distraction but as a replacement.

"I suppose the truth is, I am a sort of ghost, a leftover from another era, and I always have been. In the last century I'd have gone looking for the sources of the Nile and the true North Pole, that sort of thing. I had the income and the education and the itch to be moving. But all those places are found now, and I haven't the time or the qualifications for space travel.

"Besides, in all honesty, I'm spoiled. Those explorers I hark back to didn't come out of a world of central heating, jetliners, transoceanic telephones, and tape cassettes of Verdi operas, you know."

She had to smile. "You make yourself sound like a real bum. I've read those pieces you did for the *Guardian*."

"And you were taken in, weren't you? That was my cover. But in reality I've simply drifted through the world, the way you'd walk through your favorite old museum and nod to the pictures and the sculptures that you knew. Think of me not witnessing earthshaking events but drifting, just drifting, only pausing to shake hands, drink cups of sweet tea or palm wine or whatever with little wizened women and dried-up little chaps with hands like brown spiders, or sleek young men or stout blond women with aprons on. It doesn't matter what you talk about, or if you even understand each other's language. It's just the greeting, spending time together, and moving on again.

"Writing was an excuse. And the traveling was all the same, do you see? So there's nothing much to think about in the way that you mean."

Mars came up and put his chin on her knee, gazing soulfully up at her face in hopes of an evening stroll. She stroked the sleekness of his head, feeling the delicate shape of the skull underneath. If I say the wrong thing now, she thought, it's going to be just you and me and Brillo, kid.

"This is just what I mean," she began slowly. "Don't misunderstand me, Ricky, but I think maybe you should be saying these things to—someone else. Maybe to several people, who are all waiting for you to come and speak to them in the way that you're speaking to me now, people with a better right than mine to hear you."

"No one has a better right."

"But your own people—"

"The right you mean is mine to confer, and my own people are the people whose hands I shake, whose tea I drink, and to whom I choose to speak or not to speak. If you can't accept that, you have only to show me the door. I'm sorry, I didn't mean that to be cutting."

"Ricky, I have to ask this: Why did you come here?"

"I came because you drew me, not by conscious wish but

by physical act. It's the wall, don't you know that? The thing is magical.''

"You're not serious!'' Because she knew he was, she was afraid, although what of? She could not think what it was, but she recognized that inward flutter of fear.

"Don't you know that art is magic?'' he said severely.

"Metaphorically, of course, but I don't know anything about—well, real magic, if there is such a thing.''

"There is,'' he said grimly. "Magic brought me, your magic, the wall's magic. What keeps me here is my own choice, and your concurrence, and the work you've given me to do: this ghost. Or perhaps you've brought the ghost and me here to solve each other. What do you think?''

She did not know what to think. She leaned forward and held her cold, unsteady hands to the warmth of the fire.

So it's a lump, you great bloody fool, Ricky thought; just what it appears to be, just as you've known all along must happen sooner or later.

He drove with savage concentration, his long arms tensed around the wheel, his eyes glaring at the road back to Dorothea's. They had told him at the hospice that indeed the cancer had spread. The white, painless intrusion in his lower belly marked the pace stepping up.

He had spent the morning discussing again with them all the possibilities, had not been given any pig swill about a cure. Surgery, chemicals, radiation, he knew the drill. A great deal of misery in exchange for a little more time.

Time weak and sick as a dying dog. To hell with that.

His vision was so blurred that he could hardly see. He pulled to the side of the road and wept. Then he took out his handkerchief, mopped his face dry, and sat back in the seat to try to think. He kept the car door open for the breeze.

I'd almost forgotten the actual end. Didn't want to remember what the doctors said, don't want to now. I'm not ready to reflect on how the body shuts down. Toward the end the guts leave off churning out dung, so you don't get nagged to eat. Your bladder leaks punily down a tube. A kind of living petrification sets in. They say they can control the pain even when it gets bad, as if that means anything. Liar, he charged himself, shuddering. It means a great deal.

Here I've been chasing after Dorothea's dreams as if I had all the time in the world. What am I doing here? She was right to ask, of course she was! And all that drivel I gave her as an answer—Christ, how embarrassing! What do I shirk that needs doing whilst I potter about in Dorothea's life? Must be mad. The damned disease has eaten my brain.

Dorothea will be alive, dreaming her damned dreams, and I'll be dead, dead, dead. Dead as Danton, dead as Robespierre, dead as Bonaparte and all the other historic figures I've been telling her about, and why not? They are dead and therefore eminently suitable topics for my conversation. When I am dead, shall Dorothea dream of me?

Not likely; I'm not the right period.

Dorothea had got home before him from her morning's errands in town. Her truck was parked on the shaded side of the front yard. He could see her in the front room by the window. She was looking through that fat leather sack of a purse she carried, absorbed in finding whatever it was she sought.

He sighed, got out of the car, and entered the house.

Well, of course she knew the verdict without asking, and so she didn't ask but spared them both that. Told him furiously how annoyed she was to have lost the business card of the people who were going to come trim the dead branches in her cottonwood trees before one fell and brained someone. Would have to get a new purse in which things didn't get lost so easily, goddamn this one.

He knew what her anger was for—for him, for his news that didn't need telling. What right had she to be angry, when he was the dying one? Couldn't she see how her anger irritated him, couldn't she control herself for heaven's sake?

"I'll be leaving soon," he said abruptly. Leave, go, get the devil out of here, with my rotting body that's turning my nature to bile. She shouldn't have to put up with that (but she would if she were my true friend, if she loved me, damn her).

"But you said the other night—" Her dismay and evident pain gratified him, and then he was revolted at his own pleasure in it. He could barely look at her as she went on quietly, "I'm sorry. Are you sure?"

"Of course I'm sure!" he growled. "I can still bloody think a bit, I can still decide about staying or leaving."

"It's not because of this art class coming up next week, is it? I could always cancel, Mary would understand. She's an old friend."

"Do what you like," he said, turning away to avoid her

touching him, the touch that would melt his intention. "I'm
going to pack. Thank you for your hospitality. I hope I've
been some help with the dreams. I'll leave in the morning."

He slammed his bedroom door and sank down on his bed,
suddenly strengthless. The worst of it was that he could not
remember anything that truly required his attention elsewhere.
Not one thing.

The judge wrote, dipping ink from the bronze well in the
shape of a draped woman, half kneeling under the weight of
the ink-filled jar on her shoulder.

Dorothea woke with her skull buzzing. She sat up, scrunch-
ing her eyes shut and shaking her head from side to side. She
had a sharp cramp under one shoulder blade.

Ricky was sitting on the deep sill of the window with a
small black Pueblo pot in his hands. He turned it absently in
his fingers as if feeling it for comfort. The light was that of
late morning.

She thought, I never sleep this late. Whew, my head! Why
is Ricky here? Come to say goodbye? In his robe and pajamas?

"Ricky?" she said hoarsely. "Are you all right?"

He carefully set the pot down on the far corner of the sill
and got up. "Are you?"

"I think so. What time is it?" Her heart felt literally
heavy, as if standing up would be beyond her. Grief feels like
this, she thought, like after leaving Jack or when I used to
have those awful fights with Claire. "Damn it, I can't remember any dream at all, but I feel really—I can't exactly
explain it. Emptied. Did I say something, at least?"

"In a sense."

"In a sense?" She read the strain in his face and in the
remoteness of his tone. "What sense?"

He brought over a yellow legal pad, one of the ones he had
been using for his reading notes. The pages were covered
with methodical, ornate handwriting in pencil: not hers, and
not his either. The first page bore a salutation: *Mon cher fils*.

She stared at the pages, too frightened to speak but excited,
too.

"I heard you moving about in here, muttering to yourself
as if you were looking for something in the dark," Ricky
said. "I came in and turned on the light. You were out of bed
and your eyes were open. You asked, in French, where your
writing paper was. I gave you this pad and a pencil and I

sharpened some others. You sat over there in the chair by the little desk and you wrote for hours without speaking another word. Then you got up and fell back into bed and slept. You don't remember?''

"No," she said. The word made no sound. She cleared her throat.

"I shall never forget. You ought to have seen yourself writing this document. This—" He tapped the pages. "You'd best read it, I think."

She looked down at the pad, reluctant to read the writing. "Have you?"

He hesitated. "I began to, but it seemed—yours." He turned his hand helplessly in the air. "Anyway, some of it is beyond me. The French, I mean."

She forced herself to focus. Her palms sweated and the pad shook slightly in her grip. *'Mon cher fils, j'ai pensé cependant longtemps à votre lettre—'* She ran her eye down the first page. "Christ, Ricky, I don't even know some of these words. How could I have—? We'll have to use the Larousse, if I can find it." Triumph burst through her astonishment. She laughed. "God, I did it! I asked for something, and I got it!"

"You asked? What do you mean, you asked?"

"I went to sleep last night thinking, I want something to happen, some break, some enlightenment as to what the dreams mean. I was pushing for it, Ricky, with all my will."

"But why?"

"Because, my dear, if you go I'm left on my own with this crazy dream business. I had to try to get whatever insight I could right away, while you're still here to look at it with me."

"You mean you tried to force matters," he accused.

"Yes," she said firmly. She felt exhilarated and wanted him to share in the triumph. He had earned it.

All morning they labored over the translation.

"What the hell kind of spelling is that?"

"Obsolete, according to this entry in the dictionary."

" 'Callous' is probably a closer meaning, in that sentence."

" 'Fulling.' That's old-fashioned dry cleaning, isn't it?"

"Yes; they used to rub woolen clothing with a clay called 'fuller's earth' to remove stains and smells without shrinkage."

" 'Bitter as gall.' Not exactly an original phrasemaker."

" *'L'Ancien Régime.'* Ricky, you actually saw me write

these words in this beautiful old-fashioned hand? You know what my writing looks like. How could I have produced this?''

''I watched from start to finish.''

Once Ricky went away and returned with a bowl of fruit that he set on a chair. There was no room on the bed, which was covered with sheets of paper. He did not take anything from the bowl to eat, and neither did she.

Still in her nightgown, the one with the drooping hem and the sleeve coming out at the shoulder seam, she sat back and read the translation aloud.

My dear son,

I have thought a long time about your letter. Here is my answer, but first you must understand some matters out of my own past which perhaps throw light on my position. I have not ordinarily spoken of these things, but now the time has come.

To begin with, regardless of the foolish exaggerations to which your great-aunt Marielle is given, I have survived in the world but by the standards of many I cannot be said to have risen. Your grandfather was a landowner in a small way, as well as proprietor of a prosperous fulling works. I myself traveled far more widely as a boy than I could afford to do now. I was not sent with a lean purse to Paris to be a clerk in the law, like so many of my contemporaries, but on the contrary lived rather well. In those days Paris was smaller, and my aunt and uncle—themselves childless and thus particularly kindly disposed toward me— had a house in a suburb. They would often send me a hamper packed with excellent country food.

I was, in other words, comfortable and happy, but I was never any sort of wealthy pillar of the Old Regime, nor did I keep company with aristocrats. In fact, I was or at least became quite radical in my thinking, thanks to the company I kept in the coffeehouses. I read Rousseau and Voltaire and the rest, and I believed.

Do you find this unlikely? Yet it is true. I was not a leader, you understand—it is to this above all that I owe my survival. But I was a good follower. I was solvent, too, always ready to pay the printer and the tavern keeper and the cost of oil for the lamps by which we studied and debated how to build our dream nation of perfect law and humane justice.

I was as young as you are, as ardent as you are, as idealistic as you are, and when the Revolution came, I rejoiced, I was exalted, I felt fulfilled.

When our family's little landholding was taken, I was glad. My parents fled to Germany, where they had relatives. I was sorry about that, but I rejoiced to see the family business taken over by the local Revolutionary Council. Within six months, the business was closed forever, its assets drained and dispersed. Again, I was glad, relieved of the guilt of my comfortable young life—relieved at my old parents' expense. Yet I thought I was seeing justice done—until later, when even I had to admit in horror that what I saw about me was not justice but madness, blood thirst, and greed without limit. The promised new order arrived and devoured everything in its path.

I, fortunately, was too small to be noticed, and I had the sense to leave Paris after the fall of Robespierre, for I saw that the wave of revolutionary madness had crested and that retribution, terrible retribution, must follow. So that too—the worst of the reaction—I escaped, by going quietly home to the country.

Good luck and obscurity preserved me. My once-despised provincial cousins here took me in and spoke for me. With their aid and support I was able to live out the upheavals following Robespierre's death. I know you have never cared for Cousin Henri, and it is true that he has engaged in certain ambiguous practices in his business and has profited greatly while others have gone to the wall. Yet I owe him a great deal, for he helped me when I came wearily home, a fugitive from my own precious Revolution gone mad.

Living under Henri's protection, making myself as useful as I could in my native province, I began to see how simpleminded we young men had been in Paris, blinded by our radical ideals. I do not mean that I ever condoned the vengeful bloodletting of the White Terror, but I did begin to understand the furious anti-Revolutionary resentment from which it sprang. A conviction possessed me that we with our youthful, foolish, longing hearts had brought our country to her knees under a horde of profiteers and madmen, and I was filled with despair and shame. In the end, I did not oppose the White Terror by word or deed. I learned to be humble and to hold my peace. It is a lesson that I hope you can learn at less cost.

Cousin Henri obtained for me a place as a schoolmaster in a nearby village. I worked. I was cold and silent, and I knew others like me, men whom I avoided and who avoided me. I ventured to write some pamphlets concerning the importance of the rule of law. Recognition came. I was cheered, though surprised, to find myself appointed a defender of the law, a member of the courts of the Emperor Napoleon's government. I married your mother, a worthy woman, and in time came to love her, as I think even you will not deny.

And yes, it is true, I continued to accept such advances as came to me, for I saw that they gave pleasure to my wife and then I trust, for a time at least, to my sole surviving child, yourself. And I have remained here, in the quiet of my native province, working and writing, never more pleased than when no notice is taken of me, and in this, believe me, I am far from unique.

There are no old revolutionaries, unless you count LaFayette, who is, I think, a little mad. In making our Revolution in 1789 we unmade ourselves, and we have become something else: chastened failures who cannot be profitably judged by the standards of idealistic, romantic youth.

As for my dead friends, I honor and mourn them. They were hotter souls than I, truer to their visions, consumed while still steadfast. I no longer think of myself as one of the heroes who will set all right; and so, my dear son, I will not aid you in attempting to bring about a new revolt, a new "new order," a return to the Revolution. Indeed, I must set my face against you in this, for I have passed once through such an upheaval and I tremble to contemplate the approach of yet another.

I realize that now, in your youth, you look back on my times with romantic longing. You see these new agitations for reform and revolution throughout Europe as a revival of the glorious aspirations of those days. My son, I do not begrudge you the wish to take hold of such vital currents yourself. It is only that you are wrong. Not wrong in your objections—I agree that the gains of the Republic are being destroyed by the return to great social abuses under the restored king and the aristocrats. But do not ask me to write articles saying so for your outlawed newspapers, do not ask me to intervene on behalf of your radical friends when they are arrested, do not ask me to join you in a hopeless battle.

These days like Candide I cultivate my garden, a lesson I might have taken from Voltaire at the outset had I been wiser and less idealistic. And I uphold the law—imperfect as it is—rather than invite the return of bloody chaos.

As for your friend Moran the publisher, I have nothing to say, other than that it was foolish of you to send him to me. Whoever pried into my past and revealed to you the radical nature of my early career did not look deep enough, for that is all over. I have made my peace with the present. Therefore, I have turned Moran over to the local authorities to be returned to Paris for trial. If he—or you—persist in printing rabblerousing attacks on the present government, he—or you—must be prepared to take the consequences. And I do not intend to play a part in assuring that those consequences should be a new destruction of the public order. Quite the opposite. My past to the contrary, or rather directly on account of the lessons of my past, I stand for stability, for humble devotion to my own work and affairs, and for peace even at the price of some injustice, for fear of the alternative that I have seen made real: injustice beyond imagining and constant warfare.

So send me, I beg you, no more fugitives and no more inflammatory letters or articles. Come instead yourself. Leave the hotbed of reformism that Paris has always been and return to the true France, a land of pious and tradition-minded countrymen and townsmen who go about their business without any passion for change.

I am completing my book on the law as I have known it, my own modest contribution to the world, I believe. I wish you would read it. Since you are to judge me, as all children judge their parents, I would have you judge not by my past nor by some imaginary reformist career that you wish on me now, but by the work that I have lately chosen to occupy my time and engage my declining energies.

Your mother joins me in the earnest hope that you will come soon to see us and share a meal and perhaps some quiet talk in what is now and forever your home.

                              In love and farewell, your father.

Dorothea ceased reading, her lips trembling, her throat hoarse. Ricky said nothing. She looked up and saw his bony profile, his sunken eyes fixed on the hills beyond the patio wall.

"You saw me write all this?" she whispered. She saw the slow focusing of his mind and eyes upon her.

"Ricky, you're crying," she said stupidly.

"Weeping," he croaked, blotting at his eyes with his cuff. "Crying is noisy, it involves the voice. Why can't you Americans ever learn these distinctions?"

Near tears herself, she cried, "Oh, for God's sake!" She got up and hugged her robe around herself. She was cold. In shock, she thought numbly. I believe I'm in shock. "I'm going back to bed," she said.

He blinked at her, eyes still red-rimmed, as she went shivering past him.

He came and stood by her bed a moment, and then got in with her and drew her against him, closing his warm hands over her icy ones. For a long time they lay like that. She had almost dozed off when she felt him shift suddenly and realized that it was his erection that had been prodding her thigh, and that he was embarrassed and was trying to conceal it.

But why, when her own body was suddenly flush with appetite, ravenous and clamoring? "Ricky," she whispered, "would you like to make love?"

"God, yes," he groaned, his whole body contracting possessively about her.

"Then let's get up and brush our teeth first so we can do it properly," she said.

They did. They made long, slow, careful love, burning away for a while the chilly voice of that other life and time in the intensity of their absorption with each other. At the end she lay on her side with Ricky behind her, for he had no strength to hold himself above her. With her feet braced between his long, sharp shins, her body arched up and out, her arms stretched down her sides to clasp the backs of his hands where he held and steadied her hips, like a ship's figurehead she rode his thrusts.

Seated on a cushion on the floor, Ricky looked through the records for something to listen to over the thunderstorms that had come on with the sunset.

Prokofiev's *Romeo and Juliet*, the first suite? A bit too

youthful and dreamy and overblown, he thought, for an old
man like me. Ah, but he had not been too old today. They
had made love again, late in the afternoon, and to his joy and
astonishment he had been up to it. She had come rolling into
his arms with a great sigh, and perhaps it was from her happy
confidence that he had drawn his own strength. Afterward
he'd hiked up on his elbows, shaking his head at the opti-
mism of his cock, which stood glistening at half mast and
twitching slightly as if minded to have another go.

"Incredible," he said. "Here I am, tottering toward my
grave, and there's this rooster as eager as he was at twenty.
Pity I can't set him loose, somehow, free him from this
foundering hulk he's hitched to: Noah releasing the dove."

"A totally different situation," Dorothea had murmured,
"and besides, this bird wouldn't get far; not flapping those
fat, round, hairy little wings, it wouldn't!" And she had
hooted into his shoulder. Fat round wings indeed!

Now, sitting in the storm light after dinner, he realized that
that moment had been the first in which he had felt any
affection for his own body since sentence had been pronounced.

"Ravel, perhaps?" he said. *"La Valse?* No, we've got
enough of the French on our plate as it is."

She was sitting at the little chess table by the window,
studying the long yellow pages of their translation of the
letter. How tired she looked, he thought with a pang, slouched
there in her old corduroys and a gracefully shapeless cotton
sweater of faded maroon. "Well," she said, "this has got to
come out of the late 182Os, don't you think? Working up to
the revolt in 1832."

Tired but not the least bit scared. She astounded him. Here
they had this incredible document in their hands, a product of
her mind and hand, and she pored over it like a student. But
then she had been living for years with the amazing products
of her own mind, he must not forget that. He must not forget
how remarkable she was; not with the ordinary remarkable-
ness of someone you realize you're in love with, but the
special quality of the creative spirit and the self-reflective
mind. If anything, he thought, she must be intensely relieved
to have something concrete in her hands, something besides
her own memories of her dreams.

"That sounds like the right period," he said. Rain stippled
the window behind her. She looked wonderful against the
gray pane, wisps of hair curling on her nape. "Dorothea, I

hope you don't mind, but I've reconsidered, and I'd like to stay on a bit. I mean, in the light of that letter—"

She shot him a wide, innocent glance. "You mean the sex isn't good enough to hold you?"

He blushed and stammered, and she rescued him with her mischievous laughter that dissolved him into helpless, red-faced laughter of his own. Then, seriously, she went on.

"So it goes like this: first the wicked Old Regime, then the Revolution, then that's captured and turned into the despotism of the First Empire by Napoleon. Then he's defeated in—what, 1817? And the French monarchy is restored. The aristocrats who fled come swarming back and try to reinstate their Old Regime privileges, and the tension between them and the liberals who want to preserve the gains of the Revolution leads to a succession of messy little uprisings in the 1830s, right? Which is what it sounds as if our judge is trying to warn his kid to stay clear of."

"You've been reading my books."

She looked modestly smug. "Actually, I once knew all this stuff forward and backward, from reading about it in college—diaries, propaganda, novels, and histories: the lot. Then it all slipped out of my head, but here we are again. Peculiar, isn't it?"

"Peculiar," he repeated dryly. "Yes. And you Yanks call us Brits 'masters of understatement!' You do realize that we can't do a damn thing with that letter; nothing public, that is. We'd be branded a pair of dotty old frauds."

She said, "I don't want to go to anyone with it. This is ours, my dear: yours and mine and nobody else's. We've earned it."

"And now?" he said, sliding a record from its sleeve. "How about Brahms?"

"Good," she said. "A good background for my theory."

"Ah," he said, "I knew you had a theory."

"Yes. I think that the judge is someone from your family history, maybe an unknown or even an illegitimate kinsman. I think that he's been trying to break through to you using my dreams because you're too closed to him to receive his communications in any other form. He's using the material of his lifetime in the Revolution and after because he can get through to me that way on account of my past interest in that period. Also because there's such a strong emotional charge attached to that time for him that it boosts his signal to an intensity that even I can pick up, though, believe me, I'm no psychic!''

"And the aim of this excessively roundabout communication?" he said with some asperity. The piano quintet began, flowing into him like liquid gold in his veins. He was ashamed of his own sharpness as soon as he had spoken.

"To assure you, my dear," she said in a tone of infinite gentleness, "that it isn't all over when you die. And maybe that drifting around the world drinking tea with strangers is a good way to spend a lifetime—better than trying to make a revolution, for example."

"And," he said, "perhaps also that it's a good idea to communicate with one's kindred in the more conventional ways—letters, phone calls, even face-to-face conversations—while one still can?"

"You know how I feel about that," she said. "And how I'll miss you if you do decide to go home. Hey, come on over here and give me a game, will you? I'm tired to death of looking over and over these pages."

He hoisted himself to his feet, leaning on the phonograph cabinet—it's only love, you know, he told himself harshly, not remission—and crossed the room to sit opposite her at the little game table with its inlaid top.

"I'm not sure," he said, "that I'm willing to accept that old bastard as an ancestor of mine, no matter how obscurely connected. Judging by that self-serving, brazen attempt to justify himself, I'd say he was the worst sort of radical-turned-reactionary, probably as corrupt and cynical as they came, which was impressively corrupt and cynical, if you read Balzac, for instance. Which crooked politician of the time was it who provided the slogan of the whole post-Napoleonic age in France? *'Enrichez vous!'* he said. Make yourself rich if you can. Pack of damned war profiteers and heartless exploiters if ever there was one."

"That's exactly why I'm inclined to believe it," Dorothea said. "Because our judge is an ordinary, even a less-than-admirable type." She held out her hands, and he chose the white piece. "Your move," she said.

He studied the board. "You know," he said, "I've known some odd occurrences. I don't discount any possibility beforehand. But frankly, I don't think I need reassurance so badly as to warrant all this effort. People die. I am a person. I shall die. Why all the fuss?"

Did his voice sound bitter? He was embarrassed.

"I'm not competent to answer that," she said. "To me, any amount of fuss seems perfectly appropriate if it will make things better for you."

Lightning flared in the echo of thunder, frosting her hair with an icy light.

"Did you dream last night?" he said.

"No."

"Suppose it's all over? Now you've got the message, the judge can stop trying so hard. Or perhaps sex defuses it."

"It'll be over," she said, jumping two of his pieces, "when we don't just theorize but understand. If we ever do."

"We will," he said. "If I'm lucky, I'll see it. If not, once I'm dead I'll know the answer, won't I? Just put it to the judge, as one ghost to another: What have you been up to with all this? Then I'll come back and enlighten you. In your dreams."

"Pax," she said. "You're cutting close to the bone." She turned to the black wet window. The music—he had forgotten it—rippled limpidly. He wanted to cry. The point was not to win surrender from her. That was not the point at all. He loathed his meanness. She seemed not even to notice it, for she went on, "There is one possibility that we haven't considered, which is that I am as crazy as a bedbug and simply hallucinating madly in my sleep, and that you're taking it seriously out of an excess of good manners—the perfect guest."

He said, "You are not crazy, and I am most certainly not perfect."

They played three games, growing absorbed. At ten thirty the rain stopped. She sat back from the table. "I'm going to bed. Will you come with me?"

He had been wondering whether this moment would come. He avoided her eyes. "You don't have to," he said awkwardly. "Just because we—I wouldn't want you to feel in any way obliged—"

"I don't. I feel damned lucky."

She touched the lump under the skin of his lower belly and could not prevent herself from checking for an instant: This was it, the killer, death under her touch.

They went on without speaking of it. She came, but he didn't.

"Not to worry," he said, after. "Effect of the medication, probably." His bony arm lay across her ribs, slack and amazingly heavy. Then he added, "Doesn't it put you off a bit—this moribund carcass?"

His breath lightly feathered her shoulder, warm brush and warm brush again, while still inside her his penis wilted with small, creeping movements. Live breath, live flesh: she had not been making love with Death and must not let him think that way. Except that she had felt a lurch of panic in herself when she had touched that enigmatic lump.

She said, "It bothers me, yes."

Pause. Then he said, "Nothing good can come of this."

"Nothing has to. It's good as it is." She tried to turn to face him, but he held her as she lay and she didn't want to fight him. "We would be left wondering, later, how we would have been together. I'd rather remember than wonder."

"Ah, yes," he grated, "later: when they stick a catheter in it, and I become one great tottering system of failed and rotting pipes. Have you ever read up on cancer deaths? No, of course not, why should you? It's something one does when one first finds out."

All right, she thought, this had to come; don't let it fester, let's deal with it all right now. She forced herself to speak. "Ricky, love, I'm not perfect either. I can't promise that I won't turn away from you later because of changes in your body. And I can't alter the likelihood that you'll be dead long before I will, and that it's not fair. But I won't talk about this with you, not lying skin to skin. When we're in bed together, we're in bed. You understand?"

His grip on her body became live again, though not strong. He would never be strong again. But he wasn't playing corpse now, and he buried his wet face against the back of her neck and whispered, "Yes, I understand."

"What have you done with the covers?" she grumbled after a while. "Half of me is sticking out in the cold. My mother used to say, Never marry a skinny man. (She said 'marry,' not 'sleep with,' because she was an old-fashioned European girl.) The little bit of meat on a skinny man won't keep you warm at night, she said."

"My mother said, 'Be prudent, Ricky dear. Foreign women are usually neither as forward nor as backward as common knowledge would have them.'"

Their basic understanding held and did not need to be

remade each time they went to bed together during the week that followed. It was simple, really: Sometimes they were playful and sometimes not, and sometimes they clung together and rocked each other in silent commiseration like two frightened apes in a laboratory cage. What they did not do was tear at each other.

They filed the letter and its translation away in her desk. As if by common consent and without further discussion, they let the subject drop. This was not as difficult as she had expected; the dreams ceased, or at least were suspended for the time being.

Ricky walked less often and less far, ate less (although Häagen-Dazs vanilla ice cream could still tempt him), rested more. He came out to the wall with her only occasionally and sat reading in the shade: not books on French history any more but a novel that she had brought him from the bookstore, Garcia Marquez's *One Hundred Years of Solitude.*

Dorothea acknowledged his decline and then ignored it. Their affair was discreet in many ways, as if to shield it from the observation of unsympathetic strangers—perhaps from Death? They did not go in for hand-holdings, pecks on the cheek, and pats on the behind. He never spent a full night in her room but always withdrew to his own, well before morning. How proper he was, how articulate and courteous (except when a certain delightful silly streak came out, most often in bed). She concentrated on how English he was rather than how sick. Most often they did not have sex because he was not up to it. They merely made love.

At times she thought, All this should surely be more complex: extremes of rage, grief, withdrawal, rushing together, torment, and desperation. Instead, perhaps because she and Ricky had never imagined a shared future, the present seemed an overwhelming gift.

❧ Six ❧

ROBERTO THOUGHT Mr. Escobar looked kind of stupid up there on the band platform with the microphone, so sober-looking next to the musicians. They stood around in the scarves and belts and feathered hats they wore, looking bored while he talked. The party was roaring along already, people milling around in their good clothes looking for places to dump paper plates emptied of hot meat, cole slaw and beans, and whipped Jell-O. Nobody seemed to be paying a whole lot of attention to what Mr. Escobar was saying, and the microphone kept making squeaks and popping noises like gunshots.

Roberto was bored. He'd spent some time riding around with Horacio on his bike with the purple streamers attached to the handlebars, tearing along the rough dirt track that circled the field until people complained about dust getting in the food. Now he sat with his mother and Blanca and Great-uncle Tilo on an old blanket, wolfing down fried chicken and canned pop, looking around and ignoring his mother's comments.

She was upset about Mr. Escobar and Pinto Street Protection, like a lot of the older people on the street, and she'd been on his case to quit hanging out so much with the Maestas brothers.

"—thieves!" the microphone bleated.

Talk, talk, more talk. No inspections had been made since the street closing. Pinto Street Protection had nothing to do,

and all Mr. Escobar knew was to talk some more and get
other people talking. The Maestas brothers were not interested in taking the fight right to the construction company
themselves. It was all turning into a drag.

"Wait a minute," somebody yelled. "You mean this inspector offers money for your place after he tells you it's no
good?"

"Start over and go slower," a woman shouted. "We couldn't
hear you."

A big sweaty guy in a torn T-shirt yelled, "Music! If you
don't sing, give the mike to somebody that does!"

Roberto got up. "I'm going to get some more to drink."

"Take your plate and put it in the garbage," his mother
said. "And no beer, Roberto. You're too young."

Good thing the guys he liked to drink with behind the
bowling alley weren't around to hear that! What a bummer.

He strode away, carrying his plate and stepping around
other groups of neighbors parked on the trampled grass or
bare ground. If some of them saw him with a beer in his hand
they'd tell his mom.

He didn't need his family right now, and it sure didn't look
like Pinto Street Protection needed him. Jake and Martín
stood by the amplifiers, big strong guys who made people
look and listen just by being there. They hadn't asked Roberto to join them. His mom should know how they sort of
condescended to notice him, how if it wasn't for Pinto Street
Protection they wouldn't know he was alive.

Some of the younger guys were down by the Y construction. That was where Roberto and the Maestas brothers
had borrowed orange traffic cones to close the street with.
Now some guys had climbed the fence. You could settle
down inside the half-finished building and slug down some
beer without anybody bothering you, get a nice buzz on.
Maybe there'd even be some stuff left lying around you could
pick up and sell someplace.

The Y was going to take away the field, turn it into a
running track and a parking lot, fence everything in, probably, so why not take something back?

"Hey, Ollie!" he shouted, spotting Ollie Rivera at the
fence, just starting to hoist himself over with his T-shirt
hanging out of the back pocket of his jeans like a flag.

Ollie stared over his shoulder with his mouth open. Behind
Roberto people started yelling and screaming.

Roberto turned.

Cops in black uniforms tore through the crowd from the other end of the field. More cops spilled out of a pair of cop cars pulled up by the curb. He saw a nightstick whack down, and somebody went staggering right into a tree, blind because of his bloody hands over his face. Everybody was running and screaming every which way. Two guys charged to meet the cops with bottles in their hands.

Where were Mom and Blanca and Great-uncle Tilo? Roberto ran back to where he thought he'd left them. He swerved around a man sitting on the ground hugging his knee and groaning. Where were they, where?

Jake Maestas was hollering something you couldn't make out over the mike. Betsy Armijo, still in her bridesmaid's dress, ran past with her mouth open and no sound coming out, holding one high-heeled shoe in each hand. Like Mina, the other day, but Mina would be fighting, not running.

There was the blanket—at least he thought that was it, though it was all rucked up and trampled and there was no sign of Blanca or Mom or Great-uncle Tilo.

Shit. Where were they? He panted more with panic than breathlessness.

A cop shoved past him, pushing along some guy he had by one arm twisted up in back.

Roberto threw himself on the cop. They all fell. Something hit his head like the world falling on him, and he blacked out.

Blanca tore free of her mother's hand and ran toward the loudspeakers and the trees, across the line of charging cops.

Someone tripped her. When she got up, nursing a bruised knee, a man, a stranger, grabbed her arm and tried to pull her along with him. "Come on, come on, those cops are crazy," he panted. He crashed into a woman running across his path and Blanca spun away from him. Her chest was tightening. She thought she heard her mother screaming her name. Veering from the sound she ran into the arms of Martín Maestas.

"Go home, run," Martín shouted, pushing her away.

She no longer knew in which direction home lay. Ahead of her, people milled and shouted. Someone staggered out of the press streaming blood, openmouthed like a stunned ox in a slaughterhouse.

It's like a movie, she thought, the blood is so red.

She turned to look again for Martín, and her foot slipped

on a flattened soda can. She went down on her hands and knees. She could see Jake Maestas up a tree, kicking at the cops who clustered underneath and grabbed at him. Somebody must have stomped on the microphone, because the loudspeaker wedged between two branches let out a terrific burst of crackling explosion, like a tommy gun going off, over the screaming people.

A cop stopped running and spun around, his black boot inches from Blanca's fingers, his pistol upraised in both hands over his head like he meant to shoot the sky. Blanca saw with surprise that he was very young and that he was terrified. He was staring, she saw, at some barrels full of iced drinks. Somebody had just dodged down behind them. Blanca saw the glint of something between the barrels, and at that instant the cop brought his gun down in both hands and fired.

In her whole life Blanca had never heard anything so loud. She clamped her hands over her ears as the barrels spat splinters and rocked on their bases. Somebody heaved himself up from behind the barrels and stood there leaning on them. It was Mr. Escobar, his face blank with shock. He had a metal beer opener in one hand, and he held out the other like he was trying to show the cop his red-smeared palm. There was red on his shirtfront. The cop stared at him, wild-faced, still holding his pistol in both hands.

Blanca scrambled to her feet and ran. She could hear more shots and people screaming.

Martín was in front of her again, his shirt torn and his mouth open wide for breath, showing his empty gums. He gripped her by the shoulder and shook her.

"I told you, *hija,* get out of here!"

Out of nowhere a cop, a hurtling dark shape in his black uniform, charged. Martín dodged and kicked out. The cop jabbed the end of his nightstick into Martín's middle. Martín flipped double with a *whoof*ing sound that was lost in the other cries. More cops came running like stampeding black horses. The nearest one hiked back his stick to hit Martín again.

The time that came with the asthma moved slowly, drawing out the agony. Blanca was already in that time. In a second she would fall, writhing and breathless while everything moved away from her. Everything would happen around her to others, while she was sealed off in her cocoon of suffocation. For her, nothing more would happen but the asthma.

While she could still act, drawing on her rage at her own body's treachery, she threw herself in front of the nearest cop as his nightstick came down. She heard a great crack of sound, and she thought, as her upflung arm went numb, They exploded my arm! There was no pain. She was too absorbed in straining to expel the last of her spent breath so that a fresh one could be drawn. Not to be able to do that, that was pain.

Roberto woke up. It was dark. His head ached. Whatever he was lying on was lumpy and nasty smelling. Shit, it was that old mattress in the abandoned Estrada place. He and Horacio had snuck in here a few times to kick back and put away a six-pack. What was he doing here? He groaned. Somebody hissed at him, "Shh. Keep quiet."

"Who's there?" He was scared. His head was killing him. How bad was he hurt? He remembered jumping that cop. He sat up and groaned again, he couldn't help it. Was this jail after all?

"Talk low, Beto." Somebody came and crouched next to him, smelling of wine and sweat: Great-uncle Tilo.

"Ow, my head hurts." Fearfully he explored his tender, crusted scalp with his fingers.

"Drink this." His hand was seized and folded around the smooth shape of a pint bottle.

He swigged down a burning swallow and coughed. "What are we doing in this dirty old place?"

"They won't look for you here. They think you're on the way to Mexico already with Martín Maestas. Only keep your voice down, *hijo*. They come cruising through once in a while and you never know who's been talking."

"You mean I'm supposed to be hiding out? Why? I didn't do anything. I mean, I jumped a cop, but they attacked us, man."

"I know." Great-uncle Tilo settled himself on the mattress next to Roberto. "I saw. That cop landed on you and knocked you out. Joe Lopez jumped on him. I ran over and got you and carried you home. Only your mother doesn't want you there now because they came looking for you. Somebody's been talking, saying it was all set up by the Maestas brothers and 'Dolfo Escobar, and how you and the Archuleta twins been hanging out with all of them. It didn't help either that

they got you on the TV from the street closing, glaring out
past Jake Maestas like a wild bull.''

Bewildered, Roberto sipped from the bottle again. ''I don't
get it. Set up what? Why did the cops run crazy all over
everybody? Is Mom all right? Blanca?''

''Sure, they're fine. Thing is the cops say it was some kind
of conspiracy, a radical plot to whip up a riot in Pinto Street
because the street closing didn't get us anyplace. And then
there was the shooting. They're looking for what they call the
ringleaders.''

''Shooting?'' Roberto shivered hard. ''I don't remember
any shooting.''

''You were out cold by then. I think it was some nervous
cop who thought the microphone noises were gunshots and
cut loose, and then it went on from there.''

''What went on? Who was shooting?''

''The cops and I don't know who else. You know some
guys always carry something. It doesn't matter. The cops will
throw a few guns in the weeds there, the kind they keep in the
trunks of their cars for these kind of things, and then they'll
tell everybody we started the shooting. They have to say that.
Three people got shot and one cop. They're not going to take
the blame for that.''

''Three people and a cop?'' Roberto couldn't believe what
he was hearing. ''A cop! At least we got one of them, then.''

''Maybe,'' Great-uncle Tilo sighed. ''Anyhow, that's why
they're looking for you and Martín so hard, because a cop got
shot. That's why they better not find you.''

''I didn't shoot anybody! I didn't have a gun!''

''I just told you about the guns, *hijo*.''

Roberto felt a crazy impulse to cry, probably because his
head was so bad. ''Who else got shot? I don't understand
why anybody got shot.''

''Bennie Lopez has a bullet through his hand, he's okay. A
woman I don't know from Reyes Street, up Fourth a little,
got hit in the leg. Rudolfo Escobar got shot pretty bad. He's
still in the hospital. Critical, they say on the TV. And this one
cop, he's serious but not critical. Everybody knows 'Mexi-
cans' can't shoot straight.'' He belched. ''He probably got hit
by one of his own buddies, all the banging away they were
doing, but you'll never get them to admit that. Then there's a
bunch of people that got beat up pretty bad. Jake Maestas is
in the hospital with his ankle all smashed. They have to do an

operation on him. Our own Blanquita has a broken arm. She's got a hell of a big white cast on it and they sent her home so full of pain pills she can hardly walk. I guess they don't think they can get away with locking up a young girl like that who's got asthma. Everybody else that didn't run like hell they handcuffed and hauled off to jail.''

''But what for? We were having a party!''

Great-uncle Tilo's good hand pressed against Beto's lips, silencing him. Softly the old man said, ''They say on the news the cops got a phone call. Somebody told them that a mob from Pinto Street was going over to burn down the new Y building because of thinking it's the Y that's changed the zoning so their houses have to be condemned, which is crazy, but you know how people misunderstand things. The cops came loaded for a wild-eyed mob, so that's what they saw.''

''Who would tell them a thing like that?'' Roberto could not imagine telling such a lie. It left him awed.

''Somebody who didn't come to the party. Somebody who's all of a sudden not around, gone to visit relatives in T or C, they say. Somebody that stomped out of our house because he couldn't spy any more, once we had him spotted.''

Pete Romero, he meant. I should have fought him at the meeting in our house, Roberto thought dismally. I should have killed the son of a bitch, me and Jake and Martín should have just killed him.

Great-uncle Tilo's ropy old arm came across his shoulders and hugged him hard. ''We'll get you safe out of this mess, don't you worry, *mi hijo*. Go on and cry, go on, just try and be quiet, all right?''

Blanca had wrapped an old green sweater around her cast so that the whiteness of the plaster wouldn't gleam in the moonlight and give them away. She listened with delicious dread to every creak of branches in the bosque of willows and thorny russian olives and the soft sliding hiss of the river.

''I don't see why I got to run away,'' Beto repeated sullenly for the tenth time.

And for the tenth time Great-uncle Tilo explained. ''Not run away, just leave for a while. It's too risky for you to hang around here. You're scaring your mother to death, Beto. The cops are mad. She's afraid for you.''

''Well, I'm not afraid.''

Liar, Blanca thought. Of course he was scared, and it was

stupid of him to lie about it, but what else could you expect from Beto? He wasn't about to admit that he was plain petrified, now that the thrill of hiding out was worn thin.

If it was me, she thought, I wouldn't be scared. I'd take off in a minute and never look back. He just misses his dumb friends, that's all. I wouldn't miss anybody.

"Listen, *hijo,*" Great-uncle Tilo said. "Listen to me. I been in trouble with the cops myself, you know? Long time ago, about some railroad union business. You don't want to let cops get ahold of you, not with one of their own laying hurt in the hospital. They won't care that you're a kid."

Somebody came crashing through the undergrowth. They all froze. Blanca thought, Oh no, it's not fair, it can't be all over so quick!

"Beto?" the intruder said hoarsely. "Is that you? It's me, Bobbie. Mina sent me down here with some stuff for you."

Blanca could have laughed out loud: Cousin Bobbie from the Heights, what a dope! He could have sent them all stampeding into the river, barging in on them like this.

"Keep it down, will you?" Beto said. "What you mean, she sent you?"

"She gave me some money for you. She says you should come up to the Heights. She can find you a place to hide out until all the fuss dies down. Boy, is she mad."

"She's always mad," Roberto growled. "And I'm not going up there, no way."

Not mad enough to come down and yell at him—or give him the money—herself, Blanca noted in silence. Mina was no kind of sister, money or no money. Blanca would show them about being a sister, somehow, and do it in person, too.

"Where are you going to go?" Bobbie said.

"To Aunt Carmen in LA," Beto said. "Shit. She could drive you crazy, all that religion and running to church all the time. Anyway, what am I supposed to tell her?"

Bobbie sat down on the old half-buried timber that Roberto was sitting on, the two of them dark silhouettes against the sparkly surface of the river behind them. Bandits at night on the riverbank, Blanca thought. That's what we are.

"Mina says you can't stay with relatives, the cops will expect that. They'll come looking."

That was when Blanca had her idea. She said, "I read about some guys who ran away from the draft. They went to Canada."

"Canada!" Bobbie said excitedly. "They'd never expect that, Beto. A kid I know, his uncle lives up there. In Toronto. I could get his name for you, maybe. It's a long border up there. They can't guard it, and there's no fence. All that snow, Eskimos and wolves and things—Canada would be great."

Roberto rubbed his head where it must be bothering him again. "That's crazy! How am I supposed to get to Canada?"

Great-uncle Tilo said, "It's not so crazy if you got some money in your pocket."

And if you're not alone, Blanca thought, the idea blossoming gloriously in her mind. If they're looking for a kid on his own, running away, and instead there's a guy and his sister, traveling to visit relatives, hitching, a couple of nice kids—

Great-uncle Tilo hawked and spat in the dirt. Blanca hated how he spat all the time. She looked at the shining gobbet of spit on the ground. She had loved Great-uncle Tilo a lot when she was little. He was saying how he went across Canada once with a train. Big country, he said, but cold. Good trains.

"First you've got to get out of Albuquerque," Blanca said. With me, Beto. But she'd have to go easy on that right now or he'd spook and say no and she'd never budge him. She'd have to make him see that it was her chance to get out too. She'd have to make him swear not to tell Mom.

"I could go with you," Bobbie said eagerly. "Part of the way, anyhow. They wouldn't be looking for two guys, only one."

She could have strangled him, stealing her idea. But that wouldn't stop her. Nobody could stop her.

"I don't know," Great-uncle Tilo said, shaking his head. "It could get dangerous. You won't know how dangerous until you try. For one thing, they're looking for Martín too, remember. He's an ex-con, so they're all primed to start shooting, specially with one of their own shot already. Is it easier to slip two of you out of town, or just one? Maybe when Garduño takes his truck up into the mountains to cut piñon—"

As if that sour old man would agree to carry Beto!

Silence again. Everybody was thinking. Blanca ground her shoulder blade against the wood at her back, easing the discomfort of the cast. She was getting tired. She wished they'd get this over with so she could start working on Beto in private.

Bobbie said, "Hey. The drawing class."

"What about it?" Beto said. He sounded really cranky.

"The trip is day after tomorrow, remember? We're supposed to go in that big old van."

"So what? Man, are you crazy? You thinking I'm taking some lousy field trip now?"

"Would the cops stop a car full of kids going on a school trip?"

Hey, Mom, Blanca thought dreamily, guess what: I'm going to asthma camp in Toronto with the wolves and the Eskimos.

Ellie Stern had never seen Roberto look so subdued.

"We have a ranch south of Taos," he mumbled. "I mean we used to live up around there."

She looked at him, puzzled and wary but gratified. Had she finally broken through to him on some level, had she banished his belligerence and his bluster? With seven years of teaching behind her, she still found kids baffling much of the time, especially your more sullen, angry ethnics. She had not run into too many of them at the Marshall School in New York. Some kind of success with Roberto, here, would be all the more significant, then.

The girl, his sister, piped up. "We used to spend our summers up there." Such a clear, bright voice to come from that odd, slightly stunted body. What a striking child, with her apricot skin and honey hair; who'd imagine coarse, thickset Roberto having such a sister? Ellie had hoped for some contact with Spanish or Indian culture on her vacation out here. This seemed to be it at last, the return for her bread of acceptance cast upon the murky waters of Roberto's spirit.

She was relieved that her reaction to the street closing had not driven Roberto away. She was to have a chance now to show that though she was—not cowardly, exactly—sensible about problems like that, she was a good person.

He said, "The doctor said I should take my sister up there to spend some time with our grandma, as long as the class was going."

"The doctor?" Ellie said; surely not a trip to the country for a broken arm? "Is your sister—ah, Blanca—is Blanca ill?"

"She has asthma," Roberto said.

"It's okay," the girl said, in her curiously self-possessed manner. "I don't get attacks in cars, and anyway I have my medication with me." She tapped her battered suitcase.

Roberto stood looking down and dug in the dirt with the heel of his boot. Angry at having to ask for help, probably: the pride of the Spanish heritage. Of course they would have no money for cars or gas or bus fare to Taos. Treatment for Blanca's asthma probably devoured any spare cash they had.

Ellie said, "We're not stopping except for lunch, and that's going to be a picnic with what we've brought—is that all right? Good; glad to have you join us."

Here came Joni across the parking lot toward them with a sketch pad and a big bag of sandwiches.

Ellie introduced Blanca. "We'll be giving her a lift with us. There'll just be room: Angie's twisted her ankle again and Paul can't come."

"We're going in that?" Joni sniffed. One of the parents, a man who ran a small sightseeing operation in town, had donated the van. It was a snub-nosed vehicle in rusting gray with a once-sleek roadrunner stenciled on the side. It had three big bench seats, a single bucket seat up front next to the driver, and a cramped little stowage space in the back. Ellie unlocked the back doors so that the kids could load the food they'd brought and a big plastic jug of water.

Thank God Mary had had time to take her on a test run, teaching her to drive the thing, because now Mary wasn't coming. It was all Ellie's show. Think of it as an adventure. But she was nervous, very nervous. Dorothea Howard was not exactly a nobody, she was a very distinguished artist, and Ellie hadn't even met her personally.

Of course, having Joni Reed along was almost like having another staff member. Joni was so quick, so sure of where she was going, so adult. She wouldn't be out of place in Ellie's class at the Marshall School.

"Can I sit in the van until we go?" Blanca said. "This cast is kind of heavy."

"Sure," Ellie said. She was beginning to rather like the girl, who was certainly a great deal more open and accessible than her surly brother. "Open the windows if you like."

The three Cantus got into the back seat, the girl maneuvering her white-cased arm so that the cast rested against the window frame. Roberto reached across her to push the window out as far as it would go, which wasn't very far. The day was warm already, and the back of the van was probably going to be pretty stuffy. Ellie resolved that after lunch they would switch seating arrangements to give other people a crack at a window seat. Being fair was so important with the young.

Joyce came lolling out of the building. "Mary wants to check with you in the office before we go," she said.

Mary was absorbed in the frightening problem of a female student who had last been seen hitchhiking outside school yesterday. The child had never reached home. In the office Ellie said comforting things and gave Mary the class list with checks by the names of the kids who were going. Mary reassured her. "Please, go on, it'll make me feel better to know that something is going as planned in all this upheaval!" She swore again that Dorothea Howard would be perfectly delighted to see the class, even without Mary herself. "She'll understand. She'll be great."

When Ellie returned to the van she found that Roberto had the engine exposed and was doing something to it while the other kids watched.

"Trying to fix up the air conditioning," Bobbie volunteered. "Jeff says he heard it doesn't work."

But Roberto could not fix the air conditioning so they set out with all the windows open. Ellie left with a great sense of relief. Crisis and its atmosphere made her very tense.

Driving out toward the Interstate, she wondered ruefully how she had gotten herself into this thing. Sometimes she thought she must have been crazy to volunteer to teach in Mary's program during her vacation, and in a field that wasn't even really hers. She had done it on impulse, in response to a radio ad inviting people to come and teach something they loved and knew about. And what a relief it had been to leave her recalcitrant book project, a novel that wouldn't move, for the familiar pleasures of the classroom, only so much freer than what she was used to at home. Only nine kids! A fresh subject, her minor in college, instead of *Benito Cereno* and *Moby Dick* again!

She looked in the rearview mirror. "Joni, don't smoke in the car, all right? The rest of us have to breathe too."

In the rearview mirror Ellie saw the butt shoot out the window. She swore at a low-slung junk heap that swung suddenly in front of her without a signal. She remembered that she hadn't told Mary about her extra passengers, but with that lost girl on everybody's mind she had forgotten. Just as well. Suppose there was some school rule against taking non-school riders, after Ellie had agreed?

Jeff, in the navigator's seat, twiddled the knobs on the dashboard, but the radio seemed to be broken, thank God, as well as the air conditioner.

Roberto looked covertly at the others seated ahead of him. All Anglos. The kind of people he was heading out to spend the rest of his life with. He couldn't believe it.

Another thing he couldn't believe was that Bobbie had been right. Miss Stern didn't know a damn thing about Pinto Street. She probably never looked at any news on TV except the world news, nothing local, or she might have picked up on something. Man, was she dumb. And the rest of them were minding their own business just right.

We're going to do this. We are going to get away with it.

Canada. I'm starting out for Canada.

The familiarity of the country sliding past as they drove north made him uneasy. Pretty soon that part would run out and it would all turn strange. No more landmarks then. Involuntarily he marked them off as they flowed past: the Alameda turnoff, the Bernalillo trailer parks down below the Interstate embankment. His mind went to the scenes up ahead: the electrical station at Algodones; the yellow bluff near San Felipe Pueblo; the turnoff west to Peña Blanca and Cochiti Lake; the steep red passage up La Bajada; Santa Fe; Taos, sixty miles north; and beyond Taos, no road that he knew; and somewhere up in Colorado, mountains whose shapes he had never seen.

Near Taos was the ranch where they had all lived before his father died. He wasn't even sure he could spot the turnoff now. He didn't remember much about the place. Anyway, he would just as soon not stop there. Maybe his father's ghost, or his old grandma's that they were supposed to be visiting, might be hanging around and spot him going away. If they would even recognize him. He wasn't the fat little kid he'd been up there, that was for sure. He was sitting here with a gun in the waistband of his pants, hidden by his denim jacket.

Great-uncle Tilo had gotten the gun someplace—an old pistol, with a dull finish but oily and clean inside. Thinking about it, feeling the warming pressure of it against his belly, made him tense up with excitement. Better not fool with me, man. Better not.

He was too young for prison and he wasn't scared of the Juvenile Justice Center; he'd been there before. He was afraid of never getting that far, especially if that cop died. He was scared of being equated with the missing Maestas brother, a hard case with blood on his hands already from way back, and simply killed out of hand. It happened sometimes.

But Canada! What did he know about Canada? It's a big, cold place. A lot of the people speak French. A Spanish guy with a little cash and no job and no French and no family, what can he hope for there?

The van was slowing down. State Police cars were parked on both sides of the highway. The two lanes of traffic crawled up to cops who spoke to the drivers before passing them through.

Roberto sat clenched with fear, thinking about the gun he carried. You don't want to touch this thing unless you're going to use it, Great-uncle Tilo had said. Use it? Shoot at this cop's dark, narrow, Spanish face looking in at this car full of people? Jesus!

"What's this about?" the teacher said.

Nobody else said a word.

Roberto forced himself to breathe. He looked at the cop out of the corners of his eyes. The cop was chewing gum. He leaned in at the car window, squinting at the passengers. His partner spoke to the teacher on her side. "Driver's license and registration, please."

She dug out the stuff and handed it over. He looked through the papers. He said, "You know everybody here, right, ma'am?"

"Of course. They're my drawing class."

"Okay, go on through, please. Have a good trip."

As he stepped back, she leaned out after him. "Could you tell us what you're looking for?"

God.

"Go on please, ma'am," he repeated, and at the flip of his hand she stepped—thank God, thank God—on the gas.

Just like that. Roberto couldn't believe it. He wanted to howl with relief. Blanca was clutching his sleeve, he noticed. Bobbie, that wimp, looked green and sweaty.

Jeff, in the front seat, said, "Looking for drugs, I betcha. They always pick on kids about drugs."

"Except today, right?" the teacher said. "Not that there's anything in this car to find, I trust. There better not be."

"We smoked it all before we came," Alex said slyly.

Everybody laughed except Roberto, who was watching Joni Brown-Nose digging into her big shoulder bag. She got out a little pocket radio and switched it on. Christ. Just music, but she began to hunt along the dial.

Die, you bitch, Roberto thought furiously. Keel over and—

The teacher glanced back. "Joni, do you have to? It's been so nice and peaceful."

Joni said, "Maybe if we get the news, we'll find out what the cops are looking for."

"Illegal aliens," Alex said quickly, glancing at Roberto. Bobbie had talked to Alex; Alex knew. He was trying to help. Roberto wished he would keep his smart mouth shut.

"Oh, it's probably somebody escaped from the State Pen again," Joyce said in that spacy way she had. "They're always getting out of there. It makes you wonder why anybody bothers to stay in."

Roberto thought of Martín Maestas, wished he was with him. Martín would know how to do this really right, man. But he was off on his own. He knew how to be a fugitive. He wouldn't be rolling north with a goddamn art class, stuck in here with them while Joni Reed's radio told everybody what was up.

The announcer said it was news time. Maybe he wouldn't mention Pinto Street at all. But what difference would that make? Suppose there was another roadblock, more cops looking? Roberto knew he could not sit through another stop like that.

He said loudly, "They're looking for me."

Alex shivered with excitement. Roberto's story had wiped that namby-pamby look right off Stern's face.

She said, "Did any of you kids know about this back in the parking lot?"

Joni said, in the general silence, "Well I, for one, didn't know anything about it until just now. I don't even know where Pinto Street is."

"That's okay," Alex cracked. "Now Pinto Street has come to you; you'll get to know all about it."

Miss Stern said, "But you knew, Alex?"

"They told me in the parking lot," Alex said. "I said I was glad to be able to help."

Jeff cleared his throat. "I knew a little bit about it before, from TV. Bobbie told me in the parking lot that Roberto just needs to lay low someplace up north for a while, until things get straightened out."

Miss Stern, driving hunched over her white-knuckled hands, said, "As soon as I find a place, I'm pulling over, and you three in the back can get out. I can't possibly—Joyce, did you know?"

Joyce said, "I still don't know what the heck is going on," and that dip Cindy chimed in, "Know about what, exactly?"

Cripes, what a crew. Alex watched the road for cop cars.

Joni's radio crackled as she twiddled the dials. Miss Stern snapped, "For God's sake, turn it down, will you?" You could see her thinking, biting her lip as she drove. Figure your way out of this one, Miss Know-it-all, Alex thought.

Joni said, "I don't want to miss anything, if they talk about Pinto Street."

Bobbie said, "You won't get anything clear until we're past the Algodones power station."

Jeff swiveled in the seat to look back at the Cantus. "What are you going to do, Roberto? Where are you going to go?"

Bobbie reached over and shoved him. "Don't ask that, fool! You want the cops to worm it out of you later on? There's a plan, that's all."

Suddenly the car was full of the news announcer's voice and everybody saying "What? What's he say?" and hushing each other.

The radio clicked off on the sports scores. Joni said in a flat, tight voice, "Jesus Christ. That man died, that man who was shot."

Alex's stomach gave a lurch and he gritted his teeth. Why should it bother him? What did he care? He felt sweat run in tickling rivulets down his ribs.

Miss Stern said, "What? Who died?"

Roberto said, "Rudolfo Escobar. He owned a feed store on Fourth Street. He was at the party. The cops shot him."

Joni said, "The announcer said he was caught in the cross fire."

"There was no cross fire!" Roberto said. He hit the back of the seat in front of him with his fist.

"That's how they get you," Alex said, trying to catch Roberto's eye. I'm on your side, man. "Armed and dangerous," the announcer had said, of Roberto and that older guy, Maestas. The cop was still in serious condition. "It's how they justify shooting you down on sight."

"I'm stopping here," Miss Stern said.

Roberto said, "Just keep driving," and Joyce wailed, "Oh, no, oh, shit!" and Alex looked back and saw the pistol in Roberto's hand.

"Oh, man," he breathed, "where did you get that?"

Joyce could not eat. Roberto hadn't let them stop in Santa Fe. They had followed the road north beyond the town to a roadside rest stop with shaded tables and two chemical toilets.

Fruit and soda and sandwiches were spread on one of the tables. The kids didn't talk. Alex had taken his food over to where Roberto and Blanca and Bobbie ate seated in the van.

If one of us ran to the edge of the road and tried to flag a car down and get help, would Roberto really shoot? Joyce wondered. He's a kid, like us. But he's tough, he's a valley kid. They shoot and knife each other all the time down there, they still have gang fights sometimes. Even Bobbie looked different, excited. And that girl, Blanca, she was creepy.

Joyce looked at her sandwich. If I bite into this and taste real meat, I'll know this is all real, she thought. She did not bite into it.

Next to her Jeff ate wolfishly, humming aimlessly under his breath.

The class began to clear up, prompted by Roberto's command: "All right, let's go." Paper crackled, the lids of the trash cans rattled. Joyce could hear Blanca's lively and excited voice from the van, describing the riot and how she had gotten hurt defending one of Roberto's friends from the brutal cops. That kid was flaunting her encased arm, boasting of her war wound to Alex. Joyce hated her. If she stopped hating, she'd start being really scared.

An enormous bus swung off the highway and pulled up at the far end of the line of sheltered picnic tables. People got out: youngsters, some kind of church group with matching caps of bright yellow. Baptist canaries loud with release from the confines of their bus, they spread their white lunchboxes over several of the farther tables.

Joyce looked at them across what felt like miles of noman's-land. What would Miss Stern do now? Would she get them all killed, or save them?

In her mind's eye, she saw the teacher walk firmly over to

speak to one of the adults with the canaries. Roberto would shoot. She saw Miss Stern punched down by a bullet from behind, like somebody in a TV news clip of some horrible guerrilla war somewhere.

That's us, we're stuck here in Roberto's own guerrilla war. She's the teacher. Why doesn't she save us?

That little round lady from New York save them? Never. Roberto was pointing fiercely into the van, and they all moved slowly toward the doors.

Miss Stern stood there, looking past them, not at them. "Where's Joni?" she said.

Joyce said, "She went into the bathroom when I came out. I guess she's still in there."

"Well, go and get her," Roberto commanded, with a nervous glance at the bus people. "We're leaving."

Joyce looked at Miss Stern, who nodded. Joyce went.

The door was firmly locked. "Joni? We're going," Joyce said.

Joni answered without opening the door. "I'm staying here. You go tell them. When they're gone I'll come out and hitch a ride and go stay with a friend of mine. I won't say anything. You tell them that."

Joyce leaned against the plastic hutch, appalled. "But you can't! Joni, they'll kill you! He can shoot right through this plastic thing!" But would he, with the canaries there?

"I'm not coming out."

Joyce ran back to the van. "She won't come out," she gasped. "She says she won't tell anybody anything, but she won't come out, we should go without her."

"That sneaky bitch!" Roberto said. He would have leaped out of the van, but Bobbie grabbed his sleeve. The Cantus conferred with their heads together, their voices low and strained.

"Will they go drag her out?" Joyce whispered.

"Not in front of all those people," Miss Stern said. "They can't take the chance."

"That's right," Jeff muttered, leaning out the van door beside them. "What if they have a CB in their bus and send for help? But he can wait them out, and then go get her."

Joyce began to whimper, she couldn't help herself. If they started in on Joni, it wouldn't stop there. Why did Joni provoke Roberto this way? Even if she was safe now, the rest of them would be at greater risk because of her.

Everybody stared at the ugly plastic cabinet of the chemical toilet as if it were a magic fortress that only one could use. All scared, except for rotten Alex, who wore an expression of contempt.

Roberto said, "Everybody in the van, we're going! Hurry up, I said!"

Miss Stern got in last. She sat at the wheel like a store dummy until Roberto snarled, "I said let's go, goddamn it!"

The van lurched forward. They all looked back at the chemical toilet and the empty bus, the cheerful campers at their tables.

I'll never see my own room again, Joyce thought. I'll never see the poster of the kittens or the quill pen Aunt Reenie gave me. But though she heard the words in her mind and she felt hollow with sorrow for herself, no tears came.

I always knew something like this would happen to me, she thought. I always knew it.

In the middle seat, Cindy was crying.

❧ Seven ❧

RICKY SHOULD HAVE water with him on his drive up to the commune this afternoon. Dorothea put the water jug, freshly filled from the refrigerator bottle, into the cab of her truck.

She heard an engine down at the foot of the drive. A dented van, crowded with passengers, rumbled into the yard. The art class wasn't due until after lunch. Not the sort of error Mary Morgan, the soul of consideration, would make, but who knew about this Miss Stern from New York? Never mind, they were probably all pretty rattled by the problem of that lost student. Mary had been nearly in tears this morning on the phone about it. Ricky could still slip away without any fuss. Mentally Dorothea checked what the pantry held to suit teenage appetites as she shut the truck and turned to meet the new arrivals.

A young woman in an embroidered Mexican shirt and wrinkled jeans climbed stiffly and slowly out of the driver's seat. Clearly fatigued by a long stretch at the wheel, she stood a moment with her hand on the roof of the vehicle and her face turned away, the image of exhaustion. Thank God, Dorothea thought wryly, I didn't listen to my mother and become a teacher.

The big side door of the van slid back, but no youngsters came pouring out with radios blaring and bubble gum popping, the sort of thing Dorothea had been mildly dreading since she had committed herself to these people. Instead, out

128

stepped a very young-looking girl with one arm hiked up in a cast like a gift borne formally aloft for presentation. Dorothea's first thought was that they had sent her an elementary school rather than a high school class. This gave way at once to recognition that the person in the cast had been kept unnaturally young-looking by physical affliction; her proportions were slightly wrong, the head was too big. She must be older in years than her stunted size suggested.

Poor kid. No mother of a daughter could look at her and not be sorry for her (and glad of the normality of one's own daughter; Dorothea saw for a moment the lanky grace of dark-eyed Claire). The girl measured Dorothea with the direct look of the invalid who has come to terms with her situation and will use your own guilty thoughts against you. Good. That was surely better than cringing acceptance.

Then Dorothea heard the teacher's wavering voice, "Mrs. Howard, I'm sorry . . ."

A deep, cello-like note thrummed through her, a note of dread; she heard in her mind her own voice reciting lines from Claire's favorite childhood bedtime reading, *Madeleine:* "In the middle of the night, Miss Clavell turned on the light. She said, 'Something is not right!' "

Dismissing the image that came with this—the illustration, so sinister in its dark colors and the urgent slant of Miss Clavell's figure rushing down the corridor to see what was "not right" with her convent class of twelve little girls— Dorothea looked more attentively at Miss Stern. This isn't about tiredness or worry over the situation she's left behind in Mary's hands. This person has been drained by an ordeal, and she has brought the trouble to me.

Now the others came out, silent young people, a vacant-looking girl with a tearstained face, a gawky Anglo boy, two blond girls who stood dazedly together, a short thin boy with a sneering mouth. They all lined up in front of the dusty vehicle. Ellie Stern leaned against the front fender like a limp doll.

Last of all came two young Chicanos with identical expressions of truculent bravado. One of them had a gun in his hand, its muzzle raised. He was stocky and heavy browed and clearly scared, like all of them. But he had the pistol.

Dumb with shock, she thought flatly: You have been dreaming of violence. Here it is.

"Stand right there," the boy with the gun said loudly. "Any men around this place, lady?"

No lies, she decided. She had always been a rotten liar. "Only my friend Mr. Maulders. He's a guest in my house."

The other Chicano boy said, "Where's he at?"

"Probably in the smaller bedroom. He's a sick man."

The girl in the cast said skeptically, "What's the matter with him?"

Disliking her intensely, Dorothea snapped, "He's dying of cancer."

"Wow," the girl said, round-eyed. Who was she, this small, golden Moor of a girl with a broken arm?

"Shit," muttered the armed boy in obvious dismay. "You got a phone here?"

"Yes."

He glanced at the other Chicano. "Got your knife, Bobbie? Go find the phone wire and cut it."

Dorothea said quickly, "I think that might be a mistake. People know I'm alone with a sick guest. My friends keep in touch. Any problem with the phone will bring somebody around to make sure things are all right."

"If that was true," the boy with the gun said triumphantly, "you'd want me to cut the wires so somebody would come."

Calm, be calm, she thought, trembling inside with the effort to keep her voice reasonable. "The last thing I want is to bring any of my friends walking into this situation, whatever it is." Jesus Christ, she thought, where is all my coolness coming from? Shock? How long before it's gone and twitching hysteria takes over?

The tall Anglo boy said, "Can we go inside? I need to use the bathroom."

Bobbie-with-the-knife said unhappily, "Roberto? Should I cut the wires or not?"

Brillo came loping around the corner of the building, ears pricked up, and stopped. Dorothea saw the knuckles of the hand that held the pistol go pale.

"Brillo, sit," she said.

Brillo came over and licked her hand, panting hotly on her fingers. He sat. There was a moment of strained silence. The weepy girl hung against the side of the van like a strand of spaghetti stuck to the pot. The tall thin boy took a nervous step forward, speaking to Dorothea: "Look, I really have to go." He blushed when the two blondes behind him giggled.

"Not yet!" Roberto shouted. He was so nervous, so obviously making this all up as he went along, that against her will Dorothea felt sympathy for him. He might be a thug by nature, but he was not very practiced at it. Behind the gun, he was after all just a youngster. "Bobbie, go check out the house—where all the outside doors are, the phones, who's in there. See if there's any guns."

Bobbie went inside.

Dorothea started forward before she could stop herself. It was a violation for that kid with the knife to enter her house like that, without her leave. He would take Ricky by surprise, and what would Ricky do or try to do?

Roberto snarled a wordless sound at her and hunched over the pistol. She held herself back and waited.

Brillo, sensing the slackening of Dorothea's interest in him, trotted over to the visitors, tail wagging. The weepy girl sank on her knees beside him and hugged him round the neck, snuffling into his fur. The girl in the cast leaned on the van and kicked rhythmically with her heel at one of the tires. The two girlfriends giggled and nudged each other, subsiding instantly into vacuity whenever burly young Roberto glared at them.

Guns, Dorothea thought, sinkingly. Living in the country you had guns as a matter of course, for snakes, for the odd threatening intruder (and here he was), for deer in the fall. She thought of this boy Roberto with Nathan's old deer rifle in his hands, the pistol relegated to his friend Bobbie. Two weapons instead of one.

Brillo got nervous, licked the girl's ear, and trotted around excitedly until he found a stick, which he tried to induce one of the young people to throw for him.

"Brillo, you idiot," Dorothea said. Her voice wobbled.

Brillo lay down in the shade of the yard fence and gnawed on the stick, still hopeful, watching them alertly.

"That's a nice dog," the thin boy offered shyly.

Dorothea nodded. "There's another one, a Doberman." She spoke loudly and clearly for Roberto to hear. "He's not mean, he's just as nice as Brillo here. Nobody should be worried about him when he shows up. His name is Mars."

"They don't live in the house all the time, do they?" said the girl in the cast anxiously. "I'm not supposed to stay anywhere that there's animal hair. It could give me an attack."

"She has asthma," Ellie Stern said.

Roberto shouted, "You shut up! It's none of your business."

Dorothea said, "The dogs are country dogs. They spend

most of their time outdoors. But I can't guarantee that they haven't left some dog hair around inside.''

The girl looked apprehensive but said nothing more.

Roberto gets angry but he doesn't shoot, Dorothea thought. Not so far. But unexpected things will keep happening, and he'll keep getting angry, and eventually maybe he will shoot. While there's still time I must think. But she couldn't seem to. Her thoughts would not progress beyond that point.

Ricky appeared in the doorway. He seemed to take it all in with one glance. He stepped out and crossed the yard to stand with Dorothea. Bobbie was behind him with the deer rifle in his hands.

The girl in the cast looked at Ricky with critical interest. ''You're the one with cancer?''

Ricky gazed down at her from his gaunt height and said coolly, ''Who are you?''

The girl blossomed into childish volubility. ''I've got asthma. It almost killed me a couple of times when I was younger. I think it still could, if I was already sick with something else like flu, you know?''

''To be sure,'' he said remotely. ''I do know.''

''That's enough talking!'' Roberto commanded.

''I'll talk if I want to, Beto,'' the girl said sulkily, but she said no more.

Bobbie gave the rifle to Roberto to hold and squatted down to draw a diagram of the house in the dirt with a bit of stick. They conferred, Roberto continually raising his head to glare at them all over the muzzles of the two weapons he now held.

Dorothea heard Bobbie mention a shotgun and her heart turned over. Goddamn it, she had forgotten the damned thing. It was disassembled on a workbench in the garage. She'd meant to clean it up and give it to the fellow from the commune in exchange for work he had done on her windmill.

The ammunition was always kept on the mantel, next to the deer rifle, so Bobbie had probably loaded that by now. A loaded 30-30. Dangerous enough. And the rounds for the shotgun were there too. Nothing to be done.

Roberto took possession of all the keys she and Ricky had between them and had Bobbie lock up every door in the house that locked and both of the vehicles in the yard. Roberto did this step by step, scowling and glaring and chewing his lip, clearly desperate not to overlook anything and make some fatal error. He sent the girl—Quita or Blanca, her name seemed to be—inside with Bobbie to check out the dog-hair question. Everyone stood around waiting for them to return and being tired. Dorothea saw in the sag of their shoulders the heaviness of her own. Tension drains you.

When the two others emerged, Roberto gestured with both guns and said sharply, "Everybody inside. Single file. No, wait a minute." He had Bobbie come take the pistol and go first.

The dog jumped to its feet when they started for the door. Dorothea said, "No, Brillo. You stay here and keep watch for burglars."

The tall boy smothered a high, nervous giggle and clutched, blushing painfully again, at his crotch.

Roberto sneered, "You could have just turned around and let go. These girls wouldn't mind if they saw something any how."

Be careful, Dorothea told herself grimly. Don't let yourself hate him too soon, it could lead to a bad mistake.

They filed through the house, Bobbie and the girl Quita leading them, Roberto bringing up the rear.

Ellie Stern whispered wretchedly, "I can't tell you how—"

"I'm sure you can't," Dorothea said acidly. Christ, she was angry.

Helplessly Miss Stern shook her head. "It just seemed to happen, I don't know how."

"Think about it and maybe you will."

"Shut up, I said!" Roberto made a fierce stabbing motion with the rifle, and Ricky stumbled forward and caught himself against Dorothea.

It must have been the blurred vision of fury and helplessness at that moment that made Dorothea think she saw someone else, a shadowy flicker of movement, behind Roberto's shoulder and against the bright afternoon sun of the yard.

The key turned protestingly and locked the studio door.

Ellie went to the tall windows that lined the north wall. They looked like fixed storm panes, and they were fitted outside with black iron grillwork.

The perfect prison, she thought bitterly, an artist's studio. Sinks for water, lots of open space for people to lie down in, with a toilet off the end of the room, and no phone.

Everyone moved around the room looking it over, except Joyce, who slumped in the one chair, a big green one, and wept. Ellie knew she should go over and comfort the girl. What she wanted to do was to slap her and make the drizzling sobs stop. So she stayed where she was, looking out of the useless windows, her back to Joyce and to them all. She couldn't face them, least of all Dorothea Howard. That poor man staying here as Dorothea's guest—Heaven knew what those Cantus wanted with him, keeping him out there with them. Of all the harmless, pathetic figures, thin as a rope ladder, what could they—?

Suddenly Alex snarled at Joyce, "You're okay, they didn't lay a hand on you, so quit yowling, will you?"

Joyce's teary moaning increased in volume.

Ellie turned at last. "Alex, what's wrong with you? You act as if Joyce is the criminal, instead of these—these friends of your."

" 'Criminal,' " he mimicked. "As if that had anything to do with anything. You know, I learned more from them in one morning than I could learn in a hundred years from you and your drawings and junk."

"Alex," she said, "what is the matter with you?"

"Shit, what do you think? I'm on their side! They shouldn't have locked me up in here!"

"On their side!" Ellie exclaimed, outraged. "How can you be on their side?"

"Jesus, you're really something, you know? Pictures, books, 'Use your eyes'—what a lot of crap!" He flung out his thin, muscular arms. "If you believe in all that stuff yourself you're really a case, you know that?"

Jeff said apologetically, "He's just upset because of his buddy that got killed the other week."

"What buddy?" Ellie asked.

"You know: Peter Kesselman that was killed in a motorbike accident."

Ellie remembered Mary Morgan mentioning this tragedy, but it had slipped her mind. She said to Alex, "I'm sorry, I didn't realize. Was he a close friend?"

"What if he was?" Alex said. "He's dead anyhow."

Dorothea Howard came out of the bathroom patting her face dry with a paper towel. Her skin was red. When do I get to cry in private? Ellie thought, her eyes welling with tears.

"Can someone tell me who these people are?" Mrs. Howard said.

Everyone told her. She listened quietly. She didn't even

seem scared, you wouldn't know it if you didn't know she'd
been crying inside there.

"They're just running away from the cops, is all," one of
the Twinkies ended shyly, and they all waited for Mrs.
Howard's answer.

"Then they're not likely to stop here for long, are they?"
she suggested. "They'll rest a little, talk it over, and go on
running, I would guess. We can wait them out, if we're
sensible, without any big problems." She turned to Ellie.
"When are you all due back at the school?"

"Tonight."

She seemed to consider this carefully. "All right, listen,
people. Your parents will miss you tonight, and help will
come. But meantime everybody might as well pick a spot and
settle down. We may well be here all day, and they may lock
us up when they leave."

The kids groaned, but you could tell by the tone that they
were relieved. They believed what she said. Thank God
somebody else was ready to take over here. Ellie felt gritty
and ragged inside and out. Mrs. Howard hadn't spent the
morning in the van with a gunman, driving in constant terror
of more roadblocks, bullets flying, people maimed or killed.

The kids drifted around and settled on the floor in a disor-
derly row, most of them with their backs against the solid
wall across from the tall windows.

And now we'll have an art class, Ellie thought wildly, to
keep our little minds occupied.

She turned to stare out the windows. Scenarios of disaster
raced through her mind. Roberto letting loose with the pistol
and killing at random. Roberto and Bobbie (*Bobbie?* But
what did she really know about him?) getting drunk (there
must be liquor in the house) and turning for the fun of it to
brutality and rape. Her breath caught. Burning the place down
out of drunken carelessness, with all of them locked in here
helpless to escape. Ellie had always been terrified of death by
fire.

Joni must have told someone by now. The police would
wait until there was a chance the Cantus would be sleeping.
Then they would sneak up to the house—but the dogs, Mrs.
Howard's dogs, would give the alarm.

It didn't matter. There would be no police. Joni wouldn't
say a word, not while the Cantus were loose and might find
some way to pay her back.

Mrs. Howard was right, of course; keeping calm would save them. Then any killing would happen somewhere else, to someone else, to be seen in fragments on the TV news some night later on when all this was over.

"I'm getting hungry," Jeff muttered.

God, Ellie thought, I couldn't eat a thing, my stomach's all bunched up like a fist. I'll never sleep soundly again, never take another confident step in this sinkhole of a world, never be able to trust another stranger. They've spoiled the world for me, these damn Cantu people.

Oh, it's not fair, she mourned. How can I have come from the dangers of New York, that have never touched me, to this? It was funny, in a ghoulish way.

But it won't be so bad, it can't. Dorothea Howard lives here, she must know this kind of people, and she's not falling apart. It really will be all right, she told herself. The clarity of the light was against atrocity. The beauty of the landscape stood against it. Without some external threat to spark the fugitives' own terror, the chances of survival were good.

She walked over to sit down next to the painter. "I really am sorry," she said in a low voice.

"Yes," Mrs. Howard said. "I got that part."

Ellie steeled herself to describe the possible danger from Joni and the police. Mrs. Howard should know all about that, since she was in charge now. "Listen," Ellie whispered, "there's something else. One of my kids, on the way up here—"

Blanca was tired. She had tried to nap in the van, but sleep had been impossible. Now she sat and stared at the TV with the others. So far there was no mention of them, so she guessed that slinky bitch who got away hadn't said anything.

Good. Blanca needed some time to think and rest. It was all right with her that they sit still a little and not decide anything. The asthma didn't worry her—she'd taken her medicine and done everything right, and the dogs lived outside, not in the house. But you didn't want to overtire yourself and trigger an attack.

Besides, they shouldn't make plans, not with the cancer man sitting right there listening to every word. Blanca had found a good place to lock up the whole bunch of them, the room the old lady called her studio, but Beto had kept the cancer man out. "He's the only man in the place," he'd said, "and I'm talking to him, not some stupid old lady."

But the cancer man wouldn't talk. He just sat there with his eyes closed no matter how much Roberto shouted at him, and nobody wanted to actually touch him.

Roberto ignored him now. Only Blanca looked at him where he sat quietly on the couch with his eyes closed. He was creepy. He was like a wooden skeleton figure out of a *carreta de la Muerte.* Death wasn't coming for him; it had him. He gave Blanca the shivers but in an almost pleasing way, like a good horror movie. After all, he couldn't do anything to anybody, and no matter how scared Roberto was Blanca knew you couldn't catch cancer the way you caught a cold from someone who had it.

Roberto sat cross-legged on the rug, lovingly rubbing the parts of the shotgun with an oily rag while he watched the TV news and wrangled with their cousin. Bobbie whined and complained like a little kid. All his high spirits had evaporated when Beto pulled out the gun—Blanca had seen it happen, like a light blinking out in Bobbie's eyes when he saw the pistol—and now he wasn't just glum, he was really getting edgy. His nervousness was making Blanca nervous too.

He said that when the class didn't get home tonight, the parents would call the cops. Roberto said, By the time they do, we'll be long gone.

Feeling more and more tired as she spoke, Blanca said, "I don't know why we should go right away. There's nothing about us on the TV. Nobody knows where we are yet."

"We'll go when I say so," Beto said. "Shut up the both of you."

"What about going back?" Bobbie said. "I mean, we were just going to ride up here with these people, but now it's some kind of—well, it's turning into kidnapping, and somebody could get hurt with all these guns and all. They can really put you away forever for this stuff."

"Man, you shut your face," Roberto said viciously, "or I'll stick that rifle barrel right through your ears, man, one side to the other."

Blanca knew what the trouble was—the trouble with all of them. Though nobody spoke his name, the memory of Mr. Escobar seemed to hang in the room, making everybody feel bad. Sometimes people you knew got killed in car accidents or even in a fight if it was real bad and knives or guns came out. But this was different. A person goes to an outdoor celebration, and the next thing you know some cop, some complete stranger with no reason to hurt him, he doesn't even know his name, he shoots him! It doesn't mean anything any more that Mom always talked so warmly of Mr. Escobar but never ever encouraged him the wrong way even though she liked him so much. He was wiped right out of her life and her family's life and the lives of all his friends, just like that: gone. He hadn't been anybody special. Now he was nobody at all.

Blanca knew how it felt to have a cop bust your arm. What did it feel like to have one shoot you? (She remembered a glimpse of somebody—was it Mr. Escobar himself?—leaning on some big barrels and covered with red down the front of his shirt; don't think about that.) To die in a cold white hospital room, for no reason, trying to figure out what you did to get shot?

Bobbie said, "We could leave them all locked up here and take off, right now, while we have a good head start. But it might be better to go back and try to tough it out."

Roberto locked the shotgun together. "Okay, I got my weapon. Bobbie, you take that guy back and lock him up with the rest of them. I'm not doing my thinking with a spy from the other side sitting right there."

Bobbie picked up the rifle and stood trying not to look as if he was aiming at the cancer man, who got up slowly and walked out of the room without a word. Bobbie followed.

Blanca said, "I think we should have some dinner or something. It doesn't look like anybody's hot on our trail, and I'm kind of tired."

"You're always tired," Beto grunted. He stood up with the shotgun in his arms. "I'm going to take a look around this place myself. Stay here and watch the TV in case there's something on about us. When Bobbie comes back, tell him to stay too. I got to think about things."

As soon as he left the room, she got up and went to the carved wooden cabinet in the corner. Sure enough, inside a row of liquor bottles gleamed darkly. She uncapped them one by one and tipped them out over the windowsill to empty. The wine bottles with corks in them she threw as far as she could out into the brush. The effort made her shoulder ache, but she knew that if Roberto got hold of something to drink she would no longer have any influence over him at all. He might do something crazy and everything would be wrecked.

*   *   *

Bobbie was glad to return Mr. Maulders to the others. He hated the Englishman's cough.

The old lady was waiting. She was standing by the studio door when Bobbie opened it, and for a minute he felt a twitch of fear in his gut. What if she had a knife? He couldn't jump back and slam the door fast enough—

But she just touched Mr. Maulders on the arm as he stepped in past her and then she said to Bobbie, "It's after seven. Would you remind Roberto that we haven't eaten?"

Bobbie frowned at her. He tried to summon a rough answer, to show her he was not just a kid, he was his cousin's soldier. Drafted, for Christ's sake, the minute Beto pulled that gun in the car and everything changed. It made him want to cry to think about it. Here he was with a gun in his own hand, right now, pretending like he could shoot a person for giving him a hassle.

All he said was, "Yes, ma'am, I'll tell him what you said."

Before he could close the door, she added, "Don't forget to see that Brillo and Mars get fed too, please."

"I did that already," he said, proud to be able to tell her. "I'll take care of them, don't you worry." You had to take care of your animals, because people can sort of take care of themselves but animals can't, always. He thought about telling her his plans to become a veterinarian, but that seemed silly now. He locked the door.

Old fool, Ricky thought, raging miserably behind his closed eyelids. Weak, helpless, useless, miserable old wretch!

They had greeted him like a hero, the tearstained girl Joyce shyly rising to offer him the green chair. He had only been able to shut off their solicitude by feigning sleep, or at least an effort to sleep.

They didn't know—how could they?—how he had failed them. Sitting there in the living room with Roberto, mute and clenched with an absolute inability to act, to speak, to rise to the occasion and overwhelm this angry boy, this armed *child*, for God's sake!

I did nothing. I was afraid.

He dug his fingers into the arms of the chair. Useless. Worthless. Where was the gallant adventurer when Dorothea and these others needed him? Where was the blasé British hero, veteran of a thousand dangerous encounters, the man of cool and steady and unfailing inventiveness? Where, in fact, was Dr. Who? One may joke, old boy, but it isn't funny. You have nothing to lose, you're a dead man anyway, but you did nothing, you attempted nothing, you didn't even speak.

He opened his eyes slightly, afraid that someone might be hanging about near him. He didn't want to be observed locked in combat with his own thoughts. He longed to be alone.

Three of the youngsters had curled up on the floor to snooze or try to. The two blonds, surprisingly, were investigating the picture racks, pulling out canvases and looking at them. They murmured together, occasionally giggling over the pictures.

Dorothea was over by the loo with Ellie Stern. They had taped up a sheet of paper and were writing on it with charcoal: a list, to which one of the young people added something now, the word SOAP. The other words were TOILET PAPER, PAPER TOWELS, DRINKING CUPS, BLANKETS, and CUSHIONS. Demands to be presented to their captors, no doubt. Good, ask for the simple amenities, keep things civil. Dorothea's idea, no doubt. She kept her head. Thank God. Someone has to, and that teacher is absolutely no use at all, utterly wet.

Like me, just now.

He closed his eyes again. What went wrong, what happened?

How many young men in trouble have I run into in my travels? It's not as if this boy were the first. Hunkered down with their guns over skimpy fires, growing more callous and more reckless by the month, most of them were bad-tempered boys to begin with: then a theft, a fight, a murder sends them running for the hills. Outlawed, they stay childish, innocent in a way. A few are ideological firebrands, but even with most of those the political veneer comes well after the flight. They sometimes travel *en famille*, the girls as handy with guns as the boys.

But always before he had encountered such people from a position of strength, of a sort: acting as a foreign writer, someone who might report the rebels' side of things sympathetically to the outside. Ah, but that was because he had been from the outside and on the outside, never involved, never right in the middle of things.

And never like this: sick, weakened, dying.

Oh, is that it? The excuse? That, which ought to have freed him to act?

But I do have something to lose he thought with a wrench of anguish. I have a little time left. Months or days or even weeks, that's all I've got—how can I give up a moment of it? There is so little. It's all so imperiled, hedged in with more and more restrictions, my last scrap of time. I couldn't risk it, I couldn't bring myself to dare.

"Ricky."

Right at his ear, Dorothea's voice, and he flinched—because of how she would look at him, speak to him, if she knew what a coward he'd been, how selfish, how small. To his horror and pain he found himself wishing she would go away and not speak to him, for fear she would look into his eyes and divine the truth that would make her despise him.

"What's the situation with your medicine?" she said.

Don't make me think about that! "I can manage," he said shortly.

"For how long?"

"As long as I must." Oh, stop it, she deserves better—a straight answer. "I have one dose left," he said. "Its effects may last until morning."

"Good God."

"There's nothing to be done about it. You had better concentrate on aspects of this affair that you can do something about."

"Such as?" she said with bitter weariness.

The door to the studio swung open.

Involuntarily he remembered a desert wash tumbled full of bodies, the refuse of some brushfire war: ragged bundles of bloat, stink, and buzzing flies.

Bobbie, the young one, stood in the doorway with the rifle in his hands and looking embarrassed about it. Miss Stern opened her mouth, probably to scream.

Bobbie said, "Beto says come get some supper."

ᏮᏋ Eight ᏮᏋ

LOOK AT HER, Roberto thought resentfully. Like a general! Shouldn't have meekly let her get all that stuff on their list, but you can't leave the whole bunch of them in there with one roll of toilet paper. The place would stink too bad to go inside even if you had to.

She reminded him of the teachers he'd had in school, always so bossy. You did what they said when you were little because they were older, and later because you were in the habit. Unless you broke the habit, man.

I did. But not the rest of them.

Look at her, for God's sake! Skinny old lady with patches on her jeans, she talks and everybody jumps. Even Blanca took a hand at stirring the pot when the old lady told her to. Everybody worked.

Except Roberto. He stood munching a heel of bread with the shotgun in the crook of his elbow. Every time someone opened the door to the refrigerator they had to stop short to avoid hitting him. Roberto glared, daring them to touch him or ask him to move.

The old lady ignored him. She sent tall Jeff for drinking glasses from the top cupboard and two girls for plates and silver. Miss Stern was at the sink rinsing the things that came off the shelves dusty. The old woman didn't seem to do a lot of entertaining. Alex, scowling, was heating up two rocks of frozen hamburger meat on the range.

The old lady would step along past Alex on one of her circuits of the big kitchen and reach over his shoulder to sprinkle into the meat something from the spice rack on the wall. Roberto had had Bobbie collect all the knives and lock them in the truck. The old lady had smashed a garlic clove between two cutting boards before anybody knew what she was up to—God, he'd jumped in a cold sweat at that slamming sound.

Even the sick man was working. He moved slowly around the table setting out napkins from the paper towel roll over the sink.

The food smells made Roberto's mouth water. He devoured the rest of the bread.

Maybe now while he stood here, somebody was doing a news flash on the TV: that the land sharks were caught, the cops with the quick trigger fingers had confessed, Martín Maestas was home, and Roberto could go home too.

Boy, he must be getting soft in the head to think something like that! He was in the kind of trouble that didn't just go away. Real trouble, the kind this lady with her nice house and her friends who liked to make sure she was okay wouldn't know a thing about. The Englishman, now, he had the worst trouble there was. But the old lady made Roberto mad. She must have it real easy, a nice easy life, to be acting so confident now. She must really think nothing could hurt her. Maybe he'd show her different before he left. Hell, he was going to have to give up his own life on Pinto Street, wasn't he? Not so great, but it had suited him okay. Why shouldn't she have to give something up too?

Blanquita looked funny with her rigid arm stuck up at that funny angle. He had been crazy to let her persuade him to bring her along. How many other crazy things had he already done? Maybe he had made a fatal mistake somewhere along the line and didn't even know it.

The people he'd known who worked for La Raza, or said they did—trying to get Chicanos out of jail, trying to get the housing projects and the barrios cleaned up, and this and that—they would know better than he did how to handle this crazy mess.

But Roberto had never hung out with them. He'd hung out with the drinkers, the players, the fighters. Politics was a big bore, like most things.

So here he was, in this stranger's kitchen, with a bunch of kids and a guy dying of cancer. What had happened to his idea of slipping away alone, like a ghost with a gun in his hand, quick as a fox, a shadow?

Meanwhile, there was something that needed doing. He brushed crumbs off his chin and he motioned with the shotgun. "Come on, lady," he said. "You can leave the cooking for a minute. You got to make a phone call and tell somebody these kids aren't coming home tonight."

Her eyes narrowed. He had caught her by surprise with this, he could see, and she was not liking it, not a bit. He braced himself for an argument.

"It's late," she said. "There won't be anyone at the school now."

"Then call one of the school people at home. She can tell you who." He pointed with his chin at Miss Stern.

The old woman didn't look at the teacher. She said to Roberto, "What do you think I should tell them?"

She knows the answer, but she's asking me, making me do the work. Jesus. Playing games at a time like this. Or else she thinks I'm too dumb to think of something.

He had a simple story for her to tell. "Say the van broke down and you'll have somebody out to look at it first thing in the morning, and meantime everybody is going to bed down here overnight. Nothing to worry about, just a little mechanical problem, you understand? Not fixable right now, but no big deal to get fixed tomorrow morning."

She turned to Alex. "Lower the flame a little, you don't want that scorched. I'll be right back."

The house was like any nice old country place around here that somebody with money had fixed up: Navajo rugs, heavy old wooden chests and sideboards and things, corduroy and leather couches and chairs. You'd think a painter would want to brighten the place up a little. The pictures on the walls were on the sober side, and he didn't see her name on any of them. Ashamed of her own stuff, or what?

She kept a Rolodex next to the living room phone, like in an office. He watched over her shoulder as she flipped through it to the name *Mary Morgan*.

He mutely pushed the muzzle of the gun at her: Don't forget about this.

She got this person first try, a good sign, and explained it all.

"Don't worry," she said calmly, "everything's fine. I've got lots of room for them here. It won't kill them to sleep on couch cushions for a night, after all. I just wanted to make sure you . . . of course . . . . Heavens, no, why ferry everyone into town to spend money on a motel? Really, it's no imposition; Ricky and I are glad to have the company."

The other person talked awhile. The old woman was gazing across the room at a big Indian blanket on the wall. Suddenly she jumped, her eyes got big, and she almost dropped the phone. Roberto whipped around and stared, saw nothing, realized it must be a trick, and swung back again in a panic—but she was just standing there, the phone pressed to her ear, like before.

She said, "A little disorganized, maybe, and chagrined to have something go wrong. She's doing all right. . . . No, she's out helping them bring a few things in from the car—do you want to hang on and talk to her? There's no real need; we're fine. This outing will become part of your school history, a distinction for everyone who took part. . . .

"Good. I'll tell her. You must be very relieved. . . . Yes, it's going to be a lot of phone calls, sorry about that. You have a class list there at home? . . . Yes. . . . Really. No problem. . . . No more buses. The last bus south was late afternoon, I think. . . . Fine. I'll let you know. . . . Yes. Good night."

She hung up.

He let out his breath and jabbed her arm with the shotgun muzzle. "Why did you do that? Making me turn around like that?"

"I didn't," she said, looking blank. Then she said in this low, thoughtful voice, "Oh, you mean when I saw—I thought I saw. . . . You may as well know. We think we have a ghost here, and I thought I saw it just now: a man in a black cap and gown walking on the back patio."

He forced from his throat a guffaw of laughter. "Hey, come on, a ghost? What you think I am, some kind of retard? You think you can scare me talking like that?"

"You asked me what happened, and I'm telling you."

"Tell you what. You just shut up and go back in the kitchen." Man, that made him feel better, saying "shut up" like that to this Anglo lady with her goddamn ghost story.

In the kitchen, she went over to the range and gave the mess in the pan a couple of stirs with a wooden spoon. Everybody watched while she lifted the spoon, tasted the food, and added salt and other stuff to the pot. Then she served the teacher and all the class kids and Blanca, who lined up with a plate in her hand like the others.

He didn't like how she moved, though, sort of mechanical and forgetting things like giving people spoons. Thinking about her "ghost."

"Everybody out on the patio," he said. Show her who was scared of the ghost she saw out there. She shot him a funny look, like she was a little nervous herself. She'd have to do better than that.

They began trailing out into the patio.

The sick man stayed where he was, sitting at the table with his food plate untouched between his hands. The lady leaned to speak with him. He shook his head. He looked yellow.

"Talk louder," Roberto said. "I want to hear what you're saying."

The man didn't look at him. "I'm not hungry. I need my medicine."

Jesus, it wasn't enough to have Blanca on his hands! "Where is it?"

The man closed his eyes. The old lady spoke for him. "In the bedroom that's last down the hallway. Surely you can take Mr. Maulders there and let him stay the night in his bed."

Roberto saw how her hand lightly brushed the man's slumped shoulder. He's sick, the gesture said. He can't run away or attack anybody. Were they lovers, the two old people? Some old people were still jumping in the sack with each other when they were pretty creaky, like Horacio's grandparents. This English guy would have to be something to still get it up, dying and all—unless he was faking being so sick.

"Got a lock on the bedroom door?" he said.

"Yes, but—"

"No *but*. Which key?" He fished out her keys and held them up. She pointed. "Hey, Bobbie," Roberto called out to the patio. "Come in here a minute and go with this guy to his room. I'll take over out there."

Outside, with the old lady looking on like stone, he made them all string themselves out along the wall so they couldn't talk to each other without him hearing. He was pleased with himself, watching them eating in silent isolation from each other. One thing at a time, that was the way. Then you could keep up with all the little things you had to think about to keep on top of the situation.

He leaned against the edge of the redwood table where Blanca had parked herself with her plate.

"Do you think he needs a priest?" she said.

It took him a second to figure out she meant the Englishman. "Don't be dumb," he said.

"But maybe he's dying right now," she said. "I've seen dying people in the hospital who looked better than him."

"Look, he's not even Catholic, and anyhow there's nothing I can do about it. Just keep quiet and eat. You were so hungry, remember?"

One thing, man, one sure thing: that old lady better not say anything to Blanca about any damn ghost, or to Bobbie either, that soft little queer. If she opened her mouth about that he'd blow her head off. Blanca was the one who had believed in La Llorona, the wailing woman who supposedly wandered the banks of the Albuquerque irrigation ditches looking for kids to steal in place of her babies that she'd drowned a hundred years ago.

Something moved, crackling the brush on the hillside across from the patio. Roberto squinted up there, shotgun at the ready. It was only the black dog, digging at something under a bush. He felt his legs go weak with relief. Shit. Could have been the cops.

That was what the old lady was trying to convince him was a ghost? Damn her, thought she was so smart.

"I want some of that supper," he announced.

Blanca said, "But it's all dished out, Beto. You want some of mine?"

"No. I want some of theirs."

They all stared at him: the man with the gun who was hungry. The old lady started toward him with her plate. Jesus, was he supposed to eat from the plate of somebody who was maybe screwing with a guy dying of cancer? She must be trying to poison him.

"Not yours," he said.

"Why not?" She stopped. She sounded irritable, like his mother when things had gone bad all day at the discount store. "I'm your host and I'm offering."

"Host my ass," Roberto flashed, fed up with her. "This isn't even your house, you know that? It's a Spanish house. All that carved wood and tile floors and those *latías* up there in the ceiling. Spanish people built this house. You people stole it, that's all. Well, now Spanish people are taking it back. While I'm here this place is mine, and that food is mine too if I want it."

Jeff, who sat coiled on the ground like a snake, said suddenly, "Oh, come on, Roberto, that's crap, you know? People have been taking whole countries from each other for all of history. You just got stuck, that's all."

"No, man, *you're* stuck!" Roberto shouted. He swung the shotgun toward Jeff, who shrank back against the wall, lifting his plate shoulder high as if sheltering behind it.

"Okay, okay," he said, "whatever you say, man. Take it easy, I didn't mean anything."

That was better, a lot better. But the old lady couldn't leave it alone.

She set her plate and her water glass down on the heavy redwood table and tapped the glass with her spoon. The twinkling sound made them all look at her. "For the record, the main portion of this house was built by a family named Lobo y Vargas who ran livestock up here originally. They were wiped out in an Indian raid. A nephew named Roybalid inherited. He had a dry goods store down in Albuquerque. So far as I could find out from the records, he never came out to see the place but sold it to a rancher named Short-man as soon as his uncle's estate was settled. Shortman ran cattle, invested badly, sold in turn to an Englishman named Bellows. The Bellows's granddaughter, Nancy, leased it to a neighboring rancher until I bought it from her shortly before her death."

"So what?" Roberto glared at her. Just for an instant he saw in his mind's eye an image of a slim, dark man walking along in an orchard slapping the trunks of the twisty fruit trees, encouraging them as if they were cattle. Something from when he was a baby at the ranch, it must be, days he only knew from what Great-uncle Tilo or Mina might say. He made a fierce mental grab for the image, trying to hold onto it—that must be Dad, what did he really look like?—but the old lady wouldn't let him. She had to go on talking.

"Plenty of Spanish landholders were cheated out of their property in this state, but that doesn't seem to have been the case right here. Now that that's understood, are you still hungry?"

"Shut your mouth, I'm thinking!" But it was too late. The scrap of memory blinked out. He was left standing there like a fool.

Suddenly the teacher, Miss Stern, walked up to him and held out her plate. Her face was shiny with sweat, and he could see her trying to talk, swallowing and licking her lips, and not being able to. Too scared.

He had a headache now and he had no appetite at all. "Just set it down there on the ground," he growled. What had Dad *looked* like?

She bent and put her half-filled plate on the flagstones near his foot. Then she walked over to the back patio wall and stood holding onto it, facing away from them all.

Roberto looked down at the plate and nudged it with his boot. He said loudly to Blanca, "How can you eat that shit, anyhow?"

Moving sharp the way you do when you're mad and you don't care who knows it, the old lady stepped over and grabbed up the plate, like Roberto was nothing, a statue or something.

"Hey!" he said. "What the hell you think you're doing?"

She whistled up the hillside at the Doberman. "We don't waste food in this house. I'm going to feed this to the dogs."

"They already got fed," Bobbie said quickly.

Roberto yelled, "Fuck the dogs! You want to do something, you ask me first!" And he yanked up the shotgun and fired, felt the kick, the crash, heard the high screaming cry, heard it break off sharp. A good shot, satisfying. He felt loose inside, melted with release.

Bobbie moaned, "Shit, Beto, what did you do that for? He wasn't hurting anything."

The dog on the hillside was just a trembling dark heap now, one rear leg jerking automatically in the air. Everyone stared, except Jeff, who sat crumpled like a bag of laundry, his head covered by his crossed arms. The teacher held on to the wall with both hands. The two girls grabbed onto each other and breathed in little screams. Spacy Joyce just hugged herself and blinked.

Even the old woman was quiet now. The paper plate shook in her hands. Food tumbled off onto the paving at her feet.

You worry about me, lady, not about ancient history or some stupid ghost.

Bobbie sounded like he was nearly crying. "He's dead. I can see it from here, he's quit moving. You killed him for nothing. What did you do that for?"

Roberto stared at him. Was he crazy or what? It was to show these people not to mess with us, that's what for! To teach the old lady a lesson! And it worked too, you could see that looking around at their faces. What about that, you smart-asses? Dumb Roberto from the valley that just came along for the ride with his smart cousin to your dopey class. A shotgun made a lot of difference, more than just the old pistol alone. They'll remember.

But all he said was—and he sounded so cool, he was proud of himself—"I just wanted to make sure this old shotgun works, that's all."

What was wrong with Blanquita? She was holding her ear with her good hand, like she still heard the shotgun blast.

Well, what did you think, little sister? You wanted to come along so bad, what did you think it was going to be like?

Bobbie hadn't seen Blanca having an attack in a long time. He had forgotten what it was like, man—awful.

Beto had told him to bring one of the wooden chairs from the kitchen here to the bedroom. Blanca sat there sort of stiff with her eyes bulging and her skin sweat-shiny. She was like a pump that had gone bad, wheezing the air in and out real slow with a horrible straining sound. She was a weird bluish color, and there were big dark sweat patches under the arms of her blouse and down the middle of the back.

She looked as if she was dying. She looked mad, too. She was fighting the asthma, you could tell.

Beto was setting up the steamer for her, cursing low and steady to himself as he fiddled with the little bottle of stuff you used to keep the minerals in the water from jamming the thing. He had the shotgun right by him on the floor. That damn shotgun, why did Mrs. Howard have to have a thing like that here?

This was her room. Bobbie smelled talcum and perfume, faint but clear. The door to the closet was open a little, showing some long robes and dresses among the blouses and shirts. He stood by the writing table at the window, about as far as he could get from Blanca, feeling useless, waiting for Beto to tell him he wasn't needed any more and could go.

He thought mournfully, If it wasn't for me asking Beto to come to art class with me, none of this would be happening. I wouldn't be standing in this strange house with a gun in my hand to keep other kids in line, and Beto wouldn't have gone and killed somebody's dog. She loved the dog, too, you could tell by how she was careful to tell us about him so nobody would get worried when they first saw him, him being a Doberman. If it wasn't for me inviting Roberto along. If it wasn't—thinking like that made him want to cry. He fiddled with some pencils stuck in a pottery cup. It wasn't supposed to be like this. Beto was supposed to be on the road by now, hitching with some stranger, while I got Blanca back home.

Demanding to travel to Canada with Beto! Look at her!

Blanca began to cough again. She spat into a napkin clutched in her shaking hand.

Oh, God, Bobbie thought, praying with all his heart, oh, God, don't let me ever be sick like that. I'll be good, I'll help out at home, I'll go be a priest if that's what you want, but don't let me ever be sick like Blanca. Or sick like that skeleton Englishman, either, the guy in the next room. Bobbie had heard him coughing earlier.

It was like a hospital around here. People that sick, they shouldn't be allowed to run around loose. It was too awful for everybody else.

He wished he'd told Mrs. Howard how sorry he was about her dog.

Beto got up and stood holding the shotgun and glowering down at the steamer like he'd like to shoot the thing. When the steam finally started to come, he grunted and jerked a blanket off the bed. He put it over Blanca's shoulders.

"Shit," he said. "Well, that's that, anyhow. We're not going anywhere tonight."

Dorothea, kept out of the studio that evening to answer the phone if it should ring, sat with the two Cantu boys in the living room and watched TV. They looked for news of themselves. She watched a continual replay, inside her mind, of the death of Mars.

She was overwhelmed by remorse. What was the good of all her confidence now? You thought you could handle it, she thought bitterly. The Wise Woman of the Bookstore, so sure she could bring everybody through unscathed just by being calm, clearheaded, and firm.

When did I start to get so angry, so foolishly furious? When he forced me to call Mary and tell lies about the safety of other people's children so that those lies could be passed along to the parents. And poor Ricky! How dare these people add so much as a straw to what he carries already?

Where the hell is that ghost when I really need it? A quirk of imagination, a flicker in the field of vision, but no damn help. The first shot has been fired, and it was my fault. There could be others.

So now we're down to plain, quivering, animal fear, and maybe that's a good thing. It's real, at any rate.

At least the sister, Blanca, had the sensitivity, if that was what it was, to get sick after Mars died. Not like Bobbie, protesting but never really challenging his cousin. And never would. Goddamn these people, crashing into my life like this!

"Listen," Bobbie said tensely.

The TV announced a special report on "the Pinto Street problem," as the announcer called it. Roberto, with the pistol on the table beside him and the shotgun across his knees, leaned eagerly forward. Like a child, for God's sake, an armed, dangerous, bad-tempered child watching TV.

On the screen, a solemn-faced Chicano intoned a brief speech about real-estate fraud and political rebellion, harking back to the sixties, mentioning the Tierra Amarilla raid and its aftermath. Then a camera pan of a dirt street, small houses neat or shabby, some trailers, a man in khakis and an undershirt staring into the camera for an instant and then turning away.

What the announcer said was lost for a moment in Roberto's remark, "What's that jerk doing there? That's Betsy Armijo's brother. He lives down in the South Valley."

A civil servant with pink-tinted eyeglasses made a statement in monotone exonerating his office. There was a shot of a heavy blond man, identified as a prominent local land developer, averting his face from the camera as he climbed hastily into his car.

"Never saw that guy on Pinto Street," Roberto said.

Bobbie said, "He must have sent somebody else."

Then they were looking at two people with bloodied heads

slumped in the back seat of a police car, and somebody else knelt over a sprawled figure with its shirt rucked up, taut belly exposed. A riot, the voice-over said. A riot about the YMCA? Could that be? Pictures of two young men, labeled left-wing agitators or something equivalent in news-ese, were flashed. They had been arrested at the riot. Several others were still being sought. The wounding of a policeman and the death of a local man caught in the cross fire.

"Hear that?" Roberto demanded, turning toward Dorothea. "Well, there was no cross fire. They did all the shooting, the cops did."

Dorothea rubbed her eyes. Good Lord, she knew more about the judge's damned two-hundred-year-old revolution than she did about this story unfolding before her on television. She seldom read beyond the headlines of the papers. She was ignorant.

No, not ignorant; that was untrue. Uninformed about this particular incident, yes, but basically ignorant, no. You know. You always know, somewhere at the back of your mind.

One reason for putting aside the paper unread is the repetitiousness of the stories. It is so often the same. If it had been a white kid reaching into his pocket for his money clip, which the off-duty cop "thought was a gun," the fatal shots would not have been fired. If Pinto Street had been in another part of town, inhabited by another class of people, there would have been no riot, no police, no death.

But it's not my fault, she groaned dismally to herself. I've chosen a different kind of life, reclusive, creative. I'm not made for rough currents like these.

A wizened old man with a stained hat on was saying that the people of Pinto Street had never intended any violence, let alone burning down the Y. They had now formed a householders' block association, responsible people, no young hotheads, mind you, to deal with the city.

"What hotheads?" Roberto said. "Does Mr. Garduño mean us?"

He means you, Dorothea thought. You're the purged "wild element" that nobody has to be scared of any more, nobody has to send cops to control. Pinto Street marches on, toward moderation, accommodation, away from you, in the time-honored tradition of revolt. Ask the judge, he knows. He should come to you, my boy, not to me.

A woman spoke haltingly of her husband, the man who had
died; her bewildered, reddened eyes stared out at the camera.
Dorothea bit her lip. A person had already been killed in this
madness, and on whose head lay that responsibility, Roberto's? He had shot her dog. She'd watched him shoving that
damned shotgun in people's faces and carrying himself like a
hard-bitten desperado. Youth doesn't mean what it used to. A
man is dead, a policeman seriously injured. Keep that in
mind.

The program switched to a city spokesman who announced
solemnly that an investigation into the Pinto Street situation
had begun. Meanwhile, authorities were still looking for—

"That's your house," Bobbie said.

The camera lingered on a house with curtains drawn across
the windows, a small adobe structure with peeling stucco and
some potted geraniums outside the front door. A police car
was parked at the curb. No one went in or out of the house.
Fade-out. The smooth young announcer returned. He was as
dark as Roberto but the subtle message of his dress and
speech was, I am a different kind than those poor people in
trouble on Pinto Street. To prove it, he engaged in banter
with the sports announcer about a horse that escaped its
pasture and wandered into a bar in the South Valley. Then the
newscast was over.

"Hey, leave it on," Roberto said. "Let's see what's next."

Bobbie muttered, "I'm sick of it," and turned the knob.

"I said leave it. Turn it back, but put the sound down."

When Bobbie turned the sound off, another sound became
suddenly audible: a scratching and whining at the back door
of the kitchen.

"It's Brillo," Dorothea said. "If you just wait, he'll figure
out that he's not to sleep in the house tonight and wander off
on his own."

Bobbie got up. "I'll go talk to him, sort of calm him
down."

Screw you, sonny, Dorothea thought bitterly. That's not
good enough.

Roberto hefted the shotgun in his hands and gave Dorothea
a slit-eyed tough-guy look, making up for the absence of one
gun from the room. There was nothing amusing about his
overacting. He said truculently, "They should have showed
our side of it more. They should have talked with our mom,
too."

Their mother, who must be frantic about them. This thug has a mother.

"I want something to drink," Roberto said, looking around the room. "I bet you got some good booze here someplace."

Here we go, she thought, her whole body beginning to ache with tension. She said nothing, but he had seen her glance at the liquor cabinet, and he got up and went over to it. But when he flung the door open, no bottles winked within. The shelves were empty.

Dorothea stared, bewildered by a miracle. A small voice chimed in her heart: without drunkenness, maybe we have a chance.

"What are you, teetotal or something? Well, you got any dope, grass or like that? I heard where you artists use a lot of that stuff to help you see things in your head to paint."

She sighed. "You can tear the place apart if you like, but there's nothing to find. I'm not that kind of an artist."

"How many kinds are there?" He poked halfheartedly at the sofa cushions as if he were minded to take her suggestion. "So where's all your friends calling up to see how you are?"

"Talking to somebody else, I guess."

Trailing restlessly about the big room with the shotgun hung over his arm, he seemed very young and at a loss.

"Roberto," she said. "What are you going to do?"

"What's it to you? Anyway, why should I tell you anything? You'd just pass it on to the cops, first chance you got."

"You can't stay here indefinitely. Somebody will put two and two together and they'll come here looking for you."

"Don't tell me what to do."

"I'm only telling you what I think is going to happen," she said reasonably. "I have to. You're all here under my roof. I feel responsible. I worry about people getting hurt."

"People already been hurt," he said. "Didn't you notice Quita's arm in a cast? Or maybe that doesn't count?"

"You know what I mean."

"Sure, you mean you don't want any mess in your nice house. You can't wait to get me out of here, can you? Well, you're going to wait anyhow. My sister's with me, and she's sick. You think I'm just going to run out on her?"

Oh, Lord, she was tired. She drooped in the chair, not answering.

"What kind of ghost is it?" he said. His eyes were defiant in the lamplight.

She shook her head, sorry she'd let that slip, about the ghost.

"Come on, what is it?"

"Somebody from a long time ago and another country," she said. "It wouldn't interest you."

"That's right," he said nastily. "I wouldn't know nothing about stuff like that, right? I don't have to. I'll tell you about your ghost. You're crazy, that's all. An old lady living out here in the middle of noplace with a guy that's dying—you see ghosts because you're crazy."

"Maybe I am," she flared, "for trying to talk rationally with you!" Caution gave way. "You're a wrecker, aren't you? You scrawl your stupid signs all over every blank surface like a dog pissing on a wall, throw your damn garbage everywhere, treat the world like your private dumping ground, just for the fun of it!"

He stared at her. "Who the hell you think you're talking to? Shut your face, you dried-up old bitch, or I'll blow it off you!"

"Sure," she said, "that's your credo, isn't it? If it's beautiful, smash it; if it moves, stomp it, spoil it, crush it—you little bastard!"

He swung the shotgun so that she looked down its barrels. Here it comes, she thought, amazed at herself.

"I could bust you to pieces, I could blow you away," he said. He kicked out suddenly, knocking a porcelain lamp to the floor, where it shattered. With the butt of the shotgun he slammed through the glass panes of a book cabinet against the wall. She saw his narrowed, angry eyes as he swung back toward her, standing with his legs braced, the gun hugged tightly under his arm again.

I know you, she thought. You're what I'm hiding the wall from.

"You trying to push me into it," he said ferociously. "You want me to blast you, so you can be a hero and I can be a creepy kid who came and blew away this great old lady artist, some kind of special genius, right? Well, fuck you, lady. I'll kill you if I feel like it, got that? If I feel like it, when I feel like it, because I feel like it. You old bitch!"

Someone breathed a word into her ear: *"Canaille!"*

She snapped her head aside with a gasp and covered her ears.

"Hey," Roberto said.

"Quiet," she whispered. "He's here somewhere, he spoke to me!"

Roberto's eyes widened. Then he laughed angrily. "You never quit, do you? You think I'm some dumb peon you can scare to death with a ghost story? Fine, you show me your ghost and I'll be scared. If you can't show it, then just shut up about it."

"Get out of my house!" she screamed at him.

"When I'm ready. And when I go, I'll take somebody with me, right? As a hostage. One of those precious people you don't want hurt. Or maybe you."

Ellie sat on the closed lid of the toilet in the little bathroom and squeezed cold water from a sopping wad of paper onto her temples. All right, she thought, you didn't do so badly, and nobody got killed. Even the dog would not have been hurt, if Mrs. Howard had kept her head. After all her advice about staying calm! She was out there alone with them now, but she would be all right. They had kept the sick man, Maulders, out during the afternoon and no one had hurt him. Were they going to take each of the adults aside this way? My turn next, then.

She shivered violently and squeezed more water into her hair, cooling her headache. Her brain throbbed with the memory of the shotgun blast.

What's it like to sleep with a man who's got cancer? Maybe I've already done it. People can have cancer and not know. Anyway, poor Mr. Maulders wasn't going to be much use, that was obvious. It was up to Ellie and Mrs. Howard to figure out how to outwit the desperadoes.

Sighing, she leaned her back against the cold water tank. The damn bathroom was beginning to stink. Too many people, all of them nervous, were using it too often. The little window wasn't ventilating well.

You came out here to write a novel this summer. Well, here's your chance, no distractions at last. Write it on toilet paper, like Gandhi in prison. Or was that Hitler?

There came a timid knock at the bathroom door.

"Just coming out," Ellie said, getting to her feet.

It was one of the Twinkies, Sarah and Cindy—Ellie couldn't

remember which name went with which girl—rabbit-pale with excitement.

"Mrs. Howard's back," the girl said.

So she was—apparently unhurt, wearily settling into a corner with her blanket, looking as much like a refugee as the rest of them. Ellie carried her own blanket and her shoes over and sat down.

"How is Mr. Maulders?"

"I didn't see him, but they tell me he's all right. Whatever that means."

"Did they say when they'd be leaving?"

"No."

Ellie drew a deep breath. "I keep thinking about—what might happen. These kids, those thugs, that little monster Roberto." She hitched herself closer to the older woman. "You can make them want to go. Tell them there's a back way, a secret road that will take them around all the roadblocks and patrols and things. You could make something up, couldn't you? This country is covered with dirt tracks going all over the place, I saw them from the plane when I first came. You could promise them a quick, safe escape before the police ever catch on."

She pushed her hair back from her face, excited now, seeing it happen in her mind.

"The way they take would be one you chose to lead them right to the police. Well, no, I guess you can't be sure where the police would be, but couldn't you send these people into some kind of trap? Some place that their car couldn't get through, so they'd be left on foot for the police to find?"

Mrs. Howard shook Ellie's hand off her arm with an abrupt movement. "What the hell do you think they'd do to me, if I led them into the kind of trap that you're proposing?"

"You? But why would you be with—?"

"You don't imagine Roberto would accept this kindly offer of help from me just like that, do you?" Mrs. Howard whispered angrily. "He'd suspect the possibility of some kind of a trap; he's not an idiot. If I were he, I'd say, Sure, lady, sounds like a wonderful idea; and we'll take you with us to make sure this way out is as good as it sounds. If anything goes wrong, we'll shoot you."

"I'm sorry, I didn't think," Ellie mumbled.

"What a surprise," the painter said acidly. Then she added in a tired tone, "For God's sake, go and sleep a little if you can. I don't know what we'll be faced with in the morning, but trying to handle this situation in total exhaustion strikes me as a very poor idea.''

Ellie withdrew hastily to her own corner, where she lay curled in her blanket—the room had grown quite chilly—and her misery and rage.

Nine

ALEX WOKE IN a rush of terror, jammed up against the pipes beneath the utility sink in the corner of the studio.

He lay there hugging himself, his hands jammed tight to his mouth to keep his breathing quiet. He had dreamed of having a dog's head, seeing himself from the outside as some kind of a dog. Then somebody came along and blew the dog's head off with a shotgun, like a killing from *The Godfather*.

Already the visual details were vanishing. He was grateful for that, but the sick, gulping feeling in his stomach stayed. God, it was awful.

How could they they all be sleeping, when there was this awful thing scratching and slavering after them? Not like on the screen at all, and not like what his mother had said to him last year when Grandpa died. Nothing as kindly and wishful as that: wafting off to heaven in your sleep, what a laugh.

Death was what it was: big, mean, ugly Death.

He didn't dare close his eyes for fear of seeing more of it.

Joyce wished they would do it and get it over with.

It's not so bad, she told herself, staring up at the shadows on the beamed ceiling. I've been through it before, and it's not so bad.

That time at Tony Chester's when she had gotten so high on stuff that was stronger than she'd thought. Then Tony and

the other two boys . . . she'd known what they were doing,
sort of, and had tried to stop them. But stoned like that, what
could you do?

It wasn't so bad, not after the soreness healed up and her
mother quit asking her all the time what was wrong.

The worst was that all the boys at school knew. Girls
gossip, but boys are worse. They boast. She'd seen them
sneering or watching her as if they could see some kind of
mark on her. The worst ones grabbed at her in the halls and
said she should come blow some dope with them, they'd
show her a better time than Tony had.

The girls wouldn't talk to her at all, as if it had been her
fault.

Funny thing was, she didn't care, sort of. She had quit
talking to the other kids, at least about anything that mattered.

Another funny thing. When she'd realized she wasn't pregnant, mixed in with the relief she'd been sort of sorry. She
was sorry that it was all for nothing, nothing to show except
the shame and the whispers and this nothing feeling that had
been with her ever since.

Just nothing. Just drift along like you were out of reach,
and in a way you were. It was a kind of magic. She knew
kids who did this with music, or with books.

She just did it, drifting, answering when she was spoken
to, doing as little as she could and waiting in a flat, puzzled
way for her life to get started again. Like being at a bus stop
on some dull corner forever and ever, and the bus got later
and later, and would it ever come?

Because if not, she might as well just dump the whole
thing.

Well, something had come along, all right. She liked to
doodle with a pencil, so she'd ended up in this strange place
shivering in terror from hour to hour, waiting for it to happen
again. These Cantus were men, weren't they? Well, two men,
and the sister. She guessed she knew a little about men by
now, men and boys both. She didn't want to know any more.

This time there wouldn't be any drugs to keep everything
muffled.

One thing about drifting, you couldn't decide what you
would think about and what you wouldn't think about. Your
thoughts, like everything else, just happened to you.

Maybe they would do it to her right here in front of the

others. Well, at least then everybody would know she didn't invite them (but she squirmed inside thinking about this, and hot tears seeped from the corners of her eyes and ran down, turning ice cold in the roots of her hair). People would be sorry for her and comfort her later and say what a terrible thing.

No they wouldn't. Nobody would give a damn. And when the kids back at regular school heard, they'd remember about what happened at Tony's house and they'd laugh and say Joyce sure had all the luck.

This time she was ready. She had some pills put away. She had stolen them from her mother's medicine cabinet, a few at a time, and hidden them in a dresser drawer just to have them around if she wanted. If she got tired waiting for the bus. Too bad she didn't have them with her now. She would take them, dry even.

Even if the Cantu men got her pregnant she'd use the pills. After all, suppose it was a girl? Who'd want to bring another girl into the world, this world, full of these people?

For that matter, suppose it was a boy?

The blanket under her head was getting soggy with tears. She got up and went into the bathroom at the end of the room and stood holding the edges of the sink and crying without a sound.

Ricky woke up coughing. Someone was standing next to him: a weird, shrouded figure, with an arm raised as if to strike him—in a cast, of course, and he could make out that thick fall of hair; she had a blanket wrapped like a cloak round her shoulders. Beyond her, the cold black sky and the stars. Yes, he had dragged himself out here onto the lounge chair in the patio to try to—to try—

"You're keeping me awake," Blanca complained.

"I beg your pardon?" he replied, when he could get his breath.

She pointed over the patio wall. "I'm in the next room. I can hear you coughing."

"Sorry," he murmured. "Can't help it."

"Then there's no point in me trying to go back to sleep," she said irritably. She backed a few steps and hiked herself up on the lip of the dry fountain.

She might know. Ricky said, "Did you hear a shot earlier?"

"Hear it? I almost went deaf. I was right there." She described, vividly, the death of Mars. "Beto was just trying out that old shotgun."

Poor Mars, nice beast, what a rotten thing to have happened. But Dorothea was all right. Thank God. Ricky smiled, coughing again.

"Why are you smiling?" she said. "Doesn't it hurt when you cough?"

"Sometimes," he said. Just now the cough merely robbed him of his breath and made a tightness in his chest.

"Cancer's supposed to hurt a lot."

"If I can't get more of my medicine soon," he panted, "I'm afraid I'm going to find out."

He heard the sharp intake of her breath. "You're out of your medication?"

Medication, not medicine, saith the little expert, product of years of dosages and hospital visits. "I used it up after dinner. I'd meant to drive into town for more today, on my way up into the mountains."

"What do you take?"

"They call it 'hospice mix.' Painkillers in some combination or other."

"I wonder if any of my stuff would help," she said doubtfully.

"Small chance of that," he answered, touched, "but thank you for the thought."

"God," she said. She hunched her blanket more securely about her shoulders, leaning nearer to him and speaking in an anxious, confidential tone. "Just finding out I don't have my medication with me, that I forgot it, that's enough sometimes to bring the asthma on. Are you thirsty? I'm going to go get some juice, if there is any. I'm supposed to keep my fluids up after an attack."

"You had an attack tonight?" he said.

"I think it was just from being in a new place," she said. "You never know what's going to set it off—dust, dog hair, something you eat. I didn't know all the things they put in that supper, and I probably shouldn't have had any, but it smelled so good. I'm okay now. You want some juice?"

"Please," he said. Lately his mouth was often dry and stale-tasting, an effect of the disease.

So the child had had an attack this evening, after the death of the dog. He wanted to think about that—there was something arresting there—but he could only wonder when his own attack would come: the pain, slipped from its leash. At the first intimation he would have to send her away.

She brought him cold apple juice in a ceramic mug. The mug was heavy in his hands. The sweet juice was chilly.

"Delicious," he said. "Thank you."

She settled down again with her own cup. "What are you doing here anyway?" she said. "You should be in some famous hospital where they can do all the latest things to help you and keep you alive until somebody finds a cure."

"Been in hospital," he said. "Didn't like it. Left."

"Did you have to have an operation?" When he nodded, she went on knowingly, "I bet that hurt, didn't it? Afterward, when you woke up, I mean. I've been in the hospital a lot, but they can't operate on me. There is no operation for asthma."

"There's none for this type of cancer either," he said, "as they discovered."

"Can I see the scar?"

Well, really. But why not? He gingerly pulled up his pajama top.

"I can't see," she muttered, coming close.

He felt the touch of her fingers, light but definite, on the puckered line. He had to lean to the side to avoid getting clipped by her cast.

"That's not much," she said, clearly let down. "I've seen a lot worse from kids falling off their bikes." She sat back, still staring as he covered up again. "I guess they didn't get it all, huh?"

He shook his head, his eyes suddenly full of tears for himself, his spoiling entrails, his slowly self-destructing body. "Couldn't," he said, clearing his throat. "Had to leave me my lungs to breathe with, rotten as they are. You'd think they'd have invented plastic lungs by now, wouldn't you? But it seems an artificial heart is child's play compared to synthetic lungs, and anyhow it's too late in my own case. The filthy stuff has already spread. So I don't get to be made into a bionic Englishman. I get to be a dead Englishman, and that's no distinction; millions of them are ahead of me already."

"I've thought I was going to die a few times," she

said. "When the asthma got real bad. It was pretty scary, man."

"Terrifying," he agreed. "Sometimes I get tired of waiting and I'd rather have it over."

"That's a sin," she said quickly.

"I don't mean suicide. Just"—he tried to snap his fingers, but they would not move crisply enough to make a sound—"over. I'm told it often comes that way. The body is weakened, one picks up some sort of flu, pneumonia sets in, and that's the end. Not such a bad way to go."

She rearranged herself in her blanket. "Maybe sitting out here in the cold isn't such a good idea?"

"I wouldn't be too concerned," he said.

"Beto shouldn't have locked you in," she said. "I think he wanted to make sure you couldn't get together with the others, you know, and organize an escape. Like those Englishmen who dug their way out of German prison camps in the war."

"I'm not much good for digging."

"Are you and her in love? You and the old lady, I mean."

Ouch, poor Dorothea—but to this child even thirty would seem old, fifty totally ancient. Cautiously he said, "We're good friends."

"I saw how she looks out for you, and how you two sort of back each other up without having to talk about things first. I think you're in love with her," Blanca announced with relish.

"Really?" he said, amused but also wary. This was Roberto's sister, after all. Information about himself and Dorothea might be used against them. Name, rank, and serial number—we're way past that, but some prudence is indicated all the same. "Spying on us, were you? Caught us kissing passionately over the cooking tonight?"

"Well," she said judiciously, "love's not the same for old people, is it?"

"Yes it is," he said, stung despite himself. "Just the same, bar a few minor details. We're neither of us senile, you know, gray hairs to the contrary."

"Then there's you being sick," she went on. "Though I bet you don't let that stop you."

"Blanca, I don't wish to discuss my personal life or Dorothea's. We're both entitled to our privacy."

" 'Privvacy.' " She mimicked the short *i*. "Does everyone in England sound like you?"

"Does everyone in America sound like you?"

She giggled. Then she said, "What I think is, she's not woman enough for you. All she does is sit here in her nice house and feed her nice dogs. She doesn't even watch the TV or she'd have known all about us. She's one of these arty people with no guts, a chicken, man. Otherwise she'd have eloped with you when you were still okay."

"I never asked her to."

"Not even when you were both young? I bet you did ask her. I bet her parents were mad because you were a foreigner, and they gave her a real hard time about you. So you went traveling, but she was afraid to run away with you and came out here to sort of bury her sorrows."

What a romance! He had to smile.

Blanca said seriously, "Why do you smile like she couldn't be in love with you? You're not so bad looking, and I like how you talk."

To divert her, he said, "I did ask a woman once to come traveling with me. But she died."

"How?"

"She was burnt up in a fire."

Blanca emitted a horrified, satisfied groan. "Ugh, God, that's awful. Was she pretty?"

"Glorious." Had she been beautiful? Scarcely mattered now, did it?

"What did you do after that?"

"Got drunk, sulked and brooded, traveled."

"Dorothea should have gone with you and consoled you," she said firmly.

He almost laughed. "We'd not met then, Dorothea and I. And now . . ." He stopped uncertainly. And now, what? He thought suddenly of his own Aunt Nell and her long-time friend, Captain Carpenter. They had slept together for all those years before the captain died and widowed a dull woman who was far less devastated by his passing than poor intense Nell. One way or another, all love stories ended in parting. Not a subject fit for discussion with a child.

She said confidently, "I'm going traveling with Beto, to help him and keep him company. It's all arranged."

"Surely not!" he exclaimed. He regretted this involuntary

response as soon as it was out of his mouth. "That is—Blanca, you're far too intelligent to want to live on the run."

"What do you care?"

"How old are you?"

"Don't start that," she warned. "Just because I'm small, people always think I'm a baby."

"You're certainly not a baby," he said, irritated at his own tactlessness. "But you are young, and you do have a health condition, not to mention that cast on your arm. You'd be a serious liability to your brother, surely you must see that. He can't intend to drag you further into danger with him."

"So what am I supposed to do, then?" she challenged him. "Sit around and rot with my damn asthma? End up taking care of my mom while everybody else takes off and has a great life? That's what the whole world expects, man, but I'm not going to do it."

"Why not?" he countered sharply. "You'd probably do it very well, and there are worse fates, for heaven's sake. I doubt very much that your natural bent is for being a fugitive from the law."

"Oh, no?" she said with a surprising and unlovely gleam of cunning. "How do you think Beto got this far? He was so mad and scared after the riot, he could hardly think of a thing for himself. If I hadn't figured out how to escape, he'd still be hiding down by the river in Albuquerque. He needs me to help stop the right cars for a hitch north and to get people to help him."

Christ, he thought, this is no time for lies and fantasy. As well say if I find the right doctor my cancer will miraculously vanish.

"Nonsense, Blanca! This is nonsense, and you know it as well as I. You must see that what you've said is nothing but a story. Your brother knows, if you don't. You gave him a clear signal tonight—your attack after supper. No, let me speak. You saw the dog killed and you realized then how serious all this is, and how foolish and unfair it would be to encumber your brother with an invalid companion. So you underlined your condition with an attack."

She glowered at him. "That's the craziest thing I ever heard."

"What's happened to Roberto would have happened, more or less, without your part in it," he went on. "You are not his guardian angel, nor is he yours. He needs to be free to find the people who are essential to him, and you must find yours as well. Not merely whoever is familiar and close at hand—I mean the people you discover a spiritual affinity with.''

Excellent, he thought caustically. Do you think you're back at Winchester debating your fellow upper formers? He tried a different level.

''Think of the people who seem to take hold of your heart as soon as you meet them. Think of someone who moved into your neighborhood and you knew at once that this person would be your friend, or a teacher you loved from the first day of class.''

She shook her head in denial, her truculence replaced by confusion.

''I'm not saying this very well.'' He sighed. ''You see, I think planning for Beto seems important to you now because you don't see any life for yourself except with your family. But you must not be afraid to use your imagination for yourself, extend your vision to your own future—what you, Blanca, can do on your own in the world with the people who are meant to be part of your life. We all have to move outward from our families to find those people.''

Still no reply, and he was too tired to go on. He drifted for a minute, or perhaps it was longer, and he had to ask her to repeat herself when she finally did speak.

''Are you all right?'' she said, bent near to look at him very closely with enormous eyes.

''Just tired,'' he said.

She stood up straight, gazing loftily down on him, a pretty female goblin, bigheaded and skinny-legged. ''Then I'll go back to my room. I'm not going to talk about Beto with you any more.''

''Very well,'' he said. ''Talk about anything you like.'' But he owed her more courtesy than that after giving her such a long, sententious speech: not what she had bargained for, surely. ''Blanca, please stay. Talk to me, and later on, when I feel better, perhaps you'd like to hear about an old Englishman's travels in the world.''

''What should I talk about?'' she said warily.

''A place I shan't get to visit, I'm afraid. Will you tell me about Pinto Street?''

Before long she was caught up in her account of life in her mother's house, the neighbors, her on-again, off-again relationship with school. Sometimes he drowsed, sometimes he listened. Slowly, he began picking out elements of what she said, and these elements circled in his mind, condensing into a pattern that he felt on the verge of understanding. The incident of the neighbor boy stopped and rousted by police because he was out alone after dark in an Anglo neighborhood; comments about unemployment benefits never received because you had only fifteen days to file an appeal, and that was not enough time to find a lawyer who would do that sort of poorly paid work; people falling afoul of the welfare rules, the food-stamp restrictions, having their furniture repossessed even as the staples came out and it fell apart.

With withering scorn Blanca described how the police were trying to "explain" the riot by producing two young "radicals" they had arrested there. Ricky remembered how in similar circumstances the French police under all regimes had manipulated their own arrest patterns according to whatever was politically acceptable to the government of the day.

Dorothea's dream judge would know all about this, he thought. Is that why he's come? Is that why, if he's mine, I've brought him with me to her?

He could not hold and follow the thought, because another kept intruding, overriding everything else: Why am *I* here, talking at midnight with a child and waiting for the onset of pain? Who can need me so badly here, to bring me at such cost? Who can need a useless, craven, trembling wreck, who needs a dead man?

Ellie jerked her body from one position to another, struggling for sleep. She resisted the impulse to look at her watch. It could only tell her that her desperate efforts had taken her a mere ten minutes deeper into the night, or else that another full hour, that should have gone for sleep, had inched out of existence leaving her that much less possibility of rest.

She had a sudden, brilliantly clear image of herself standing in bright sunlight, very young in jeans and a western shirt, looking down in astonished wonder at something incredible. A monarch butterfly, almost as big as her childish hand, had come fluttering through the air and had landed on the buckle of her belt. There it perched, slowly flexing the brilliant panels of its wings like a gift from some unimaginably benevolent and powerful source.

She had been what, nine? Ten? She never could pinpoint her few memories of childhood. It was one of the summers she had spent at camp. She had stood holding her breath for a long time, in anguish that some twitch of her body might send the bright creature flying again.

The butterfly had clung there, seemingly oblivious to any threat or danger. She had even walked around behind the cabins without disturbing it, avoiding the other kids and not telling a soul at the time because she knew they would spoil it if they could. When the monarch had finally flitted up and away from her, she had not felt abandoned. She had been the girl the butterfly came to, and the fact that the butterfly left again had no bearing on that singularity.

One sunny passage of perfection, indescribable to others (as she had discovered afterward) and never again achieved. . . .

That small Ellie, slim and exalted in her beloved cowboy clothes—her belt buckle had been a nickel-plated relief of a broncobuster—and graced by an inexplicable, transitory wonder, was at the high point of her life. Unknowingly, that child stood on a summit. Ever since: downhill.

Roberto dreamed of scorpions, the kind they show in the movies, close up so you can see how ugly they are, like they're more than just—well, bugs.

They were on everything, just laying there, waiting for him to touch something, sit somewhere, take a step even.

He grabbed the blankets off his bed and began slamming around with them, trying to sweep the scorpions off the dresser top and the windowsill. But they clung to the blanket and crawled toward him, or they flew. The air was full of buzzing scorpions.

He woke up twisted in a blanket on the floor, gasping for breath.

Just a room, a room in the old woman's house. The TV was still on, a blank gray screen; that was where the buzzing came from. The thickness of the air; that was moisture from Blanca's steamer burbling away in the other room where it was set up on a stack of books next to her bed.

Bobbie was asleep on the couch with his knees up, snoring, his head thrown back and his mouth wide open. A wonder he didn't have his stupid thumb in his mouth. He had wrapped himself in an old Navajo blanket taken down from the wall, a dusty, raggy thing.

Why the hell wasn't he outside, on watch? No, Roberto remembered now; he had been going to take the first watch himself, prowling out there to make sure no cops snuck up on them. Only he'd fallen asleep in front of the damn TV instead. Shit.

The house was so quiet. No faint lively music from a late-night party down the street, no traffic, no sirens. Just the hissing of the TV.

The goddamn TV news. He'd expected them at least to talk with his mother. How do you feel, Mrs. Cantu, about what your son is doing? They always asked about feelings, like feelings were news. You'd see a lady with tears all over her face because of a dead kid or something, and some jerk would stick a microphone in her face and ask how she felt.

He looked at the black windowpanes, thinking apprehensively, I should go out and have a look around. I should get the hell out of here anyhow. This place. Silent, like under a spell. So where was this ghost she was so hot about?

Mrs. Howard was something weird, all right. Her and this walking dead man she had living here. He must have come to get cured by her, because he knew she had secret witch powers, man. There was sure something going on between those two.

And wasn't everything working out just like a witch would plan it? Blanca sick, Bobbie as good as out cold, Roberto himself dozed off in front of the TV while the cops sneaked up? For all he knew those kids in the class were tunneling their way out of the studio right now. Shit, if she wasn't a witch, wouldn't he have bashed her one when she called him a bastard?

That was what he knew his teachers in school had always wanted to say to him; you could see it in their faces: bastard, bum, all the rest. What did she say? He didn't remember, that's how much it meant to him, man. She'd said it all out loud and right to his face, and only a witch would have the nerve to do that. But here he still was, guns and all. So big deal.

Lucky that Angie didn't come, or fat Paul—less people to handle. Not too many for himself and Bobbie. Bobbie the wimp, well, he was doing okay for a wimp. Maybe he'd remember how to be a man before this was all over, maybe he'd be a pretty good guy to have along, not just a walking whine you needed to hold another gun. Too bad Blanca was a girl and stuck in that cast, or she'd be great. But Bobbie would do. Things could be worse. A guy could be completely on his own in this thing.

He got up and moved around the room, carrying the shotgun. Broken glass crunched under his boot sole. Busted the place up for her a little; she'd remember him, all right.

He shouldn't even be thinking about her and her shitty ghost. He should be thinking about taking off for Canada in the morning. Man, there would be some scene with Blanca, she was so set on going with him. As if he could take a little crip like her with him! She'd fuss and scream, maybe even pretend to have an attack, but she'd be all right. Bobbie might catch some shit, but Blanca would go home, back to Pinto Street. Nobody would dare do a damn thing to her, because she was so delicate and all.

Tomorrow. I couldn't leave before, not with her sick like that. But tomorrow morning I'll go. Be great to get out of this witchy old house, too.

Meantime, to take his mind off how weird it was, why not get something going with one of those chicks locked up in the studio? Cindy and Sarah in their tight clothes. They kept hanging on each other and staring, man, you could tell they were interested: watching every move, watching the man in charge. And that other one, the soppy one, Joyce: she was more scared, and she probably thought she was too good for it and would put up a fight. Would that be so bad, to have a little wrestle and then stick it to her? He remembered now that Alex had once told him something about her putting out for a couple of guys from her school. Anglo guys, probably. Well, he could show her something, all right.

And they'd come across. They'd have to. They were in a spot where they couldn't say no, which was exciting. You could have one of them if you wanted. More than one. Or have one now and take the other one as your hostage and screw her later.

His mind veered from the complications of taking one of them along. It wasn't time for that yet. Stay with now, just go take one for now. No point waking Bobbie and inviting him in. He was too chicken. Tell him in the morning, watch him squirm.

Roberto stepped out into the hallway and stopped, listening.

At least that mothering black dog, that you wouldn't even see in the dark until it was right on you, wouldn't come around. He was glad it was dead. It was like a witch's black cat.

Shit. He'd started to have a hard-on, thinking about those chicks, but it was gone now. You wouldn't get anywhere with them anyhow, not with that old bitch looking on. She'd freeze your balls with her stare.

He remembered going in there earlier, taking Mrs. Howard back inside. Those two girls had some pictures out on the floor. Pictures by the old lady, he guessed. There was one of a wild-looking guy with long hair and a tough, mean face. It had really jolted him. So ugly! What would you make a picture of a face like that for? Maybe it was part of the magic? Maybe that was what the ghost looked like? Maybe that was why the old lady had no pictures of her own hanging on the walls of her house; maybe her stuff was too strong, it could do things to people, so she kept it out of sight in that studio.

He imagined her squatting in the middle of the floor in there while the others slept, making a drawing in blood by moonlight, a picture of Quita, maybe, or of himself: laying a curse. What was the use of heading out of here if there was a curse laid on you by a witch? Shouldn't have talked to her like that or busted up her living room, but shit, she asked for it, man. She really did.

I can stop her, he thought. Go right over there and blast her. No talk, no time for magic, just step outside and aim in through one of those big windows and let her have it, man. *Blam!* She's gone.

Quickly, silently, he went out the back door from the kitchen and stood listening in the night. Oh, it was cool and clean-smelling out here. The moon was big and glowing. It felt so good to be outside all alone, in the quiet. Like last year before Mina used the car all the time, when he used to drive up into the Sandias before going to work. He'd take that old bow of Jimmie Archuleta's and hunt deer before anybody else was awake, even. He never got any, but man, that had been something. He'd been going to do it again this fall, but now he'd be someplace else.

He liked this too, right now: being the only one awake, free, moving around quiet in the dark in his own kind of country.

Something moved, over past the low patio wall, something sniffed and whined. Roberto stared, his scalp creeping. Then he laughed. It was the other dog, of course, the gray one that looked like a clown, what else could it be? Not the dead black one, that he could just make out lying still on the hillside. Now, that would be something, the ghost of a dog!

He let himself out the gate and the gray dog came and sniffed at his hand with its sharp, cold nose. He scratched its curly head and breathed deep.

He should be looking around to make sure about cops.

But he knew in his guts there weren't any out there: no ghosts, no cops. The night felt friendly. When the dog went trotting away down the arroyo behind the house, he followed, moving quietly the way he knew how to do from hunting, happy in the pattern of hard black shadows and bright slaps of chilly moonlight across the sandy ground.

Could just keep walking, he thought, hit a road someplace. Hitch a ride, disappear. Let them all wonder. The invisible man, gone without a trace, no more decisions to make about other people, no hollering and tears from Blanca, write a postcard home from Nome. Home from Nome, that sounded funny.

Something winked and flashed in the moonlight ahead. Some kind of building, one of those metal kind, to shine like that? In front of some sort of a dark hill? More cautiously, he advanced, while the gray dog loped on ahead out of sight.

It was not a building. It was a whole hillside, a rib of rock sticking up out of the ground like a wall and covered with bright and dark veins, sparkling and darkling like the side of some fantastic huge spaceship.

He moved closer, the shotgun a comforting weight in his hands. Like the magnified eyes of a million insects, darkly gleaming rounds of glass peered out of the rock at him, next to a ripply sweep of something satin-silver: tabs from aluminum pop cans? And wire, rusty wire, flowing long like the hair of a woman with snarls in it? He stared and stared, walking slowly along and touching it: pitted glass, rusty metal, slick plastic, all the darks and lights the moon showed him. Old beer cans, velvety dark with rust. Bottle caps, the heads of nails, old ones and new ones clustered together.

I can't believe my eyes, he thought. This was what it was like, to not believe your eyes; his eyes felt like they were pushing wide open in his head trying to take in everything, it was so damn big, all these streamers and waves of brightness and darkness rippling across the rock where someone's hands had fixed them.

Something brushed his knee. He jumped, swinging the gun, but it was only the curly gray dog. It stood watching him, one paw raised, delicate and nervous.

Her dog. It had led him here.

Small footprints in the sand at the bottom of the wall. Her prints. Her work.

Suddenly the night wasn't his any more. It was hers. This was her mark on it, on this whole place, night or day. He hunched his shoulders.

Those were just washers there, and little cogwheels from all kinds of busted old machines. Just any old junk. You can't make real magic out of junk, nobody could. He was walking around all wide-eyed in front of a big rock wall covered with pieces of goddamn junk you could pick up any day on the road or in your own back yard!

He uttered a raucous shout of laughter.

There was no ghost, and this great glittering thing like the wing of an intergalactic bird was just a lot of glued-together trash.

He put the gun down; if he fired, the slugs might ricochet off the uneven surface and hit him. Instead, he hurled a rock at the wall.

The rock rebounded with a dull sound. He swore and threw another. On the third throw, something shattered and splinters of glass gleamed for an instant in the moonlight.

I'll show you ghosts and magic, you crazy old *bruja!*

Bobbie woke up alone and scared. The TV was hissing. Roberto was gone.

Bobbie had dreamed that he sneaked up onto the hillside while Roberto wasn't looking and found the dog was still alive, he could save its life.

Just a dream. I wish I'd never come here. Can they put us in jail for killing Mrs. Howard's dog?

I need somebody to talk to.

He got up and pulled on his boots. Roberto would be out on watch, most likely, but Blanca was probably sitting up, sick, and happy to have company.

Just to be safe, he took the 30-30.

The room Blanca was supposed to be sleeping in was empty. The air was rich with steam. The bathroom door was open; she wasn't in there. She was probably just in the kitchen looking for a midnight snack.

The next door, the door to the sick man's room, was wide open. Nobody was in there either, just rucked-up sheets on the bed. God, had the old guy been faking? Had he fooled Blanca into unlocking his door, and then grabbed her and hid her someplace?

Bobbie heard a voice over the thunder of his pulse. The tone was conversational, the voice was the skinny man's with that faggy accent. He was out there, talking, in the little patio beyond his empty bedroom.

Bobbie crossed the darkened room as quietly as he could and pressed himself, rifle at the ready, to the wall beside the open door to the patio.

The skinny man lay on the reclining chair in his pajamas, a pillow behind his head. Blanca sat on the edge of a little stone fountain, her back against the central pillar of it, her feet hanging out of her blanket in midair.

"—in the South Valley," she was saying, "and he's a real radical. I think he used to be a member of the Brown Berets, so he's pretty militant for a priest." She opened her blanket and spread it, settling it higher on her shoulders. There was something batlike in the gesture that made Bobbie's skin crawl. Maybe he even made a sound, because suddenly she looked right at him and said, "Bobbie, what are you doing?"

The man turned to look at him too. It was just like having a skull look at you, with big hollows under the cheekbones. The two faces like two skulls, the blanket lifting like bat wings, Blanca's cast sticking up like a thick white bone—

"Looking for you," Bobbie said. His voice squeaked, damn it.

"We were just talking," Blanca said.

"In the middle of the night, out here? Beto wouldn't like it."

"I'm afraid my coughing woke your cousin up," the man said.

Was he mocking Bobbie, looking at him like that with those black caves of eyes?

"Blanca, you're not supposed to be out here," Bobbie said. "Not with him. He's a prisoner, like the others. He's not allowed out of his room unless one of us is with him."

"I am one of us," she said. She had always been such a smart-mouth.

"You're a girl," he retorted, "and you're sick, and you've got a broken arm. I don't want you alone with this guy." Because what, exactly? He couldn't say. "Get inside," he said to Blanca.

"We are inside," she answered, pointing to the adobe wall that surrounded the little patio. She looked exasperated, like he was just a bothersome little kid. "Nobody's going anywhere."

He had to do something, he couldn't just let her brush him off like that. Roberto would say he was a pussy, letting her boss him. Not that you could do anything to Blanca herself. Roberto would beat the shit out of you for trying, like those guys he hurt once for calling her Tattoo after the dwarf on "Fantasy Island."

Bobbie turned the muzzle of the rifle on the sick man. "All right," he said, managing not to let his voice crack this time. "You tell her to come back inside with me or I'll shoot you."

If he looks in my eyes he'll know I can't, Bobbie thought, nearly sick with nerves. He knew he could never have killed the dog, for instance, the way Roberto had. Except he felt light and almost dreamy-headed right now, and he had the spooky feeling that if the man didn't obey him, his trigger finger would tighten all by itself and fire off the rifle.

The man said, "Blanca, I think you'd better go in." To Bobbie he said, "Young man, may I ask you to see what you might bring me from the liquor cabinet?"

Oh, shit, Bobbie thought, it must be hurting him. The cancer must be chewing on him. "Sure," he said, and he herded Blanca hurriedly into the house ahead of him.

"There's no booze," she said in a funny, worried voice. "I looked."

Bobbie went and sat with her in her room because he didn't know how to go out there again and tell the guy there was nothing to drink. Blanca wouldn't talk to him, but he didn't care. As long as he didn't have to stay up all by himself.

*   *   *

I don't want to, Dorothea thought, waking unwillingly.

Ellie was right, of course, damn the girl. Roberto would take a hostage when he left, he had said so. And it ought to be me.

She groaned and buried her face in the quilt she lay rolled in on the studio floor.

Mercilessly, methodically, her mind plotted it out: If they take one of the kids from the class, the chances are increased that something will happen to that kid, either because of meanness or because the kid can't stand it and tries to get away. Ellie Stern is little more than a kid herself, Ricky is too much of a problem and doomed anyway so they won't consider him, and that leaves me. I know the country. I have some self-control, at least, no matter how thinly worn at this point. I would have a chance.

I should have said it already: Take me, I know a quick, secret back way. He'd be out of here by now, these kids would be safe.

She imagined herself trudging along a roadside somewhere in the wilderness or across a desert, failing for want of water. Or hurt, maimed, raped, dying in some culvert with the trash and the ants because Roberto panicked or got angry or maybe just bored. How long before any one would find me?

I could still do it. Tomorrow, first thing. I could try. But it's nonsense; I'm no youngster, to take on such a role. This is not the Scarlet Pimpernel vs. the dreaded M'sieu Robert.

She smothered a weak giggle with her hand.

No no, murmured someone, very close, a voice she did not know—a male voice, unknown but shockingly familiar. *He is Monsieur no one, he is a ruffian.*

She opened her eyes.

In the corner where the north wall of windows met the solid wall at the end of the room, a dim figure stood: a man, a person of shadow standing in shadow, with a face she could not discern. No image of his features produced itself in her mind, familiar as he was—not very tall, rather stiff in posture with the feet braced apart. How well she seemed to know the worried hunch of his shoulders, the way he held his hands hooked together in front of him over the curve of what she knew would be an incipient potbelly.

Oh, she thought calmly, it must be a dream.

One of the children sighed and kicked the wall in sleep.

Dorothea sat up slowly, gathering the quilt about her to keep in the warmth of her body. The air in this corner of the room seemed suddenly arctic.

Take no chances, came the visitor's voice, insistent and hissing, *with such a person!*

Who are you? her mind replied. She didn't want to speak aloud and wake the others. This visitor was for her alone and she knew it: after all this time.

That you should ask that, child!

Child? She smiled slightly. If he took her for his own son, they must be pretty myopic over there on what she had heard called portentously the Other Side. How can I smile when I am so frightened? she thought. But of course it was only a generalized fear; no ghost that belonged to Ricky would wish to do her harm, she was sure, and now she faced the real threat of the Cantus. That did tend to put a mere phantom in the shade.

He stood so that she could not see his face. Good, she thought; it would be like Ricky's face.

Why have you come? she asked.

He cocked his shadowed head, just out of range of the moonlight, and she was suddenly filled with the old terror that he might misjudge and show her his face, if he had one. She slitted her eyelids, ready to blink him out if that happened. *I wrote to you,* he replied without sound in the breathless spaces of her mind. *You never answered.*

I didn't know how, she offered, abashed.

No? At a loss for an argument? How unlike you, my child! How refreshing! He must have laughed. She didn't hear anything like laughter, but she saw his shoulders move and a glint from where light touched something on his hand—a ring? He leaned toward her. She heard a shifting of clothing and she shrank back, clutching the edge of the quilt.

Don't be silly, she lectured her terror. You've no fear to spare for him. But why does he appear to me, not to Ricky directly? He should go to Ricky.

Did you speak? the visitor inquired.

She shook her head, a great muscular effort which produced a minuscule motion.

Good. You are in great danger here, and so it is appropriate that you listen. I have been here before you and I know. You are considering some romantic and perilous ges-

ture, some heroic action, against the wild beasts who have invaded your life. But I tell you, there is nothing to gain by such efforts, not against the rabble when they become great. Romance and heroics are nothing, phantoms, illusions of youth. Power is real, in a king's hands or a peasant's, and it can crush you in the wink of an eye. I have seen strong men, great orators and movers of men's souls, borne down inexorably by the juggernaut of political passion. All my life I have seen it. My child, I do not wish to see you destroyed.

A message, she thought, staring at the wink of jewelry on his hands, his unreal hands. He's come to tell me what he knows, the distillation of his life's experience, to help me save myself and Ricky. Can that be it?

Slowly she formed an answer: You were not destroyed.

Exactly!

She heard as if from a distance her own whimper of fear. He gave no sign that he had noticed anything. If this doesn't get itself over soon, she thought, I'm going to break down and scream, and if I start I won't be able to stop. None of them will see him, they won't feel the chill he brings. They'll just think the old lady has cracked up.

I was not destroyed, the shadow continued, *because I acted on what I learned. I withdrew, I found a corner for myself in which I could live my life productively, quietly, with a modicum of happiness even! Not troubling my neighbors, not mixing in great and dangerous affairs any longer, none of that. I set to work to produce for the world whatever modest achievements lay within my power. This humility is what heroes lack, and it is what ruins them. Do not try to be a hero, my child. I have known many of them in my lifetime. I have shared their wine and their hopes. But they are dead.*

Don't worry, she thought dully. The best I've done so far is to insult Roberto until he broke a few things. This is me, the great creative artist as she really is: a coward. Ricky was right about that. I'm not the one who's dying, and I'm not about to risk my life. That's what I've been learning from Ricky; how I don't want what he's got, which is death. So don't worry about me. I've already found my safe corner, and I'm not about to give it up.

Bitterly she stared at the shadowy visitor, thinking, Am I like you? Is that why you come to me instead of to Ricky?

When the moment comes, remember the virtues of reticence, modesty, practicality. Deny your foolish impulses, avoid the heroic gesture. When the moment comes, my child, think of me and stay your hand. Give them someone else.

He reached toward her across the intervening fall of moonlight. She was caught in an icy rush of terror that prevented her from crying out, but her own hand flew up to ward off his touch. She saw with straining eyes the brightness of shirt cuff beneath the sleeve of the black gown and the inner round of the ring gleaming on his finger.

His fingers, shockingly warm and plump and slightly damp, caught her own—she was the cold one, a woman of ice—and she gasped at the contact. The pressure of his ring bit slightly into her skin as he tightened his grip and gave her hand a shake as if for emphasis. The unmistakable sensual reality of that rigorous hand taking hold of her lifeless one pressed her into a nauseated faint.

❧ Ten ❧

DOROTHEA WOKE FEELING stiff and chilled. She groaned and turned on her side, tugging her ragged quilt free from where it had bunched under her hip. Her joints ached from the pressure of the hard floorboards.

It was light. Some one was crying, soft puppylike sounds: that girl Joyce, the one who looked like a battered child but without any visible bruises. Everybody else seemed to be still sleeping.

Dorothea sighed and got up to go sit beside the girl. "Hey," she said softly, "you're going to scare me if you keep that up. That would please Roberto, and it will also make your face red and sore."

Blub-blub.

"It can't go on forever, you know." God, how lame. But she couldn't say, They'll leave soon, because then someone would say, Who will they take with them? And it could so easily be this girl, an unbearable thought.

"I hate being afraid," Joyce muttered fiercely. "I'd rather have them hurt me, I'd rather be hurt and get it over with, than just sit here being so scared!"

Dorothea wanted to pat the girl's hair, but she felt she didn't have the right. She owed the child something, though; something instead of the protection a grown-up should be able to provide. "Listen," she said, "did you notice anything odd in here last night?"

Joyce shook her head.

"Well, I did. You talk about being scared! I woke up and saw a ghost in here."

That did it. "A ghost?" Joyce gaped at her with red-rimmed eyes.

"Yup." This is what a cowardly old woman is good for—telling stories. "It's the ghost of a man who lived in France during the time of the French Revolution. He was a lawyer, like so many of the men who made the revolution, and at first he was all for it. But later, when it turned into a bloodbath with the revolutionaries chopping each other down right and left for being not revolutionary enough, or too revolutionary, he ran away and hid in the country.

"I think he became a provincial magistrate of some kind, a local judge, and all through the crazy times afterward—Napoleon, constant warfare with the rest of Europe, and then the restoration of the monarchy—he went along doing his judgely job and getting rich off shrewd investments. He was probably dabbling in army supplies and confiscated real estate, like many another comfortable bourgeois of the time, a regular pillar of the community, a staunch supporter of law and order."

Joyce sniffled. "Sounds like all those sixties people, those hippies and all, that my dad says are working on Wall Street now."

"Yup," Dorothea said.

"I bet you were too scared to say anything. You know, tell him he shouldn't have sold out like that."

Say anything? Dorothea thought caustically. Honey, I agreed with him, but it didn't make me like him any better. She sighed. She felt really old this morning, and very depressed.

"What would a ghost come here for?" Cindy said. She and her friend Sarah had edged nearer and were listening too.

"Because he's sorry," Sarah answered quickly. "It's always because they're sorry about something."

"Why does he come?" Joyce said.

Dorothea looked from one vivid young face to another. "I think my friend Mr. Maulders brought him along, to tell me something I needed to hear for this situation right now. Though the ghost thinks he's home in France, talking to his son. That's who he seems to think I am. He tells me to be careful, be prudent, be circumspect, be safe."

Sarah said, "What's 'circumspect'?"

The door opened. Bobbie stood there, rifle slowly swinging to cover the whole room. Now Dorothea heard the phone ringing, and she began to quake inwardly. When the moment comes, stay your hand—was this the moment? She remembered the pressure of the judge's ring. If she looked at her hand now, would she see an imprint, a sign of that warm, moist grip, that seal of his fearfulness to hers?

"Ma'am?" Bobbie said. "Beto says come answer the phone, please."

Everybody sat up, blotchy-faced with sleep. She could sense the muzzy echo of her own panic in them.

Dorothea rose, her knees wobbly, and forced herself to go with Bobbie. Just keep your head, stay calm, be careful.

In the hallway Bobbie said, "I'm sorry about your dog."

He held himself straighter today and spoke more firmly. She decided she'd liked him better the other way.

Roberto was sitting on the tall kitchen stool with his back to the corner. He looked tired, scruffy, and tough.

"Answer it," he said, "and watch out what you say."

Stay your hand. For God's sake, what else could she do? Roberto's shotgun—her shotgun in Roberto's hands—lay across his knees. The judge knows nothing I don't know, I had the message before he ever arrived: I'm an artist, not a member of a SWAT team.

The voice was Frank Sanford's, calling to find out whether Ricky would be coming in to the hospice today to pick up more of his medication. Frank said he was surprised to see from his records that Ricky must be nearly out by now.

She had not once thought of Ricky's exposed situation during all that long night. Blinking back tears of anger with herself, she said, "He drove up into the mountains, but I think he plans to stop by later on today or maybe tomorrow."

Frank sounded worried. "He's not cutting back on his dosage, is he?"

She said she didn't think so.

Frank wanted to talk: Was she doing all right, would she like him to come out and discuss anything with her while Ricky was away?

"No, thanks, Frank, I'm fine. I'll come see you sometime soon at your office, though, all right? I do have some things to talk about with you, but not now." Not now, not now, go away and don't endanger me, Ricky, all of us any further.

But he was talking again. She reached the end of her self-control.

"Got to go now, Frank," she interrupted. "I have some guests and they want their breakfast. Goodbye, thanks for calling."

She hung up.

Bobbie cried, "She told! Beto, she told!"

"I said I had visitors," Dorothea said. "Not what kind of visitors they were. Having guests is normal around here this time of year."

Roberto scowled at her, biting his lip. "Well, we'll find out, won't we? If a bunch of cop cars come whooping up the drive, that'll tell us something."

"We can't sit around and wait anyhow," Bobbie said miserably. "Beto, we've got to go, we've got to get moving!"

"Not on an empty stomach," Roberto said. "I want breakfast."

You'll have to take someone; take me. The words formed themselves in Dorothea's mind. She contemplated them help-lessly, no more able to speak them aloud than she was able to fly.

"But Beto—" Bobbie whined.

"Listen, meantime I don't want any more phone calls. You don't have to cut any wires, Bobbie. Just unplug that phone." He was staring at Dorothea with a hard, mean look. "Toss it in the arroyo."

Bobbie did as he was bidden, leaving Dorothea alone in the kitchen with Roberto.

I wonder, she thought, how much more of this I can stand. Her body felt light and wobbly. She should eat something and see that they all got fed, of course, the time-honored responsi-bility of women. The thought of food made her stomach clench. Tell him to cook his own goddamn breakfast.

Stay your hand. Survive. What the hell use is it having a ghost take all the trouble to come and tell you how to save your life if you don't use what he tells you? He came to you last night because you're the one in a position to act; Ricky isn't. Stop blaming yourself and take advantage of what you've got: good advice, sanction from someone who ought to know, confirmation that your instinct for personal survival is right. Don't offer yourself. "Eggs," she said.

Roberto shrugged.

He's angry, she thought, because he knows I'm not going

to give him a chance to "blow me away" and he despises me for it. Well, let him. Christ, her body was sore from sleeping on the floor.

She broke eggs into a bowl. The clean surfaces of the shells felt like satin to her touch. All her senses were vitalized by tension and by fear. She poured the beaten eggs into a heated pan.

"That stuff smells funny," Blanca said. She had installed herself at the counter with a bowl of cereal and was watching Dorothea cook.

Dorothea added another dollop of soy sauce. "It's egg foo yung, a kind of Chinese omelet," she said.

"I don't like Chinese food," Blanca said, wrinkling her nose. "But Ricky might like some."

Ricky! How had Blanca come all that way from "You're the one with cancer?" Dorothea said, "How is Ricky this morning?"

"I don't know, exactly. Last night he couldn't sleep, and I was wide awake myself, so we sort of talked most of the night—until Bobbie came around playing big shot and made me go back to my room. Ricky seemed pretty good when I left him."

God, what wouldn't Dorothea give right now to have the whole damned lot of them vanish like smoke so that she could crawl into Ricky's bed, twine herself among his scarecrow limbs, press against his knobby crate of a chest, and lull herself to sleep with the dogged rhythm of his heart.

"Is that stuff done?" Blanca said. "I'll take him some."

She looked worn but alert this morning; she had clearly taken pains to brush her thick hair and wash up, though her blouse had a drip spot on it and the ironed-in crease was gone from her jeans. Her face seemed slightly puffy, accentuating the sensuous quality of the golden-skinned face, the luminous sweep of the brow under the thick, weighty hair. The sockets of her eyes looked bruised, apparently from lack of sleep as well as the effects of her asthma attack the evening before.

Bobbie came trailing in. "Nobody around," he said. "But they'll come sometime. We got to go, Beto."

"We should eat first," Blanca said primly, tasting what Dorothea had spooned onto her plate.

"You're not going anywhere, don't worry," Roberto said.

"I'm going with you," she said.

"Hell you are."

"Beto!" she wailed.

"I can't have you getting sick. Give me some breakfast."

"I won't be sick." Blanca held out a plate and Dorothea filled it. The girl gave the plate to Roberto. "I'm fine this morning. It was only the dogs' hair anyhow, and when we're out of here, that won't be a problem any more. Come on, Roberto. I'm coming with you. It was all my idea."

"No," Roberto said, with his mouth full.

"Bobbie's going, and he's only your cousin!"

"I have to," Bobbie mumbled wretchedly.

"You?" Blanca cried, outraged, turning on Bobbie. "You shouldn't even be here! It was all my idea, not yours!"

"Go take that guy his breakfast," Roberto said. "Nobody's going anywhere yet awhile."

Blanca slipped off the stool and went to her brother. "Okay, but don't you try to sneak away without me, Beto. I won't let you. I'll make a lot of trouble."

He reached out and grabbed her good arm and shook her. Her hair bounced, her jaw dropped, her plaster-cased arm jigged briefly in the air as if she were dancing. She was clearly too startled to utter a sound.

Roberto said, "No more trouble, Quita. Now, go on."

And she went.

Sarah, the taller of the Twinkies, came red-faced to Ellie and whispered, "Miss Stern, what am I going to do? I've got my period."

Damn. "You don't have anything with you?"

"No. I'm early by a couple of days, and I didn't expect to be away so long." Her lips quivered.

"Go use some toilet paper from the bathroom." Thank God somebody had thought to ask for a fresh supply last night. "Or better yet, there's a roll of paper towels in there now. Use some of that."

Sarah stood there. "Yeah, we thought of that, Cindy and me, but I thought maybe you might have a Tampax with you?"

"I'm sorry, Sarah, I don't."

The girl nodded and headed for the bathroom.

Ellie climbed stiffly to her feet. "All right, everybody," she said. "Let's try to clean ourselves up a little. We're not animals, even if we get treated as if we were."

Mechanical speech, mechanical action, she thought, as they straggled into a line for the use of the bathroom. You go through the motions to fill the time.

She remembered last night's vision of her butterfly visit, and she had the curious sensation that today she was living in some sort of obverse of that vision: the mechanical opposed to the spontaneous, the drearily horrible set against the vividly wonderful. And this misery could no more be fully described afterward—if there were to be an afterward—than that joy could be.

"Aren't they going to feed us breakfast?" somebody whined.

Click went something (she imagined) inside her, and she told them in falsely confident tones that of course they would be fed. Meantime, she had them take some of Dorothea's pictures out of the racks to look at. The kids responded sluggishly, but they did as they were told.

The idea of invading Dorothea's privacy in her absence filled Ellie with mean pleasure. She was so nasty with me last night, she thought, and it wasn't fair. I was right. She could save us, she should save us. She's had a whole life already, more than a lot of people get.

Her thoughts, panicky and childish, revolted her. You're a teacher, she told herself angrily. So teach!

"All right," she said, "let's leave the pictures for a while, and after we all have breakfast maybe Mrs. Howard will talk with us about her work. Meantime, we'll do some drawing of our own. Pull out those newsprint pads and pass around some charcoal from that tin box over there. Come on, Mrs. Howard won't mind. Spread out, give each other some room. The light's good and there's lots to see out of these great big windows. Or draw each other, if you can stand to."

That got a giggle. She felt a rush of warmth for them, and then a spasm of rage on their behalf. Would any of them ever again look at a painting without feeling echoes of this time? Would they ever think of an artist without thinking of Dorothea—prisoner in her own home, powerless against armed criminals? What a lesson!

Ellie drew the sink in the corner, ignoring the hungry hollowness in her belly.

Someone tapped on the glass.

Everyone stared.

A man stood outside, a tall man with bushy hair and a push-broom mustache. He had a roll of papers in one hand.

He wore a corduroy suit and a bolo tie and dusty boots. The fingers that drummed the glass were big and square-ended.

Scrambling to her feet, Ellie went to the window.

He mouthed a word at her: *Dorothea,* of course. He was looking for Dorothea. He knew nothing. She must do it all. Her heart's thunder filled her mind.

The kids crouched wordless on the floor with their sheets of paper while she searched for a catch to open one of the windows. The catches were recessed, hidden in the frames. She found one, but it stuck. She struggled with it two-handed, trying to get a grip with too many fingers on too small a flange of metal, while the man shouted idiotically through the glass, a far-off voice like a voice in a dream: He had something for Dorothea, where would he find her?

Jeff tried to help her dislodge the catch.

Joyce rushed up, a piece of paper in her hands. It had writing on it. She pressed the paper to the glass.

The man turned his head; waved to someone else they couldn't see; gave them all a quick grin (don't worry, here she is, thanks all the same), and strode away toward the corner of the building without looking back. Ellie saw him raise in a flourish the papers he carried, saluting, she supposed, Dorothea.

He had not seen the written words, that was sure: HELP WE ARE BEING HELD HOSTIGE.

"I didn't write it dark enough," Joyce said in a small, desperate voice. "I should have written in charcoal, but I had this pencil in my hand."

Jeff hit the glass with his fist and sobbed out a string of obscenities. He moaned, "We should have shouted. He'd have heard. Why didn't we just yell?"

From the other side of the room, Alex said, "The Cantus would have heard you too. They'd have come in here shooting, man." He looked at the sheet of paper dangling from Joyce's hand. "When they see that maybe they'll shoot anyhow."

One of the Twinkies began to cry. "Shut up," whispered the other one, hugging her. "Shut up, Cindy, shut up!"

"What's going to happen?" Cindy sobbed. "Why are they going to shoot us?"

"Shhh, shut up, come on," Sarah said tenderly.

Ellie stood by the windows, straining to see if the man

outside might possibly come back this way. No, of course he wouldn't.

My God, she thought, we lost our chance. Why do these kids listen to me at all, why should anyone listen to me? She caught Alex watching her with a look of bitter satisfaction that made her want to smack his face for him. She would have, by God she would have, except she was afraid that once she started hitting him she wouldn't be able to stop.

Jeff cleared his throat. "Joyce. You could tear that paper up small and flush the pieces down the toilet inside. Give it here, I'll do it."

Ellie pushed past Jeff and grabbed the paper out of Joyce's hands. "I'll take care of it."

Miraculously, she did. She put the paper on the floor and began drawing on it with big, black strokes of the charcoal. She drew the dog Mars, his corpse sprawled so that the body and limbs covered the incriminating words Joyce had written; she drew him as she had seen him lying on the hillside after that thunderclap of a shot.

Here came George, wheeling from the studio windows when he saw Dorothea. This is it, she thought, conscious of the absurdity. A line from a hundred bad movies: This is it. She smoothed down the apron she had thrown on to cook breakfast in.

Be careful, be safe, the judge told you that. Remember.

Behind her, at the window and the front door, the two Cantu boys had their guns ready, their fear ready. She stayed at the corner of the house so they wouldn't panic at losing sight of her. Let George come to her, he'd shown himself willing to do that often enough.

He did, cheerful as ever. He'd brought copies of the poster for the concerts with her drawing on it. He didn't ask why she looked disheveled, why her hands trembled, why there were people locked up in her studio. He apparently saw nothing.

The trick now would be to edge him into his car again and away. Thank God he was biddable. She could easily draw him back around to the front of the house just by drifting in that direction herself.

Isn't it amazing, she thought, I see not only what's around me but something that isn't, really—a ghost—and George sees nothing of what's right in front of his eyes.

Her resolve wavered. He was so close, so damned stupidly

oblivious. She wanted to tell him right out. He was a man of the world, or so he thought, a man who wanted to be the mediator between herself and the commercial parts of that world. Let him mediate this, by God! But he wouldn't. He would find some way to make things worse.

She imagined Roberto's heavy, angry face peering at her over the shotgun barrel. You've had your chance for heroics, she told herself, and you decided. Just do what they told you to do. It's all you're capable of anyway.

"Not bad," she said, glancing at the poster with a professional eye as she came around the corner of the house, George bouncing along beside her. The reproduction really was handsome.

"Not bad?" he expostulated. He was practically dancing. "It's beautiful! I was pretty relieved, to tell the truth. You know what a mess they made of the flyers for the craft show last fall. But this—I sat down with them and made them understand we wanted a first class job, and that's what we've got. I'm proud to show it to you."

She glanced over her shoulder at the front door, which stood slightly open. "Look, George, I have this class of kids visiting today—"

"Oh, yeah," he said, "that must be their van. I wondered who that bunch was. Pretty small class; lucky for you."

"You saw them?" she stammered.

"Sure, in the studio. They were all drawing away like mad, very earnest looking."

"Oh, they're a very earnest group," she said inanely. "I'd ask you in for coffee, but they've gone through the place like locusts. I'd forgotten about teenage appetites."

"Dear Dorothea," cried George, flinging up his arms with such abandon that she flinched, in a panic that the watching Cantus would take this for a sign of comprehension or a signal to an army of cops in the hills—

All that happened was that George leaned down and embraced her, wrapping her in his cablelike arms and his aftershave smell. "It's me that owes you hospitality! Sometime soon we are going to have a historic meal." He stood back, holding her shoulders and smiling down at her. "Maybe I'll hire the Trujillo brothers to do a real old-style barbecue in the back yard, and we'll have some people in to share it.

"Actually, it would be a shame to pass up the chance to do some fund-raising for the concerts at the same time, wouldn't

it? If we could just have the barbecue in a place that was big
enough—''

Shit, she thought, George wants me to let him and Leroy
Trujillo run the whole thing *here*.

"But your privacy is important to you," he added quickly,
with an ingratiating smile. "I wouldn't dream of imposing on
you."

I have just the site for your party, George. We'll put up a
tent and have an unveiling, a surprise for you. Isn't a wall
covered with a work of art a passable symbol for oppression
transcended? But I can't promise anybody anything this morning, so you must be content with something else from me
now: your life, George. Let me give you your life.

She put her arm through his and turned him toward his car.
Nice to be able to do something for somebody, even if it's
only George. "Come on, George, I have to get back to my
guests. I promised them a critique of their work."

"What, food and a critique too? I hope they're paying you
for this, Dorothea."

Steered to the car by her, he sat sideways in the front seat
while the air conditioner blew out the sun-heated inside. He
talked about publicity. He interrupted himself with a happy
laugh and leaned out of the car to greet Brillo, who came
rushing up to lick George's face.

Dorothea froze. Christ almighty. Surely, without doubt,
from where he sat George could see Mars lying black and
bloated on the hillside behind the house!

"Down you go, boy," George said, giving Brillo a solid
but friendly shove. Dorothea caught hold of the gray dog's
collar and held him by her side. George pulled the door shut.
"Okay, Dorothea. You take care of yourself. I don't like to
see you looking so tired."

He revved the car and pulled away in a spit of gravel.
Brillo lurched suddenly forward, pulling his collar from her
grasp, and went galloping after the car, a thing he hadn't
done since he was a pup. Dorothea yelled after him, but he
vanished around the first of the driveway's curves. Just as
well, really: best of all if he were to follow George all the
way back to town, out of danger, but that was too much to
hope for.

She felt dizzy with strain. She turned.

There was Mars's body, an odd-shaped splotch on the

dun-colored slope, legs stiffly outthrust. Could George have taken him for a shadow?

Here came Roberto, running toward her with the pistol in his hand. He jabbed her in the ribs with it. He looked where she was looking, and she heard him curse under his breath.

"I don't think George noticed," she said. "He's not the kind of a man who notices things."

Roberto prodded her with the pistol. I didn't say anything, she thought over and over. I didn't do anything. Don't kill me. You can't kill me, I had this special advice and I followed it. I was careful, I said nothing.

Blanca pushed past Bobbie at the door. "It wasn't somebody from the hospice, was it?" she asked.

Dorothea shook her head.

Roberto slammed the front door shut behind them all and set his back against it. "Goddamn you, you old *bruja*," he snarled. "You told him, didn't you? You sent him for help. I saw how he drove out of here—tore down the driveway like a bat out of hell, man."

"She wouldn't do that," Bobbie said. "Too many people could get hurt." He gave Dorothea a look that seemed close to tears.

"When he hugged her," Roberto insisted, "she whispered something to him."

"Jesus," Bobbie said weakly. "We really got to get out of here now."

Dorothea thought, He'll take Joyce. He'll take a pretty girl, not a dried-up, shaking, safe old woman.

"I'm ready," Blanca said. "I packed up my steamer and everything."

"Inside," Roberto said. He herded them back into the living room. "I got to think a minute."

Wouldn't it be funny, Dorothea thought, if I became someone else right now, if all of a sudden my heart stopped stamping and I became cool and purposeful and threw away the message of the ghost. If I said, Roberto, take me with you. Maybe in the next instant. But instant followed instant, and she did not.

"Let's go, if we're going," Bobbie said desperately. "Even if she didn't say anything, even if that guy doesn't know, we can't stay around here forever! Somebody will come!"

"Leave him alone," Blanca said. "Beto knows what to

do. He knows we have to go. I'm going to get my things and put them in the truck. And I want to say goodbye to Ricky.''

Roberto said, ''We'll go. But if that guy really doesn't know, if he doesn't say anything, there's no point tipping off the next one to come rolling up to the front door for whatever. We don't want them poking around any sooner than they have to. We'll take her truck, so they'll see it's gone and they'll think she's down in town or something and they'll just take off again. But we got to get that damn dog off that hillside. Anybody can see it from the front yard.''

Bobbie protested, ''Why waste time on that? They could be here any minute.''

''Keep your shirt on, we're going. It'll take a little while to pack up the truck anyhow. We should have some water and food and stuff with us. Then we're going to lock Blanca up with her precious Englishman in there so she can't hassle us, and we're going to get out of here. We'll take one of the others in the truck with us for insurance. There's room for three up front.''

Dorothea stood rigid. She could not speak.

Bobbie licked his lips, looking dismayed. ''Who're we going to take?''

''I don't know.'' Roberto looked at Dorothea, hard-eyed. ''One of the girls, they won't be hard to handle.''

''Beto, we're going to have enough on our hands without somebody else in the truck,'' Bobbie said.

''You think I'm just going to head out with the two of us and no protection? Anybody knows better than that, man. We'll take somebody. But first you go get that dog and toss it down in the arroyo.''

''Not me,'' Bobbie muttered. ''I don't want to mess with that stinky old dog carcass.''

Roberto said, ''Well, I'm sure not going to do it.'' Then he grinned. ''I know,'' he said. ''Go get old Alex. He's been dying to help us out all along, right? Here's something for him to do.''

Bobbie held the 30-30 on Alex, who trudged up the hill ahead of him carrying a coil of rusty wire to drag the dog with. When Bobbie looked back over his shoulder, he could see Roberto standing down in the back patio outside the kitchen, shotgun in his hands, watching.

Alex was still crying. Roberto had let him think they were

taking him out to hang him with the wire. As soon as they were out of earshot Bobbie had told Alex it was only the dog's carcass they meant to move, but the guy couldn't seem to quit crying. It was embarrassing.

"Let's go, man, all you got to do is move the dog," Bobbie said again. He was anxious to get it over. Any minute the cops could be swarming all over the place. How could that guy not have seen the dog, how could he not have guessed something was wrong?

Alex moaned and rubbed his eyes and stumbled as he walked.

Bobbie could smell the dog already. Poor dog, nothing but bug food now, he thought. His stomach squirmed. He looked back down at Roberto, wishing they were farther away from him. He could still see Roberto's mean face. Roberto yelled something.

"Do it," Bobbie urged Alex.

"Well, how?"

"Make a noose, you know, twist the wire. You can slip that over his head and, like, drag him."

Alex looked as if he might throw up. He rubbed his palms on his jeans.

"Come on," Bobbie said. He stared around, trying to see if there were any cops sneaking through the piñons.

Alex knelt down and started working on the wire. Then he jabbed at Mars with a chunk of wood, levering the head up so he could slip the noose over it.

Bobbie watched out of the corners of his eyes, thinking about that time he found a dead goat in a neighbor's yard. That was on Pinto Street, when he'd still been real little and hadn't known any better than to go poking at the dead thing. All he remembered clearly was how stiff and heavy it had seemed, like a toy made with badly cured leather and stuffed with horsehair.

The dog's head lolled against the stick, empty-eyed, gaping. That's how you look when you're dead.

Alex pulled at the wire. It tightened around the dog's neck. His uncle had once told him how in the old days they had to figure how much a man weighed before they hung him because the force of too long a drop for his weight would jerk his head right off his body.

The dog's corpse moved like something in a bad dream. He

nearly threw up. There was a pinkish, raggedy hole in its side with white splinters sticking out.

He could see Roberto watching them from the patio. Funny how the house from here was just some old building, unrelated to the prison of the studio, which was all Alex really knew of it—that and the kitchen.

I'm not going back in there, he thought. Next time it could really be me, not a dead dog, with wire around my neck.

"Where'm I supposed to put this?" he said.

"Beto says just haul it down into the arroyo there," Bobbie said.

Alex wrapped the hem of his shirt around his hands and laid hold of the wire, gathering his legs under him like he meant to stand up and start dragging the dog.

Roberto had to be a good shot or very lucky to have hit the dog from down there with just the patio floodlight to see by. Maybe good and lucky both.

I can't believe I'm going to do this, he thought, feeling a muscle twitching in his thigh. What if it's too heavy? Down below he saw Roberto kicking at the base of one of the patio benches, bored, only looking up the hillside now and again.

Alex surged up out of his crouch, heaving on the wire with both hands as hard as he could. For a second, when he hit the weight on the end of it, he thought, It's not going to work, the head will come off—

Then the round-bellied carcass came up and up and arched clumsily through the air straight at Bobbie. Bobbie threw up the deer rifle crosswise in both hands to fend the thing off, his mouth wide with revulsion. The corpse struck him and sent him staggering backward down the slope.

Alex sprinted for the skyline.

Dorothea stood by the living room window, looking out. Soon she could celebrate a lucky escape with Ricky while Joyce or Cindy or Sarah or even Ellie jounced along in the truck between the two Cantu boys, trembling with fear. Right and proper, according to the judge. Think of it this way: You may not be more worthy of survival than any of them, but are you less so? That's what the judge would say. He warned you. Save your life, save your talents, take no risk. There's a reason you're here at the window watching the mob (two boys and their victim!)—standing in the judge's place. Listen to the judge, he knows. Give them what they want—a sacrifice—and they'll let you keep your life.

What kind of a life? Like a great black muffled bell the future tolled in her mind: an endless round of self-loathing and self-justification after the word came back, this child or that one got killed or hurt or psychologically maimed, even, in her place. And there was not a thing she could do to prevent it, because the judge had spoken to her animal core that did not want to be hurt, let alone to die, itself. The judge had told her what she wanted to hear.

Something moved on the patio, catching her eye: Roberto, staring up the hillside, flinging the shotgun up to fire.

"The fucker's getting away!" he screamed.

On the hillside, Mars's carcass slid sideways into a rock. Bobbie scrambled for the rifle he had dropped. Alex lunged toward the crest of the hill. Astonished, Dorothea saw Alex's angular shoulders and elbows and big, driving feet all thrusting desperately for the safety over the skyline.

Now. *This* moment. *This* sacrifice, Alex's head on a pole, Roberto's future impaled with it. All she had to do was— nothing.

Roberto's mouth twisted into a tiger snarl. He hunched over the gunsight, and the muzzle tracked Alex's pounding progress up the hill. The hammers cocked with a fat, rich sound. Alex seemed to run so slowly.

How simple. One does not permit children to murder children. Dorothea moved.

A howl of protest filled her mind and something plucked violently at her left hand as she plunged across the doorway and outside. Go to hell, ghost, she thought. She threw herself across the patio and upon Roberto as if smothering a live grenade. Thunder engulfed her and something hard hit her a swift double wallop in the side and flung her down.

A weight stamped down on the bricks, right next to her face: Roberto's heavy boot as he reared up above her with the empty gun raised to bring down and brain her where she lay. She could not hear—her ears rang brilliantly—but she could see him: a child bringing death.

The stock of the shotgun crashed down near enough to fill her nostrils with brick dust, and then down again on the other side of her head. Roberto grunted with the furious effort of his blows. How funny that all that concentrated energy did not seem to do the job: she was still alive, unable to draw a

breath to laugh with at the absurdity of it. The stock of the
shotgun split with a sharp sound and Roberto bellowed something in Spanish and slammed the gun like a baseball bat
against the trunk of the big cottonwood. The gun flew out of
his hands and clattered onto the table, the bench, the flagstones.

Up on the hill Bobbie shouted, "Should I follow him?"

"What the fuck for, you dumb asshole?" Roberto howled
back, his hands clenched together. "He's gone, that's all,
you retard, you let him go!"

Dorothea could not breathe. Not shot, she was sure—the
recoil, of course. The stock had kicked her a good one. Can't
breathe. Does Ricky feel anything like this? Or Blanca, having an attack? Jesus.

She fell thankfully into a darkness in which she did not
need to breathe.

Great, man, Roberto mourned, now you busted the shotgun.
All you got left is that rifle and the pistol Great-uncle Tilo
gave you. Super. Shit. Wonderful. Better get going and run
away because you got no firepower to speak of and they are
going to come and get you for sure.

Here came Bobbie, that stupid cunt. If he tripped carrying
the 30-30 like that he might blow his own head off, with
luck. Running down the hill and whining like usual: "Beto,
we got to go right away, let's get out of here quick!"

Roberto's hands still stung from the impact of smashing the
shotgun. He tucked them into his armpits and hugged himself
with his arms. He didn't want Bobbie to see him cry. Not
because of his hands hurting, either. It was frustration, that
was all. And there was Blanca at the door, staring out with
that goddamn eternal curiosity of hers about things that were
none of her business. What would she know about his frustra-
tions? She'd just see her brother crying, that's all, and she'd
be scared, and what good would that do?

I could have killed that kid, he thought. Maybe I've killed
the old lady. Maybe she's dead from the recoil. Some witch.
Why is the whole world such a bunch of hopeless *wimps?*

"I'm going to go load the truck," Bobbie dithered. "I'll
come get you when I've checked it out, all right?"

He didn't wait for an answer. He went. Speaking of wimps.
And I was thinking I wasn't too bad off, having him with me.
Jesus, how desperate can you get? This is all Bobbie's fault.

Roberto looked at his sister. "Get back inside. Tell your

English guy Mrs. Howard's okay, right? He must have heard the shooting. He'll be worried, won't he? Well, go tell him!''

The old lady wasn't dead. She looked up at him and groaned. Just an old lady with a couple of busted ribs, man, you couldn't do that to a *bruja*.

"Shit," he said, dabbing at his nose with his cuff. Never been so damn mad. Would have shot that dude right in the back, man, and he deserved it, the sneak. If I could have even hit him at that distance. He was pissed off to have lost the chance, but it was funny how now he was relieved, too. So much his legs sort of gave out. He squatted down on his haunches.

"Can you sit up?" he said.

She was just an old lady, like his Aunt Lucy or his Aunt Carmen, for cripes' sake. He couldn't leave her laying there on the bricks, with the stars on them where the shotgun stock had come bashing down. Whoo, man. What a dumb thing to do! But he was so mad, it was all so unfair—he was still mad, he was still busting with tears, like a baby, and he wasn't even sure why.

Funny, touching her finally. Like after a wedding or something and all the old aunts and people like that hugged you and patted your back. Not like grabbing a chick, none of that at all. And he wasn't scared to touch her either, like he had been before when he thought she was a witch.

He reached down and took hold of her. She had thin arms under the flannel sleeve, but not flabby. It was probably good exercise, gluing things to that rock out there, but don't think about that; she might pick up about what you did there right out of your head the way people do sometimes even if they're not witches.

He helped her sit up. She grabbed his wrist a moment, gasping, before she would let him release her to lean back against the trunk of the cottonwood with its fresh scar where the shotgun had hit it.

"Goddamn it," she whispered.

He liked that.

"Better go," she gasped.

And suddenly he just boiled over; he leaped up and started screaming and stomping around, spewing it all out: "Why the hell *should* I? Everybody keeps telling me to get out of here and *I'm not going to.* I live here, this is my place, why should I run away? I can't just run away, goddamn it! That's my street and my friends and who's going to help my mom out? She's a widow, and Great-uncle Tilo's a wino and all my friends are down there; who the hell's going to be my friends in Canada, for Christ's sake? I don't have friends in Canada, I'd never have friends in Canada! I can't just drive away with that shivering litle cunt Bobbie. Jesus, I'd be better off with that gray dog of yours, it's got more sense! Bobbie and some weepy Anglo girl whining and moaning the whole way and who knows what she'll do soon as you turn your back—shit on that! What would happen to Blanca? You tell me that, what would happen? You can stop telling me to run away, everybody can just quit that. I'm not going.''

His face was all wet and his voice kept cracking like a kid's. He steadied himself against the redwood table and tried to take deep breaths.

"Guns," she whispered. "You only have . . . two guns . . . people will get . . . killed and . . . you'll still lose out . . . in the end. You can't—''

"I just got through telling you not to tell me what to do! Jesus, don't you listen? What you want me to do now, give myself up like some dope in a movie? Lady, they'd blow me away; there wouldn't be enough left to fill a coffin! You think I'm going to let them get their hands on me?''

"Maybe not if . . . they know somebody's . . . watching,'' she said. "Keeping track. Somebody famous, Beto. Got this damned importance . . . never wanted it . . . useful now. Use it. Good for something.''

He rushed on, borne along on his own rage and despair. "I'd rather—I'd rather load up the truck with the ammunition that's left and drive right into the cops and shoot into the bullets and blow us all sky high, like those guys in Lebanon did to those marines. I'll do that before I'll run away to goddamn Canada or LA or Mexico or anyplace!''

"Don't fight them,'' she said in that same painful gasp. "Beto. I'll speak . . . for you. Help the best I . . . can. Could be a lot. Try me.''

He stopped raging. She meant it, he could tell. And he already knew how tough she was, how she could damn well get what she went after. If she wanted to help him, shit, she could probably really help. She was what she said, a famous artist, he had seen the proof himself. Seen it and tried to trash it, man. What a fool he was. Dancing in the moonlight, busting up his own one chance to come out of this alive and home where he belonged, with his own.

"You won't want to help," he said, hunkering down again to her level but unable to look her in the eye. "You'll want me dead more than anybody else will."

"Oh, Beto," she said. He saw her face go all crimped with pain and her eyes shining out so bright at him, waiting for it; she knew, all right. "Beto, what did you do?"

"I just saw it there," he said sullenly, "and I couldn't help it. I had to do something. So I did. You could fix it. All you got to do is glue some things over where I busted it and nobody would know the difference."

He couldn't stand it, the look she gave him. He really couldn't stand it.

"It's not my fault," he stormed. "I didn't ask to get chased up here by the cops! I didn't ask for all this trouble!"

She kind of caved in right in front of him, going so slack against the tree trunk that he was afraid she would die right there, as if he had killed her not with the shotgun but with the rocks he threw last night in the moonlight.

"Hey, I'm sorry," he said anxiously. "I mean, I know it must have taken a long time to make that thing. You can see it was a lot of work."

She seemed to come back from someplace way deep inside herself where she'd gone to cry privately about the ruined work. She looked at him with this very calm, very tired look and went right on as if he hadn't said anything about that.

"Listen," she said. "Get the phone. I'll call . . . Frank at the hospice. He can bring Johnny Sanchez . . . out with him. Johnny's . . . a policeman but . . . calm by nature. Won't panic, do . . . stupid things—helicopters and sharpshooters— none of that. Good chance, if you . . . stay close to me . . . with the others. No guns. With the class. Can you try?"

Wow, was he tired all of a sudden. He couldn't tell what was going on any more. Well, maybe what, but not why. He sat down on the flagstones. "Thanks for offering, I guess, but I think it's more likely they'd just kill me, you know? Because of the cop that got shot in the riot, and Mr. Escobar being dead and all."

"You really don't . . . want to go to Canada."

"Shit," he said. God, he did not want to go, he did not want to leave his street and his friends and his family. "If I did, I'd be long gone out of here, wouldn't I?"

"Then don't. Can't guarantee anything." She winced. "Do my best. Will you . . . take a chance?"

Oh, man, is this crazy. But suppose it worked? He blinked at her. He worked himself up to it and he nodded, quick and short, and it was like the weight of the whole sky just slid right off him.

He jumped up to go get the telephone from where Bobbie had dumped it down the arroyo. He ran out the back gate and plunged down the side of the arroyo, lifted on a blast of terror and exhilaration.

Jake and Martín—if Martín ever came back—would get some story from him, when he got home to Pinto Street.

Blanca watched the patio gate swing behind Roberto. She stepped away from the doorframe, where she had been standing to listen. She couldn't hear it all, but she'd heard enough, all right. Her face felt hot and red and she knew she was working up to a super fit but she didn't care. It would serve them all right if she died right there, her blood on their heads.

She went out, turning to keep from catching the cast against the doorway, and stood over the old lady.

"He's not going to Canada, is he?" she said. "You stopped him. You sold him some story about being a good boy and giving himself up to the law. You old creep!"

The old lady squinted up at her. "You should be . . . glad. He couldn't . . . have taken you along."

"He would have! I'd have made him take me, I can always get him to do what I want! You don't know anything about it! We were going to go together, we were going to get away, far away where nothing is the same, and you spoiled it! You ruined everything!"

"You could have died," came the whispered answer. "Both of you, any of the rest . . . shooting, deals, all that . . . too dangerous."

"Dangerous for you, you mean," Blanca sneered. Her heart pounded. She kicked at the wreckage of the shotgun. She felt explosive with her own fury. Damn that Beto, damn him for ducking out on her! Damn this old bitch for making him do it! She hoped the old lady was really hurting right now, she sure deserved it.

"Help for Ricky, too—sooner."

"First place we stopped, I'd have slipped away and tele-phoned for help for Ricky, without giving my name or anything. Did you think I'd just leave him like that, locked up and waiting? I'm his friend. And now they'll lock us all up and I'll never see him again and I'll never ever ever get out of here and I hate you so much—if I had a gun, I'd shoot you myself, right now. You've ruined it all!''

The old lady's eyes closed. ''Make yourself sick,'' she murmured.

''I don't make myself sick, it's other people that make me sick!'' Blanca cried. ''You make me sick! Beto makes me sick! Everything and everybody, you all—make—me—sick!''

Ellie sat at the end of the big bare room, leaning her head against the wall and looking out the window. There was nothing to see outside, no movement, and no sound since the shots. In here the kids were quiet, listening as she listened.

In books they talked about the sweat of fear, usually the ''rank'' sweat of fear. She kept thinking she could smell her own sweaty clothes and skin.

The key grated in the door lock.

She went rigid with a blast of energy that shocked her. Oh, God, I am afraid to die.

Bobbie opened the door and looked in. He smiled a peculiar, tremulous smile (is that how a killer smiles before he pulls the trigger?) and said in his old, shy tone, ''Everybody can come on out now.''

A trap, Ellie thought. We walk out and they shoot us and drive away laughing and splashed with our blood. I came here to write a thriller, not to be in one. Oh, but it's not funny, it's not funny at all, and there was this whinnying laugh trying to squeeze out of her throat. . . .

Joyce said in a tiny voice, ''What are you going to do?''

''Nothing,'' Bobbie said. ''It's all over. They want you to call up the guy at the hospice, Miss Stern. For Mr. Maulders. He's pretty bad.''

I don't believe it, she thought, but already she was moving forward. She could not stand to be cooped up in here another moment, not if they blasted her to bits on the threshold as she emerged.

''This way,'' Bobbie said, trotting ahead of her eagerly.

In the living room, Dorothea was sitting in the leather chair near the fireplace looking haggard. Roberto stood next to her holding—a glass of water. The pistol was gone from his belt, the shotgun had vanished.

"I'll just go get rid of this," Bobbie said, and he trotted out the back door and across the patio with the rifle. They all watched him toss the weapon out over the back patio wall into the arroyo and turn and come trotting back.

"I'd like you to call for me," Dorothea said laboriously to Ellie. "For Ricky really, if you would. Please."

She indicated the telephone on the sideboard, where someone had plugged it in.

"Are you hurt?" Ellie was acutely aware of the theatricality of the moment: the whole class of kids at her back looking and listening and drinking it all in, afraid to utter a sound until they knew how things stood, no more ready to trust this sudden freedom than she was herself. Blanca, that horrible child, had curled on the couch with her plaster-cased arm sticking up and her color very poor. She glowered at the hearthrug as if to ignite it with her gaze.

"Ribs broken," Dorothea said, "I think. An accident, really. Tell you later."

In the back of Ellie's mind an unctuous little voice observed, "Now everybody can see what happens to the brave ones. She brought this on herself somehow."

Whatever "this" was. There seemed to be no blood on Dorothea's clothing, but she was clearly injured. And the atmosphere was so odd. Dorothea looked strangely composed despite her pain, and were those aspirins Roberto was handing her, with the water to wash them down with? What the hell? Are we really free?

Jeff said, "Where's Alex?"

Bobbie said, "He's okay. He got away."

Now Roberto spoke. "We had a little trouble. Alex was supposed to help bury the dog. He made a run for it instead. I was going to fire after him like a warning shot, but Mrs. Howard stopped me. The recoil from the shotgun caught her in the ribs, but I think she's okay."

Joyce said, "Then someone should be coming soon?"

"Yes," Dorothea said.

At this there came a ragged cheer from the kids.

Ellie had never had a broken bone in her life. God, it must hurt. She walked over to the phone, floating in a sort of cinematic dream in which she saw herself simultaneously with feeling herself move.

Bolder now, she said, "What about that man who came by here?"

Roberto looked blank for a moment, as if she were talking about something that had happened ages ago. Ellie had the oddest feeling that while she'd been locked up here in the studio, something had moved up the clock hands for the people outside, pulling them on ahead of her.

"Oh, yeah, him." Roberto frowned. "Mrs. Howard sent him away. I don't know if he caught on or not."

Jeff said uncertainly, "Uh, what about Mr.—ah—Mr. Maulders?"

Bobbie looked unhappy. "He said to leave him where he is. We made him as comfortable as we could, with water to drink and blankets and everything. He won't have to be alone there for long."

Everybody was watching Ellie. It's up to me to break the spell, she thought. God knows what comes next. How the hell am I going to write about this when I don't really understand it at all?

She cleared her throat. "What's the number at the hospice?"

❧ Eleven ❧

BOBBIE STAYED NEAR Mrs. Howard and Miss Stern. He was nervous about what might happen now that he and Roberto had gotten rid of their guns. Not that they had long to wait—the guy at the hospice had said he'd come right out, soon as he located this cop Sanchez that Mrs. Howard knew personally.

As soon as Miss Stern had finished the phone call, Blanca had asked how long before somebody came. Now she was sitting next to Bobbie on the couch, looking mad. She jumped up, just like that, and said, "I'm going to go tell Ricky. Somebody should stay with him."

Mrs. Howard talked easier after those aspirins Roberto had given her. She said, "Certainly, go and tell him relief is on the way. But don't be surprised if he'd rather be by himself until Frank arrives, Blanca. It's only because there's nothing any of us can do for Ricky ourselves."

"A real friend can go and sit with him," Blanca said nastily, and she walked out of the room.

Nobody followed her, and that was good, but Jeff was looking around and he said, "Hey, we've been cooped up a long time. Is it okay if I go take a walk outside?"

"Of course—" Miss Stern started, but Mrs. Howard cut right across her without raising her voice, just talking.

"No," she said. "No one is to go out, please, until Frank gets here. I want us all together and in plain sight when the police come. No mistakes now, people, not when it's almost over.''

Nobody argued.

In a few minutes Blanca came back in looking shaky. She sat down by herself on a blanket chest next to the TV and didn't look at anybody or say anything.

If only everybody could forget the whole thing, Bobbie thought. I've never been in trouble, no arrests, no kind of record. What's going to happen to me now? My whole life could be spoiled. But at least I'm not driving around with Roberto with the cops chasing us. It could be worse. One thing, next time somebody's in trouble, I'll keep my big mouth shut and let them find their own way out.

Roberto came and sat next to him. ''Hey, bro,'' he said. ''Don't look so down. We made a good try, right? But the old lady was too much for us. She's a *bruja*, did you know that? If we'd of tried to run, she'd of witched us right into the hands of the cops. I'm not afraid of anybody, but there's no point fighting a witch.''

Bobbie, taken completely aback by this idea, said, ''What do you mean, a witch? There's no such thing!''

''No? How you think Alex got away? You think he did that on his own, that jerk? What about this ghost that's wandering around here, and that great big wall the old lady's spirit helpers made for her out in the desert back of this place? She didn't say so, but I bet she's got some Indian blood, you know? Look at her from the side, you see what I mean? Indian blood and Indian magic. You don't want to take chances with that.''

He told Bobbie about wonders and amazements, and Bobbie listened, enthralled.

Joyce couldn't believe it. She sat playing cards with Sarah and Cindy—Sarah always carried a tiny dog-eared pack with her—playing badly because she kept glancing over at where Mrs. Howard and Miss Stern sat with the two Cantu boys. Everybody was just waiting, but this time it was supposed to be waiting to get free and go home.

All that crying for nothing, she thought, picking up one of Cindy's discards. All that being scared and it comes out fine. She felt jangled and twitchy, and she could tell Cindy felt that way too.

Suddenly Cindy put her cards down. ''Hey, is anybody

going to believe this when we tell them? Nobody will ever believe us!''

Sarah giggled but it ended up a catch, like when you cry.

"I tell you what," Cindy said. "I think we should commemorate the whole thing, what do you think? I mean do something to mark it, that it really happened."

"Well, what?" Joyce said.

Cindy looked over her shoulder at where Blanca sat by herself with her encased arm propped on the sill of the window next to her. "Why don't we all write our names on Blanca's cast?"

Joyce was up before any of them. She went over to Blanca. "Hi," she said. "How are you doing?"

Blanca looked away and didn't answer. The other girls crowded around. Cindy had fished out some colored pens from her bag. She handed a red one to Joyce. "Listen, Blanca," she said, "you know how people put their names on a cast and decorate it? We'd like to write on your cast, so there'll be something to remember us by."

"I don't want to remember you," Blanca said in this thick hateful voice. "I don't want to remember anything."

"Too bad," Sarah said. She had green eyes like a cat, and now they got narrow and sly, and she lunged forward and grabbed Blanca.

Without even wanting to, Joyce flung herself after Sarah, and suddenly the four of them were rolling around on the floor in a tangle of flailing limbs and fury. Blanca was grunting and gasping from where she got hit. Somebody aimed wrong and kicked Joyce in the knee and she yelled and tumbled free, holding her leg.

Somebody grabbed her hair—she looked up into Roberto's face that was like a fright mask of anger—and then Jeff tackled him and Miss Stern was standing up and watching with her mouth wide open and not a sound coming out and Blanca was screaming, "Leave me alone, I don't want you writing on it, let me go!"

"Stop!"

It was Mrs. Howard who had spoken. She only had to say it that once. Joyce leaned over and grabbed at Sarah's shoulder because Sarah still had hold of Blanca by the waist. "Hey," Joyce whispered fiercely, "she says quit it."

They all broke away and sat panting and sniffling and nursing their bruises. Blanca sat up silently, her hair a wild tangle and a drippy scratch over her left eye. Bobbie had a bloody nose which he kept wiping on his shirt and then looking at the stains like he couldn't believe it.

Miss Stern said sharply, "All right, everybody, what was that all about?"

Cindy, looking up from a torn buttonhole on her blouse, said sulkily, "We wanted to write our names on her cast for her to remember us by, that's all."

"I don't want your dirty names," Blanca spat out.

"Who cares what you want, you creep?" Cindy said. "You and your creepy brother, we should take you in the bathroom and stuff your head down the toilet, you little—"

"That's enough," Mrs. Howard said.

"—freak," Cindy finished, baring her teeth at Blanca like a dog.

Joyce hugged her aching knee and was glad she had fallen out of the fray early on. She was ashamed to have anything to do with Cindy and Sarah now. Trying to take it out on a kid with a broken arm because they didn't dare take on Roberto or even Bobbie!

Mrs. Howard went on. "You are all still in my house. No one is to bother anyone else for as long as we're together here. Are we going to tell people later that we survived being held hostage at gunpoint but couldn't control ourselves afterward when the danger was over?"

You had to remember, Joyce thought, she's the only one that really got hurt. You could hear it in the tired, thready sound of her voice. She's the one that got hurt, and her dog got killed, and she says take it easy. What an amazing person. How did a person get to be like that?

When you quit being scared, that was when you could ask questions about those things.

Joyce hugged her knee tenderly, thinking, I don't mind having a sore knee. It's like a war wound, even if nobody ever knows that but me.

"Do your ribs hurt a lot?" Ellie asked. Could you die of broken ribs, if you were an older person? Dorothea looked terrible.

"Not so bad. Be worse tomorrow. I'll have a hell of a bruise. Like the time a horse kicked me." Dorothea chortled faintly, stopped with a gasp, her hand to her side. "Christ."

"Too bad you don't have at least a bottle of Scotch or something."

Dorothea shook her head. "I wouldn't want any. Liquor makes me too sleepy, and besides, on top of lots of aspirin—better not."

"Aspirin!" Ellie said, shooting Roberto a killing look where he stood slouched at the front window, his back to them all. "What was Roberto doing, showing what good care he takes of his hostages after he's broken their ribs?"

"It's over," Dorothea said. "We're all in pretty good shape, even me. Don't exaggerate how bad things were, Ellie."

Ellie gaped at her. "Don't exaggerate? What is there to exaggerate? We're alive and together by the skin of our teeth and you know it!"

"All the same," Dorothea said in a fading voice, "no great harm."

"Didn't he try to kill Alex, didn't you stop him from committing a murder? Listen, I was half minded to join in when those kids jumped Blanca just now."

"I know you were," Dorothea murmured. Her eyes were closed again.

"Well, can you blame me? We could have been killed here!"

"But we weren't," came the patient, exasperating answer. She's treating me like a kid, Ellie thought. She took my class right out from under me just now, after all I've done with them, and now I get this? Who the hell does she think she is?

"I don't get it," Ellie said, her jaw clenching painfully with tension. "Are you on their side?"

"I'm on the side of keeping the all-around damage as minor as possible."

Ellie felt as if the floor had lurched under her feet. "You're going to help them, aren't you? You're going to minimize the whole affair and try to get the law to go easy on them—that little thug and his rotten, weird sister and that snake of a cousin! It's a wonder you didn't actually help them get away!"

"If they'd still wanted to go, I would have," Dorothea said.

"Even if he might go murder other people because you aren't on hand to prevent it?" Ellie was outraged. "If the courts turn him loose because you take his side, and he goes on and actually does kill somebody like Alex later on, how will you feel?"

Now the painter's eyes opened, and there was an angry shine in them. "Those are not my choices," she said. "I can't live his life for him. My choices had to do with what happened here. I made them. His choices belong to him."

Her eyes swimming with tears of frustration, Ellie punched the arm of the chair with her fist. "I don't understand!"

Dorothea said, "Would someone please bring me a glass of water?"

Each time Ricky said to himself, This is frightful but I can stand it, the pain got worse.

His pain had never been like this. He could visualize perfectly the hot wires—not white-hot yet, but a dull red—being drawn tight along his bones, scorching grooves in the calcium, pressing toward the marrow.

The more you fear it, the worse it will be. That was what the doctors said about pain and fear.

Deep pain, this was, as opposed to the sort of surface pain that made the lightest touch, the mere weight of a blanket or a sheet, unbearable. What happens when the wires reach the bone centers and there is nowhere else for them to go, and they lodge there and begin to burn hotter, scarlet and then white-hot?

They had left him alone in the small patio at his request. The wrong request. Should have asked the boy to shoot me. Never imagined it could be like this.

Blanca saw how bad it was getting and she fled, while I was still telling myself it would soon be over, it was all right. But first she told me, my young friend in the cast, that help was coming. Frank. Did she lie? Would she? Why would she? He's coming, he is coming, only it takes so long.

Nothing else mattered. Not what had happened or might yet happen (Frank was coming).

He will come. He must. She said so.

Deep pain. Squinting up at the bright sun in its faultless blue setting, panting through his dry mouth, he thought, This can't go on. Every motion made it worse, and yet he moved weakly in the lounge chair, twisting in a slow underwater motion from one position to another, trying to escape the pain. He tried to distance himself from it, to rise from his body like an astral spirit and observe with Olympian detachment his own struggles. He groped after chants and spells he had heard healers use in huts, in tents, under brush shelters.

He made frantic promises to a God he hadn't believed in
since he'd been very young and still didn't believe in. He
watched the hands of his wristwatch creep.

Alex was too tired to run any more. His shirt stuck to his
back. Jeff was the runner, not Alex. The soil gave under his
sneakers, dragging him down. His scalp felt scorched by the
sun.

If anything terrible was happening back there because he
had escaped, it wasn't his fault. At least now somebody was
going for help.

If he could just find the road.

He knew the others would tell the cops and everybody that
he, Alex, had sided with the Cantus. Helped the Cantus,
even. They'd take it out on him. So it was a good thing for
Alex to be the one to go get help.

Where was the damn road? He was getting thirsty. He was
lost. Nobody had ever taught him to tell direction by the sun.
He looked at it helplessly. It just hung up there and burned at
him. How could you know which way it was going? Well,
this was morning still, it must be rising; that meant over there
was east.

Great. This did not tell him where the road lay.

He tried to remember the orientation of the house. All he
could think of was looking down into the courtyard and
seeing Roberto with the shotgun.

That sound, God, he had almost been knocked off his feet
just by the roar of that gun. Sure he'd be hit, he had kept
running away from the blow that must come. When he'd
realized it wouldn't, he'd wanted to laugh and laugh, but that
would have slowed him down so he hadn't let the laughter
out.

He'd kept running, and there had been no more shots.
Yeah! Missed me, man. You all missed me.

But where was he now? He stopped and stared around.

Down the arroyo, something glittered in the sunlight, wink-
ing and gleaming in the air.

A mirage, he thought. I'm dying of thirst, I'm starting to
see things. I got away, and now I'm going to die out here in
the damn desert, it isn't fair! He shut his eyes, his breath
sobbing dryly in his throat, and tried to remember when he'd
had his last drink of water. Oh, God, I'm going to die
after all!

He turned and scrambled up the side of the arroyo, frantic for a sight of something manmade, a road, a house, a fence.

Help me, somebody! I got away, I can't get lost and die out here! I have to live so I can get help!

Footprints. Some one had passed this way, going someplace. He followed, weeping as he trudged along.

Ahead of him, a fold in the ground rose in a low ridge, and on it lay a building. Morning shadows reached out from the cinnamon walls. Quiet reigned. Peace.

Alex quickened his pace, then suddenly moaned to himself and dropped on all fours, trying to hide behind the yellow grasses.

It was the painter's house, the desperadoes' last stand, the terror from which he had only just escaped. He had come back.

Dorothea leaned back in the leather chair with her eyes closed. A mean ache chased up and down her side, and pain bit with every breath. Her body's ills seemed to her a just penance for not being able to do better for Ricky.

She couldn't stop listening. Beyond the occasional desultory remarks and conversations in the room around her, she listened for the sound of Frank's station wagon. But beneath this she knew she was listening in fear of hearing something else: screams, Ricky's screams.

You see, my child, I warned you, mourned the voice she knew.

Her eyes flew open. The living room was quiet, offering nothing unusual to her sight. There were only the kids scattered and talking in low voices or sitting quietly. Jeff was reading, Joyce was watching Dorothea with a wide, luminous gaze. Ellie Stern, looking fretful and upset, sat at the chess table, writing on a yellow pad.

Dorothea did not see the ghost; she could tell by his voice that he was behind her chair, standing over her: *I warned you, and I was right!*

No, she answered quietly in her mind, not turning. And I'm not your child.

You always say that when we disagree, came the querulous reply. *You always say that, and it changes nothing! What have you done, you hothead, you fool! The security I so carefully fashioned for you is shattered, your chance for a peaceful and prosperous life is forfeit. How could you do this?*

What? she thought. Across the room someone laughed. She closed out the sound, shutting herself inside her own head with the voice of the judge. *What are you talking about? I don't understand you.*

No, it is I who cannot understand you. (What was that sound, that dry, faint rasping? Like hands rubbing themselves together in distress, so familiar a sound. From when Ricky had sat vigil in her bedroom those early nights of the dreams? Appropriate, that a ghost from Ricky's ancestry should echo that gesture.) *What good can come of all this uproar? Do you think your heroics can change the world? You only bring danger on yourself, the unpredictable eye of public notice, the scars of injury.*

She hunched her shoulders, feeling the chill of his presence again. She wished he would stop talking and go away. Couldn't he see that it was all over, her course was set? Couldn't he see that apart from the nagging concern for Ricky and the unremitting pain of her own side, she was settled, and liberated, and glad?

Look, she replied reasonably, it's not hard to understand. I couldn't stand by and let one kid slaughter another just because I was scared.

What was that scent, cloves? smoke? and a wine scent, some kind of spiced wine breathed close over her. Her side flamed. Must be delirious, she thought, arguing in my head with a ghost. Where the hell is Frank? Maybe I'm hurt worse than I think I am. She could hear the TV sound on very softly—some of the kids must be watching, good—at the same moment in which she smelled the wine on the ghost's breath as it leaned closer above her in its vehemence.

Prudence is not fear! Is it wise, is it brave, to end up here, like this? To bring me searching for you in such a place, stepping among the rows of the dead killed in riots looking for my own, my only child?

Ellie still wrote, the kids sat watching football or playing cards. What dead? Could he mean the casual ties of the abortive 1832 uprising against the restored monarchy? Was that where the judge's rebellious son had ended up?

Something light as the touch of a bird's claw brushed over her hair. Her skin tightened and her breath caught in her throat, but within herself she was not frightened, only impatient and worried. What did he want with her now that the matter was resolved?

Why are you so afraid? she challenged.

After a still moment the answer came, intense and rapid: *You can only ask such a question because you have been sheltered in the haven I made for you, earned for you, the haven that you have thrown away, and by what right?*

She thought out her response slowly. A haven is only a haven, not the world, and no matter who makes it or earns it, it can't be forever. If you don't return to the world, once you've had the benefit of your haven, then the world will come to you. It has surely come to me, armed with anger and guns. Didn't it come to you? If it didn't, why not?

Ah. You bought off the world, right? You bought your peace and prosperity and security. At what cost, I wonder?

You know nothing, cried the ghost. *Nothing! How dare you speak to me of costs? A dead dog, a dead child? These are nothing, nothing! You fool! An entire farm family hung up to their gateposts like sacks of rags, children, dogs, and all, does that mean anything to you? Bodies floating down from two towns upriver where half the men rose from their drink and talk at a tavern and fell upon the other half, who were drinking and talking at a tavern across the square—talking politics of a different stripe—and slaughtered them, and threw their corpses off the town bridge. Neighbors accusing neighbors falsely in order to obtain their neighbors' best fields, madwomen in an asylum raped and murdered as they wandered out dazed and mumbling to greet their revolutionary liberators, what can you know, with no memories of these things? Battlefields of dead all across Europe, is that how you think of it, illustrated with colorful paintings of heroes and valiant cavalry charges and impudent cartoons showing bold workingmen standing up to the oppressions of a royal tyranny? But you have to have seen it happen right at hand, body by body, scream by scream, the dog-torn filthy corpse rolled carelessly into a ditch and left there for days as a warning—*

The voice raved and wept on and Dorothea sat battered by the ravaged emotions of a phantom. I must be mad, she thought. He certainly is, and with reason. But doesn't he see that it's the shedding of blood, if only a small amount—the blood of Roberto, of Bobbie or Blanca or any of us, if things go wrong when we're found—that I am trying to prevent here?

His voice changed as he moved nearer and farther from

her, and she realized that behind her chair he was pacing back and forth. The floorboards creaked slightly. No one else seemed to notice.

To have survived at all, he hissed, *and then to live carefully, managing and more than managing in the greedy, scrambling world of profit that succeeded our world of blood and fury—how dare you sneer at me for that? The costs were mine, and I took the gains too. I was entitled to them, and I do not apologize! It is you who should apologize to me, for your recklessness and your contempt!*

Oh, enough, stop it, she retorted, twisting in her chair to try to see him—could she see him now? But it hurt too much to turn. What did you do, judge, sell rotten grain to the army, bad boots, short rations? What's this tirade supposed to excuse—a radical turned exploiter and profiteer, traitor to his own, a smug scourge of the left in the name of the fat-bottomed powers that be? Is that why you hide your face from me? Who are you to me, with your whining excuses; why do you haunt me? I'm nothing to do with you, and I don't want you!

She heard again that rustling sound of dry skin on skin, and his agonized whisper came. *You will never understand. I cannot tell you, nothing I say affects you. I don't even know you. Who are you, who are these people, what is this place?* The voice trembled with such anguished terror that she felt afraid herself. *Why am I here? What has happened to me? Who are you?*

She managed at last to turn slightly in her chair, and she saw him hovering beside her, the translucent shape of his body, his hands clasped together and winding and wringing each other, eloquent of agitation.

Like Ricky, his descendant.

No. Not like Ricky, not at all—this was not Ricky's gesture. Electrified by memory, she stared at the writhing hands. Ricky rubs at the back of his neck. But she knew the ghost's gesture, she knew it in her muscles and the deep-grained memory of her nerves.

She had to see the face. With a convulsive effort that made her gasp, she reached up and caught his wrists, her fingers closing on icy flesh. She pulled.

He stumbled forward with a cry, and she saw a shadowy disturbance of the air and a distortion of the wall beyond him, and she saw his face, gaping with panic—and did not know it.

Yet knowledge pressed for recognition, and in a moment would burst dreadfully upon her. Whose face looked like that, broad at the brow and narrowing neatly to the jaw, the lips curled at the corners and bracketed with fine, precise lines, the nose aquiline and the eyes large, dark, and hooded? Not Ricky, nothing like Ricky. Who was this, with his white hair curling damply at the bluish hollow of the temple?

His eyes opened wide, his lips parted. *"Your face is mine,"* he whispered, *"but you are not my child!"*

She was flooded with recognition and an upwelling of pity, and she tried to offer comfort. "Not the son you wrote to," she murmured, "but in a way, your child."

Someone was calling her name, a nagging distraction she shrugged off. All her attention was on the judge, who tried with a frantic cry of rejection to pull away from her. She clung to his hands. He fell downward, into her, like an arctic wind breathed into her tissues through the contact of their hands. The icy infusion settled softly into her flesh and her bones, where the last of it was warmed away as rapidly as evaporation on a hot, dry day.

He was gone, spent, accepted—home at last.

She sat in the old leather chair in her own living room with Ellie Stern standing over her and anxiously calling her name while the kids of the class looked on.

Oh, damn these people, couldn't they let her alone, at this moment at least? How often do you get to literally come to yourself? How often do you feel such peace?

Outside came the roar of a motor, Frank at last, with (if they were lucky) Johnny Sanchez of the Taos police force.

Dorothea gathered herself, cleared her throat, and took a breath (*agh,* damn it). "Roberto, Bobbie, come here," she said. "Blanca, you too. I want you all right here by me when the police come."

Because nobody was going to shoot at Dorothea, no matter how nervous they were or what they expected to find here in the studio.

❧ Twelve ❧

DOROTHEA INSISTED THAT Claire come inside. Claire was driving the truck for her while she was on the codeine pills for her ribs but insisted on sleeping down the road at the Willises' ranch, probably to give Dorothea and Ricky the run of the house at night.

Claire's normally brash manner underwent a puzzling sort of dimming at the prospect of entering Dorothea's house. She shook her long hair back from her face and said, "All right. I'll make you some coffee, how's that?"

"Thanks, hon, that would be lovely." Dorothea could not get over how much like little-girl-Claire this grown Claire looked, soft-faced and solemn-eyed. In her letters she was so much older and more severe. Have I been quarreling all these years through the mails and over the phone with a mere front? No, no, don't oversimplify. She is my youngest, Claire, but she's also this adult stranger with her own life. Damn, I'm glad she came.

She had hoped to find Ricky outside in the big patio today. He never used the little one adjoining his bedroom any more. Instead, as usual with him now, he lay stretched out on the couch in the big front room, her old afghan pulled loosely over his body, pillows tucked behind his head and shoulders. The radio was on softly, the dial turned to the classical station.

Claire gave him a hearty, "Hi, Ricky!" and hurried on into the kitchen with her arms full of stuffed grocery bags.

Ricky's dark shirt hung on him as if on a wire hanger; his belt was buckled through a fresh-punched hole to hold in the slack folds of his trousers. His neck was a knobbed, fragile stem too delicate to hold up the bony sculpture of his head. Face and hands looked outsized, vital, preternaturally rich with character, hooked to that sketch of a body.

"How was it?" he said. He sat up, swinging his legs over the edge of the couch with deliberation and effort. She sat down facing him in one of the big leather chairs. She had been to Albuquerque to speak yet again with Mrs. Garcia, the probation officer in charge of the Cantu case.

Dorothea talked easily of the trip down. As she spoke she began to see how one might frame Ricky sitting there: his dark clothes, the furry gray corduroy of the couch, the pale skin of hands and face, the bright afghan lapping a pink and vermilion corner over his rail of a thigh. She could feel her hand jump with an impulse to paint him just as he was, quietly dying in the mellow afternoon light.

How would you show in the picture the pain that his medication controlled? How would you show the distance he had traveled lately, all unwilling? Sometimes now his eyes would take on a remote and shuttered look that it hurt her heart to see.

For the moment, however, he was attentive and interested. "Sounds as if she still hasn't made up her mind, then."

Mrs. Garcia's job was to speak with all the parties involved and then advise the Children's Court Attorney whether to bind any or all of the young Cantus over for trial as adults. Alternatively, she could recommend a disposition that would result in some form of probation. Dorothea had been arguing all along for probation.

"She admitted today that I baffle her completely."

"Because you're the only one to have been physically injured but you aren't howling for blood," Ricky said, nodding. "She must find you utterly inexplicable."

"This time she went so far as to suggest that I may be suffering from something they call 'hostage syndrome,' where you start identifying with your captors. She's no fool, Ricky. The first time we talked, she asked me about my kids, whether any of them had ever been in trouble with the law. She suggested point-blank today that I see in Roberto something of my own younger son in his more wayward, draft-dodging days.''

"Poor woman," Ricky observed calmly. "She hasn't a chance in hell of working out the truth, has she?"

"Not unless I tell her, and I have a feeling that she's not much on mystic revelations, so I'm not going to.''

The radio whispered a banal, familiar theme. She got up.

"I'm going to put something on the phonograph. One more hearing of the 'Bolero' and I'll turn into a pillar of salt. Any requests?"

He murmured, "You've got some late Haydn quartets there, I believe."

In the kitchen the phone rang and Claire answered. She uncomplainingly fielded the calls—not so many of them now, thank goodness—from news and media people, friends, sympathizers, critics, nuts of the extreme right and left, members of civil rights and ethnic or minority rights groups, law students, prophets, politicians.

Ricky cocked his head in the direction of the kitchen. "Mrs. Garcia calling, no doubt," he observed with amusement, "to make an appointment for your next discussion."

Dorothea groaned. "I hope not. She quizzed me pretty closely today, even asked me if I'd been in communication with the Cantu kids or their mother. Undue influence on a sentimental old mommy could explain me, I suppose. I assured her I've been avoiding any such contact for exactly that reason."

"Well, what do you think of Roberto's chances?"

"The best I can persuade myself to think on any given day," Dorothea said grimly. "I'm doing all I can for him, but he hasn't made it easy. And some of the other kids' parents are out for blood, believe me—among other things, it looks as if Mary's school is going to be shut down even if they don't get sued to blazes. I must admit, I find it hard to figure out how you put a dollar value on what we all went through."

"For some of them, I would imagine the value would be a plus rather than a minus," Ricky said, "although I wouldn't say such a thing aloud to anyone but you."

"I know. I can't very well tell Joni Reed's mother that I'm not very impressed that the kid has been having nightmares ever since. In the first place, Joni missed the worst of it thanks to her own quick-wittedness, which should be worth something to her self-esteem. And in the second, I'm an old hand at weathering nightmares myself, aren't I?''

Ricky said, ''Do you think another statement from me might be of help?''

Dorothea shook her head. She yawned. The codeine did that to her sometimes. ''You've done more than your share, love. And the Cantu kids have a few other things going for them. The results of the Pinto Street investigation are helping tremendously.''

A complex case was being built by the state against the fraudulent developers who had tried to steal Pinto Street and against the police who had answered the riot call. It had recently come to light that one of the developers had a friend in the police department who had been acting for the developers in various ways, most of them having to do with the distortion or suppression of information. The whole thing stank higher and higher and promised a sizable battle in court down the line.

''I do have my doubts sometimes,'' she admitted. ''I can't deny that Roberto has the makings of a real thug. Or he could become one of any number of other things, couldn't he? I don't want to try to write his romance for him. It may turn out a good deal grubbier and smaller in scope than I hope for him, but whatever it is, it'll be his.''

''I believe you've come to like Roberto,'' Ricky said.

''Oh, I don't know. Youth is attractive, kids themselves are. Their easy bafflement. Their amateurish defenses and tremendous vulnerabilities. I've had kids of my own. I'm not proof against any of it.''

''I have none,'' Ricky said, thoughtfully drawing the edge of the afghan through his fingers. ''And I'm not either.''

''And another thing. I remembered something the other morning, something I normally don't think much about. Do you know what I did when I left Jack? The last thing I did? I went out into the garage and used every bit of my strength to tip over that old printing press I'd been using, trying to smash it to pieces.''

She stopped, thinking back to that dank work space of her married days, with the fluorescent bulbs she had installed herself to have light to work by.

''I confess, the connection escapes me,'' Ricky said.

''I was angry. I was furious. Angry with myself for having put it off so long, afraid I'd given Jack and the kids everything and they didn't even appreciate it. Afraid I was starting too late, you see? That I would never catch up and make a serious career as an artist. And afraid to leave, too. I was just boiling with rage and fear, Ricky. I've never felt that way since, not even when Nathan left—not until that evening when Roberto and I ended up shouting at each other and he smashed my lamp. He reminded me what those feelings are like. I think he's been living with them for a long time. I guess I understand him a little better, remembering that, than I'd like to. So I can't just write him off, can I?''

"You can," Ricky said, "if you want to."

Dorothea leaned back. "Then I guess I don't want to."

The phone rang again and Claire called, "Mom? Did you want to speak to George?"

Ugh. No. But it had to be done. Ricky gave Dorothea the victory sign as she headed for the kitchen.

She leaned against the wall, watching her daughter deftly making, of all things, crepes to go with the tea. Watching this soothed her, and she needed soothing, for she had to calmly, steadily, and repeatedly tell George that no, he would not be allowed to come out early, ahead of the scheduled mob, and show his personal bigwigs the wall. No. No. No.

But you must, he said, I can do so much for you: my friends, my contacts, important people, I've told them all about you, I could have arranged a tremendous event for you if you'd let me, at least let me improvise, let me, let me.

No. Dorothea stayed with it, noting with surprise the racing of her heart. How angry he made her, and how unsettling that she should also be a little afraid. She wondered if she had made it clear to Ricky how valuable it was to her to have remembered how to be really, cleanly, knowingly angry and to act on it, a debt of sorts owed to Roberto. Saying no to George felt good: thrilling, because fear was being denied its absurd, obscure power. Not that she had a great deal of choice. If she were to hang up, that would be George's excuse to drive out and continue the conversation.

No, she said again, watching Claire's slender body doing its crepe dance at the stove. No. You and your friends can come out with everyone else or not at all. And if you do try to sneak back there beforetime, I will raise such hell that your name will be black, stinking, volcanic mud in the art world forever after, my lad. Yes. I mean it. Over and over.

In the end, it was he who hung up (How can you do this to me?). Dorothea, delighted and relieved, laughed.

"Great, Mom," Claire said. She knew all about this. She was the one who had handled the invitations to the first viewing of the wall.

Dorothea indicated the delicately rolled crepes on an old silver tray that she never used. Claire had even polished the tray. "You've got to show me how to do that before you take off again."

Claire flashed her a quick, taut smile and rolled a new skin of batter swiftly around the pan. "Arthur called yesterday, did I tell you?" The younger and sweetly prodigal son, heard from again. "While you were out walking. He's upset to have missed you again. He thinks you're ducking him. You know how sensitive he is."

"We've all survived Arthur's sensitivity this long," Dorothea replied testily. "I suppose we can get through this bout as well. It would be so much better if he'd just accept the fact that it's all going to set itself right without him, that's all."

Arthur had to stay with the latest of the string of rock groups he had been managing. He worried, it seemed, from this or that hotel room between gigs and between tokes.

Bill, the older boy, handled things differently (always had). He'd sent a telegram from Tokyo, and there had been one exhaustive, efficient phone call in the middle of the night. He would come and see her when he got back. His mother's assurances that she was well, that things were in hand, that Claire was here to help, had satisfied him. No doubt he thought this was a daughter's proper place and duty, though Claire would mince him for saying so.

"Okay," Claire said, switching off the gas, "that should be enough to hold you."

She carried the tray inside and set it on the table in front of the couch. Dorothea followed, admiring her daughter's style, proud to show her off a bit before Ricky.

"Only two cups?" Ricky said. "You're not eating with us, Claire?"

The edge in his tone surprised Dorothea. Even more surprising was Claire's sudden frowning confusion. She still looked about six when she knit her brows like that—only then she'd had bangs—and poked out her lower lip.

She said, "I can't stay, really. My editor wants to talk some more about the article, maybe expansion into a series.

She's calling me soon, down at the Willises'. I'll see you both later.''

And she tossed off the apron, grabbed her suede jacket, and fled.

"Dope," Dorothea said, trying to chew one of the crepes before it dissolved ethereally in her mouth. "These are delicious, and she's too thin. Did you ever see her when she was in her teens? Plump as a partridge, and now look at her."

"She's afraid," Ricky said.

"What?"

"She's afraid. Of me, of the damned cancer."

"Oh, Christ." Dorothea set the coffeepot down and stared at the beautiful spread of food. "Are you sure?" But she knew. Of course Claire wouldn't eat here or sleep here. She was scared of somehow picking up the cancer from plates and utensils Ricky had used. She was afraid of breathing air that had been tainted by his tainted lungs.

"It's nothing new," Ricky said. "I've seen it before."

"I'm sorry, love," she said.

"Don't be so sorry that you let the crepes go cold. You're right, they are delicious."

Ricky heard Dorothea crying and took his morning juice to her room. She was sitting up in her bed and crying full-heartedly, noisily, wetly, into the top bedsheet, which she had gathered to hold to her face.

Well, he thought, Frank had said this kind of thing was to be expected after what she'd been through. He wondered if there had been other outbursts. At least he could be moderately sure this wasn't about himself.

He knocked on the doorframe. "May I come in?"

Blubbing and blotting away with the sheet hem, she nodded.

He padded over in his pajamas and slippers and stood looking down at her. One way or another, he thought, we are managing to squeeze in nearly everything we might have had in a lifetime together, including this. My, doesn't she look a mess, poor girl.

"What's it about, do you know?" he said.

"Just woke up and exploded," she gasped. "Is this what Frank's been trying to warn me about? It's horrible."

"Snuffle, snuffle," he said. "As if you'd muffed it instead of pulling off a glorious victory. And still working at it, manfully and well, if I may say so." He sat down beside her and hugged her against him, taking care to choose the side on which her ribs were whole. There was no place within reach now to set the juice down. Ah, well. Funny thing, too, how no juice he had tasted since could approach the wonderful cool sweetness of the glass that Blanca had brought him on that terrible night. "You're making the sheets all wet."

"Laundry tomorrow anyhow," she said, her face muffled in his shoulder. He loved the feel of her sleepy, loose weight against him, all trusting and helpless. At least at moments like this he could feel himself in some sort of authority, a sensation he found increasingly hard to come by these days.

"I think," he said, "you miss your ghost."

At this she began to laugh as well as cry and ended up gulping down hiccups.

"Careful," he said, "or you'll have orange juice in your hair."

"Poor ghost," she said, relaxing against him as the weeping fit passed. "So terrified, and trying to terrify me too, for my own good. The funny thing is, it wasn't about the details of history at all—all that good stuff you dug up for me in the books I brought you. It was about the effect of those terrible times on a vulnerable soul. He was ruined, Ricky. Pathetic. But even if fear is the only possible, reasonable response to your situation, you can't let fear run your life. Well, you can; but it won't be much of a life."

"You think you've truly made your peace with him, then?"

"I think so. I think I let him have his fear, poor bastard, but for myself—I grew past it, that's all. I went on to something else, and that let me take him in as he was."

"Put him to rest. Well, it's the damnedest ghost story I've ever come across: your own past self coming to haunt you, and with a message it's your job to ignore, what's more! It's all upside-down, Dorothea. Shockingly unconventional."

"But satisfying," she said, sounding peaceful now. "After all, who could possibly haunt me as effectively as I could haunt myself? What could I learn more from than from my own past lifetime?"

"Reincarnation!" He snorted. He couldn't help it; every time this came up he had the same reaction.

"He was me, Ricky, as I was in a former life," she said earnestly. "I'm sure of it. What have you got against the idea, anyway?"

"It's such a tearoom-gypsy notion," he said irritably, pull-

ing away from her and propping himself against the head-
board of her bed. "All beads and incense and Madam Arcati
shenanigans, or else a lot of pseudo-eastern mystical solem-
nity! And either way it's belittling, don't you see? So damned—
convenient. Death's a lark, not to worry, back again sucking
your bottle before you can say Jack Robinson!"

She smiled. "My own feeling has always been, 'What, you
mean I have to come back again? I've just managed this time
by the skin of my teeth, next time might be worse!' But when
I recognized him—God, Ricky, it was the creepiest moment
of my life, I swear. I thought, It's me, and oh, the poor
creature. Even though he didn't look exactly like me—it was
that difference that threw me at first—I didn't have a doubt in
the world."

"How, not exactly like? Blue-jawed? Hairy-eared?"

Dorothea burrowed past him to dig a tissue out from under
her pillow. "Move, come on." She blew her nose. "The
main difference was that his eyebrows were spiky and tan-
gled, like a cartoon wizard's."

"A lot of old codgers have wizard brows," Ricky said.
"There are even barbers who offer to singe them flat for you,
to make you look younger. Your ghost needs a better barber."

"Why do you take that jeering tone whenever the subject
comes up?"

"Why do you always defend him? Love me, love my
ghost?"

"I think you're just annoyed that you didn't figure it out
yourself. But who in the world could have guessed? Our
cultures don't even recognize the phenomenon as real! What
tickles me about the whole affair is the way it shows that
people are too narrow in their thinking about reincarnation,
trying to confine it to bloodlines and physical inheritance.
When you think of it, there's no good reason why a nonphysi-
cal transfer like the reincarnation of a soul should have the
least connection with the fleshy old family tree."

Ricky rubbed at his nape. "So perhaps we do get another
chance, is that the conclusion?" He did not know why he
fought this idea so stubbornly.

"I think it means that though history doesn't repeat itself,
certain patterns do. If you're stuck somewhere, if you're
being held back by some trauma from a former life, you get
to tackle a similar problem from another angle, in another
setting, so you can beat it, put it behind you, and move on.

My ghost didn't come to show me what I am but what I had been and what I had to grow beyond. That's what I think.''

"Here's to that thought, then," he said, lifting his juice glass to her. "I think we could all use that kind of opportunity, one way or another." And then, because she looked so small and warm and red-nosed wth weeping and because he missed her horribly across the foot-and-a-half of space between them, he put the glass down and held out his hand. "In the meantime, would you mind if I just lay here and hold you for a little?"

That afternoon Dorothea did her own driving. Brillo and the knapsack of tools and supplies rode in the back of the truck. She regretted giving up the slow, thoughtful stroll to the wall, the rewards of the gradual approach, but Ricky was weaker than he had been. And there was no longer any reason to avoid laying a telltale wheel track along the arroyo.

She parked without looking at the wall, hoping that this time she wouldn't want to throw up or faint when she did see it. Ricky climbed carefully down. He was slightly wobbly under the stronger dose of hospice mix they had him on now. They left the truck doors open so it wouldn't turn into an oven.

She turned quickly away from the wall, her eyes wet. It was no good, she couldn't get used to it. She had been mad to agree to show the thing. It had not been obliterated—that was beyond even a half hour of Roberto at his most destructive—but it was not what it had been, what she had set out to make and what she had made. It was changed by the destructive hand of a stranger.

"Come here, sit down," Ricky said. He had spread the old blanket in the shade of the juniper. Dorothea sat, her back to the wall.

Brillo sprawled, grunting with pleasure. Ricky scratched the dog's stomach. "When are you going to get another dog?" Ricky said. "Brillo's lonely."

"Um," she said.

"Such a pity about poor old Mars," Ricky went on. "The only victim, in the end. He had such a sweet nature, the most innocent creature here, except for Brillo."

Dorothea stared at him from under her hat brim. He was bareheaded as usual, reddening on forehead and nose. She would never forget the sight of him being lifted out of the patio strapped into the lounge chair, his hands like white marble claws clutching at Frank Sanford's sleeve, his mouth stretched in a frozen, soundless scream.

"Not the only victim," she said in a small but stubborn voice.

He sighed and coughed, covering his mouth. "We've been over this. It wasn't your fault that Frank had such trouble locating what's-his-name, and frankly I'm glad he stuck with it and didn't settle for some more excitable officer. You did the best you could."

"The best," she said with deep self-disgust.

To her astonishment he sang in a creaky voice, " 'We were the victims of circumstances.' My dear Dorothea, I was and am still the victim not of any person but of this damned disease."

It made her angry that he tried to make light of that horrible experience to spare her feelings. No one had spared his.

"What other arrangement could you have made with Frank that would have been better?" he said.

"I don't know; something. When I think of you abandoned for almost an hour—"

"Don't think of it," he said. "What's the good?"

She shook her head. "I can't help it."

"Well, there's no arguing with the unreasonable," he remarked. He rumpled Brillo's ears and bent closer, picking the burrs from the matted fur. He added mildly, "Oh, I admit I sent a few wild curses your way while I was—waiting. There was little that I didn't curse during that time, and my curses were no more rational than my prayers were. I, now, this self that speaks to you today, won't have you feeling accountable. I can't stand the idea of the splendid finale of our mystery all gummed up with guilt."

"Oh, Ricky—"

"You got rid of one ghost, Dorothea. Don't replace him with some maudlin image of me. Let me be Ricky here, Ricky now, Ricky sitting in comparative comfort on this scratchy blanket and giving Brillo a heavenly scrooch round the ears and even, God help you, on occasion a song."

If you ask it, how can I not?

"No more dreams?" he inquired.

She hesitated, acutely conscious of the spoiled work behind her back. "I did have a dream last night. All I remember is that a voice said, very matter-of-factly, 'Fame is creeping upon you.' ''

"And?"

"That's it. I remember feeling a little nervous about this creeping fame, but the dream certainly didn't qualify as a nightmare. And there was no sign at all of the judge."

"You are eminently one of those upon whom Fame ought to creep," he said. "It's creeping right now, I expect, very quietly." He resumed his singing:

" 'No sound at all, we scarcely speak a word.

A fly's footfall would be distinctly heard.

Tarantara, Tarantara . . .' "

"Well, if this creeping fame is supposed to be on account of the wall," Dorothea said, "it's probably all off."

"No, I don't think so. Come, my dear, turn round and look the thing in the face."

She looked. If she tried to say anything, she would cry, and she was fed up with crying. Her eyes were still sore from this morning. Besides, what was there to say? Only that she could not even see where to begin to attack the damage now any more than she had at her first confrontation with what Roberto had done.

"It looks to me," Ricky said, "as if it's primarily that vein of glass pieces that's suffered. The rest—the scratches and the dents—that all looks inherent in the materials."

"Stop trying to make me feel better," she said through clenched teeth. "I was crazy to let Claire arrange a viewing."

"Why did you?"

"I just said, because I was crazy. There I was, fresh from this insane experience, and somebody should have stopped me, or stopped Claire." No, that wasn't fair. "It was because I couldn't face the idea of touching it ever again, not after what Roberto did to it. I just wanted to get it out into public sight and *over*."

"Then stick with that. Why try to fix it?"

Helplessly she spread her hands. "I just thought I might be able to do something—but it would take ages, Ricky. And I don't have the heart."

"Then do as you originally planned," he said. "Let it go as it is. Frankly, I rather like it."

"Oh, Ricky, stop! Don't sit there and tell me soothing lies!"

He turned his steady blue gaze on her. "I'm not lying.

Don't you see that where the bottle bases shattered, they look like stars? Think of that painting of Van Gogh, you know the one: 'Starry Night.' Wheels of light being borne along on visible currents of darkness, very powerful. Only yours are wheels of splintered glass. I like the way it looks. And besides.''

She refrained from telling him that she thought Van Gogh's work showy and heavy-handed. "And besides what?''

"I think the boy made you a spirit door, an exit for your soul from the perfection of the work.''

She was speechless.

"Forgive me,'' he said, "if that's a presumptuous thing to say.''

"No,'' she said softly. "It's not. Thank you, Ricky.''

"Oh, thank Frank, it's a notion I picked up talking with him.''

They looked together at the wall's shimmering face.

"It's quite magnificent, you know,'' Ricky said in a low voice. "I can understand Roberto's needing to make his mark on it. May I make my own contribution?'' He took off his wristwatch and carefully detached it from the expandable metal strap. "May I?''

"Show me,'' Dorothea answered, "where to put the glue.''

In silence she made the mixture and applied it where he pointed: the lower left quadrant. He opened the watch and spread it open so that both the engraved inner lid and the face, with its second hand still sweeping, were visible.

Now at last she recognized the quiet void behind her own eyes, the place where images of the next stage had always formed and did no longer, as a result not of shock or defeat but of completion. There was nothing more to do. Not one thing. Her hands hung empty and heavy at her sides.

"Is that all right?'' he said doubtfully.

"Yes.''

"It was the spell Roberto broke, you know: the spell, not the work.''

The spell that had brought him, he'd said once.

She turned to him. "You're leaving!''

"I think I'd better, don't you?''

"Listen, if it's Claire, if she's making you uncomfortable—''

"No, no, I'm making her uncomfortable, but that has nothing to do with it.''

"Oh, hell, Ricky, you can't! We've come all this way

together, and now you want to duck out and leave me hanging? I want to be with you till it's over. I've earned that, damn it!''

"You won't have time," he said with a grimace that he must have meant for a smile. "After all, 'Fame is creeping upon you.' No, no, I'm sorry, I've said it wrong, trying to be clever. I mean only that with your enchantment over, the stream of your life is already carrying you on. You need to be at liberty to go with it. You would only feel badly that you couldn't attend to me as you wished to, or you'd neglect the new opportunities coming to you and then I would feel badly.

"Oh, in God's name, Dorothea, don't fight me, help me! I don't know how to do this, I don't even know for certain that I'm right. It doesn't make you wise to have cancer, you know. I'm the man I was before, but there's this disease eating my life. Help me.''

Anger and tears half choked her. She stepped away from him quickly because she wanted to hit him, seize him, bind him to her forever.

"Oh, you bastard," she sobbed.

He hung his head. "You were right, you see. There are other matters for me to attend to, people to see, words to say. I thought about this in the hospice, when they kept me those few days after Roberto. But first I needed—I needed you.'' He was blushing painfully, a deep red bloom shading his sallow skin. "I needed to act, to accomplish something, I suppose, even if it pertained to nothing more substantial than your dreams. One needs to know that one is not yet dead, you know. One needs evidence.

"Well, I got it. But that's over now, and I mustn't hide here with you from what remains for me to do. That would be cowardly. You are a brave person. The spectacle of my cowardice would disgust you. You wouldn't love me any more, Dorothea. Or if you did, I shouldn't deserve it. And I couldn't bear that.''

She could stand still no longer. "You goddamned English," she raged, striding up and down before him with her fists clenched at her sides. "You are so damned articulate. You say it so well. Do you think that makes any goddamned difference?''

"Shall we go back now?" he said.

She grabbed the glue pot up from the sand, ignoring the

twinge this gave her injured side. "We're not done talking about this," she warned.

Walking back to the truck in the late light he held her arm, his hand resting as lightly as a leaf of old paper. Her fury melted, her resistance vanished. She recognized an ending when she saw one. She drove them home with the water sliding ceaselessly from her eyes and drying on her cheeks.

They had offered Ricky a wheelchair, but he preferred to walk while he could. At the other end of the journey, after sitting so long, he suspected that he would need that sort of aid. Meanwhile, he sat down across from Dorothea in the coffee-shop booth, propped his elbows on the scarred table-top, and wondered how far it was to Gate Eight.

He wore a lightweight suit and carried his nylon flight bag. Inside he had packed his shearling slippers, Dorothea's departure present to him. They were for the plane, and, knowing how chilly the air conditioning could be, he intended to use them. But he was damned if he would go shuffling round the airport in slippers beforehand like some Methuselah from an old-age home.

Dorothea looked tired. More than likely she had slept no better than he had last night.

He ordered coffee for them both from a square, smiling waitress with red tints in her hair. Then he and Dorothea returned to the subject of their conversation: the police. Ricky had dutifully checked in with them, or rather checked out, before completing his travel plans.

Not worth more than a passing remark, perhaps, but he wanted to hear her speak while he still could, regardless of the topic. He doubted he would write to her, preferred it that way actually. Make an end here, and she would play her part. Curious how this dying business conferred certain leadership responsibilities.

"I would say," he remarked, "that your police handled me with a decidedly light touch. I think I frightened them; hardly surprising, given the state I was in when they found me. At the hospice a young officer whose nose kept twitching like a rabbit's wrote down my answers to his questions. I suspect he'd heard that people with cancer stink horribly. He was trying to pick up the scent to see how awful it was, as you'd poke your tongue at a sore tooth to discover how badly it hurts."

"Ugh, Ricky," she protested, but she giggled.

He laughed too, a soft "haw" of derision, pleased to have amused her. Yet they hurt, these live moments: bright-edged reminders of all he was losing, the costs of this farewell.

A silent farewell for the moment. She stirred her coffee, one hand to her forehead, her fingers slanted to hide her eyes from him.

He took a square sugar packet from the bowl on the table to play with, tapping first one point on the tabletop and then another. It was really best for him to go, but he could not bring himself to explain fully. It had to do with that night and the morning after, of which he seldom spoke.

At a certain point he had clawed his way so far out somewhere from his agonized body that only the threads of pain themselves had held him. When he had been brought back from that dimension and found that he was not to die after all, not just yet, something in him had remained suspended, waiting. He probed sometimes after the memory of that sensation of stretching away thinner and thinner into a different air.

He did not actively want to die, far from it. But since he had some sense now of what death might be like when it did come, as it must and soon, he was always on the alert for its approach: listening. You could not do that and be with the people about you, whose ears were tuned to other rhythms.

And your eyes to other visions, perhaps. That last time at the wall he had found himself impressed as always, but no longer bewitched, and it was not a matter of the alterations Roberto had made. For him, the spell was over.

He wondered what Claire's art people would see, feel, and say when they stood before it. They would not stand unmoved, he was certain of that. Whatever they saw, it would not be exactly what he had seen, that original magnificence shared only by himself, angry Roberto (who had changed it) and Dorothea. He took a degree of satisfaction from this and was glad Dorothea could not read his mind and see it there. Her sun-browned, fine-boned face across the table from him was absorbed in what she was doing now. She had taken out a felt-tipped pen and was doodling on her napkin.

He said, "What have you drawn? It looks like a figure from some Renaissance fresco."

She turned the napkin and showed him a sketch of a woman, draped in the style of artistic convention that had nothing to do with actual clothing, bent under a vessel she carried on her shoulder.

"She's a statuette," Dorothea said. "A bronze figure, perhaps eight inches high, with ink in that bowl she's shouldering. This is the inkwell I used in my dream, when I wrote the judge's letter."

Something about the drawing bothered Ricky. "Well used, by the look of it. Did you mean for this bit of her robe to be broken off like that?"

"That's how it was in the dream," she said. "Lord, when I think of the detail work I put into those dreams! Anything for verisimilitude."

"May I keep this?" he said.

"Of course," she answered, low-voiced. "I wish I had something better to give you."

He folded the napkin carefully and tucked it into his pocket.

"Poor ghost," she murmured, "you could almost say that I haunted him, couldn't you? Imagine, waking up suddenly to find that the person he'd been talking to all along wasn't his wayward, radical son at all but a stranger, over fifty—and a woman! No wonder he gave up—"

"—the ghost," said Ricky promptly.

Dorothea groaned. "Bad," she said appreciatively. "Very bad. Lord, what a business. I was so sorry for him at the end, the poor, terrified, rationalizing, disoriented mutt. He *was* a bit blue-jawed, you know? Poor thing, having to get himself shaved every day. You know, Ricky, if there's one thing I've never wanted to be, it's a man. No offense."

"None taken," he said. "For my part, I can't say I've ever been attracted by the thought of being a woman. But I can see the point of having to be each sex, in various lifetimes, so that nothing vital to the species' experience is omitted from one's curriculum."

"What about animals? Coming back as members of other species?"

"No," he said gravely. "Can't see you as a llama. There wouldn't be enough to learn, I should think, not for the kinds of situations we human beings get into. What would the experience of even the wisest Andean llama have had to offer you on the subject of Roberto and his conflict with the law? Precious little, don't you think?"

"Assuming," she said, "that the major purpose of coming back—"

"If we come back."

"—and of remembering—"

"If we do remember."

"—is educational."

"Can't think of any other point to it, offhand."

"No, that makes sense to me too. Although I still have moments," she said, leaning nearer so that the booted and sprawling lunchers in the next booth couldn't hear, "when I think we must both be crazy."

And I still have moments when I know it's all a drama we dreamed up between us to give me an excuse to stay with you, and to try to ease my terror, he thought. Steam dawdled from the cup in front of him. He forced himself to speak lightly.

"No, no, my dear, crazy would have been you recognizing me as Danton himself, or beastly little Robespierre, and maybe as Lancelot to your Guinevere—a whole convoy of exalted lives lived together from the Stone Age onward."

"I'm not greedy. We've done all right here." She reached over to take his hand. He saw that on the back of hers, under the skin, were a few of the age marks that sprinkled his own hands.

"Right," he retorted. "Then why are you weeping? I'm sorry, Dorothea, I didn't want you to weep. Well, perhaps I did, a little." He dug in his pockets for a handkerchief to offer her.

Blotting her eyes with her sleeve she said, "People cry in airports." Dark blotches of moisture spread on her purple shirt cuff.

One of the men in the next booth was staring at them.

Ricky said, "Was that my plane they just announced? I never can hear what they say over those damned bleating speakers."

"I'll go find out," she said, rising. "You get the bill, all right?"

Paying the bill, he watched her from the register desk. She leaned into her forearm beside the wall phone, her face hidden from him.

Can't stand much more of this, he thought. Either of us.

"That was the first gate announcement," she said, meeting him outside the coffee-shop door. "Gate Eight."

"Let's go, then," he said. "I hate hanging about."

Desperation made the walk to the security counter seem

short, even brisk. She walked close enough to brush against
him, and he kept the nylon bag slung on that side, between
them, warding her off. His medicine was only effective against
certain kinds of pain.

At the security counter he had to give up the bag. He
turned toward her, unable to speak. She could go on with him
to the gate if she wished to. He hoped she would, he prayed
she wouldn't.

She stepped against him, her arms lightly encircling, and
he stooped to embrace her. He smelled a fragrance in her
hair, something floral—not a sweet perfume but a green and
tangy scent like cut stems.

This brought a flash of memory: his sister Margaret, small
and solemn, snipping roses, as she had often seen her mother
do, for a play party. Oh, she had caught it later on when the
poultry shears were missed from the kitchen and the rosebush
found butchered. Lord, how many years ago? More memories
pressed, a deep stream patiently crowding for entry. Why,
yes, he thought, his heart oddly lightened, but not just yet.

Dorothea's lips brushed a kiss onto the corner of his mouth
and she stepped away and said intensely, "Next time, if there
is a next time, I'll know you right away, damn it. We'll do a
whole set together, how's that?"

We just have, he thought, but I'm game for another if you
are. He said, "That's the nicest folie-à-deux anyone's ever
proposed to me. You're on."

And then they parted and he watched her walk quickly
away.

Later, on the plane, he grew tired of the book he had
bought for the journey, and hunting through his pockets for
something to use for a bookmark he found the napkin Dorothea had drawn on. He flattened the paper out and studied the
drawing, struck again by that peculiar detail of the broken bit
of projecting drapery. Imagine conceiving of the object complete with damage like that! What a mind! She should be
writing novels, she'd do better than the poor sod whose book
lay in his lap.

The figurine is damaged, he thought with a blinding flash
of memory, just as it was when I saw it myself, years ago
now, in the little museum of a French town somewhere near
Saint-Vallier.

Dorothea has never laid eyes on that inkwell. She's never
been to France, and that tiny place didn't even have a catalog

of its collection, let alone photographic postcards. She can't have seen it.

Except in her dreams. Except through the eyes of the judge, scratching away with pen and paper a century and a half ago.

"Christ Jesus," he whispered.

The stewardess was heading his way, all smiling concern. Hastily he folded the napkin and slid it into the nylon flight bag at his feet. He pretended to be reading his book, and after hovering a moment above his stubbornly lowered head the stewardess passed on to a tanned gangster in sunglasses behind him.

Christ Jesus, Ricky breathed, seeing nothing on the page in front of him. His eyes watered and his hands shook, but beneath his agitation he felt calm and *amused*—as if he had always known that the ghost had been real.

"But it's so early," Claire said blearily.

Dorothea gulped her coffee. "I know. I just want a last quiet look at it before the locusts descend." Today the photographers and reporters, lined up with alarming efficiency by Claire, were coming to see the wall. Something—the secrecy—was going to be officially over. Dorothea had wakened with a taut, dark feeling in her chest, like dread.

"They're not locusts," Claire said. "They're some of the best art photographers and journalists in the business. If you've changed your mind, you should have told me before."

Snappy; oh, dear. Poor Claire, she had always hated early rising, and here she had pulled out all the stops professionally to round up these people. Her reputation was on the line.

"I haven't changed my mind," Dorothea said. "I'm just a bit sensitive, I suppose. Put it down to leftover irritation with Ellie Stern and her plan to write a book about it all. God almighty! I have a feeling George has put her up to it. Did you know he's been seeing her? Well, they deserve each other. Anyway, you can blame her if I'm a little edgy, all right? It doesn't mean I'm going to mess up this—event."

"I'd like to come with you," Claire said. "The others can find their way without me."

"But you're not even dressed!"

"Give me five minutes. Please, Mom. I'd like to."

Dorothea had wanted to see the wall by herself, but what the hell. She let Brillo out of the back room. He frisked in the arroyo, waiting with her. The sun was just up and the air was crisp.

Claire came. They walked.

"This is the first time in years that I've come down here without tools or anything in my hands," Dorothea said. "Feels funny."

Claire, hunching along with her hands jammed in the pockets of her windbreaker, said, "It's funny to think of you trotting out here almost every day, all by yourself, making that thing, and nobody knowing. So much of women's art is like that—nobody knows, nobody notices. That's why it's so crucial to have these people come today. A couple of them are really important in the women's press."

"I know," Dorothea said, not wanting to go into all this again.

"Have you thought some more about those foundation women?"

Several calls had come, once the word was out, from a feminist culture foundation. They were all excited about building a museum of women's monumental art around the wall.

Something of the sort was bound to happen, she supposed. One way or another, people would come and stare and talk nonsense about the wall and expect her to talk nonsense too, but more artistically. Someone would want a soft-drink concession, and there'd be toilets set up, and white stones laid to mark the trail to the wall for those mad or devoted enough to want to walk. The wall would acquire its satellite sculptures of human use: the drinking fountain, the curved plastic sun shelter for viewers by the busload, the garbage cans, the guardhouse.

This is my land, she thought. I could prevent all that, at least until I myself was dead and maybe after, too.

"I am thinking about it," she said.

"It's a great idea. The work needs to be seen by lots and lots of people. I think it's a masterpiece."

"You do?" Dorothea glowed with pleasure, feeling foolish for being so easily flattered.

"Didn't I tell you that?" Claire, wiry and taller than her mother, bounced along on the balls of her feet, speaking eagerly. "I do. I think it's wonderful, and important, and you could do such fantastic things with it—think what it would mean if you let the foundation build here. They could have exhibition space and maybe some day studios and living quarters for artists, and courses to help women artists get along in the world, and you could funnel through all kinds of programming for poor women and women of color and their kids to get them involved. After all, you have these big Spanish and Indian populations here. If you left the land to the foundation, they'd never have to worry about getting kicked off—''

"Thanks," Dorothea said dryly, "for planning the rest of my life and beyond. It sounds a little super-public for my tastes."

"You still won't accept it, will you?" Claire said with exasperation. "Even while you use your influence to save those grubby Mexican kids, you deny that you have any clout at all—''

"They're not Mexican," Dorothea interrupted firmly. "Their ancestors came from Spain and got here before ours did. And they're no grubbier than any kids their age, either."

"And you refuse to help your own."

"My own? You mean women, as a class. I don't know that I understand 'helping' a whole class of people. And I'm not helping the Spanish-American population at large either, if that makes you feel any better. I'm trying to keep a very crude corrections system from pulverizing a few individuals who've stumbled clumsily into its way, that's all. They happen to be Hispanics in a time and a place where that signifies to people who count votes, but I'm not running for office. What makes sense to me is that the Cantus are kids I've come to know, kids I feel some responsibility for."

"But you've got to see beyond that!" Claire pressed urgently. "You don't owe those people anything. You owe your talented sisters, especially in these god-awful reactionary times! You're an artist first, an important woman—''

Dorothea caught her arm to stop her and stood facing her. "I do owe, believe me, where the Cantus are concerned. As for the other—well, look, my darling, I accept that there's going to be a furor over this piece of work, and a lot of attention, most of which I won't want. I'll accept some of it anyway, to find out what it's good for, and because I think it's time. But if you think I've become somebody different— some arm-waving demagogue, some aspiring congresswoman or board member or tireless cross-country lecturer or administrator of a desert school for poor women artists—you are setting yourself up for disappointment."

Claire didn't answer.

"We could both end up wishing we'd never taken a walk this morning or had these people come. I don't want that. I'm rolling, Claire, at my own speed, turtlelike though it may seem to you. Don't push me, all right?"

"Okay," Claire said. "I'm sorry. But you'll let me advise you a little? I do know about the ins and outs of feminist politics, and that's just as important in the arts as anywhere else. You put that on top of the regular politics of art, and it's a real backbreaker."

"Believe me," Dorothea said grimly, "I'll take advantage of all the expertise I can get."

They stopped in front of the Indian pictographs.

"God," Claire said in a low voice. "You can almost feel them watching you—the spirits of the old people who put those marks there. Didn't it feel spooky, working with these images watching over your shoulder like this?"

"To tell the truth, once I got to work I forgot about them."

They turned.

Part of the wall was in sun, part in shadow.

"God," Claire breathed again. Suddenly she grabbed Dorothea and hugged her hard. "I am so proud of you!"

"Thanks, love," Dorothea said, patting her on the back. "It does look pretty good from here, doesn't it? Scars and all."

"It's magical!"

"That's what Ricky said. He said my finishing the wall was what brought him here, and the ghost too."

"Ghost? What ghost?"

"Um—well—" Oh-oh, what have I said? First she thought I was wonderful, now she'll think I'm nuts.

"What ghost? Come on, Mother, tell me!"

Haltingly, Dorothea told her.

"You're kidding!" Claire cried. "You can't mean it! That actually happened? And it's all over, and I missed the whole thing? Why didn't you call me, I'd have come right away! God, all my life I've hoped for something like that!"

She seemed near tears.

"But I never thought you had any—any metaphysical leanings, Claire. You never indicated—"

Claire swung away from her. "Never mind, I guess I just missed out. It was only intended for you anyway, judging by what you say. You and Ricky. I'd have just been in the way."

Dorothea took Claire's face in her hands. "Don't be jealous of Ricky, love. I needed him here, and he needed to come and help me. It may have been his last effective action in this life. In any case, he was entitled, don't you think?

"Now it's your turn. Aren't you telling me yourself that I stand on the verge of a whole different kind of life as an artist? Ricky was a sort of medium for me with my ghost. Now you're going to be my medium, to help me navigate through a world I've avoided for years."

Claire said, "If you'll let me."

"I'd be grateful," Dorothea said. "Just try to remember that I'm older than you and slower and more scared, all right?"

"And you'll let me read the—the judge's letter?"

"On the understanding that nothing about it gets into print anywhere," Dorothea said sternly. "Is it a promise?"

Claire put out her hand. They shook.

Dorothea walked down to the wall, and Claire had the sense to stay behind and let her be there by herself. Dorothea glanced back and saw her daughter standing, hands in pockets, hair lifting on the morning breeze. A good kid, a surprising kid, though more grown-up than kid these days; try to remember that.

Right over there was where Ricky used to sit, in the shade of those twisted junipers, watching or reading. She could see him lifting his book, holding it open and shaking the sand out of the pages after a scut of wind had bullied past.

She sipped cool water from the plastic bottle she had brought.

A huge, mockingly diverse, and rich monument for Ricky— was that what she had been fashioning all this long time? "Ricky's Headstone." Not, come to think of it, a bad title for the thing, if you wanted to avoid inanities along the lines of "Opus X."

Ricky's Stone: courses of studded wire, porcelain curves, shards of sand-frosted glass, brash splinters of plastic—all pieces that her hands remembered holding, her eyes remembered placing, but beyond her now and moving as she watched. Her assemblage of these remnants of the past would travel farther into the future than she would. Traveling—did she see an illusion of motion? How odd; it was like the seconds-long sequence in an underwater film where a school of fish hovers briefly before they all flicker and are gone.

A school of souls, each trailing its wake of older lives, the
wakes interwoven with each other all the way back, and
weaving forward to interweave again in the unguessable future: why not? All of us weaving together, flowing and
changing, meeting and passing, meeting and dancing, meeting and fleeing each other, flicking away from meeting here
only to meet and merge there, and all the time scarcely
knowing it. Some perhaps never knowing it, swimming blind
their whole course until the end, and others coming with a
start to suspect and look about them at all this company
shimmering through the greatest sea.

As for these intruders whose arrival she anticipated with
amusement, resignation, and dread, weren't they up there
too, swimming on the rock? And Ricky?

Brillo trotted up, and she knelt and leaned her forehead
against his woolly one. He tried to lick her face and patted at
her leg with a delicate forepaw. She was acutely aware of the
gritty sand under her palm, the label of her new shirt sticking
her in the back of her neck—and no one sitting under the
junipers.

The mosaic wall was just a decorated ridge of stone standing against a sky that dwarfed it. Busywork, embroidery to
fill the time, whatever Ricky said or Claire said or anyone
said. These people will come and discover that I'm a fraud.
It's not what Roberto did. Ricky was right, they won't even
notice that. It's me. A jumped-up collage-maker with delu-
sions of grandeur.

No. There it was again, a faint shimmer of vast and
multiplex movement, intimations of a pattern making itself in
the flicker of an eyelid. What she had seen in that first instant
and now again was too much to hold in the mind for very
long. Maybe for those who could see, even if only for a
second, the cliff face could stand as a sign of our true depth,
our speed, our beauty.

I was not wrong in withdrawing into making this thing only
in trying to stay with it past its completion. And I am right
now to leave it.

Brillo barked. A jeep was grinding its way down the
arroyo.

Today *Art Directions*, tomorrow the world.

Claire took charge, making introductions, looking very
sophisticated and shining with pride. Thank God there were
only five of them, eager people with pads and cameras and

tape recorders no bigger than a cigarette pack. George was not there. Sulking, no doubt. If he couldn't have it his way, he wouldn't have it at all. Too bad.

They loved the wall, took pictures, made notes, asked questions. Claire lounged against the side of the jeep, shooting Dorothea a shy smile of commiseration every time their eyes met.

My new life, Dorothea thought ruefully. Why is Claire smiling over the ruins of my precious solitude? Because she thinks I could get to like all this razzmatazz. Could I? Sure. The whole point in letting go of what's behind you is to leave you openhanded for what's already blowing toward you from the future.

She had an inkling of the first thing to come after the wall: a painting of Ricky as she had seen him that day on the living room couch with the brightness of the afghan lying over his leg. And then perhaps other portraits from memory.

"What do you call this work, Mrs. Howard?" a man was saying.

Do you name it Ricky's Stone and end up explaining? The hell you do. Besides, the wall isn't only Ricky's. It's for the judge too, and the young Cantus, and others.

"Spirit Shoal," she said. There: named, completed, done.

" 'Shoal?' " the man said, writing on his pad. "As in shoals of fish?" He squinted. "Yes, you could see it as a great, barnacled fin cutting the water. Are you concretizing here the geological history of this area, the fact that all this land was once covered by an inland sea?"

"Well, I hadn't actually worked out anything like that," Dorothea said, taken aback.

One of the others, a sleek black woman with a fleecy vest that was soon going to roast her now that the sun was well up, waved her arm. "I noticed the Indian rock art over there, facing this work of yours. Did you mean to suggest that much of what archaeologists attribute to primitive 'men' is work left behind by women of early times, women like yourself making use of whatever comes naturally to hand?"

Well, I'll be damned, Dorothea thought, looking from one of them to the other. They look at the wall and they see time: geological, historical, some kind of time. This is where you really let go or not—let the work take off and be whatever it can be, or shackle it with your own intentions, kill it with possessiveness.

"Could be," she said cheerfully.

Besides, they're right, by God. Isn't time the medium of all those interwoven lives I saw there, bringing us together and apart and together again?

"I'd like a shot of you with your daughter and the poodle, Mrs. Howard," one of the photographers said.

The letter found Blanca at the asthma camp, where the juvenile court judge had insisted that she go. She hated the camp, just as she had known she would. Her mattress sagged, the kids in her bunk were noisy and silly, and someone had stolen her comb. They watched you like a hawk here. She would have spent her entire time in the crafts room carving soapstone, but they wouldn't let her. They had all these activities, and they made you do them all.

If you had an attack, nobody was impressed. They weren't actually mean, but they treated you so matter-of-fact, and everybody else went on about their business. She had no TV and not enough to read. After a while you got bored being sick and got up, even if you didn't feel great. Nobody made a fuss about that, either.

Every day you had mail call at lunch and then a rest hour when you could write letters or sleep.

The letter Blanca got was in a thin, bluish envelope, and the stamps were foreign. The return address was St. Christopher's Hospice, London. The name of the sender was G. Eric Maulders.

Blanca put the letter on her pillow and looked at it for a while. Nobody took any notice. The girl in the next bunk was sleeping. Nobody came sneaking over to Blanca's bunk to whisper with her. Blanca had made no friends here. She didn't want to.

She opened the letter.

It was written in blue ballpoint on flimsy stationery, like tracing paper.

My Dear Blanca,

You will have been told, I imagine, that I was too ill to respond to your card or your phone messages during the remainder of my stay in New Mexico. This was true in the sense that although physically far better off than I was the last time you saw me, mentally I felt a great deal nearer my death. Frankly, I did not wish to nourish ties to a world I must so shortly be leaving. I may have been mistaken in this, and I apologize for any hurt my silence caused you.

Since settling in here, I have thought of you often. You have a clever, restless, observant mind, Blanca, and it seems to me that you would make a good traveler.

Not all travels are happy ones, as you know. Your brother would not have enjoyed wandering in Canada. I have a sister who returned from an early journey forever changed for the worse (not so severely changed, however, as I had thought, as I have lately discovered). But one need not be a fugitive or an exile to fare forth, and I believe that for an eager, questing mind like yours the risks are worth the gains.

Do you recall my telling you that night of a friend from India (Sikh, but not, lucky man, sick, as you at first supposed)? He has turned up and visits me here frequently. I am reminded by him of many people I have met in my travels whose spirits have warmed at once to mine and for whom I in turn have felt an immediate liking that made the most alien settings and situations seem less strange and the world itself a less lonely place. I think now it is not so bad a thing to rove over the world clasping the hands held out to you. You may in that way meet those heart's kindred of whom we once spoke.

In that way you and I, against all probability, managed to meet, however briefly. I hope that despite the negative aspects of that experience, when you can venture forth again you will. I feel certain that there are many lives your life could cross to their great gain and your own.

To that end, I am making you a modest bequest in my Will. Given current economic conditions, by the time you reach your majority this money, no matter how wisely invested in the interim, will probably buy you little more than a one-way bus ticket to Denver, Colorado. The legacy is intended as an aid only, and with luck by that time you shall already be away on your own.

On the other hand, if I have misread you, or if you change very much between now and then and find you would prefer to use this sum for other purposes, by all means feel free to do so. My intention is to help you to free yourself, not to constrain you in any way.

It rains here nearly all the time, but at least people know how to speak properly. They say "privvacy," not "pry-vacy." Good luck to you, my dear young friend. Don't trouble to write a reply. They assure me here that the end is very near. I find that I hardly mind.

Your old friend, Ricky

P.S. I regret being unable to write this letter in my own hand, but in the past few days my vision has gone very bad. Therefore I am dictating to a companion who is very discreet and who assures me of the privacy (see pronunciation instruction above) of this communication.

R.

The letter was on such fragile paper that, subjected to many rereadings, many foldings and unfoldings, parts of it became illegible. By that time Blanca knew the contents by heart.

ACE
SCIENCE FICTION
SPECIALS

Under the brilliant editorship of Terry Carr,
the award-winning <u>Ace Science Fiction Specials</u>
were <u>the</u> imprint for literate, quality sf.

Now, once again under the leadership of Terry Carr,
<u>The New Ace SF Specials</u> have been created
to seek out the talents and titles that will lead
science fiction into the 21st Century.

__	THE WILD SHORE	08887-4/$3.50
	Kim Stanley Robinson	
__	GREEN EYES	30274-2/$2.95
	Lucius Shepard	
__	NEUROMANCER	56959-5/$2.95
	William Gibson	
__	PALIMPSESTS	65065-1/$2.95
	Carter Scholz and Glenn Harcourt	
__	THEM BONES	80557-4/$2.95
	Howard Waldrop	
__	IN THE DRIFT	35869-1/$2.95
	Michael Swanwick	
__	THE HERCULES TEXT	37367-4/$3.50
	Jack McDevitt	

AWARD-WINNING
Science Fiction!

The following authors are winners of the prestigious Nebula or Hugo Award for excellence in Science Fiction. A must for lovers of good science fiction everywhere!